KT-116-661

SKYBREAKER

KENNETH OPPEL

Hodder
Children's
Books

A division of Hachette Children's Books

Copyright © 2005 Firewing Productions Inc
Illustration copyright © 2005 Kirk Caldwell

First published in Great Britain in 2005 by Hodder Children's Books.
This paperback edition published in 2006.

The right of Kenneth Oppel to be identified as the Author
of the Work has been asserted by him in accordance with
the Copyright, Designs and Patents Act 1988.

2

All rights reserved. Apart from any use permitted under UK copyright law,
this publication may only be reproduced, stored or transmitted,
in any form, or by any means with prior permission in writing from the
publishers or in the case of reprographic production in accordance
with the terms of licences issued by the Copyright Licensing Agency
and may not be otherwise circulated in any form of binding
or cover other than that in which it is published and without a
similar condition being imposed on the subsequent purchaser.

All characters in this publication are fictitious and any resemblance
to real persons, living or dead, is purely coincidental.

A Catalogue record for this book is available from the British Library

ISBN-10: 0 340 87858 4
ISBN-13: 9780340878583

Typeset in Bembo by Avon DataSet Ltd,
Bidford-on-Avon, Warwickshire

Printed and bound in Great Britain by
Clays Ltd, St Ives plc, Bungay, Suffolk

The paper and board used in this paperback by Hodder Children's Books
are natural recyclable products made from wood grown in
sustainable forests. The manufacturing processes conform to
the environmental regulations of the country of origin.

Hodder Children's Books
a division of Hachette Children's Books
338 Euston Road
London NW1 3BH

Kenneth Oppel wrote his first novel at the age of fifteen, and enterprisingly sent it to his favourite writer, Roald Dahl. Publication soon followed, and since then he has written more than twenty books, including the bestselling *Silverwing* trilogy, for which he has won many awards in his native Canada. He recently won the prestigious Canadian Governor General Award for *Airborn*, which is being developed as a major motion picture. He lives and works in Toronto with his wife and three children.

Praise for Kenneth Oppel:

Skybreaker: 'Fasten your seat-belt for some terrific reading . . . this is the kind of adventure that children love best.' *The Times*, Children's Book of the Year

'For children of ten-plus, Kenneth Oppel's *Skybreaker* is an irresistibly ebullient blend of adventure, mystery and romance set on an airship concealing a fortune in gold. It dragged my son back to enjoying reading.' *New Statesman*, Children's Book of the Year

'You won't be able to put down this ripping good yarn . . . Like its predecessor, *Skybreaker* is distinguished by stellar prose, engaging characters, and a minute attention to detail that makes even the most fantastic elements totally believable: indeed, you'll ache with disappointment that this world doesn't really exist.' *Quill&Quire*

Airborn: 'A terrific, rollicking adventure set in a Victorian world traversed by airships . . . Matt is a lovely hero – fearless, smart, irreverent, sunny and agile as the young Indiana Jones . . . *Airborn* bounces along, filled with irresistible optimism and a zest that makes you hope for a sequel.' *The Times*

'This is gripping stuff.' *The Bookseller*

'Brilliantly done . . . *Airborn*'s contained world is totally absorbing, cleverly plotted, a terrific read.' *The Irish Times*

'A tightly plotted, fast-paced adventure with engaging and humorous characters.' *Times Educational Supplement*

'*Airborn* is a satisfying rip-roaring adventure . . . Oppel writes with clarity and passion, particularly in his descriptions of the natural world and the world in the sky, and the plot fairly zips along, but there is also a reflective quality to his writing, and he is not afraid to tackle the issue of death . . . If you liked *Mortal Engines* and Harry Potter, this is for you!' *BooktrustedNews*

'In crisp, precise prose that gracefully conveys a wealth of detail, Oppel imagines an alternate past where zeppelins crowd the skies . . . The author's inviting new world will stoke readers' imaginations.' *Publishers Weekly*

'Spectacular . . . A master stylist, Oppel keeps his prose as streamlined and fast-paced as ever while feathering his tale with flight-inspired allusions to the Icarus myth and Peter Pan . . . *Airborn* is a soaring aerial joyride.' *amazon.ca*

'From the soaring success of his *Silverwing* trilogy, Ken Oppel takes his readers even higher in the skies . . . A tautly paced adventure, solidly built around character . . . The action is at times heart-stopping, the dialogue lively and convincing. Oppel's images take lasting root in our memories.' *Quill&Quire*

For Julia

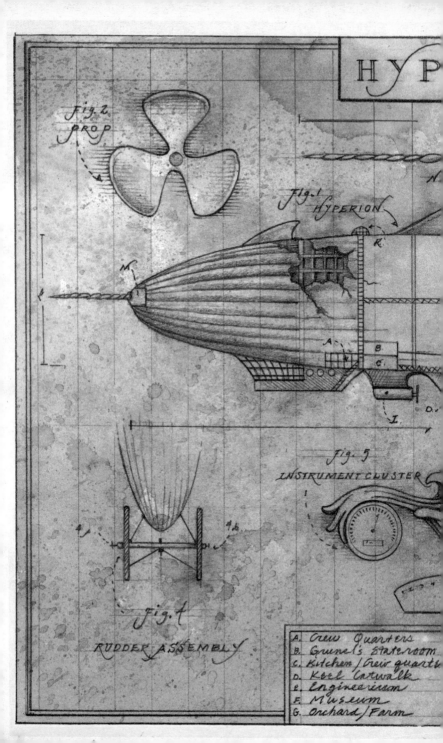

HYP

Fig. 2
PROP

Fig. 1
HYPERION

Fig. 5
INSTRUMENT CLUSTER

Fig. 4
RUDDER ASSEMBLY

A. Crew Quarters
B. Grunel's Stateroom
C. Kitchen / Crew quarters
D. Keel Catwalk
E. Engineerium
F. Museum
G. Orchard / Farm

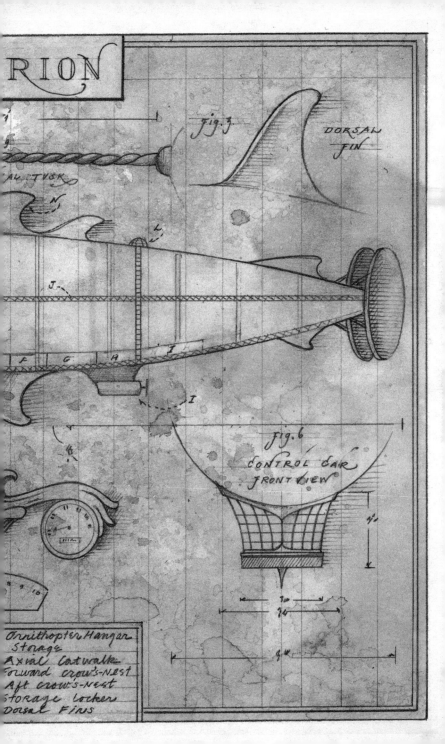

RION

fig.3

DORSAL
FIN

AL TUSK

N

L

J

F G G H I

I

fig.6

CONTROL CAR
FRONT VIEW

Ornithopter Hangar
Storage
Axial Catwalk
Forward crow's-Nest
Aft crow's-Nest
Storage Locker
Dorsal Fins

1

THE DEVIL'S FIST

The storm boiled above the Indian Ocean, a dark, bristling wall of cloud, blocking our passage west. We were still fifty kilometres off, but its high winds had been giving us a shake for the past half hour. Through the tall windows of the control car, I watched the horizon slew as the ship struggled to keep steady. The storm was warning us off, but the captain gave no order to change course.

We were half a day out of Jakarta and our holds were supposed to be filled with rubber. But there'd been some mix-up, or crooked dealing, and we were flying empty. Captain Tritus was in a foul mood, his mouth clenching a cigarette on one side, and on the other, muttering darkly about how was he expected to pay and feed his crew with an empty belly. He'd managed to line up a cargo in Alexandria, and he needed to get us there fast.

'We'll clip her,' he told his first officer, Mr Curtis. 'She's not got much power on her southern fringe. We'll sail right through.'

Mr Curtis nodded, but said nothing. He looked a little queasy, but then again, he always looked a little queasy. Anyone would, serving aboard the *Flotsam* under Tritus. The captain was a short, stocky man, with a greasy fringe of pale hair that jutted out beyond his hat. He was not much to look at, but he had Rumpelstiltskin's own temper and when angry – which was often – his fist clenched and pounded the air, his barrel chest thrust forward, and his orders shot out like a hound's bark. His crew tended to say as little as possible. They did as they were told and smoked sullenly, filling the control car with a permanent yellow pall. It looked like a waiting room in purgatory.

The control car was a cramped affair, without a separate navigation or wireless room. The navigator and I worked at a small table towards the back. I usually liked having a clear line of sight out the front windows, but right now, the view was not an encouraging one.

Flying into a storm, even its outer edges, did not sound like a good idea to me. And this was no ordinary tempest. Everyone on the bridge knew what it was: the Devil's Fist, a near eternal typhoon that migrated about the North Indian basin year-round. She was infamous, and earned her name by striking airships out of the sky.

'Eyes on the compass, Mr Cruse,' the navigator, Mr Domville, reminded me quietly.

'Sorry, sir.' I checked the needle and reported our new heading. Mr Domville made his swift markings on the chart. Our course was starting to look like the path of a drunken sailor, zigzagging as we fought the headwinds. They were shoving at us something terrible.

Through the glass observation panels in the floor, I looked down at the sea, three hundred metres below us. Spume blew sideways off the high crests. Suddenly we were coming about again, and I watched the compass needle whirl to its new heading. Columbus himself would have had trouble charting a course in such weather.

'Two hundred and seventy-one degrees,' I read out.

'Do you wish you were back in Paris, Mr Cruse?' the navigator asked.

'I'm always happiest flying,' I told him truthfully, for I was born in the air, and it was more home to me than earth.

'Well then, I wish *I* were back in Paris,' Mr Domville said, and gave me one of his rare grins.

Of all the crew, he was my favourite. Granted, there was little competition from the hot-tempered captain and his stodgy, surly officers, but Mr Domville was cut from different cloth. He was a soft-spoken, bookish man, quite frail-looking really. His spectacles would not stay up on his nose, so he was in the habit of tilting his head higher to see. He had a dry cough, which I put down to all the smoke in the control car. I liked watching his hands fly across the charts, nimbly manipulating rulers and dividers. His skill gave me a new respect for the navigator's job – which, until now, I'd never taken much interest in. It was not flying. I wanted to pilot the ship, not scribble her movements on a scrap of paper. But working with Mr Domville I'd finally realized there could be no destination without a navigator to set and chart a course.

I did feel sorry for him, serving aboard the *Flotsam*. It was a wreck of a cargo ship, running freight over Europa and the Orient. I wondered why Mr Domville didn't seek out a better position. Luckily, I only had to endure it for five more days.

All the first-year students at the Airship Academy had been shipped out on two-week training tours to study navigation. Some shipped on luxury liners, some on mail packets, some on barges and tugs. I'd had the misfortune of being placed on the *Flotsam*. The ship looked like it hadn't been refitted since the Flood, and it smelled like Noah's old boot. The crew quarters were little more than hammocks slung alongside the keel catwalk, where your sleep was soured by the stench of oil and aruba fuel. The hull looked like it had been patched with everything including cast-off trousers. The engines rattled. The food quite simply defied comprehension. Slopped on to the plate by the cook's rusty ladle, it looked like something that had already been chewed and rejected.

'Think of this as character-building experience,' Mr Domville had told me at the first meal.

Why the illustrious Academy used the *Flotsam* as a training vessel I couldn't guess, unless they were wanting to teach their students how to mutiny. Captain Tritus,

I'm sure, was glad of the fee the Academy paid to place me on board. For a heap like the *Flotsam*, it might have made the difference between having enough fuel or not. It made me long for the *Aurora*, the airship liner where I used to work before starting my studies at the Academy. Now *there* was a ship, and Captain Walken knew how to run it, and take care of his crew.

When I looked out the window again, I wished I hadn't. We'd been making for the storm's southern flank, but it now seemed to be moving with us, spinning out its dark tendrils. I looked at Captain Tritus, waiting for him to change our heading. He said nothing.

'Have you ever flown through the Fist?' I asked Mr Domville in a whisper.

He held up a single finger. 'We were very lucky.' He coughed, and seemed to have trouble stopping, so I uncorked the canteen hanging from the chart table and poured him a cup of water. He didn't look at all well.

'Thank you.'

The control car was suddenly dark as cloud engulfed us. Mr Curtis quickly switched on the interior lights, which did little more than illuminate the instruments and gauges, making skulls of the crew's faces.

'All engines at full,' Captain Tritus said. 'We'll punch through shortly. Hold her steady, Mr Beatty,' he told the helmsman.

This was a tall order, as the wind was battering us from all sides. The control car darkened further. Rain lashed against the windows. Someone switched on the wipers, which only smeared water across the glass. The lamp over the chart table swung crazily.

'Speed?' barked the captain.

'Forty-three aeroknots, sir,' replied Curtis.

'We should do better than that with engines at full.'

'Not against these headwinds, sir.'

All around us were the unfriendliest clouds I'd ever seen, mottled grey and black, fuming. They looked so dense it seemed a miracle we were not already shattered against their bulk.

Without warning the *Flotsam* dropped and my feet nearly left the floor. I grabbed the table's edge. The crew staggered off balance. Mr Schultz was thrown off the elevator wheel, and for a moment it spun unattended before he and Mr Curtis launched themselves atop it, and fought to level off the ship. We were caught in the storm's massive downdraft.

'Two hundred metres, sir,' said Mr Curtis.

Two hundred metres! That meant we'd already fallen one hundred!

'Elevators full up,' ordered the captain.

'They're full up already, sir,' Mr Schultz replied.

'One hundred and eighty metres,' reported Mr Curtis.

I could not see the altimeter, but I could hear it. It fired a sonic pulse at the ground and used the speed of the returning echo to calculate our height. With every pulse, the altimeter gave a loud BEEP, and then a fainter beep as the echo returned. At normal cruising height of three hundred metres, there was about two seconds between the beeps, and you noticed it no more than your own heartbeat. Mr Curtis must have adjusted the sound, for now the beeps seemed to blare through the entire car. *BEEP . . . beep . . . BEEP . . . beep . . .*

I looked down through the floor panels. All I saw was cloud, but my stomach told me we were still falling, though not as fast.

'Steady at one hundred and forty metres, sir,' reported a relieved Mr Curtis.

I drew in some breath, and then the ship plunged again. Weightlessness soared through me once more. I was not afraid of falling, but I was afraid of hitting water.

'One hundred and fifteen metres!'

BEEP, beep, BEEP, beep . . .

'Jettison all ballast tanks to two-thirds!' roared the captain.

I heard the metallic *thunk* of the hatches opening, and the brief rush of water as it sped seaward.

'One hundred!'

'Wind measuring force twelve from the south west!'

It was like riding surf: you'd feel the ship struggling to stay level, and then lurch back down with a tremendous bang that shook her entire frame. The machinists in the engine cars must have been holding on for dear life, praying the support struts did not shear off.

We were lighter now, but it did not seem to be slowing our fall. I looked at Mr Domville. His eyes were fixed on the chart, even now updating it. His hand did not tremble.

'Eighty!'

BEEPbeep, BEEPbeep . . .

'Jettison tanks to one-half!' shouted the captain.

'Sixty-five!'

'Lift, you wreck,' cursed Captain Tritus.

The engines' roar, amplified by the dense cloud, reverberated through every beam and rivet. I hated to think of the strain on the elevator flaps.

'Fifty, sir!'

Be-be-be-be-be . . .

'Jettison all tanks!' bellowed Tritus. 'Every last drop!'

Only when disaster was imminent would a captain order such a thing. I looked down through the floor windows, saw nothing but grey, and then suddenly we dropped through it and I gave a shout. The sea was not fifteen metres below us, looking like shattered glass, great cracks of wind-lashed spray cutting diagonally across the jagged surface. I wanted to shut my eyes but couldn't.

Beeeeeeeeeeee . . .

The altimeter was one long continuous sound. The crew grabbed hold of whatever was nearest. The sea would have us. I did not think of my mother, or father, or sisters, or Kate. My mind was empty. Then, all at once, I felt heavier.

We were rising!

'Twenty-five metres!' shouted Mr Curtis.

'Seal the ballast tanks!' barked the captain. 'Save what you can! We'll need it.'

'We're out of the downdraft, sir,' said Mr Curtis, looking queasier than ever.

'This is not over yet,' Captain Tritus muttered darkly.

He was right. Only seconds after he spoke, I was suddenly heavy as an elephant, my ears shrieking with the sudden change in altitude. Beside me, Mr Domville's knees buckled, and I had to grab him to keep him from collapsing. After breaking through the downdraft, the storm's updraft had us now. With no cargo, and barely any ballast, we were already dangerously light, and with the tempest's explosive energy beneath us, we careened sickeningly heavenwards. The beeps of the altimeter became less and less frequent, and then grew so faint I could scarcely hear them.

'Should we vent some lifting gas, sir?' Mr Curtis asked.

Captain Tritus said nothing.

'Sir?' the first officer repeated.

'Let her rise!' Tritus snapped. 'We're better off high until we clear the Fist.'

'Eighteen hundred . . . nineteen hundred,' said Mr Schultz at the elevator wheel, reading off the altimeter, 'two thousand and climbing . . .'

Still the wind thumped and pummelled us. Blinking away my light-headedness I got back to work with the business of the charts, directions and drift readings and wind speeds. I marvelled at the steadiness of

Mr Domville's liver-spotted hand. Even as the ship was tossed about, his notations were crisp and clear.

'You've got a magical hand, Mr Domville.'

'It's the only competent part of me,' he said, and started coughing again. I passed him more water, then zipped up my jacket. At these heights it was much colder. Mr Domville took his breaths in raspy shallow sucks. The higher we climbed, the harder it was for our bodies to get enough oxygen.

'Two thousand, three hundred metres,' announced Mr Schultz.

I watched Captain Tritus nervously. We were going too far. Like all airships, the *Flotsam* relied on hydrium, the most powerful of lifting gases, to give her flight. The hydrium was contained safely in enormous balloon-like cells within the ship's hull, but at two thousand, six hundred metres, as the outside air pressure dropped, the hydrium would swell dangerously. It might easily rupture the impermeable fabric of the cells.

'Begin venting in all cells to ninety-five per cent capacity.'

All shoulders relaxed as the captain gave the order. The *Flotsam* exhaled into the sky. Our ascent slowed, but still we rose.

At three thousand metres the *Flotsam* gave a great shudder and ploughed through the clouds, leaving the storm behind us. Suddenly it was so bright, I had to squint. The sun blazed in the western sky. I turned to look out the rear windows of the control car, and saw the dark, roiling canyon wall of the Devil's Fist behind us.

'Good,' was all Captain Tritus said. He wasted no time lighting up another cigarette, and even offered his carton to Mr Curtis, Mr Beatty and Mr Schultz – something I'd never seen him do before. He was clearly in a celebratory mood.

'Never let it be said you can't pass through the Devil's Fist, eh? Vent the gas cells to ninety-three per cent, and level us off.'

It was lucky we were so light, or he would have had a hard time staying aloft with our gas cells so depleted. As it was, with nearly all our ballast gone, we'd have to valve even more when we came in for landing in Egypt. This would be an expensive voyage for the *Flotsam*, for hydrium was costly.

At the moment though, not even Captain Tritus seemed upset by his misadventure. We were lucky to be alive. For the first time in my life, I caught myself wishing for land. Tritus was reckless, and I did not trust him. The storm could easily have torn us apart like a kite. Just five more days and I would be back at the Academy.

'Are you all right?' I asked Mr Domville. His fingers were very pale, and his nails had a blue sheen to them.

'I don't do well with high altitudes,' he said.

I'd had little experience flying at these heights, but had read about its possible effects on crew. Altitude sickness affected everyone differently. It was called hypoxia and it could give you a headache, or it could kill you, depending on how healthy you were, and how high. Right now all I felt was a faint pressure against my temples.

'We're bound to descend before long,' I said. 'Now that we're clear of the storm.'

Mr Domville made no reply, conserving what little breath he had.

'Crow's-nest reporting!' The muffled voice emanated from a metal grille, the end point of the long speaking tube which connected the bridge to the forward observation post high atop the ship.

Captain Tritus pulled the brass mouthpiece sharply towards his face. 'What is it?' he said, mouth clenched around his cigarette.

'Vessel to the south south east, sir! She's very high. Maybe seven thousand metres.'

All the crew looked at one another. It was virtually unheard of for a ship to fly so high. It must be a mistake. Maybe he was seeing a cloud, or even a nearby bird, and mistaking it for something far away.

'Say again, Mr Sloan!' Captain Tritus barked impatiently into the mouthpiece.

'It's definitely some kind of vessel.'

The captain removed his hat, grabbed his spyglass and stuck his head out a side window. Wind blasted at his hair, though I noticed it scarcely moved, being so well greased to his skull. He pulled his head back in with a curse.

'Can't see a damn thing.' He took up the mouthpiece. 'Not been drinking I hope, Mr Sloan!' he bellowed, and it was not a joke. 'Don't lose sight of it now, we're coming about!' He turned to Mr Schultz. 'Angle us up eight degrees or so. Let's see if we can spot Mr Sloan's ghost ship.'

The *Flotsam* turned, and Mr Domville and I were busy for the next few minutes, updating the chart, which now resembled the scribblings of a lunatic. I felt our nose pitching up as the elevator flaps pushed our tail lower. It was an ungainly angle, and one that strained both engines and fins, but it would give the captain a better vantage point.

'We're aimed right at her now, Captain!' I heard Sloan say over the speaking tube. I wanted to rush forward and peer through the windows, but I could not leave my station. Captain Tritus scanned the skies with his spyglass.

'Zeus's throne,' he muttered, and I must say, a cold tingle swept my arms and neck. 'Something's up there. Cruse, try to raise her on the wireless!'

Since there was no proper wireless officer aboard the *Flotsam*, the task fell to the assistant navigator – me. I hurried to the ancient radio beside the chart table, hoping I'd remember what to do with the bewildering array of knobs and switches. I pulled the headphones over my ears and lifted the microphone. The radio was already tuned to the universal airship frequency.

'This is *Flotsam*, hailing vessel heading south south west from bearing ninety degrees, twenty-eight minutes longitude by nine degrees thirty-two minutes latitude. Please reply.'

When I heard nothing, I bumped up the wattage, and tried twice more, without success.

'Nothing, sir,' I told Captain Tritus.

'Try the distress frequency.'

Rapidly I turned the needle to the proper location and listened. Soft static whispered over my headphones.

'There's nothing coming in, sir.'

'Not surprised,' muttered Mr Domville. 'At that height, unless they had tanked oxygen, they'd all be unconscious.'

He was right. All the flight manuals said that at altitudes over five thousand metres, supplemental oxygen was mandatory. And the cold would be something else altogether, far below freezing. What had happened to drive her so high? I wondered if her engines had failed, or maybe she'd jettisoned too much ballast, and the storm's updraft had lifted her to this deadly height – a fate that could easily have been ours.

'Her propellers aren't even turning,' Captain Tritus remarked, spyglass to his eye. 'What a wreck! She's older than the pyramids. Can't make out her name . . .' He pulled the mouthpiece close. 'Mr Sloan, have you got her name yet?'

'It's . . .' There was a lengthy pause. 'Captain, I'm not entirely sure but I think it's the *Hyperion*.'

Without a word Captain Tritus dropped the mouthpiece and once more lifted the spyglass to his eye. For a long time he stared.

There could be no one in the control car who hadn't heard of the *Hyperion*. She was a ship of legend, like the

Marie Celeste, or the *Colossus* – vessels that had set out from harbour, and never reached their destinations. The *Hyperion* was rumoured to be carrying great wealth. She may have crashed, or been pillaged by pirates. But no wreckage was ever found. Over the years sky sailors sometimes claimed to have spotted her, always fleetingly and from afar, and usually on foggy nights. Before I was born there was a famous photograph that was supposed to be of the *Hyperion* sighted over the Irish Sea. My father had shown it to me in a book. It was later exposed as a fake. She was a ghost ship – a good story, but nothing more.

'It's her,' the captain said. 'By God, I think it's her. Look!' He thrust the spyglass at his first officer. 'Curtis, can you see her name?'

'I can't quite make it out, captain.'

'You're half blind, man! It's clear as day. Cruse, get over here! They said you had sharp young eyes. Take a look!'

Eagerly I hurried to the front of the control car and took the spyglass. When I worked aboard the *Aurora* I'd spent many hours in her crow's-nest, doing lookout duty. I had plenty of experience with a spyglass. Before I raised it to my face, I sighted the ship with my naked eye. I reckoned she was over five kilometres away, no larger than a cigarette, pale against the distant darkness of the storm front. Quickly, before her position changed, I lifted the lens to my eye. Even with my feet planted wide for balance, and both hands on the spyglass, it was

15

no easy feat to get a fix on her. Whenever I came close, the *Flotsam* pitched and tossed, and my view would skid off into cloud and sky.

Glimpses were all I caught:

An enormous engine pod, its paint stripped away by the elements, glistening with frost.

A control car almost entirely encased in ice, light flashing from a cracked window.

Wind-blighted letters barely visible on her flayed skin: *Hyperion*.

'It's her,' I breathed.

It sent a chill through me just to see her. How could she still be up there, so high? What spectral crew had been guiding her across the skies for forty years?

'We'll have her!' said the captain. 'Mr Domville, mark her location on the chart! Prepare to drop some ballast, Mr Curtis.'

'Sir, we're already at our maximum height,' the first officer reminded him.

'It's the *Hyperion*, Mr Curtis. By all accounts she's a floating treasure trove. I mean to claim our right of salvage. We'll tow her in!'

His speech failed to rouse an enthusiastic cheer, but no one dared contradict him.

'We've already jettisoned nearly all our ballast,' Mr Curtis pressed on uneasily. 'To reach her, we'd have to lose it all.'

'So be it. The *Hyperion* will be our ballast when we bring her down.'

'But we'll also be needing to vent more hydrium so we don't rupture the gas cells.'

'Correct, Mr Curtis.'

'Sir, we may be too heavy coming down.'

'Fuel, too, can be dumped. Follow my orders. That's all that's expected of you.'

I watched this exchange, barely breathing, for I could see that Captain Tritus was hell-bent on reaching the *Hyperion*. He would risk his life, and all of ours, for this chance at riches. When Mr Curtis said no more, I could not hold my tongue.

'Sir, if I might have permission to speak.'

He glared at me, but said nothing, so I hurried on.

'At seven thousand metres the *Flotsam* might suffer. Her engines weren't designed for such high altitude. And the crew—'

'That's enough, Mr Cruse! Remember you're a trainee, and here under sufferance.'

'Sir, I'm just concerned that hypoxia—'

'Return to your post and keep your mouth shut! I'll be making a note of this insubordination. I've got no patience for snotty-nosed Academy brats.'

I went back to the chart table, my face burning. Nothing short of a mutiny would stop Captain Tritus.

'We'll make a homesick angel,' the captain told his crew.

A homesick angel was a steep and very fast ascent – like an angel speeding heavenwards – usually only made in emergencies. I suppose he was hoping that if we did

17

it fast, we'd suffer less from altitude sickness as we climbed. He was trying to cheat Mother Nature.

'We'll be there in under ten minutes,' Tritus assured his crew. 'We'll take up the *Hyperion*'s bow lines and make them fast. Now then, blow our forward tanks, Mr Curtis!'

The hatch forward of the control car opened and through the window I saw a ragged column of our precious ballast fall away to the sea. With our bow much lighter than our stern, the ship's nose pitched even higher. I heard the *Flotsam*'s powerful engines roar to full power, labouring to drive us up into the sky.

'Speed, twenty-two aeroknots,' said Mr Curtis.

'Four thousand metres,' reported Mr Schultz.

'This is madness,' I muttered to Mr Domville. He gave a curt nod, and I could tell he was holding himself very tightly, trying not to shiver. I looked at the thermometer mounted against the nearby window. The mercury was just falling below freezing. Mr Domville deftly updated the chart, marking the *Hyperion*'s longitude and latitude. I looked at the numbers.

The captain's laughter made me turn, for it was not a sound I'd heard before. It was a harsh, strangled thing – really not the kind of sound you'd want to make in public.

'Imagine the look on their faces when we come into harbour towing the *Hyperion*, eh?' Captain Tritus said, mightily pleased.

He reached for his spyglass, and dropped it. Stooping

to retrieve it, he teetered clumsily for a moment. Tritus gave another laugh as he finally scooped it up and held it to his eye.

'Amazing luck!' he said. 'Just waiting for us all these years, eh, Mr Beatty?'

'She is indeed, sir,' Mr Beatty replied cheerfully from the rudder wheel. He was smiling.

It was starting. I remembered the symptoms from my textbook. Hypoxia might come on as a feeling of tremendous well-being, even euphoria, so you wouldn't notice that your vision was failing, and you were getting clumsy and weak. You might not even start to feel short of breath before you suddenly went unconscious, your brain and body starving for air. If you were healthy, you could last a bit longer, but Captain Tritus and his crew were not healthy. They were all great lumps and smokers, and they would not make it to seven thousand metres. I turned worriedly to Mr Domville. His health was poor to start with. He kept blinking, and his breathing came in ragged puffs, as if he was running.

'Mr Domville?'

'I need a stool,' he gasped.

I dragged one over for him, and helped him perch on the edge, his upper body hunched on the chart table. It seemed an effort for him to keep his head up. I took off my jacket and placed it over his shoulders.

'Four thousand, five hundred metres, sir!'

Negative three degrees it was now. A fine icy lace was spreading across the windows.

'Sir,' I called out to the captain, 'Mr Domville isn't well.'

The captain didn't hear, or if he did, he ignored me.

'There she is, gentlemen,' he said, pointing out the windows.

We were within two kilometres now and I could see the *Hyperion* much more clearly. She was an immense, old-fashioned ship, the likes of which I'd only seen in photographs. She seemed as much a vessel of the sea as the air. She looked like a Spanish galleon shorn of her masts and sails.

'Five thousand!'

The faint pressure at my temples had amplified. My heart raced.

'Just a few minutes more,' the Captain promised his crew, 'and you'll all be rich. Are the men stationed at the tail cone, Mr Curtis?'

Mr Curtis looked confused. There was a layer of sweat across his waxy face. 'No, captain.'

'I gave you the order,' shouted Tritus, suddenly enraged. 'We need four men at the stern to take the *Hyperion*'s bow lines!'

'Sorry, sir, I must've forgotten.'

'Hurry, you damn fool. We want this done as quickly as possible!'

Mr Curtis staggered to the ship's telephone. He almost tripped, and Mr Beatty started laughing, and couldn't stop.

The idiots were getting drunk on the thin air, and no one seemed to notice.

'Five thousand, three hundred metres,' said Mr Schultz, his voice slurred.

Mr Beatty's laugh turned into a cough. No one was smiling any more. I saw several of the crew holding their cheeks and temples and ears against the pounding pressure within.

Pressure. With a sick jolt I suddenly remembered the hydrium, how it would be expanding dangerously as the pressure dropped, straining the goldbeater's skin which contained it.

'Sir,' I called out to the captain, 'the gas cells need—'

A great tearing explosion rocked the ship, throwing half the crew to the floor.

Enraged, the captain looked about as if someone had slapped his great red face. He should have known instantly what it was.

'We've lost gas cells number nine and ten,' reported the first officer dopily.

'Curtis!' Tritus alone seemed to have the energy to raise his voice. 'You were supposed to be venting as we climbed!'

'You didn't give the order, sir,' he wheezed.

'Of course I did! Do it now, you idiot, before all of them rupture!'

Mr Curtis sleepwalked towards the gas controls, and I could not bear to see him move so slowly. The cells would all burst in a moment. No one else seemed to be helping, so I ran to the board and started opening the valves. Mr Curtis finally reached the controls and together we vented enough hydrium to prevent another explosion.

'Thank you, Mr Cruse,' he said wearily.

I was shivering badly now. I was slender, and did not have much between me and the elements. The tips of my fingers were numb. My vision had contracted to a narrow tunnel. When an alarm blared through the bridge, it took me a few seconds to understand what I was hearing, as if my very thoughts had started to congeal and freeze.

'Engine number . . . two's . . . down,' Mr Beatty hacked out between his coughs.

The engines were starving in the thin air, just like us.

'Maintain course,' Captain Tritus commanded.

A second alarm sounded over the first.

'Sir,' Mr Curtis said, 'engine four has stalled.'

'Almost there,' said Tritus. 'All we need do is put a few lines on her, and then we'll descend.'

I looked at Mr Curtis, his face sallow, his lips blue-tinged.

'Sir,' he wheezed, every word an effort, 'we're at . . . half power. We'll likely . . . lose all the engines . . . if we continue.' Curtis was capable of no more, for he sank down on his haunches, his head drooping as he struggled for breath.

'Maintain course, we're grand,' muttered Tritus. 'She's within reach. Imagine their faces . . .'

Through the control car window I saw her, the *Hyperion*, looming large. Her massive flanks glinted with frost. Her windows were black. For a moment, my mind wandered. What if she really was filled with treasure? We were so close, and would it be so hard to throw a few lines on her and take her back to harbour? What would my share be? Beyond one of the *Hyperion's* black windows, a pale face bloomed and I jolted in shock. I blinked and then saw nothing except ice.

I turned back to the chart table. Mr Domville was collapsed on the ground. I moved towards him, and it was like moving through water, every step slow and laboured.

'Mr Domville!' I turned him over on to his back. He made no reply. His face was grey. My numb fingers could barely feel a pulse at his throat.

'Captain, Mr Domville is unconscious!'

As if from far away, I heard a great bang and suddenly icy water was pouring over me. I gave a curse, but the cold sharpened me up. A fresh water tank must have burst overhead, drenching the rear of the control car. The chart table, and all Mr Domville's careful markings, were obliterated.

'Someone . . . tend to that,' slurred Captain Tritus, his eyes fixed on the *Hyperion* through the bridge window. No one moved. Mr Beatty had stopped coughing and was slumped against his wheel, and I could not tell if he was conscious. Mr Schultz was barely managing to stand.

I looked at the water puddling on the floor and saw a skin of ice already forming on its surface.

'Captain!' I shouted. 'We're too high! You'll wreck the ship!'

The captain could no longer hear. He was humming contentedly to himself as he watched the *Hyperion*. His fingers clumsily tried to extract a cigarette from his case, but couldn't. They all scattered on the control car floor and he laughed. The sound came out like a gasp. He tried to bend down to pick them up, and fell to his knees. Like all his crew, his lungs were scarred from years of smoking. My vision swam and puckered but I was still on my feet, and I was alert enough to understand that we would all die if we continued to rise.

I knew I had hardly any time. My fingernails were rimmed with blue. My skin tingled all over, just as it does when your foot's gone to sleep. I felt a huge plunging sensation pass through me, and worried I'd soon black out.

Laboriously I walked to the elevator wheel and pushed Mr Schultz out of the way. He made a small grunt of objection, but sagged to the floor, too weak to stand. I gave the wheel a few hard turns, angling the ship lower.

'You little whelp!' Tritus wheezed.

Through my scarred vision I saw the *Hyperion* floating up out of sight as we began to drop.

'I'll see you in the clink for this!' Tritus hissed, but made no move to stop me. No one did, they were all so weak.

Next I staggered over to the gas controls and vented just a little more hydrium, enough to level off the ship properly and keep us on a gentle descent. A huge weight was against my chest, forcing the air from my lungs. The sky did not want me to breathe.

At the rudder wheel I turned us back to our original westward bearing. I fixed my eyes on the altimeter, just to make sure we were indeed falling, for I no longer trusted my senses. We had only two engines, little hydrium and no ballast, but if we were lucky, we would make it to the nearest harbour.

2

THE JEWELS VERNE

A private elevator, its interior gleaming with mirrors and brass, rocketed me diagonally up the south-east pier of the Eiffel Tower. The elevator soared past the tower's first platform, and at the second, slid gracefully to a halt. A sombre attendant in a black suit snapped back the mesh screen and I stepped out into the swirl and scent of a bustling restaurant. Guests chattered, waiters moved about in an intricate ballet, cutlery clinked and glasses pinged. My eyes were instantly drawn to the floor-to-ceiling windows. Here, at two hundred metres, the Jewels Verne had an airship's view of the entire city – one usually reserved only for the rich and famous.

Trust Kate de Vries to choose the fanciest restaurant in all of Paris.

I suppose she thought I'd enjoy being aloft.

I looked around at all the fine ladies and gentlemen, the extravagant hats and suits and furs, and could easily have been back aboard the *Aurora*, serving in the first-class dining lounge. Certainly I would have felt more comfortable. But right now I was a guest. At least I'd had the sense to wear my Academy uniform, second-hand though it was. I felt young and poor and altogether an impostor.

The maitre d' strode towards me. His busy eyes flitted over me, picking out the worn cuffs, the ghostly trace of a stain on the lapel. Six months ago, when I'd bought the uniform, it had seemed crisp enough in the dim glow of the shop. But here, in the dazzle of the restaurant Jewels Verne, I might as well have been draped in rags. I now wished I'd splashed out and bought a brand new uniform, like all the other students. But after watching my pocketbook for so long, it had seemed extravagant. And I always knew that my mother and sisters could make better use of the money. Even though I paid for all my tuition and room and board here in Paris, I still felt guilty I no longer had my cabin boy's salary to send back home to them in North America.

'Monsieur has a reservation?' the maitre d' inquired, consulting the vast leather-bound notebook on his walnut lectern.

'I believe it's under de Vries.'

'This way.' He gave me a rather resentful look and quickly led me to the most out-of-the-way table he could find. My heart sank, not because the table was near the kitchen doors, and beside a window which looked on to the great wheel and cables that operated the elevator – but because Kate was not yet here.

I'd intentionally arrived twenty minutes late, hoping to avoid this. Kate was always late. So a while back, I'd decided to be late too. See how she liked that. But if I were five minutes late, she would be ten. If I were twenty, she would be forty. I didn't know how she managed it. My efforts were quite futile. It was all the more irritating today since the note she'd sent this morning had been extremely precise. 'At twelve-thirty *sharp*,' she'd written, underlining 'sharp' as if I was the one who needed reminding.

'Would monsieur like to order something from the bar?' the maitre d' asked as he pushed in my chair.

'I think I'll wait till Miss de Vries arrives,' I said.

'Of course.'

I'd been back in Paris less than forty-eight hours. After the *Flotsam* had made an emergency landing in Ceylon, it was in no fit state to take flight again. Mr Domville, still slipping in and out of consciousness, was sent to hospital. I'd wanted to stay on to make sure he was going to be all right; I'd even offered to help with repairs to the *Flotsam*, but Captain Tritus made it clear I was no longer welcome. He told me to keep my mouth shut, and sent me packing. There was nothing left to do but arrange my own passage back to Paris.

I wished Kate would hurry up. Between her classes and mine, it was no easy feat to see each other. She'd arrived in the summer, three months ago, with her frightful chaperone, to find a place to live while studying at the university. I knew that Miss Simpkins did not approve of our friendship. Even though I was now a student at the esteemed Airship Academy, she still remembered me as a cabin boy, and did not feel I had any right to be socializing with young Miss de Vries. We socialized anyway, at least once or twice a week, usually at Kate's apartment, where Miss Simpkins would sit in a corner of the room, pretending to read. I wondered if she'd be coming to lunch. I hoped not. I had so much to tell Kate.

I watched the elevator gears turning for a while, and then swivelled round so I could look into the heart of the restaurant. I figured I was the youngest person here by about thirty years.

I spotted the Lumière triplets, the three most famous film makers in the world, arguing over the last chocolate éclair. At another table, a man who looked suspiciously like the Great Farini was entertaining his lunch guests by balancing a bottle of champagne on his palm while pouring it into a crystal flute poised on his pinkie. Across the great room a flamboyant lady bedecked in peacock feathers was banging her fist on the table and talking loudly to a group of appalled, mustachioed gentlemen. I recognized her picture from the newspapers. She'd struck gold in the Yukon and with her new fortune was trying to buy the Eiffel Tower and have it transported back to Canada, girder by girder. So far, no luck.

I looked at the ornate clock. Kate was now over half an hour late. A waiter with excessively oiled hair came by and asked me if I was ready to order. When I said I was still waiting for my friend, he gave me a very dubious look and marched off. I saw him whisper something to the maitre d' and they glanced balefully over at me. My cheeks burned.

To distract myself, I gazed out the restaurant's great windows. The Champ de Mars was a busy airfield, and the sky was dotted with ballons-mouches, the small sightseeing airships that flew tourists over the spires and garrets of the city. Winged ornithopters juddered across the drizzling October sky, accompanied by their insistent mosquito-like drone. Some of them came quite close to the Tower, as there were docking trapezes for them beneath the second platform. The Eiffel Tower's very summit, however, was reserved for the most exclusive airship liners, and as I watched, rapt, one floated in with stately grace to dock.

'Perhaps monsieur is getting peckish now.'

With a jolt I realized the waiter was back at my elbow. He was smiling, but I'd seen happier faces on taxidermy. The oil in his hair would fuel the city for a month. I knew I had to order something, or they would turf me out.

I picked up the menu. It felt heavy. The prices were printed in tiny, swirly script. Maybe they kept them small and almost unreadable so people wouldn't go crazy and start hurling themselves out the windows. But I couldn't imagine anyone here would think twice about paying a week's salary for a bit of barnyard chicken.

I started to have very unkind thoughts about Kate.

She'd sent me to the most expensive restaurant on the globe, and she was late. Not just a little late, or charmingly late, but very, very late now. She would take one look at the menu and say it was her treat. But I didn't want it to be her treat. I wanted to pay for myself, and she was making that impossible.

My eyes swept the menu's creamy pages. I figured if I spent nothing for a week, I could maybe afford a flavoured water.

'An Acqua Sprizzo, please,' I said with a world-weary air.

'Very good, monsieur. And something to accompany it perhaps?'

'No thank you.'

'Perhaps some smoked salmon?'

'Thank you, no.'

'Just a little something from the menu to nibble on?'

I looked up at him and could see he was enjoying himself. I didn't understand this fellow at all. In all my years serving aboard the *Aurora*, I had never tried to embarrass someone, or make them feel ill at ease.

'Waiters in a fine establishment such as this,' I told him quietly, 'should listen to their guests, not harass them.'

He looked at me, his mouth twitching, but said nothing. 'I'll bring your Acqua Sprizzo, then, monsieur,' he said.

The water would buy me a few more minutes. After that they'd probably heave me down the elevator shaft.

I'd been all eager to see Kate. Now I was feeling flustered and angry. I hated that. Why on earth had she

31

asked to meet here? Couldn't she understand I had very little money? I suppose she thought I still had heaps from the reward the Sky Guard had given me after our adventures last year. We'd discovered the secret island stronghold of Vikram Szpirglas's notorious air pirates, and helped capture some of them. But the truth was, that reward money was enough for my two years' tuition to the Academy, my room, board, and clothing, with just a little left over to help out my family back in Lionsgate City.

My heart sank when I saw the maitre d', followed by the greasy waiter, strutting purposefully to my table. He bent down, his breath unpleasantly warm against my ear.

'Perhaps monsieur would like to follow me quietly to the elevator so as to avoid any further embarrassment.'

'But I ordered a flavoured water!' I objected.

'Yes, and we doubt you will be able to pay for it.'

'How do you know?' I said angrily.

'Please, monsieur. You are a boy.'

'I'm a student at the Airship Academy!'

He compressed his lips disdainfully. 'Anyone, I think, can buy an old uniform at a thrift shop.'

'I am waiting for a friend,' I said, trying to sound affronted, and hating that my voice trembled.

'We rather think there is no friend, and you are merely escaping the rain. Come now.'

His hand closed around my arm, and I pulled it free, furious. He took hold again, tighter, as did the waiter, who had stepped around behind me, and grabbed my other arm. I would not be manhandled by these two. Just let them try and move me to the elevator!

And then an amazing thing happened.

A waiter came crashing out through the kitchen doors, as if someone had hurled him. He gave a terrified look back over his shoulder as a small but furious man in a chef's hat appeared in the doorway.

'*Imbecile!*' the chef shouted. 'Next time why don't you just put your whole *hand* in the food, hey? Yes, your whole hand, or maybe your *face*! I arrange the food on the plates with care, are you understanding what I am telling to you? It is part of the art form of cooking, yes? A lovely plate of food is a thing of beauty! And then you, *numbskull*, come along and put your fat greasy *fingers* all over my plate, and *shake* the plate, and move my food all around the plate until it looks like pigs' vomit!'

'Chef Vlad!' I cried out in delight.

The chef turned. The anger on his face washed away in a second, replaced by astonishment and then confusion as he saw the maitre d' and the waiter, their hands still gripping my arms.

Chef Vlad Herzog marched to my table and looked at the maitre d' severely.

'Monsieur Gagnon, is there some problem here?'

'Not at all, Monsieur Vlad. Just ejecting this ragamuffin.'

'Ragamuffin!' The anger was coming back into Vlad's face. 'Am I hearing you call this gentleman a ragamuffin?'

'Well . . .' said the maitre d'. I felt his grasp loosen and fall away.

'Do you know who this is?' demanded Chef Vlad.

'No,' whimpered the maitre d', looking around at the audience of delighted diners.

'Here, sitting at this table, is Mr Matt Cruse. He is a good friend of mine. We sailed together aboard the *Aurora* when she was taken over and nearly wrecked by Vikram Szpirglas. You have heard of him, yes? This young man was in every newspaper in the world. Matt Cruse, pirate slayer, do you hear? A hero!'

'Yes, Monsieur Vlad.'

'Shoo, then,' said the Transylvanian chef with disdain. 'Shoo–shoo and do whatever paltry little thing it is you do here. Shoo now.'

The maitre d' slunk away, and the waiter tried to follow but Chef Vlad caught him by the lapel. 'You, stay here. You are going to bring Mr Cruse a bottle of the '43 Champagne d'Artagnan, and bring him some smoked salmon, and the salade du fermier. He is hungry. You are hungry, yes, Mr Cruse?'

'Starving, Mr Vlad,' I said with a grin. 'Especially when it's you doing the cooking.'

'You flatter me shamelessly. I like it. Good. Bring him all these things now,' Vlad snapped at the stricken waiter, 'and whatever else he so desires. Make sure his glass is never empty. If a plate is finished, bring him another. And bring the bill to me. Do not harass him with it. That would be an atrocity I could never forgive. In my

34

country we deal with these things very seriously. Am I making myself clear?'

'Yes, sir, Monsieur Vlad,' said the waiter, hair oil running down his sweaty cheeks.

'Now go. And wipe the grease off your face. It is unsightly.'

The waiter limped off.

'Mr Vlad, really, this is too generous.'

'Not at all,' he said, sitting down. 'I am honoured to feed you again. You are dining alone?'

'No. I'm waiting for Miss Kate de Vries. Do you remember her?'

'Of course I am remembering her! She was your accomplice, yes? A fine young woman. So you are dining with her. Well, well, well . . .'

I blushed.

'I will cook you a special meal,' Chef Vlad announced. 'Something to impress your lady.'

'She's not my lady.'

'She will be after she sees the champagne and the food I am about to make you.'

'Really, Mr Vlad—'

'You must trust me. Chef Vlad is not without experience in winning favour with the feminine heart.' He gave a quick smile, as if remembering one, or possibly more, great romantic conquests in his past. 'The young lady, as I recall, was a great fish enthusiast, yes?'

I nodded.

'For her, the arctic char . . . and you, how could I forget? Smoked muscovy duck.'

I smiled. He remembered everyone's favourite meal.

'I will take care of you, Mr Cruse. When Miss de Vries arrives, you will have a feast before you!'

'Thank you very much.'

I was aware that the other diners were watching, and wondered if they'd all heard Mr Vlad's grandiose introduction of me.

'How long have you been working here?' I asked. 'I didn't know you'd left the *Aurora*.'

'Four months ago. After our little tête-à-tête with Mr Szpirglas, I decided the air was no place to cook to the best of my abilities. My feet may not be quite on the ground here, but it is better, I think.'

'The *Aurora* must miss you and your food.'

'Yes,' he said. 'This is true. Many of the officers wept openly. But to cook in Paris, at such a restaurant as this, has many compensations. And you are studying here, are you not?'

'The Airship Academy.'

'Very good, Mr Cruse. Very good.'

'Maybe when I have my own ship, I can convince you to come aboard.'

'Ha! Maybe so, Mr Cruse. With you as captain, I need fear no pirates, no!'

'It's good to see you, Mr Vlad,' I told him. 'I've missed you all.'

A sous-chef in a floppy white hat appeared in the kitchen doorway, looking desperate.

'Monsieur Vlad, le consommé!' he whispered.

'Idiot!' roared Vlad, standing. 'Can I entrust you with nothing?' He turned back to me, all smiles. 'These Eiffel Tower idiots. They have much to learn. Enjoy your meal, Mr Cruse.'

'I will. Thank you very much.'

With that, Chef Vlad strode into the kitchen, shouting abuse at his stricken assistants in a variety of languages.

Moments later, my waiter mutely returned with a platter of smoked salmon and capers and all sorts of breads and crackers to eat them with, and an enormous bowl of the most delicious-looking salad I'd ever seen. The champagne cork shot out with a celebratory pop. My flute sparkled and fizzed as it filled.

There's nothing like a sip of champagne to cheer you up. All those bubbles give you quite a lift.

Kate was forty minutes late now, but I didn't feel so upset any more. I fixed myself some smoked salmon and sipped at my champagne, and enjoyed watching the other guests. The Great Farini smiled at me and lifted his glass high. The Yukon gold lady winked at me. I winked back. I was feeling on top of the world. Kate would come in and find me waiting with champagne, and an array of delicious food, and a whipped-looking waiter who would hustle over whenever I glanced his way.

The drone of an ornithopter rose above the restaurant's

buzz. I turned and glanced out the north-facing windows to see a small single-seater flying towards the Eiffel Tower, at the same level as the restaurant. At first I watched with interest, then growing alarm, as the ornithopter, feathered wings flapping furiously, did not bear away or dip down to the landing docks below the platform.

The diners nearest the north windows had also noticed and were looking at one another in consternation.

'Look out!' a man bellowed, and dozens of guests scattered, knocking over cutlery and wine glasses and chairs in their panic.

The ornithopter careened ever closer, and just before it came crashing through the glass, it banked more sharply than I thought possible, and veered off around the corner. The restaurant had windows on all sides, and I had an almost uninterrupted view of the ornithopter as it made a dizzying circuit of the Eiffel Tower.

A cheeky daredevil this pilot must be, for as he came around for the second time he lifted a hand and cheerfully waved at the very diners he'd just sent scattering. I couldn't get a very good look at his face because it was hidden behind flight goggles and a leather helmet. Then he swung away in a wide three-sixty-degree turn, and made a proper approach to land his ornithopter below the Eiffel Tower's second platform.

Waiters hurried to restore order. Tables were re-laid, chairs righted, complimentary wine and champagne poured to soothe rattled nerves. It took only moments before everyone was chatting and eating again, and the whole incident might never have happened.

Another bottle of champagne and platter of salmon had appeared on my table, even though I hadn't finished the first ones yet. I was hungrily eyeing the salad when I heard an excited murmur ripple through the restaurant. I looked up to see an ornithopter pilot striding out of the elevator, leather helmet and goggles still on, beaded with dew. Everyone watched, wondering if this could be the same lunatic who'd nearly berthed his ornithopter in the restaurant.

I swallowed, for it seemed he was headed straight for my table.

He pulled off his helmet and a mass of dark auburn hair spilled out. Off came the goggles and I was looking at the beaming face of Kate de Vries. I could not speak.

'Hello!' she said brightly.

'That was you?' I managed to say.

'You're not the only one who can fly now, Mr Cruse.'

'When did this happen?'

'I've been taking lessons in my spare time.'

'It's incredible! That was quite a fancy trick at the window.'

'Oh, that. I was completely out of control. I'm amazed I didn't smash myself to bits. Champagne! What a brilliant idea!'

Her legs were shaking, and she sat down. Her eyes were rimmed red from the goggles. I poured her a glass of champagne and she drained it in two or three swallows.

'Ah, that's better.' She looked at the label. 'Good heavens, this is awfully fancy.'

'It's nothing,' I said.

'Well, it's my treat.'

'It's on me today.'

'Gosh, certainly not. I invited you!'

'I insist.'

She lowered her voice. 'You have seen the prices, haven't you?'

I shrugged with supreme indifference.

'Well, thank you very much. They might have given us a better view,' she said, frowning at the great elevator wheel at our window.

'I was rather enjoying it,' I said defensively.

'Boys like mechanical things, don't they.'

'Gears and cables and wheels. That's all we can cram into our tiny little brains. I can't believe you're a pilot now!'

'I prefer the word aviatrix. It has more zing to it.'

'It's very zingy,' I agreed.

'Anyway, that's why I picked the Jewels Verne. I was hoping you'd see me as I came in to land. You did see me, didn't you?'

'Everyone did. You caused quite a stir.'

'Those trapeze landings are very tricky, you know!'

'I can imagine.'

'Are you impressed?' she asked.

'Very.'

Though, truth be told, I didn't know exactly how I

felt. Flying wasn't just a hobby for me, it was something personal, all wound up in my bones and veins. It was *my* thing, and I wasn't at all sure I liked sharing it with Kate. Especially since she was brilliant at so many other things.

'I just thought it might come in handy,' Kate said. 'Seeing as I intend to lead a life of dazzling adventure.'

'When did you manage to take lessons?' I asked her.

'Well, I have no classes at the Sorbonne Tuesday and Thursday mornings, so I thought I'd put the time to good use.'

'Who's been teaching you?' I demanded, suddenly suspicious.

'A charming young gentleman called Philippe, as it turns out.'

'Oh really?'

'Yes. He's an instructor at a small flight school in the Bois de Boulogne. He had impeccable references, I might add. And he's so kind. He's offered to give me some extra lessons for half his usual price.'

'I'm sure he has.' I didn't like this at all. This Philippe had probably seen more of her than I had over the past few months.

'I guess Miss Simpkins was there the whole time,' I said hopefully.

'Fortunately, these ornithopters only seat two. Marjorie had to wait in the lounge, which was quite all right by her.'

I couldn't imagine that Kate's parents approved of her learning to fly, and said so.

Kate gave a Mona Lisa smile.

'Ah,' I said, 'of course. They don't know. But didn't Miss Simpkins tell them?'

'Marjorie and I have a wonderful arrangement now,' Kate said, unable to hide her delight. 'A while back she had a bit of a romance. With a real bounder actually.'

'A bounder?'

'Yes, one who bounds. Away. A rascal, you know. But Marjorie fancied him, and they had a bit of a fling. Anyway, I turned a blind eye to that, and in return she now turns a blind eye to some of my little projects.'

'It sounds like there's a lot of blindness going round,' I said.

'It's very convenient. And we get to have lunch just the two of us.' She squeezed some lemon juice on a large piece of smoked salmon. 'This is quite a spread, Matt. I've never seen a waiter more attentive.'

'Well, it seems they've . . . *heard* of me.' I shook my head humbly. 'You know, my little adventure aboard the *Aurora*, and all.'

'It was my adventure, too,' she said, rather put out.

'Ah, but you didn't defeat Vikram Szpirglas in single-handed combat on the ship's tail fin, did you.'

'You told me he *slipped*.'

'Well, I gave him a good shove.'

'Hmm.' She narrowed her nostrils for a moment – an old trick of hers when she wanted to put someone in their place – but then she smiled. 'I missed you these two weeks. So how was your training tour? You're back early.'

'Ah, well, there's a story to that.'

'Was the ship as horrible as you thought it would be?'

'Much worse.' I smiled. I'd been dying to tell her all about my ill-fated flight aboard the *Flotsam*.

'Can't wait,' she said. 'And I have some exciting news too!'

'Well, you go first,' I said, practising gentlemanly restraint.

'You sure?'

'Go ahead.'

I didn't actually think she'd take me up on it, but she did. She reached inside her aviatrix jacket and took out a folded newspaper.

'You haven't seen today's *Global Tribune*, have you?' When I shook my head she opened the newspaper and lay it flat on the table. In amazement and dismay I stared at the headline:

HYPERION SIGHTED

Beneath it, an artist had drawn a rendition of the famous ghost ship.

I'd been scooped.

'Apparently,' Kate enthused, 'some cargo ship spotted it over the Indian Ocean. Isn't that fabulous!'

I grabbed the paper. Someone aboard the *Flotsam*

must have sold the story to the newspapers for quick money. Captain Tritus would be furious; he'd told his crew to keep it secret, for he intended to salvage the *Hyperion* the moment his ship was repaired. Given the *Flotsam*'s condition, that wouldn't be any time soon.

'I remember my grandfather telling me about the *Hyperion*,' Kate said. 'Have you heard of her?'

'I saw her,' I said, still reading.

'What?'

'I was on that cargo ship.'

Kate snatched the paper away from me.

'The *Flotsam*,' I told her. 'That was my training ship.'

'No!'

Immediately I felt better, just looking at the astonishment on her face.

'You *saw* the *Hyperion*?'

I nodded, took a slow sip of my champagne and put the glass down carefully, savouring the moment. Here I was dining in the fanciest restaurant in Paris, drinking the finest champagne in the world, and, best of all, seated across from a dazzling young lady, who was hanging on to my every word.

'I was going to tell you right away, but you said you had exciting news.'

'You should've just told me to put a cork in it.'

'I'll remember that next time.'

Between us, we'd pretty much finished off the salmon and the salad as we'd talked. The waiter whisked away our plates, and I'd scarcely taken three breaths before new ones were set before us.

'Arctic char,' Kate said in delight.

I looked over her shoulder to see Chef Vlad peeping out through the doorway. He smiled, gave a little wave, and disappeared back into the kitchen.

'Tell me everything,' Kate commanded, and set to her meal.

In between bites of my delicious duck, I told her the whole story, glad that we were seated a ways off from the other diners. I didn't want anyone else hearing. Every time the waiter came near to see how we were doing, Kate dismissed him with a little imperious wave. She was a very satisfying audience, I must say, her big brown eyes never straying from me as I spoke. Halfway through my story she took my hand under the table and the unexpected warm touch of her sent a hot rush through the hidden parts of my body. I stumbled over my words.

'Keep going,' she said impatiently.

'Sorry. You just distracted me.'

'Should I let go?' she whispered.

'No, I like it.'

I continued on, and during the most dangerous and exciting bits, I felt her squeeze my hand hard.

'Gosh,' she said when I'd finished. 'How terrible about Mr Domville.'

'When I left Ceylon, he was still in hospital.'

For a moment she said nothing. 'But it's really up there. The *Hyperion*.'

'Way up there.'

She leaned forward. 'Do you know what's aboard?'

'Gold, they say.'

'Oh, yes, gold,' she said dismissively. 'But do you know what else?'

'Lots of very frosty corpses.'

'Possibly. But listen. The *Hyperion* was owned by Theodore Grunel.'

'The inventor, I know.'

'Not just any inventor! He built most of the great bridges in the world. Plus the underground railways of Europe. Oh, and the tunnels beneath the Strait of Gibraltar and the English Channel.'

'The internal combustion engine was his, too,' I said.

'I was just getting to that. It made him immensely wealthy. And after that he invented all sorts of other things. He was brilliant, but very, very odd, by all accounts. Lots of strange habits. Didn't like people much. He had a son and daughter, and didn't get along with them at all, especially the girl. She married someone he didn't approve of, apparently, and they never spoke again. Cut her off completely. Anyway, that's not important. When he got older he became more and more reclusive. He would take long mysterious journeys. No one really knew what he was doing any more. Then one day he disappeared. He left behind a statement announcing he was leaving Edinburgh and moving to America. Just like that. He'd had his own special ship built in secret, to carry all his belongings. He'd handpicked the captain and all the crew. They say that ship was carrying his entire life, everything he owned!'

She looked at me triumphantly.

'So there's also some very nice furniture aboard,' I said.

'He wasn't just an inventor. He was also an avid collector. He had one of the most extensive collections of taxidermy in the world.' She paused, and lowered her voice. 'He had specimens he never showed to the public.'

My skin crawled. 'Like what?'

'No one knows. Some people say he had animals that had been extinct for centuries, or creatures everyone thought were imaginary. And it's all up there in the *Hyperion*. The entire ship is like a floating zoological museum – a museum that's never been seen before.'

'That's something.'

'I don't give two hoots about the gold! But wouldn't I like to see his Bestiary! Why don't we get her?'

I gave a laugh. 'Just like that?'

'Why not?'

'She's too high. She can't be reached.'

'Just because you failed.'

'If we'd gone any higher, we'd all have died.'

'Well, there's got to be some way.'

Kate was not one to let a little trifle like death stop her. Looking at her eyes, I could tell she was serious, and with some alarm, I started to feel her gravitational pull.

'She's drifting at around seven thousand metres,' I said. 'It's freezing cold up there, and that's not the worst of it. The air's too thin to breathe. And at that altitude, the gas cells explode, and the engines fail.'

'Because the air pressure's so low, is that right?'

I nodded, impressed. 'The internal combustion engine wasn't designed to work at those heights.'

'What about turbo-charging?' she suggested casually.

I looked at her carefully. 'Now you're scaring me. You've been thinking about this already, haven't you!'

'A girl's permitted to think, isn't she, Mr Cruse?'

'Why do I have the terrible feeling you've already made plans, and I'm just getting mangled into them?'

'But it is possible, about the engines, isn't it?'

'Theoretically, yes. If you pumped air into the engines, to keep them at sea-level pressure, they could operate at any altitude. Or you could just pressurize the entire engine car.'

Kate nodded innocently. 'Just something I read about. A type of ship called a skybreaker.'

I sighed. I didn't want to go encouraging her.

'So you've heard of them?' she asked.

'Well, we've talked about them in class. I think only a few have ever been made, and most are still in the experimental stage. There are lots of problems with them. It's not just the engines. At high altitude your hydrium expands so much you'd have to vent huge amounts of it. And if you vent too much, you lose all your lift, and

48

then you're finished. It almost happened to us in the *Flotsam*.'

Kate nodded thoughtfully. 'I'm sure some clever fellow could solve that problem.'

'There's not much point,' I said, and then started thinking about it a little more. 'Although . . . you would be above the weather, which means you wouldn't have to fly around it when it's bad. And the thinner air means less resistance, so you'd go faster on less fuel.'

Kate was beaming at me.

'But this is all hypothetical,' I hurried on. 'As far as I know no one's got to that stage yet.'

'I get the feeling you don't really want the *Hyperion*.'

'No sense yearning after what we can't have.'

'I think that's precisely the point of life,' Kate insisted.

'Well, I'd find some other impossible dream that's safer. Anyway, say you did find a proper skybreaker. Not many captains would be willing to risk their lives on something so dangerous.'

'Oh, come on! If there was treasure waiting for them?'

'Rumoured, not proven.'

'Grunel was one of the richest men in Europa.' She lowered her voice to a whisper. 'Matt, how many people would have the *Hyperion*'s coordinates?'

'Mr Domville, if he recovers. Tritus might remember them, but probably only a general idea. Same with the bridge crew. The chart was completely ruined by water. I saw it when we landed. You couldn't read a thing.'

'You remember, though,' she said.

I nodded. 'But it doesn't matter. The *Hyperion* is drifting. She's carried along by the winds at seven thousand metres. I saw her almost three days ago. Who's to say where she is now?'

This did seem to stump her. 'But you have a rough idea of her direction and speed?'

'Very, very rough. The winds change all the time. She could be anywhere over the globe by now.'

'Your whole attitude is very defeatist,' Kate said.

'Not defeatist. Honest. I just like my goals a bit more attainable.'

'How frightfully practical of you.'

For a few minutes we ate in silence. The champagne didn't taste as fizzy as before.

'You know, I'm rather peeved with you,' she said.

'I can see that!'

'On quite a different matter, actually. I've heard there's a ball at the Airship Academy next weekend.'

I'd been hoping she wouldn't find out. 'Yes . . .'

'Were you planning on going?'

'Well, I—'

'Because if you *were* going, and *didn't* invite me, I might be a little miffed.'

'Miffed?'

'Put out. Upset. Angry even.'

'If I were going, there's no one else in the world I'd rather invite.'

'I'm glad to hear it,' she said. Her expression was a mixture of longing and expectation – and something else: mischief. 'Gosh, I haven't been to a ball in ages!'

It was a formal affair, the Autumn Ball, with mandatory black tie for the gentlemen. There was a sumptuous dinner in the grand hall, and afterwards dancing. Aboard the *Aurora*, I'd spent years around ladies and gentlemen in all their best finery, but I'd been serving them. I couldn't imagine being one of them. I wouldn't fit in, just like I didn't fit in here in the Jewels Verne. Most of my fellow students at the Academy were older than me by at least a year, and many of them were from very wealthy families. Half the time I felt I should be serving them drinks.

'Why don't you want to go?' Kate asked.

I was too embarrassed to tell her how expensive the tickets were, and that I could ill afford them – or the cost of renting a dinner jacket for that matter.

'Would Miss Simpkins even let you go with the likes of me?' I asked.

'The blind eye, remember.'

'This might take two blind eyes.'

'I'll get her a cane.'

'I don't know how to dance,' I admitted, which was true enough.

'Ah. I could help you out there. If I were invited, that is.'

I took a breath. 'Miss de Vries, would you do me the honour of accompanying me to the Autumn Ball?'

'I think I'm busy that evening, actually.'

'What?'

'Only joking.' She couldn't stop herself laughing. 'I'd love to come. Thank you very much. Lovely. That's that settled.'

'I'm glad you can tick that off your list,' I said, grinning.

'There's still the *Hyperion*.'

'You're really serious about this, aren't you?'

'Someone's going to get her. Why not us? Grunel's collection should be brought back to earth and put in a museum.'

'A museum named after you, perhaps?'

'Perhaps. I don't understand why you're not more interested, Matt. You'd get awfully rich!'

I wondered if she wanted me rich, but said nothing.

'I must fly,' she said, looking at her wristwatch. 'I'll be late for class as it is.'

'How much champagne have you had?'

'Just the one glass. I'm very responsible, I'll have you know. I'd offer you a lift, but it's only a single-seater.'

'Oh, that's all right,' I said. 'It's just a quick walk along the river for me.'

'You don't trust my flying, do you?'

'I just don't care for ornithopters.'

'Have you flown in one before?'

'Well, no.'

'Widen your horizons, Mr Cruse.'

'You're quite right.'

I stood and pulled out her chair.

'You're sure about the bill,' she said softly.

'It's all taken care of,' I assured her.

We made our way to the elevator. The maître d' smiled weakly as we passed.

'Merci beaucoup, monsieur,' I said to him. 'My compliments to the chef.'

We asked the elevator man to take us down to the ornithopter hangar. Stepping out, I could see the docking trapezes and great pulleys and tracks that moved the feathered craft to their berths, and back to the launch position at the platform's edge.

'Mine's the lovely coppery one, over there,' Kate told the harbour master proudly.

'Very good, Miss de Vries. We'll move it into position for you. Won't be a moment.'

There were not many people about, and I took Kate's hand and drew her into a hidden corner. I pressed her against the girders and kissed her. Her mouth felt a little hard at first, for I'd taken her by surprise, but then it softened into mine, and for a few delicious moments we were back in the island forest where I'd first kissed her, and tasted her lips and tears mingled. I wanted all of her, all at once, every scent and surface of her. I wanted to bottle her like ambrosia.

'A kiss like that,' Kate said when we finally drew apart, 'is usually followed by a proposal of marriage.'

'Is it now?' I said, smiling, but feeling a bit sick at the same time.

'In many circles, yes. But I think that's a very

old-fashioned way of thinking, don't you?'

'Absolutely.'

'You should really get to know who you're kissing before any of that.'

'Very modern of you.'

'Anyway,' she said, 'I don't think either of us is interested in that marriage nonsense.'

'No,' I said with relief, then looked at her. 'You mean you think the idea of marrying me is nonsense?'

'That's not what I meant.'

'Oh.' I wondered if she was being honest.

The idea of marriage was absolutely terrifying to me, but I hoped she didn't feel the same. My friend Baz, who'd worked aboard the *Aurora* with me, had got married in Sydney a couple of months ago, and I'd been at his wedding. I kept staring at him as he walked down the aisle, not quite able to believe he was going through with it. I kept waiting for him to hurdle the church pews, vault through a window and keep running into the Australian outback. But he didn't, and suddenly I did not understand him, or feel I could talk to him as I had. He was married now. Different. He certainly seemed his usual jovial self at the banquet afterwards. But seeing his beautiful bride on his arm made me feel young and faintly ridiculous. There was no one in the world I wanted to be with more than Kate, but I did not want to marry her, not yet anyway. I still had nearly two years left at the Academy. And I was not at all sure she would even say yes.

'Your ornithopter is ready, Miss de Vries!' the harbour master called out.

We walked out to the edge of the platform, where her ornithopter was hanging expectantly from its trapeze.

'Thank you for a delightful lunch,' Kate said as I helped her up into the cockpit. 'And thank you for inviting me to the ball. It's a shame I'll probably miss it.'

'Why do you say that?' I asked in surprise.

'Because I'll be on my way to the *Hyperion*. And you will too.'

She gave me no time to reply, for she'd started the ornithopter's engine, and it made quite a roar as it got the wings flapping. I stood back, shaking my head. She flashed me a smile, adjusted her goggles and hat, and revved the engine to full. When the wings were ablur, she gave the harbour master the thumbs-up. The trapeze released, and down she plunged in her ornithopter for a few heart-stopping seconds before levelling out and soaring skyward.

3

PUTTING ON THE RITZ

The sky had cleared by the time I got back to the Academy. In the porter's lodge there was a message waiting for me from the Dean, Mr Ruprecht Pruss. *At your earliest convenience*, he had written, which I took to mean right away.

I started down one of the great stone hallways towards his office. Narrow arched windows let in streams of late afternoon sun. The Academy was largely deserted, everyone still out on their training tours. Mine had been cut short five days. Coming home early was virtually unheard of, and I felt like a failure. I was worried people would think I'd been kicked off my ship because of incompetence or recklessness. I wasn't surprised Dean Pruss had summoned me. I hadn't even had a chance to write my formal report yet, but I suppose he wanted to know first-hand why I was back so early. I waited only a few minutes in the vestibule of his office before his secretary told me to go in.

'I understand you're a celebrity once again, Mr Cruse,'

the Dean said, motioning me to one of the chairs before his grand desk.

I was never quite sure when Mr Pruss was being sarcastic. I took aerostatics with him, and though he rarely spoke directly to me, he sometimes talked about me, before the entire class. 'Of course, not all of us here have been fortunate enough to land a three-hundred-metre airship on a sandy beach, like Mr Cruse' or 'It is never advisable to have a fist fight on the airship's elevators when in flight, as Mr Cruse might attest.'

At first I'd felt flattered to be singled out like this, but after a while, it started making me uncomfortable, as if I were some kind of a circus freak, and Mr Pruss the mocking ringmaster.

He'd been a distinguished pilot until a motorcar accident had confined him to a wheelchair. Some people said the accident hadn't just damaged his legs, but had left him all twisted up inside too. It seemed perfectly understandable to me, for it would make me bitter too, to be landlocked so.

On his desk I spotted today's newspaper, with the news of the *Hyperion* on the cover. He swirled it around for me to see.

'This is quite a story,' he said. 'It's true, I take it?'

'It is, sir.'

'Perhaps you could give me your personal account.'

As succinctly as I could, I told him of our voyage through the Devil's Fist, and then skyward to try to salvage the *Hyperion*.

'You disobeyed the captain,' was the first thing Mr Pruss said when I finished, and it shook me.

'Not directly, sir. He wasn't thinking properly, because of the altitude. He never actually told me not to vent gas.'

'But he did not order you to do so.'

'No.'

'Or to turn the ship around?'

'No, sir.'

'You realize what you did was a serious breach of aeronautical protocol.'

'Yes, sir.'

'It was, in fact, mutinous.'

I drew a sharp breath. Mutiny! 'We all would have died, sir.'

'Perhaps, yes.'

I wondered if Mr Pruss would rather I had done nothing and sent us all to an icy airborne grave.

'So are you a hero, or a mutineer, Mr Cruse? An interesting question, don't you think?'

I did not find it at all interesting. 'At the time, it seemed the right thing to do, sir.'

'Well, given Captain Tritus's conduct, I doubt this question will ever be posed in a formal Sky Guard tribunal. The *Flotsam* used to be a perfectly respectable vessel, you know, before Tritus gained its command. We certainly won't be using it again for our training tours. Would you agree with that, Mr Cruse?'

'I would, sir.'

He rolled his wheelchair back from the desk and moved around to the side, where a patch of sunlight warmed the wood. Maybe it was just the light, but for the first time, the hardness in his face seemed to disappear and his eyes took on a kindly glow.

'I saw her once, too, you know. The *Hyperion*. We were off Rio de Janeiro and we spotted something above us, very high. We couldn't read her name, but I saw her profile. I knew there were no ships of her type still sailing. It could only have been the *Hyperion*.'

'It was quite something,' I said.

'You know who the *Hyperion* was carrying, do you?'

'Theodore Grunel.'

'Very good. Reputedly carrying his life's belongings and riches. And who should telegraph me this morning but the Grunel family? Yes, quite a surprise. One of Theodore's grandsons, Matthias. Once they saw the story in the papers, they made enquiries. Apparently Captain Tritus refused to speak to them. Then they managed to get a hold of the ship's transit papers in Jakarta, and found the name of the navigator.'

'Mr Domville,' I said.

'That's it. They were hoping he might give them the last coordinates of the *Hyperion*. But apparently he has died.'

For a moment I could say nothing, I was so dismayed. The one decent man aboard the whole wretched ship.

'When?' I asked.

'Just last night, of respiratory failure.'

If only Tritus had turned around earlier – or I had. 'I'm very sorry to hear that,' I said.

'Yes. Very upsetting. It seems Matthias Grunel discovered your name listed as assistant navigator in the ship's papers. He's wondering if maybe you can shed some light on the location of the *Hyperion*. He'd like to meet with you.'

'He's here in Paris?'

'Flew in this morning from Zurich. I told him I was doubtful you could be of any help. The navigational charts are no doubt with Tritus.'

'There are no charts,' I said. 'They were destroyed when a water tank burst.'

'Ah. So presumably no one has accurate coordinates.'

I hesitated a moment and then said, 'I saw the exact coordinates as Mr Domville wrote them down.'

'Planning a little treasure hunt of your own, Mr Cruse?'

I gave an uncomfortable laugh. 'No, sir, not at all.' But I thought of Kate and all the grand plans she'd already made for us. Dean Pruss was staring at me, and for an uncomfortable moment I wondered if he was going to ask me for the coordinates.

'It would be a foolhardy pilot who tried to reach the *Hyperion* at that height,' the Dean said.

'I agree, sir.'

'Still, given the ship's contents, some may try. If I were younger, and had my legs, maybe I'd be foolhardy enough too, who's to say? I wouldn't be surprised if the Grunels

60

offered you a small reward for any information. That could hardly be unwelcome, eh?'

I wondered if he too saw the scuffs and scrapes in my uniform.

'What you tell them is your own business, of course. The *Hyperion* doesn't belong to anyone any more. Not until someone boards her and claims the right of salvage.'

I thought of Kate, of how much she wanted that frozen bestiary. I thought of all the money, glinting coldly in the ship's vaults. Even Tritus did not have her coordinates – a rough idea at best, given his airsick brain. The thought of him claiming the salvage was revolting to me – after what he'd done to his ship and the crew.

Someone's going to get her, Kate had said. Why not us?

I'd been holding my breath, and now let it out in a silent gust. Kate could dream if she wanted, but the *Hyperion* was probably untouchable, and anyway, I had more pressing things on my mind. Exams were in less than three weeks and I had a lot of studying to do. If anyone was going to undertake a risky salvage attempt, it seemed right it should be Grunel's own family. Best to give them what they wanted, take the reward money, and be done with it.

'He asked if he could see you at eight o'clock,' Dean Pruss said. Across the desk he slid a thick card embossed with the insignia of the Ritz hotel. In beautiful script was written: *Matthias Grunel, Trafalgar Suite.*

'Of course.' I took the card.

'Be careful, Mr Cruse. The Grunels may not be the only people seeking those coordinates. This afternoon, apparently, there was someone asking for you at the lodge. I've instructed the porters not to give out any information about you.'

'Thank you, sir.' I felt a first flicker of apprehension.

The Dean looked at me carefully. 'You seem a sensible sort, Mr Cruse. I don't think you'll be one to go chasing after phantom gold.'

'Absolutely not, sir.'

'Good lad. I daresay your thoughts are on your upcoming exams.' He looked at a ledger on his desk. 'I see your marks in aerostatics and physics are far from satisfactory.'

'I know, sir.'

'Instinctive ability will take you only so far, Mr Cruse. Theory and mathematics are equally, if not more, important. Past heroics will not win you a flight certificate. You've got a great deal of work ahead of you if you plan on passing your second term.'

'Yes, sir.'

He rolled himself back behind the shadow of his desk. 'And if I could have your full written report by the end of the week, that would be most appreciated.'

The Academy was built around a large quadrangle, with a wide arched entranceway overlooked by the porter's lodge. The dormitories occupied the south and east wings, and were divided into several houses. I was lodged in Dornier House, on the second floor, in a room just big enough for a narrow bed, a chest of drawers, a desk, and a closet. My window looked out on to the quad. It was noisy on the weekends, especially in warm weather, when the students drank and caroused until all hours. Right now, the residence was eerily quiet, and I didn't like it. Apart from the prehistoric caretakers treading the hallways, there were only a few teachers, clerks, and a handful of upper-year students who, for one reason or another, hadn't gone out on training tours.

In the great dining hall, the rows of long wooden refectory tables were all but deserted as I ate my supper. For company I had only the giant portraits of famous aviators and past deans looming over me. Clement Ader, Billy Bishop, Amelia Gearhart, Henri Giffard, Camille von Zeppelin. It was humbling company to be in, and I'd certainly been humbled since coming to the Academy.

I was not the star pupil everyone had expected. Before working as a cabin boy, I'd attended school for only a few years. I could read and write. I could add, subtract and multiply. But at the Academy, I was suddenly expected to know all sorts of fancy math, with symbols I'd never seen before. Working hard, I could just manage the Latin, and the expository essays, and the history, but those numbers vexed me no end, jittery and slippery as eels. I just could not make sense of them. It seemed like all my years aboard the *Aurora*, watching and listening in the control car, counted for nothing. I had launched a three-hundred-metre airship; I had flown her. But I could not explain it all in equations and scientific laws. Some nights I would glare at the pages in my textbook, and I might as well have been trying to read Egyptian hieroglyphics. I told no one of my difficulties. I was too humiliated. I had dreamed of attending the Academy; all I'd ever wanted to do was fly.

I looked up into the pale eyes of Dean Pruss's portrait, and swallowed down the rest of my food with some difficulty. He was right: instinctive ability was not enough. I was not good at school, but I would work harder. If others could learn it, I could learn it. I would work until I mastered those numbers and made them do their tricks for me. I gave the Dean's portrait a wink and left the dining room.

Nearly all the windows were dark as I crossed the quad. I'd be glad when everyone returned from their tours and the Academy was back to its usual bustling self. My heels clapped too loudly against the paving stone. Maybe it was the Dean's words about a stranger asking for me, but I felt ill at ease. My eyes fell into their crow's-nest rhythm, scanning the horizons for hidden dangers. I hurried into Dornier House, feeling silly.

I had a little time before heading off to the Ritz, so I buffed up my shoes and put on a clean shirt. I hoped my uniform was enough to get me past the doorman.

'Where you off to, then?' Douglas, the night porter, called out as I passed the lodge.

'Oh, just a meeting at the Ritz,' I said.

'Quite the man of the world now, aren't we!'

I gave a cheery wave as I pushed through the great oak door and started down the steps. At the bottom, I glanced back over my shoulder. To the left of the Academy's vaulted entranceway, someone was standing in the shadows amongst the ornamental shrubs and trees, not exactly lurking, but not really wanting to be noticed either. I did not stop, but kept walking, and turned on to the busy avenue that ran along the river.

It was raining lightly, so I unfurled my umbrella. After twenty steps I looked back towards the Academy and could no longer see the figure by the doors. There were plenty of people behind me on the pavement now, most with their faces half hidden beneath their umbrellas.

Horse-drawn carriages and motorcars vied noisily for space on the road. Barges and pleasure boats glittered on the water. Across the Seine, the city glowed invitingly. The man at the newspaper kiosk gave me a friendly nod as I passed.

The whole idea of being followed seemed idiotic right now, shenanigans from a penny novelette. Cutting across Place de la Concorde and into the Tuileries gardens, I left behind the crowds and noise. It was suddenly darker among the trees, the sound of motorcars and horses dulled. My unease returned. Up ahead a great fountain trilled water. I turned on to a path that would take me more quickly back to the street.

'Excuse me.'

I doubt I would have stopped if it hadn't been a girl's voice.

I turned. It was a gypsy girl, no older than me. She wore a long leather coat. An exotic scarf was wrapped around her head, strands of night-black hair hung damply across her face and forehead. She did not have an umbrella. From the moment I set foot in Paris I had been warned about the gypsies. They'd rob you blind, a train porter had told me; they didn't even need to touch you, a shop owner had commented, they could spirit your pocketbook from your vest just by looking you in the eye.

'Do you have a minute to talk?'

Her accent was English, I noticed. 'I'm in a hurry,' I said to her.

She took a step closer. I watched her hands.

'I just want to talk to you.'

I stepped back. 'No, I really must go.' I'd heard the pretty ones sometimes distracted you while two or three of their burly men came up behind and thumped you on the head.

'You can't be afraid of me,' she said, half amused.

'I don't know you.'

'Are you Matt Cruse?'

'How did you know?' I asked foolishly.

'Monsieur, is this woman troubling you?'

I turned to see a gendarme approaching with a lantern and a billy club.

'No, officer. But I must go. I'm late.'

The gendarme turned to the girl. 'You heard the gentleman now, he doesn't wish to speak with you any longer. Are you living here in Paris, or just passing through?'

'That's none of your business.'

'It's precisely my business when dealing with your sort.'

'And what sort is that?'

'Gypsies, mademoiselle.'

'I'm a Roma.'

'Call it what you will . . .'

I walked away, feeling guilty at leaving the girl in the clutches of the gendarme. But I was truly unsettled now. Was she the one lurking in the doorway of the Academy? Had she followed me all the way? Perhaps Dean Pruss was right, and there were many people hungry for information about the *Hyperion* who might wish me harm.

I quickened my pace and within minutes I was in the Place Vendôme, encircled by sparkling restaurants and bars and boutiques. The Ritz, with its blazing windows and honeyed stone, radiated luxury and safety. An enormous doorman, clad in a brass-buttoned coat that looked like it could sink a battleship, stood before the hotel's entrance.

'Can I help you, monsieur?' he inquired.

I pulled Grunel's card from my pocket and held it out to the doorman. He glanced at it, and then pushed the door wide.

The Ritz had no lobby. I'd heard they didn't want to give room to undesirables who might come hoping for a peek or photograph of the rich and famous. I stepped quickly towards the elevators.

'Which floor, sir?' The elevator boy couldn't have been more than ten. He looked tired, the poor lad. I hoped they didn't work him too hard here. Paris was filled with young boys, and girls too, working hard, their eyes ringed with soot and exhaustion.

'The Trafalgar Suite, please.'

As he was closing the mesh screen, I saw the gypsy girl rush into the hotel, nimbly pulling free from the doorman's grip. Her eyes swept the hall and locked with mine.

'Matt Cruse, wait!' she called out, hurrying towards me, but the elevator was already starting to rise. 'Just a moment of your time, please!' she shouted as we lifted out of sight. The last thing I saw was the doorman striding angrily towards her, telling her in no uncertain terms to clear off.

'Pestering you, is she, sir?' asked the elevator boy.

'I don't know her,' I muttered. And yet she had known my name. My heart was pounding. She was just a girl – not some hooded thug – but the blazing urgency in her face and eyes shocked me. I wondered who on earth she was.

'Old Serge will have her out in no time,' said the elevator boy. 'Now then, the Trafalgar Suite is just down the hall to your left, sir.'

'Thank you.'

I gave him all the spare change in my pocket, and made my way to the door. It was a vast expanse of darkly lustrous, coffered wood, with a single button in the middle. I pressed it.

The man who opened the door was dressed in a velvet dinner jacket. He was a big fellow, and might have appeared a brute except for his trim ginger beard which lent him an air of distinction. He smoked a long brown cigarette.

'I'm Matt Cruse,' I told him.

'Matthias Grunel.' He held out his free hand and we shook. His grip was powerful. 'Please come in.'

He led me through a small foyer into a large sitting room, sumptuously decorated with enough brass and gilt and leather to put the king of Bohemia to shame. The walls were panelled, with an elaborate crown moulding at the base of the ceiling; the fireplace was marble, no doubt Italian. Enormous sprays of fresh flowers were arranged on the various sideboards and bureaus and tables and armoires.

'Thank you so much for coming,' Grunel said. 'Would you like to sit down?'

I lowered myself into an armchair so deep I nearly fell backwards. I perched on the edge, suddenly not knowing where to put my legs and hands. I wished Kate were here with me. She'd know what to do amongst fancy people.

The curtains were still parted, giving a wide view of

the Place Vendôme. Drizzle glittered in the spotlight beams aimed at the great bronze column in the square's centre. Hieroglyphs swirled around it, all the way to the top, where a statue of Napoleon stood, looking quite smug.

'Cigarette, Mr Cruse?'

'No thank you.'

'A whisky? Or something else perhaps? Port, brandy?' He gestured to the array of crystal bottles on the drinks table.

'Thank you, no.'

'Too young for such bad old habits.'

He poured himself a tumbler of some amber liquid and sat down opposite me on a sofa. 'It really is awfully good of you to come. Mr Pruss has explained why we're here, I imagine.'

'He has, yes.'

'I'm sure you can understand how we, my family, would like to reclaim our grandfather's belongings.'

'Of course.'

'Mr Pruss said you were one of his top students.'

'If he did, he was being very kind,' I replied.

'You were working as navigator aboard the *Flotsam*, yes?'

'Assistant to Mr Domville.'

'I understand it was a pretty rough ride.'

'It was indeed.'

'But it must have been something to see the *Hyperion*.'

'It really was very strange, sir.'

His sleeves were just a little too short. I might not have noticed it, except that he had astonishingly hairy wrists and forearms, and whenever he lifted his cigarette to his mouth, or reached for his tumbler on the side table, his sleeves would shoot up and reveal his hairiness. Matthias Grunel was wealthy as sin, so why on earth would he be wearing an expensive jacket that was too small for him? I'd worked three years aboard a luxury airship liner, and one thing I'd noticed about the rich: their clothes always fit. I wondered if Matthias Grunel had already squandered his family's fortune, and was now down and out, just trying to put on a good show.

'You're a resourceful young fellow by all accounts,' said Grunel. 'Your Dean wasn't sure how much you might remember, but obviously we'd be extremely grateful for any information you could give us. And my family feels very strongly that, if we do recover the *Hyperion*, you should receive a full five per cent of its value.'

'That's really too generous, sir.'

The newspaper had calculated the airship's contents at fifty million europas. Whether this was a reasonable guess or complete invention, I had no way of knowing. But that would mean two and a half million just for me. It was too mind-boggling a sum to even contemplate. It was enough for five lifetimes.

'We would insist,' said Grunel with a smile. 'After all, without your coordinates, how else could we hope to

71

find the ship? It's been a source of great sorrow to me, that my grandfather was never able to fulfil his final wishes. My grandfather was a very loving man, Mr Cruse.'

Matthias Grunel faltered for a moment, perhaps overcome with emotion. He stood and turned his back to me, staring out the window.

'He would have been so distressed to think that his beloved son and most cherished daughter – and all their offspring – had never benefited from the fruits of his great fame and industry. If we can recover the *Hyperion* – and my grandfather's body – I feel his soul will at last be able to rest in peace.'

He turned towards me, and exhaled a long rapier blade of cigarette smoke. I swallowed, feeling queasy.

This man was not Matthias Grunel.

I'd suspected it the moment I'd seen his sleeves ride up. And now I knew it with sickening certainty. It was the mention of Grunel's cherished daughter. Hadn't Kate told me Theodore Grunel had had a falling out with his only daughter? Cut her off without a penny? Kate would not get a detail like that wrong; she was a voracious and attentive reader. I trusted her completely. Ginger Beard here was an impostor.

From the drinks table he picked up a notepad and pencil, and brought them over to me.

'If you were working the charts, you probably have a pretty good idea of the *Hyperion*'s coordinates.'

I took the pencil and started writing some numbers,

then scribbled them out and put on a show of chewing my lip and frowning.

'What was it now . . .' I muttered. 'You see, sir, we'd just gone through the Devil's Fist and were mightily off course . . .'

I was not going to offer up the coordinates to this impostor, whoever he was. My only thoughts now were of getting away.

'I'm sorry, sir, I don't know what the Dean told you, but my memory's never been my strong point – and the air was so thin up there, we were over five thousand metres you know. I don't think my brain was working its best.'

'Ahh . . .' said Ginger Beard. 'Of course. But you can probably remember the rough coordinates, no? The charts would surely have been before you the whole time.'

'I know, sir, it's just . . .' I screwed my eyes shut, tapping my pencil against the pad, trying to look a proper imbecile. 'It's very embarrassing, sir, please don't tell the Dean.'

He was smiling hard at me, but it was not a kindly smile.

'Just think of the reward that could await you. Think hard now.'

I took a deep breath, wrote down a set of coordinates that were off by several hundred kilometres, and handed them over.

'There! I think that's it!' I said, standing up. 'I really

should get back now, if you don't mind. Exams are coming up and—'

'Strange though,' said Ginger Beard, and I felt myself start to sweat beneath my arms. 'I thought the *Flotsam* was bound for Alexandria over the Indian Ocean. These coordinates are well over the subcontinent.'

Only a mariner of the sea or sky could glance at raw longitude and latitude and fix them instantly on a map.

'Oh,' I said, downcast. 'I've bungled it then. I'm sorry I'm not more use to you.' Heart pounding, I turned and stepped towards the door.

'Lads!' Ginger Beard shouted. 'I think our boy needs some help remembering!'

The room was suddenly full of men, striding in from various doorways. Unlike Ginger Beard they wore no velvet smoking jackets. Clad in dark trousers, coarse shirts rolled back to the elbows, boots and caps, they emanated the unmistakable whiff of oil, aruba fuel and hydrium which marked them as airshipmen. Two of them seized me by the shoulders and pushed me back into the centre of the room, face to face with Ginger Beard.

'Don't lie to me, boy,' he said. 'You're no simpleton.'

'I really don't know,' I insisted, seeing the exact coordinates swirl before my mind's eye. Part of me wondered if I shouldn't just tell, and be done with it. But if I were to tell them, they might just as easily bundle me out the window to keep me eternally quiet.

'Shall I give him some stars to see?' said one of the men, pulling back his fist.

'No,' Ginger Beard said sharply. 'Show some respect, Bingham. This is Mr Matt Cruse, pirate slayer. We know all about you, Cruse. Read about how you bested our late lamented colleague, Mr Szpirglas.'

With a sickening jolt I wondered if these scoundrels were the last dregs of Szpirglas's crew, come to wreak their revenge.

'Don't worry,' said Ginger Beard with a wink, 'there was no love lost between me and Szpirglas. He and I parted ways years ago! I'm no pirate. That's nasty, coarse work. My name's John Rath. My colleagues and I, we're employed by some of the finest people in London and Paris. You'd be surprised. Think of us as private investigators.'

I said nothing.

'I'm here to make you a proposition, Cruse. I like what I've heard of you. You're a smart lad. Not nearly as gullible as that Dean of yours. He went for my Matthias Grunel story hook line and sinker!'

One of Rath's men gave a snort of derision.

Rath nodded appraisingly at me. 'And anyone who can send Vikram Szpirglas to a watery grave is worth ten of these great hulks behind you – no offence, lads,' he said to his henchmen. 'I think you and I can do business together, Mr Cruse. What say you? There's money in it. Plenty. You like money, don't you?'

I said nothing, but I thought of the elevator boy. I

thought of my second-hand uniform. I thought of my mother, her finger joints swollen and shiny with rheumatism, wincing as she sewed.

'It's very tempting,' I said. Maybe if I played along, I would find a chance to break free.

'Good then. What say we take you for a little ride, and talk some more. Convince you,' said Rath. 'And if not, dangling over the river from three hundred metres can often be very persuasive. Come along, gents. We're checking out!'

Two of them grabbed my arms and started marching me out of the room. John Rath downed his drink and grabbed a full bottle of whisky.

'I've quite enjoyed putting on the Ritz,' he said. 'But only a fool would pay for it.'

Out we went. An elderly couple was walking down the corridor towards us, but shrank back in terror as the men shouted at them to clear off. I considered bellowing for help, but doubted it would do me much good. We reached the stairwell. Rath kicked the door open, and up we went. At the top of the stairs, they flung another door wide and I was dragged out on to the roof of the Ritz. Drizzle wet my face.

The glow from a large skylight illuminated the underbelly of a small airship, hovering silently a metre or so off the roof. It was tied up with only bow and stern lines. As we moved towards her, twin propellers gave a cough and began to turn.

'Get him on board,' said Ginger Beard.

I gave a mighty jerk and twist and was free, but it was no good. One of the men kicked me on to my knees, and they had me again, and tighter than before. From the airship, a gangway sprang down, revealing a rectangle of pale light. Ginger Beard led the way.

A smudge of movement caught my eye. A shadowy figure slipped from the darkness of the roof and crouched before the ship's bow line. With a quick tug it was loose. There was shouting from the control car, and a spotlight flared from its underside.

The shadowy figure ran, grabbed hold of the forward landing wheel and gave a strong shove. The ship was lighter than air, and moved easily, swinging in a swift, wide arc, held only by her stern line.

'Steady her!' Ginger Beard shouted to his men from the hatchway.

The ship came straight for us, propellers whirling. We all threw ourselves to the gravel roof. The airship roared overhead, buffeting me with its engine wash. With a start I realized I was free.

'Come here!' one of the pirates barked, lunging at me on all fours.

I kicked him in the chin, scrambled up, and started running.

Someone touched my arm and I looked to see the gypsy girl keeping pace with me. Her headscarf was gone and her long black hair was tucked inside the collar of her overcoat.

'This way,' she said, veering towards the roof's edge. 'Can you jump?'

'Oh, I can jump!'

'Then *jump*!'

She sped ahead and leaped without even hesitating. Her leather coat flared out behind her like wings, and I thought, I'd like a coat like that. She touched down on the next building, arms wide for balance. My strides lengthened and I took flight, my body thrilling as it soared over the lane far below. I hit the gravel running and caught up with the girl. Blinking away the rain, I turned to look back at the Ritz. A couple of pirates stood at the roof's edge, silhouetted briefly by their airship's spotlight as it soared over them, heading for us.

'There!' I puffed, racing towards an access door jutting from the roof. The ship's drone deepened. I rattled the door but it would not budge, rickety as it was.

There was the crack of a pistol, and we cowered as the airship shot overhead and began to turn. We had to get off the roof, but I could see no other exit.

'We've got to jump again,' said the girl, and launched herself into a run. We only had a few precious seconds before the airship was upon us. There was only one other building close enough; it was not so very far, but it was lower than the Ritz and would be quite a drop. We had only a moment to pick a likely spot, then sped up and soared across – and down, landing hard amongst chimney stacks and wooden water tanks.

Cloaked in shadow, we ran across the long stretch

of rooftops, leaping alleys when needed. The airship hounded us, its spotlight fixing us time and time again. They'd dropped a couple of men down on to the roof and we could hear them behind us, trying to hem us in.

'Aim for the legs!' I heard Rath shout at them from the airship above, 'I want them alive!'

This was not an encouraging thing to hear. Up ahead, I could see the roof ending, and beyond that a great canyon between us and the next building.

'It's big,' the gypsy girl panted.

'Too big,' I said.

To our left and right were high brick walls, no ladders or likely footholds to be seen. We were cut off. Before us, the roof angled down sharply, a slate toboggan ride, ridged with garret windows.

'You've no fear of heights,' puffed the girl.

'None,' I said.

'I've heard that about you.'

The airship skidded overhead, and gunfire pockmarked the shingle. The ship's wake nearly toppled me over. The gypsy skipped over the roof's edge and skidded crazily down the slate. She grabbed a weather vane, twirled round it, and swung herself in through the open window of a garret. I heard a shriek of surprise from inside.

I could only follow. Down I went, surfing on slate, and hoping I would not overshoot the weather vane. I clutched at it and felt it bend far out, nearly spilling me off the roof altogether. My feet scrabbled against the shingles. Before me, the airship was turning and I saw Rath leaning out of the hatch, pistol cocked. I heaved myself through the open window.

It was not a graceful landing. Some bit of furniture shattered beneath me, and there was the sound of broken glass, and I was sprawled on the floor in a most undignified manner. I scrambled to my feet and found myself in a bedroom. An attractive young woman in her corset and petticoats stood screaming at the gypsy girl in French.

'Pardonnez-moi, mademoiselle,' I said. 'Just running for our lives.'

We hastily found the door of the apartment, and clattered down the corridor and into the stairwell. The sound of our wild breathing reverberated off the walls. I was barely aware of my feet touching the steps. Everything was a blur. Suddenly we were outside in the dark and drizzle, and we hurled ourselves down a narrow cobbled street, and then another, intent only on escaping the sound of propellers.

4

NADIRA

We ran for a good long time, and it was only a stitch in my side that made me stop. I stood with my hands on my hips, breathing hard. I had no idea where I was. I listened and could not hear propellers.

'I think we're OK now,' the girl said, her voice hoarse from exertion.

'Thank you,' I said, 'for helping me, up there.'

'Will you talk to me now?'

'Who are you?'

'My name's Nadira. We can go in there and have a hot drink,' she suggested, pointing up the cobbled street to the bright window of a café.

I hesitated. True, she'd helped save me from John Rath and his men, but who was to say this was not just another trap? My knees felt wobbly and I wanted to sit. It was probably a good idea to get inside, in case anyone came looking for us.

Inside the noisy café, Nadira led the way to a table near the back and asked the waiter for two coffees. She tried to gather her damp, wild hair into a braid. Long tendrils escaped and floated along her temple and cheek. I knew very few young women, and certainly none who wore leather overcoats. I shouldn't have agreed to this. She was a gypsy. Everyone had warned me.

The coffee arrived. I'd always liked the smell better than the taste, but I was chilled and shaken enough to appreciate the hot jolt of it down my throat.

'I could've warned you about them,' she said. 'If only you'd listened.'

'So you know them?' I asked suspiciously.

'I know who they are.'

'That's being evasive.'

'I don't work for them,' she said, 'if that's what you mean.'

'Who do you work for then?' I asked.

'No one. Myself.'

She was very pretty and it made me uncomfortable. Was that why I was still sitting here? Or was I genuinely, dangerously, curious? I found the way she looked at me unnerving. Her gaze had a locksmith's insistence. I didn't know if her dark eyes held curiosity, wariness or even hatred for me.

'I thought you'd be bigger,' she commented. 'All those stories about you in the newspaper.'

'Well, they tend to exaggerate, don't they?'

'They certainly do.'

I hoped she didn't think me a paltry specimen. 'How did you find me?'

She took another sip of her coffee. 'I've got a business proposition for you.'

'You want us to team up and salvage the *Hyperion*?' I suggested.

'That's right,' Nadira said. 'There's a fortune on board, and I want it. You have the coordinates, don't you?'

There was no risk of our being overheard in the din of the café. We had to lean across the table even to hear each other. Mingled with the damp odour of her leather overcoat was a warm, faintly spicy smell. Cumin, maybe. Working around Chef Vlad's kitchen for years, there weren't too many spices I wasn't acquainted with.

'I don't think I'm interested,' I told her.

'Is it because I'm a gypsy?'

I did not answer.

'You don't know anything about the Roma, do you?' she demanded. 'I mean aside from the fact that we're all pickpockets and brigands?'

'No, not really,' I replied.

'You shouldn't believe every nasty rumour you hear.'

'I'm sure you're right.' I felt ashamed.

'So, what do you think? Can we work together?'

'I don't even know you,' I said.

'No, but you need me.'

'I do?'

Nadira reached a hand down through her collar and lifted out a thin leather case that hung around her neck. With her long fingers she snapped open the clasp and drew out a tarnished brass key. An ingenious-looking thing it was, and obviously quite old, with all sorts of prongs that folded out from the central shaft, and revolved around it. It was as much a puzzle as a key. I'd never seen anything so intricate.

'It looks like it could unlock the gates of heaven,' I said.

'Almost.' She deftly folded it up and slid it back into the leather pouch. I tried not to look at the smooth dusky skin of her throat. 'It unlocks the cargo holds aboard the *Hyperion*.'

'How do you know?'

'I have it on very good authority,' she said.

'Where'd you get the key?'

She did not even blink. 'That's my business.'

'Did you steal it from John Rath?'

'No. He found out I had it, and came looking for me. I did a little spying, and overheard them talking about you. They said you had the coordinates. So I got passage to Paris as fast as I could. I wanted to warn you.'

'Where are you from?' I asked.

'London.'

I'd suspected as much from her accent. She'd come all the way from Angleterre to find me. Had she travelled alone – practically unheard of for a girl in proper society? And who had paid her way? Or maybe she had her own means. I imagined she must be entangled in some dangerous criminal underworld. How else would such a valuable key have come into her possession? She dressed like a man. She spied. She could leap across rooftops and dodge bullets. Altogether she was a mystery.

'You have the coordinates,' she said, 'I've got the key. We need each other.'

I shrugged. 'Locks can be broken.'

'Not these ones.'

'You seem to know an awful lot,' I said, 'but you're not telling me much. Why should I trust you?'

'Look,' Nadira said, leaning even closer to me. Her teeth were very white against her skin. 'Grunel knew there were air pirates about, and he didn't want to take any chances. The cargo holds are all ferro-titanium cages, and they're booby-trapped. If anyone tries to get into them without unlocking the doors, they blow up. Grunel only had one key made, by some fancy locksmith in Switzerland. But the locksmith was so proud of his special key he couldn't shut up about it, and word got out to a group of pirates. They paid the locksmith a visit, and found he'd kept his designs. They held him at gunpoint until he made them their very own copy. Then they shot him.'

'And somehow,' I said, 'you've got that copy.'

'It was a gift.'

'Quite a gift.'

'The pirates never did find the *Hyperion*. That's what I was told. It just disappeared. Everyone assumed it had crashed into the sea. The key lost all its value. It was just a curiosity. Over the years it passed from person to person. My father won it in a card game and gave it to me when I was eight.'

'Your father's not interested in this venture?'

'He's dead.'

Suddenly I felt very tired. 'You can't know if that key's the real thing.'

'It's the real thing,' she said, quiet but fierce.

'We should be talking to the Sky Guard,' I said, 'or the Airborne Police.'

'What on earth for?'

'John Rath and his men were shooting at us!' I exclaimed. 'They're dangerous.'

'We'll avoid them. If we go to the Sky Guard they're going to want your coordinates, and my key. There's no way I'm handing it over.'

'I really don't want to get involved with this,' I said.

'You're already involved,' she told me. 'You're the only person on the planet with the ship's coordinates.'

'I'll go to the newspapers then. They can publish the information for the whole world to see, and then I'm through with it.'

She looked at me silently for a moment, then gave a nod. 'You're not interested? Fair enough. Just give me the coordinates. I'll have a go.'

I made no reply.

'See!' she said. 'You *are* interested!'

'Honestly, I don't know.'

'You can't pass this up,' she insisted. 'We need this, you and I.'

'What do you mean?' I felt like she'd tossed a rope around us both and cinched it tight.

'I think you know,' she said. 'You're not from money. The newspapers said you have no father, but you've got a mother and sisters back home to take care of. All you had was a cabin boy's salary and that's gone now you're at the Academy. It's going to be a struggle.'

She seemed to know a lot about me. I didn't know whether to be flattered or alarmed.

'You're trying to make a go of it on your own,' Nadira said. 'And so am I. We need big breaks.' There was such urgency in her face. 'This would be the biggest break of all.'

I sighed. 'I think I should be going.'

'Where?'

'The Academy,' I told her.

'You might have company waiting for you.'

Goosebumps erupted across my belly and neck. She was right. Rath and his men knew exactly where to find me.

'I'll have to tell the Dean,' I said. 'He was fooled by—'

'Who says he was fooled? Maybe they offered him a cut.'

'No,' I said, 'he's not in on it. He got tricked. Rath said so himself.'

'Go then,' she said miserably. 'No one's stopping you.'

I put some money on the table for the coffee, and got up.

'Don't you even want to know where to find me?' she asked.

'No.'

'One-nine-nine rue Zeppelin,' she said. 'It's near the aeroport.'

'I know where it is.'

She held my gaze. 'Remember, you can't do this without me.'

'So you've said.'

'Well, you can't.'

'Goodbye,' I said. 'And thank you.'

I was grateful to be back on the street, in the night's cool drizzle. After walking for half an hour, it all began to seem like a dream: John Rath at the Ritz, the rooftop chase, the gypsy girl who came to my rescue. I looked about me. The buildings were so solid, the flagstone hard beneath my feet. My eyes grazed the faces of the men I passed, but all I saw were ordinary people going about their normal lives. The air smelled like stone and cold trees and the river.

I wasn't far from the Academy now. Down the boulevard I beheld its impressive façade, warm and welcoming in the glow from the streetlamps. I was exhausted. I wanted sleep. At the bottom of the steps I hesitated, then told myself I was being silly. In the morning I would talk to the Dean, and then I would go to the Sky Guard and tell them everything. I walked through the entrance archway.

I couldn't see Douglas in the porter's lodge. A mug of tea was steaming on his desk beside the late edition of *La Presse*. I walked on into the quadrangle. Usually it was bathed in the light from the surrounding dormitory windows, but now it was murky. I looked up at Dornier House and picked out my window. Behind the glass something shifted.

Electricity jolted through my body, and I actually let out a gasp. I spun around and ran back to the porter's lodge.

'Douglas!'

There was no reply from the back room. Perhaps he was doing his rounds, or had been summoned away on some urgent business. I stood, frozen for a moment, unsure of what to do. The great clock in the hallway ticked. Far away I heard a door creak. A few footsteps, then silence.

I fled. Perhaps I was unwise, and cowardly, but I wanted to get out of the building. I dashed out the main doors and back on to the street. I stood for a moment, comforted by the passing carriages, and the moving constellation of airship lights overhead. A gendarme strolled past on the other side of the street. I wondered if I really had seen someone behind the window. One thing I knew for certain. I could not sleep in my own room tonight.

Kate's house was on the Île St-Louis, a little island floating in the shadow of Notre Dame. I took the footbridge behind the cathedral to the island's tip, and headed down the Quai de Baudelaire. The street was an unbroken wall of baroque mansions, rising like a glorious fortress over the river and the city's Left Bank. Just looking at all those grand houses made me feel poor. Kate's was number twenty-six.

Deirdre, one of her maids, opened the door to me. I knew she was from the same country as my parents, but when once I'd tried using my few words of Gaelic, she had pretended she didn't understand me, and refused to reply. Now that she was a maid in a fancy Parisian mansion, I supposed she was embarrassed by her birthplace. It had made me feel sad, and vaguely humiliated.

'Monsieur?' she said with a disapproving air.

For the first time, I realized I must look a sight, my uniform all crumpled, my overcoat dirty and grease-stained, and torn where a pocket had been ripped out during the chase. No doubt my face was gritty with soot and sweat.

'I am very dirty,' I said in my poor French.

'Yes, you are very dirty, monsieur, it is true,' she replied, without any hint of amusement.

'I am calling for Miss Kate de Vries.'

'At this hour, monsieur? It is late.'

'It is not so truly late.'

'Was she expecting you?'

'Yes. I mean no.'

Deirdre hesitated, as if wondering whether I even deserved to be admitted. Eventually she held the door open a bit wider and I squeezed inside. The ceiling soared overhead. "A cosy little place in Paris" was the way Kate had described it to me. 'It's not an entire house, only the first two floors,' she'd pointed out when I first visited. 'Just somewhere I can rest my head while I study at the Sorbonne.' Many people could rest their heads here. About forty-nine, I reckoned.

'If monsieur would care to wait here, I will see if Mademoiselle de Vries is receiving visitors tonight.'

'You are very kind,' I said, or it might have been, 'You are a knee.' I wasn't sure. French was a vexing language. I never knew which letters to pronounce and which to ignore. I decided I should talk faster, slew everything together, and see how I got by. It was lucky for me all my lectures at the Academy were in English, the international language of aviation.

Deirdre was just starting upstairs when another maid burst out from a doorway and started hissing at Deirdre so rapidly I had not a clue what she was saying. Clearly there was some unpleasantness going on in the kitchen.

'Please wait,' Deirdre told me, and disappeared.

I waited a minute, and then a minute more, and wondered if I'd been forgotten. I could go into the kitchen and remind Deirdre I was still here, but why bother? I knew where Kate would be this time of night. Upstairs in her beloved library.

The great walnut staircase curved gracefully up to the second floor. My footfalls were muted by the oriental runner. Halfway up, I realized that this was probably a very foolish move on my part. If Miss Simpkins were to come across me, she would accuse me of slinking around the house unescorted. But it was too late now, and I could see the library door, just slightly ajar, spilling light into the hallway.

As I drew closer I heard voices. One of them, I was certain, did not belong to either Kate or Miss Simpkins. I peeped through the crack in the doorway.

There was a gentleman in the library. He was turned away from me, but he looked tall and broad, impressive in his suit and gleaming leather shoes. Hands clasped behind his back, he was admiring a glass case which contained some zoological specimen Kate must have purchased in Paris.

'Miss de Vries, this creature is vicious to behold.'

'Nonsense,' said Kate, sitting in an armchair near the fireplace. I could see her in profile, her face flushed – I hoped only from the merry blaze in the hearth. 'It's a marsupial, Mr Slater. Its cousin is the kangaroo. You're upset by the teeth, perhaps?'

'It's an ugly thing,' he said. 'It reminds me of my aunt.'

At this, Kate laughed, a sort of high tinkling wind-chime laugh that splashed cold through my body. That was a laugh I had considered mine alone. She had no right to go trilling it out for someone else. I had never heard her mention this Mr Slater.

'You certainly are an accomplished young lady, Miss de Vries,' he said, turning to her.

I saw that he was indeed a dashing fellow, perhaps in his early twenties. All I knew for sure was that he was older than me, that he cut the figure of a fine gentleman, where I still looked a boy. I tried to see if Miss Simpkins was in the room with them. What on earth were they doing alone?

'And what about you, Mr Slater?' Kate asked. 'Your own accomplishments are very impressive indeed.'

To hear her praise him so warmly made my mouth dry with jealousy and indignation.

'Ah,' Slater said, trying to sound modest, but clearly pleased. 'So much of what happens to us in life is luck, don't you think?'

He came and stood beside her chair, one hand resting on the back.

'I don't agree with you there,' Kate said. 'I think we make our own luck.'

He pursed his lips thoughtfully and gave a small manly chuckle. 'A fine notion to be sure. But chance runs like a river through all our lives, and being prepared for surprise is the best we can do.'

'How fatalistic of you,' said Kate.

'Not at all. I didn't say we had no control of our lives. Quite the contrary. I think the man who is dealt bad luck, but makes good despite it, is the most noble of men.'

'And does the same go for women?' Kate inquired.

'When I say *man*, naturally I mean *woman* too.'

'I prefer to say it aloud,' Kate remarked.

'Completely understandable, Miss de Vries.'

'Thank you, Mr Slater.'

Every charming word they exchanged was like a stake

driven into my chest. I should have left, but I could not. Rivets held my feet to the ground. I was no more capable of movement than the Eiffel Tower.

'Actually,' said Slater, 'I much prefer to have the word *woman* on my lips.'

As I watched in icy horror, he leaned towards her, and I knew he was about to kiss her. I could not see Kate, for Slater was blocking my view. As if from far away, I heard a door open, and someone must have entered the library, because Slater stood upright and turned with a graceful smile.

'Ah, Miss Simpkins, we were wondering when you'd rejoin us.'

'I was just looking for my book,' said Miss Simpkins. There was a girlish, slightly constricted quality to her voice I'd never heard before. 'I must have left it here. Ah! There it is.'

'I'm amazed you have so many books on the go, Marjorie,' I heard Kate say dryly. My view of her face was still blocked, but I imagined there was a small smile on her lips as she looked at her chaperone.

'Really, you two,' said the chaperone, 'it is getting rather late.'

'Yes, I must be off,' Mr Slater said, looking at Kate with merry eyes. With a laugh he added, 'I fear Miss Simpkins sees me as a disreputable suitor.'

'Dear sir, not at all,' said Miss Simpkins, coming into view. The colour in her cheeks was high, and she seemed rather flustered. 'You are clearly of the most reputable sort. It's such a shame that my Kate seems to have a penchant for the disreputable kind.'

'Really?' said Mr Slater. 'How intriguing.'

'Marjorie, please,' said Kate, sounding annoyed.

'She prefers cabin boys,' Miss Simpkins said with a titter.

Mr Slater gave a laugh. 'Oh, this must be the famous Matt Cruse, the young lad on the *Aurora*.' He didn't say it mockingly, but I didn't like the tinge of amusement in his voice. 'Rather taken with him, were you, Miss de Vries?'

Kate said nothing. I still could not see her face. I counted my seismic heartbeats, waiting, then turned and walked away, fast.

Halfway down the stairs I passed Deirdre, who stared at me in shock.

'Monsieur! This is not right!'

'No, it's not right at all,' I said bitterly.

I hurried out the front door and on to the wet cobbled street. It was raining heavily now, and I ran along the Quai de Baudelaire, towards the midnight bulk of Notre Dame. I had no destination in mind, I just kept running, taking corners and bridges as they loomed up in my smeared vision. On the left bank, half soaked, I took the stairs down to the river and found a dry spot underneath a bridge. It was cold. The wind played bassoon through the girders and cables of the bridge's underside. For a long time, I just stared at the dark water, flowing like mercury into hell's caverns.

Then my thoughts began to run swiftly. What was she doing with that man? How long had she known him? They seemed very familiar. She laughed for him. Maybe she'd even touched him, or let him kiss her earlier. At the mere idea I felt a volcanic rage in my heart. Slater was tall and handsome and wealthy by the look and sound of it.

I was once a cabin boy. Now I was a student. I would never be wealthy. If I ever managed to graduate from the Academy, the best I could look forward to was an officer's salary – a year of which would buy the rugs in Kate's apartment. She was ashamed of me. She thought I was absurd. She could not even say anything when Slater and Miss Simpkins mocked me.

Before meeting Kate, I'd never thought much about money. I did now. I thought of money all the time. It was everywhere. I saw banknotes and coins flashing between the gloved fingers of gentlemen and ladies, brighter than gold ingots. I saw money in my fellow students at the Academy, in their clothes and shoes and pens. I saw it gleaming like jewels in Kate's dark hair. I saw it like a sheen on her lovely lips. I counted it in the stars.

I'd been a fool to think it wasn't important. When my mother's hands became too swollen and painful to work, and my sisters got older, they would need money more than ever. I did not want them to worry, or lack for things, or have my little sisters marry men they didn't love, just to make ends meet. I wanted to take care of them. Without money, I was useless. Without money I could be mocked and thrown out of restaurants and pushed aside for the likes of Mr Slater.

The night passed, taking forever and no time at all. I shivered and pulled my tattered coat around me and felt good and sorry for myself. But before the rising sun had painted the highest gargoyles of Notre Dame red, I had made a decision.

5

AT THE HELIODROME

I went to the Banque du Quebec and withdrew everything in my savings account. At first I didn't think they'd let me, I looked so scruffy after spending the night under the bridge. But after comparing my signature with the one on file, and a few whispered words with the manager, the teller counted out the flimsy notes before me. Holding them in my hand, it seemed a trifling amount. I wondered if any decent captain would agree to charter his ship to a sixteen-year-old boy, even with the promise of a cargo bay crammed with riches. I sealed the money in an envelope and hurried out to rue Avro to catch a tram.

I knew I was being rash, and wished I had a steady mind to counsel me. I thought of Captain Walken and Baz. But Captain Walken was piloting the *Aurora* over the Orient this season, and Baz was on leave with his new bride on an island near the Great Barrier Reef. Both had always given me good advice. I didn't know who else to turn to. My professors at the Academy were knowledgeable, but distant, and I didn't feel any special connection with any of them. I dared not approach Dean Pruss, for I knew he would threaten me with expulsion if I carried out my mad scheme.

I hopped on to the tram bound for the Bois de Boulogne and was lucky enough to find a seat. How I wished I could talk things over with Kate. But I refused even to consider it. She had betrayed me. Whenever I thought of Slater bending towards her, a searing wave of humiliation and anger and jealousy broke across me, and I had to clamp my teeth to stop myself baying like a lunatic.

Kate wanted the *Hyperion*.

But she would not have it. All her money could not buy it for her.

It would be mine to claim. I would return to Paris a rich man, and the custodian of a coveted zoological collection to boot. And then we'd see if I was so easy to dismiss.

The skyways over Paris were always busy, but they became even more congested as we neared the airship harbour. Some of the luxury liners, like the *Aurora* and *Titania*, moored at the Eiffel Tower, but most airships, and all the commercial vessels, docked at the Paris Aeroport, amid the vast parklands of the Bois de Boulogne. I knew the area well, since all the Academy students came here regularly for lessons and training flights.

Ranged along the outskirts of the aeroport were enormous fuel silos, bearing the crimson insignia of the

Aruba Consortium. It was hydrium that gave airships their lift, but it was aruba fuel which powered their hungry engines. For that matter, it was aruba fuel that heated and lit Paris, and practically every city in the world.

At the last stop, I hopped off the tram. Overhead, airships circled gracefully, waiting for the harbour master's permission before making their final approaches. The sight of all those ships in the sky never failed to stir me. Even after six months in Paris, I still felt a bit lumpen on the ground, as though it wasn't just my body that moved more slowly but also my mind. Everything seemed to take longer. Sometimes I'd catch myself staring at the clouds scudding overhead and wonder why my life wasn't moving at the same speed. It gave me some comfort now to think I might soon be on one of these ships, bound for the high sky.

I walked along rue Zeppelin, looking for the address Nadira had given me. I now understood the desperation I'd seen last night in her eyes. I wanted the *Hyperion*. I saw its icy hull before my mind's eye and it seemed an Aladdin's cave that could solve all my problems. I didn't know if this fancy key of hers was just a hoax, but if Nadira was brave enough to try to salvage a ship at seven thousand metres, she might be a valuable shipmate.

The street was lined with ship's provisioners, and rooming houses for the harbour's constant ebb and flow of sky sailors. After the grand boulevards of central Paris, rue Zeppelin had a down-at-heel look. Even at this early hour of the morning, there were loud sailors reeking with drunkenness, prostitutes standing boldly in doorways. One caught my eye and winked, and I was afraid she might step up and try to talk to me, so I looked straight ahead and hurried on. None of this was new to me; I'd seen my share of air harbours around the world.

Nadira's address was a rooming house above a sailmaker's shop. It looked a little more presentable than most, and as I went through into the courtyard, I was met by a jolly-looking landlady mopping the flagstones.

'Ah, the gypsy princess, but she's gone out, my dear.'

'I don't suppose she said when she'd be back?'

'No. But if you tell me your name, I'll let her know you called.'

'Matt Cruse,' I said, wondering if I should be giving out my name.

'Ah, well in that case, mon cher, she left a message for you.'

She disappeared inside for a moment, leaving me alone in the courtyard. Through the ground-floor windows I could see a team of sailmakers sitting at long tables, painstakingly stitching together great bolts of goldbeater's skin into airship gas cells. Hydrium was the lightest gas in the world – or how else could such enormous vessels take to the skies – but it was also wily, and it could make its escape through the tiniest of gaps. The goldbeater's skin was made from cows' intestines, specially treated so it was impermeable.

The landlady returned holding a sealed envelope.

'There you are.'

'Thank you very much.'

Nadira must have been pretty sure of me to leave a note. Her handwriting was crimped and awkward, not so unlike mine. 'At harbour master's, trying to find a ship. Meet me there.' And that was all. Quite presumptuous of her really. I wondered how much experience she had with ships. Certainly she seemed plenty capable in every other way.

The Paris Aeroport was the largest in the world, and it took me almost half an hour to reach the harbour master's office, walking past countless open-air berths. Tethered to their mooring masts, the airships floated three metres above the ground. All around me were passengers boarding and disembarking, stevedores lowering freight from cargo bays, sailmakers patching, engineers and machinists inspecting fins and engines.

The harbour master's offices occupied a remodelled hangar, and inside was all the bustle of the Stock Exchange. Hundreds of clerks went about their frenzied business of tracking the comings and goings of vessels from around the world; customs officials checked cargos and paperwork; officers negotiated their berthing fees and made out work orders. There seemed no method in the place, and I wondered how I would ever find Nadira in all this.

I made my way over to the great wall where all the day's shipping news was posted. Here, you could find the name of every vessel in port, her captain, cargo, berth, engine size. I knew what I was after. A powerful tug with plenty of engines that could haul the *Hyperion* back to earth. But none of the information posted on the boards would tell me if the ship was capable of high flight. I was doubtful we could even find such a ship.

'I've got an interesting lead,' Nadira said, suddenly beside me.

No hello, no sign of relief that I'd actually shown up. Gone were the trousers and leather overcoat. She was swathed in a beautiful orange sari, and I must say, she looked altogether dazzling in it.

'You've been busy,' I muttered.

'I saw no point waiting. I didn't know if you'd come. There's a ship at berth thirty-two.'

'A tug?' I asked.

'Salvage ship. The clerk said it had set some sort of record for above-cloud flying.'

'Really?' I scarcely knew whether to believe it.

'According to the shipping news,' Nadira said, 'she's not going anywhere this week. And the name's promising too.'

'What's that?'

'The *Sagarmatha*,' she said. 'It's the Nepalese word for—'

'Everest. I know.'

'We should go look at her.'

She knew enough to call a ship a she, and I wondered if she'd spent a lot of time around harbours and airships. She certainly seemed to have no fear of rooftop acrobatics. I remembered the way she'd surfed down the slate, pirouetted round the weather vane and launched herself through the garret window. It was quite something.

We left the swirling crowds of the harbour master's office and set off for berth thirty-two.

'How were you planning on paying for the charter?' I asked her.

'I wasn't.'

I stopped. 'Then what were you planning?'

'We offer the captain a cut.'

That was certainly preferable to spending all my savings.

'How big a cut?' I asked.

'I thought you weren't interested in money,' she remarked.

'Oh, I've changed my tune.'

'I was thinking fifty per cent,' she said.

That didn't seem unreasonable, since he was putting up the ship and the fuel, and bearing a huge weight of the risk.

'And how were you planning on splitting the rest?' I asked.

'Half and half.'

'Fine.' If there were millions on board, as everyone seemed to think, there'd be enough for everyone. 'But I want all the taxidermy.'

'The what?' she asked.

'Dead animals, stuffed.' I cleared my throat. 'Apparently Grunel had quite a big collection aboard.'

'You're welcome to it,' she said.

'Thank you. We need to be careful. We'd better make sure we trust the captain and crew. That key around your neck is easily stolen.'

'Only from my dead body,' she said.

'They might not have a problem with that,' I told her.

'What about you? Once you tell them the coordinates, what's to stop them from tumbling you out the hatchway at three thousand metres?'

I thought for a moment. 'Well, it would be awfully poor manners.'

I think she smiled, but I wasn't sure. 'We need to find someone with impeccable manners then.'

Berth thirty-two was inside the new Heliodrome, at the north end of the aeroport. All of Paris was buzzing about the Heliodrome because it had just been officially named the largest man-made structure on earth. Its vast dome rose up over the aeroport like some enormous mosque, with minaret control towers soaring from its four corners. Within, it offered protected mooring for countless airships.

We stepped inside. The ceiling was so high you could be forgiven for thinking it was the vault of heaven itself. Enormous retractable doors on all sides allowed airships to enter and exit wherever the winds were most favourable. One was just coming in now, a mid-sized liner called the *Pompeii* which was being walked in by the ground crew. The *Pompeii* was two hundred metres long, but within the Heliodrome she looked like a child's toy.

A network of pedestrian catwalks was suspended high above the floor, so as not to interfere with the movement of the airships or ground crews. We started up a spiral staircase, and climbed the two hundred and fifty steps to the catwalks. I paused, taking in the stunning view. I could see the entire hangar and there must have been close to a hundred ships currently docked inside. I asked someone where berth thirty-two was and got pointed in the right direction.

An entire section of the Heliodrome was devoted to shipbuilding, and I saw some massive alumiron skeletons, all their ribs and vertebrae showing. Another ship was closer to completion, and the sailmakers were inflating the huge gas cells within her mainframe. Still others were being fitted with their outer skin. From start to finish, the building of an airship could take years.

We were half way across the Heliodrome when, to my astonishment, I saw Kate de Vries walking towards us along a converging catwalk. She wore a purple tailored suit with a fur collar and cuffs, and a wide-brimmed hat sprouting violet feathers. Beside her strode Mr Slater. We came face to face and stopped, fourteen storeys above the earth, in the dead centre of the Heliodrome.

'Miss de Vries,' I said.

'Mr Cruse,' she returned. There was a terrible moment of silence as everyone looked at everyone else. No introductions were offered.

'Might I have a moment alone with you?' Kate said to me.

'I don't see why not.'

'Excuse us just a moment please.' She smiled politely to Nadira and Mr Slater and the two of us walked off a-ways.

'So who's your charming gypsy friend?' Kate asked conversationally.

'That's Nadira.'

'Lovely name,' she said.

'Isn't it?'

'Have you known her long?' Kate inquired.

'Practically forever. I'm surprised I never mentioned her to you.'

'Look,' Kate said, putting a hand on my arm, 'I've been trying to reach you at the Academy. Where have you been?'

I moved my arm away. 'Making plans.'

'Deirdre told me you called last night,' Kate said.

'Yes. I spied you with your gentleman friend. Mr Slater I believe.'

She smiled. 'I can explain.'

'You don't need to explain anything. I'm turning a blind eye. Just like Miss Simpkins.' I wished I had been blind, rather than see Slater bending over her. 'You can do whatever you want.'

'You think I'm interested in him?' said Kate.

'I saw you kiss him.'

'*He* tried to kiss *me*!'

'And did you let him?' I demanded.

'Fortunately Marjorie entered the room.'

I didn't think that exactly answered my question. 'It's none of my business anyway,' I said coldly.

'Ah, but it is your business, very much so.' Her eyes twinkled. 'It's *our* business.'

'What're you talking about?'

'That gentleman over there,' she said, 'is going to fly us to the *Hyperion*.'

'I never said I was going.'

'Of course you're going,' she said.

'Maybe I am, but who says with you?'

'Oh, stop being dramatic, Matt. Mr Slater has a ship that can go very, very high.' She raised an eyebrow significantly.

I stared stupidly for a second. 'You're not serious.'

'He built one,' Kate told me. 'Just six months ago.'

'A skybreaker?' I breathed in amazement. I looked over at Slater. 'He's awfully young to have his own ship. Does he come from money?'

'Made every penny himself, I gather,' Kate replied. 'He struck out on his own, and did awfully well.'

Ship owner and captain both. I felt my jealousy re-ignite.

'How did you find him?' I wanted to know.

'Philippe, my ornithopter instructor, put me on to

him. So I asked Mr Slater over last night to see if he would be a suitable pilot for us.'

'I gather you found him agreeable.'

'He's a very brazen man,' Kate said. 'In normal circumstances, I'd never associate with him. All I care about is his ship. So there. You aren't allowed to be angry with me any more. But I must say' – her eyes strayed towards Nadira – '*I'm* wondering if I should be angry with *you*.'

'I just met her last night. I had a little adventure with pirates.' Very quickly, I told her about my encounter at the Ritz, and how Nadira had helped me escape.

'So you were going to team up with her instead of me?' Kate inquired with frightening calm.

'I thought you were all cosy with Mr Slater!' I protested.

'She's a complete stranger, Matt!'

I raised my hands, trying to shush her.

'Don't shush me,' she said, eyes blazing. 'I hate being shushed.'

'Then you should talk more quietly. Listen, she has the key.'

Kate faltered. 'What key?'

'To the *Hyperion*'s cargo holds. She says they're booby-trapped.'

'A likely story,' she sniffed.

What about Slater? Do you trust him?'

'I think so, yes.'

'How much have you told him?' I asked.

'Just that I had the last known coordinates of the *Hyperion*.'

'That was cheeky.'

'It did the trick,' Kate said. 'He's willing to take us.'

'I want to make sure I trust him,' I said. 'He's not the only ship in town. We've got our own lead on a high flyer.'

'The *Sagarmatha*? Berth thirty-two?'

'Oh.' I took a breath. 'Slater's ship, is it? Well, we'd better introduce everyone then.'

We walked back to the others. Slater was gazing patiently out over the Heliodrome, and Nadira was staring hard at me. This was going to be complicated. Slater turned and strolled towards me, hand outstretched.

'Hal Slater,' he said. His grip was stronger than I liked.

'Matt Cruse.' I squeezed back as hard as I could. He squeezed even harder, then let go.

Nadira looked at me. 'You didn't tell me you already had partners.'

'I didn't last night. Mr Slater here is captain of the *Sagarmatha*. And Kate de Vries is a friend of mine with a special interest in the *Hyperion*'s cargo.'

'How do you do?' Kate said, offering Nadira her hand. Nadira took it reluctantly. She didn't look at all pleased.

'Obviously we have some things to discuss,' said Slater. 'Perhaps we could do so in private aboard my ship.'

'I think that would be a good idea,' I said, not liking the way he took control.

He was a handsome devil, and naturally I hated him

on sight. He had a broad forehead, high cheekbones flushed with good health and vigour, blue eyes, and a square jaw. Wavy blond hair was swept straight back from his forehead, though I was happy to note that his hair was thinning somewhat at the temples. I thought his nose a bit bulbous – Kate, I hoped, might say it lacked refinement. And this too: he looked the slightest bit too big for his suit, like his body was merely putting up with it. It wanted boots and a leather aviator's jacket. I wondered if Kate had noticed the two small holes above his left eyebrow where a ring had once pierced his skin, a common enough fashion among sky sailors – and pirates for that matter.

Slater led the way along the catwalk. Trailing in his dashing wake, I was aware of my torn and dirty overcoat, my scuffed shoes. I must have looked a proper beggar.

I kept hoping for a glimpse of his ship, but she was berthed directly behind an enormous Russian liner. It wasn't until we were heading down the spiral stairs to berth thirty-two that I got a good look at the *Sagarmatha*, and she completely stopped me in my tracks. She was a beauty.

'Smitten already?' Kate quipped as she stepped around me.

Just looking at her made my stomach clench with envy. If the *Aurora* was like a magnificent blue whale, the *Sagarmatha* was like a tiger shark. I reckoned she was about fifty metres from stem to stern, maybe ten high, and all muscle. Her outer skin had been reinforced with an exoskeleton of ultra-light alumiron, to protect her, I supposed, from the scuffs and collisions inevitable in salvage work. But the *Sagarmatha* did not look scuffed or scraped at all: she was pristine. The copper of her oversized engine cars gleamed as if hand-polished. Like the ship's hull, the entire control car was sheathed in a kind of protective filigree, without a patch of tarnish or rust. Spotlights and mechanical arms and coupling gear bristled from her underside.

'What do you think, lad?' Slater asked, waiting for me at the gangway.

'Not bad for a tugboat,' I said.

'Oh! A tugboat!' he exclaimed, looking wounded. 'You are unkind, sir! Come aboard and have a look around. Let me change your mind. The *Sagarmatha*'s a beauty. Her name is Nepalese for—'

'I've sailed past Everest several times.'

'Ah! But have you ever sailed *over* her?'

The summit was nine and a half thousand metres. 'It can't be done,' I said.

'Can't it?' He gave me a wink. 'I could sail over her; I could probably give her a good tug if need be.' He nodded at the massive starboard engine cars. 'Notice anything special about them?'

I took a closer look and gave a gasp of amazement when I saw they were totally sealed, only the shaft and propeller sticking out.

'They're pressurized,' I said.

'That's right. Don't have to worry about thin air stalling my engines.'

'What's their maximum altitude?' I asked, wanting to sound knowledgeable.

'Haven't found it yet.'

'How do you stop your gas cells blowing?'

'She's designed to carry two extra cells, empty,' Slater said. 'When my hydrium expands too much, I route it to the overflow cells.'

'And if they fill?'

He smiled. 'Ah. That's a little secret of mine. Can you guess?'

'You've got a compressor on board and you pump the hydrium into tanks.'

'You're a thinker,' he said.

We stood staring at each other appraisingly. I heard Kate clear her throat.

'Sorry, ladies,' Slater said, turning unapologetically, 'just a bit of man talk. After you.'

Once up the gangway, I noticed that he was careful to lock the hatch behind us. Slater led us along a clean, well-lit corridor which had carpeting, and a brass railing running along one side.

'The mess is just through here,' he said, opening a door and ushering us inside.

This was no tugboat's mess. It looked more like a gentlemen's club. One side of the room had a generous dining table, set atop a Persian rug, and surrounded by elegant high-backed chairs. Through a wide archway was the lounge, filled with leather armchairs of dark green, and cognac, footstools and side tables, and a few enormous potted plants. There was a small but well-stocked bookcase, a rack of newspapers, and a gramophone. Against the wall, a fine mantelpiece was built around an electric fire. There was a small bar in one corner, its counter made of a dark tropical hardwood. The room was amply lit, from overhead lamps but also from a long panel of reinforced glass set into the floor. A faint aroma of cigar smoke lingered in the room. Not even the officers on the *Aurora* had such a fine lounge.

'Surprised, Mr Cruse?' Hal Slater asked.

I was indeed. Though the ship was a commercial vessel, Slater had obviously not stinted on the interior. Most freighters and tugs I'd seen were a gloomy webwork of catwalks and platforms, with hammocks strung between girders.

'It's very well appointed,' I remarked.

'This is my one and only home,' he said. 'I like to have a few comforts at day's end. Now let's all have a seat.'

We settled ourselves around one end of the dining table. Kate and Nadira sat side by side, both gazing at me, and looking thoroughly displeased. I could not help staring back, for they made quite a contrast: Kate's pale skin and elegant purple suit, Nadira's dusky skin and exotic fiery sari.

'Do we clash?' Nadira said dryly.

'We certainly do,' said Kate. 'Would you like me to move?'

'Don't trouble yourself.'

'Shall we begin?' said Slater. 'Miss de Vries has already apprised me of the situation, and I *am* interested in the venture. But it seems to me it requires a great deal of secrecy. How shall we all be satisfied our partners are trustworthy? For my part, I have no quibble with Miss de Vries, or Matt Cruse. But Miss Nadira here worries me.'

I was both startled and impressed by his bluntness.

'She has a key that opens the cargo holds,' I said, and repeated for Slater the story I had told Kate.

'Let's see this key, then,' said Slater.

Nadira took it from its pouch and put it on the table.

Slater poked at it with a finger. 'It's a pretty little thing. But for all I know, it might be the key to your luggage.'

'How do we know you're not working for John Rath and his pirates?' Kate asked.

'Why would I have helped Matt Cruse escape from them?' Nadira shot back.

'To make him trust you,' Slater said coolly.

'It's too fancy,' I said. 'On the rooftop, those men had me. They would have beaten the information from me, or worse. They didn't need some complicated scheme to get the coordinates.'

Slater said nothing. Kate looked at me, and I couldn't tell if she was convinced, or just surprised I was sticking up for Nadira.

'You say these fellows came looking for your key,' Slater said to Nadira. 'How is it they knew you had it?'

I felt a fool I hadn't asked the same question last night, and now wondered what her answer would be.

'They knew my father,' Nadira said. 'He used to work with them.'

'Oh ho! A pirate's daughter,' Slater laughed. 'Mr Cruse, what fascinating company you keep!'

It was a damning piece of information, to be sure, and I was amazed she'd admitted it so readily. Angry too that she'd omitted this detail when talking to me last night. My face was hot. I'd been too trusting and hasty; I felt a complete amateur.

'My father left when I was nine,' Nadira said. 'The last time I saw him was seven years ago. He made his choices; I've made different ones.'

'Where is he now then?'

'Dead.'

'And this John Rath, is your family still on friendly terms with him?' Slater demanded.

'No. I haven't seen him since my father left. But Rath came looking for me, a couple of days ago, in London. A neighbour knocked on the door and said some gadjo was asking around for me.'

'What's a gadjo?' I asked.

'An outsider, someone who's not a Roma. No one was in any hurry to help him. I wanted to know what he was after, so I followed him from a distance. He and his men went back to a tavern and I listened in on them. They started talking about how the *Hyperion* had been spotted and how they needed the secret key. Until then,

I was never completely sure if my father was telling the truth about it; he made up a lot of stories. Rath must've remembered my father giving it to me. Then they talked about Matt Cruse and how they were going to get the coordinates from him.'

Slater looked at her suspiciously. 'I don't trust you.'

Nadira made no reply.

'I trust her,' I said, not knowing quite why. Maybe I just wanted to contradict Slater.

He gave an amused sniff. 'Look, lad, I'm susceptible to a pretty face, too, but I wouldn't mix it in with business.'

'That's got nothing to do with it,' I said, feeling my cheeks burn yet again. I glanced over at Kate. She was looking at me. 'If the ship's booby-trapped—'

'If,' said Hal Slater pointedly.

'If it is, we need the key.'

'A key that might not even work,' said Kate.

Nadira gave Kate a long hard look. 'Mr Slater has the ship. Mr Cruse has the coordinates. I have the key. What exactly do you have?'

For the first time Kate looked flustered, and I felt immediately protective of her, I'd so rarely seen her at a loss for words.

'Well, she did find Mr Slater,' I pointed out.

'We were just on our way to find him ourselves,' Nadira countered. She turned her cyclone eyes back on Kate. 'Is it because I'm a gypsy, or because you're afraid I might cut into some of your loot?'

'I'm not interested in the loot,' Kate said disdainfully. 'There's a collection of taxidermy I want.'

Nadira turned to me. 'I thought *you* wanted the dead animals.'

I shrugged. 'It's just clutter to me.'

'I don't care who gets them,' said Nadira. 'It's the money I want.'

The two girls stared at each other, fuming.

'As far as I'm concerned, this is Miss de Vries' charter,' said Slater. 'She approached me, and she's agreed to pay my fee and all my costs in the event we don't find the *Hyperion*.'

'Exactly,' Kate said, with a grateful nod to Slater. 'That's my contribution. Money.'

'Money won't open the cargo bay doors,' Nadira remarked.

'It would be a shame to get all the way up there and be blown to bits,' I said, trying to lighten the mood. 'I think Nadira should come. Anyway, she's good in a scrape.'

'The final decision's not yours,' said Slater.

'Yes it is,' I said, bristling. 'This is my trip. Without my coordinates no one goes anywhere.'

'Wrong. Without my ship no one goes anywhere.'

Nadira stood up with a disgusted snort. 'I wish you all luck. I'll find myself another ship.' She walked out the doorway and kept going.

Hal Slater grinned at me. I glared back.

'We reach the ship,' Slater called out, examining his

fingernails, 'and if your key works, you get a cut. If it doesn't work, you get nothing.'

I heard returning footsteps. Nadira poked her head around the doorway.

'That suits me. Because if my key doesn't work, we're all dead anyway.'

'Excellent,' said Slater. 'Come sit down. I can get you to the *Hyperion*, but my share is ninety per cent. You three can squabble over the rest. And Miss de Vries is welcome to the animal carcasses.'

'We want forty per cent,' I said, amazing myself.

Slater shook his head. 'I'm shouldering all the risk. Ten per cent is a generous finder's fee by any stretch of the imagination.'

'You try finding her without my coordinates,' I said.

'Matt . . .' Kate said.

'You might not care about the money,' I told her, surprised by my sudden flare of anger, 'but I do. So does Nadira.'

'You're overestimating the value of your coordinates,' said Slater with an indifferent shrug. 'They may not be that helpful, if she's drifted.'

'Fine,' I said, 'why don't you just close your eyes and pick a point on the map? You wouldn't be interested in this trip if you thought my coordinates were useless.'

Slater stared at me hard; I forced myself not to look away.

'I take eighty,' he said, 'you keep twenty.'

I turned to Nadira. She nodded.

'Good,' said Slater. 'Since Miss de Vries claims she doesn't want a cut of the money, you two will be very rich. You can take me out to dinner at the Jewels Verne when we get back.'

'When can we leave?' Nadira asked.

'This afternoon.'

'This afternoon?' Kate said in surprise.

'Every minute we wait, the more the *Hyperion* drifts,' Slater said.

She looked at me. 'Told you we'd miss the Ball.'

'Get yourselves ready,' Slater said, 'and be back here at four o'clock, latest. Talk to no one. Cruse, I'll need those coordinates.'

'You can have them when we're airborne.'

Slater was about to protest, but then he just grinned.

'You're a smart lad,' he said.

6

A RATHER HASTY DEPARTURE

We left Slater to muster his crew and prep the *Sagarmatha*. Outside the Heliodrome, Kate had a motorcar waiting.

'Hop in,' she said. 'I'll give you both a lift.'

'I'll walk,' Nadira said. 'It's not far.'

'Are you sure?'

She nodded.

'See you at four,' I said, as I climbed in.

Kate gave the driver instructions and then closed the screen so we could talk privately as we headed back into the city.

'I don't think she likes me,' Kate said.

'I'm not sure she likes anyone.'

'Well, I think she likes you. She kept looking at you.'

'I didn't notice,' I lied.

'It was very chivalrous of you, leaping to her defence all the time.'

'I just didn't like the way Slater treated her.'

'Do you trust her?' Kate asked.

'Don't you?'

'Not particularly,' she said.

'But you have no problem with Slater.'

'He's quite straightforward. He just wants money. I don't know if it's that simple with Nadira. She's a bit of a mystery. Pirate's daughter and all.' She paused reflectively. 'Gosh, I wish I were a pirate's daughter.'

'You do not!'

'Oh, come on, it'd be fabulous. Everyone would think I was frightfully alluring and mysterious.'

'You're already alluring.'

She looked a little hurt. 'Not mysterious?'

'You're too talkative to be mysterious. It all comes out sooner or later. Sooner mostly.'

'I just like everyone to know what I'm thinking,' she said.

'That's awfully considerate of you.'

She jabbed me in the ribs. 'Well, come on! If we all knew what the other person thought, we could just get on with things much more easily. She's very beautiful. And extremely capable. Getting over here all by herself. She can't have much money. But she's obviously got big plans. I've always admired people who start with little and really work hard to make something of themselves.'

I nodded, hoping I, too, was included in this. But then I thought of Slater and how young he was to have such a fine ship – or any ship at all. I wondered how impressed Kate was with him, whether his type of accomplishments appealed to her. But if she weren't impressed with a man who'd made his fortune in the air, why would she be impressed by me, who had neither ship nor fortune to his name?

I wanted to dig a little more into her cosy meeting with Slater last night, but Kate had apparently decided the conversation was over. She produced a notebook and began writing down all the things she would need to bring on the trip.

'Aren't you making a list?' she asked, looking over at me with some disapproval.

'I don't have that much to bring.'

'I've got loads,' she replied, and went back to scribbling.

I asked her to drop me a block away from the Airship Academy. If Rath and his men were lying in wait for me, I didn't want to take any chances. I went around the back, where a door was usually left ajar by the kitchen staff. I was in luck. I took a stairway down into the steam tunnels. Enormous water pipes ran along the walls, chugging and gurgling, as they carried hot water to the Academy's many bathrooms and radiators. In cold weather, students sometimes used these tunnels to get to the dining hall, rather than cross the quadrangle. I navigated my way to the basement of Dornier House, then climbed the stairs to my room.

At the doorway I hesitated, remembering the figure I'd seen behind the glass last night. But it was daylight now, and even if there had been an intruder, surely he was long gone. Carefully I unlocked the door and pushed it open. The room was so small, there could be no place to hide. Just to be sure I bent down to check beneath my bed, and then opened the closet door wide. The room showed no signs at all of being disturbed. No scattered papers or strewn bedding, no broken chairs or upended tables. I got busy.

I changed out of my uniform, dragged out my duffle bag, and started packing. Shirts, trousers, underwear, socks, sweaters, the warmest coat I had, the pair of mittens my mother had knitted for me back in Lionsgate City. I tossed in my aerostat operations manual, my mathematics of flight text, and celestial navigation handbook, figuring that I'd have time to study during the journey there and back. If I had any hope of passing the upcoming exams I needed to use every spare moment.

Assuming I was even back in time for the exams. I looked at the schedule I'd pinned above my desk. If I missed my exams, I got zero. And that would make it next to impossible to pass the year. For a moment, my sleepless night under the bridge caught up with me, and all the electricity that had been fuelling me fizzled out. What sort of fool's errand was I embarking on? For so much of my life, I had dreamed of attending this Academy, and one day being an officer and even captain of some fine vessel. If I missed my exams, or failed the year, they might kick me out altogether.

I looked at the notebooks on my desk, the numbers and symbols and scribbles and crossings out. If I stayed I might fail nonetheless.

But it would not matter if we found the *Hyperion*. If

we found riches, I would not need to serve on a ship. I could buy my own, and be captain, like Hal Slater. All these ifs were strung together like an icicle ladder in the blazing sun. Fantastical as they were, they did give me some comfort.

I sat down at my desk and started a letter.

Dear Mother, I wrote.

And stopped. What could I say to her?

I'm embarking on an idiotic and dangerous quest. I'm writing this to you in case—

A letter from Paris to Lionsgate City via regular delivery, would take almost two weeks, by which time I was almost certain to be back in Paris. Was there any point worrying my mother? Better not to tell her at all, then. But I couldn't help wondering what would happen if some disaster befell us. She would never know what had happened to me. The thought made me gloomy, and doubtful about the whole affair once again.

Writing a letter that will only be read if you're dead is an odd business, and I felt suitably ghostly as I scribbled a few lines to my mother, telling her what I was about to undertake, and what I hoped to gain from it. *If you're reading this, it means I've failed at what I tried to do, and perhaps it was very foolish. I wanted to make sure we always had enough, and that we wouldn't have to worry, or feel sad or desperate.* I signed it with love, sealed it, and then wrote a second letter to Baz in Australia, telling him everything, and folded my mother's letter into the same envelope. I told Baz that if he hadn't heard from me in more than a month, he should assume the worst, and forward the letter to my mother.

Then I scribbled a note to Dean Pruss, saying I would be absent for a number of days, without giving any specifics. I'd mail both letters on my way to the Heliodrome, and put my money back in the bank. It didn't seem I would need it after all.

I wondered what counsel my father would have offered me. From my desk I took the brass compass he'd given me when I was a child, and carefully placed it in my duffle bag. He died when I was twelve, but he was still often in my thoughts and dreams. I finished packing. Probably I should have made a list like Kate. I hefted my bag. I couldn't remember it ever feeling this heavy.

You're looking at it all wrong, I tried to tell myself. Think of this as another training tour. With a bit of luck and fine weather you'll be back in Paris not much later than the other students, only you'll be coming back rich as the King of Babylon.

I arrived at the Heliodrome at three o'clock, and made my way to the *Sagarmatha*'s berth. Setting eyes on her again, I felt a familiar, giddy swirl in my stomach – the feeling I got whenever I was about to embark on a ship. It wasn't so unlike the first time I saw Kate de Vries, and something in me seemed to know right away that things would never be the same again.

Slater's crew was busy fuelling the ship, topping up her gas cells with hydrium, loading cargo – and Hal

Slater was directing them all like a conductor, though a talkative one who wasn't afraid of colourful language.

'Good,' he said when he saw me. 'Dump your bag in the mess for now and lend a hand with the loading.'

I wasn't sure this was exactly the kind of relationship I wanted with Slater, him ordering me around like crew, but there was a restless fluttering in my stomach, and I was glad enough to work.

I walked up the gangway, turned down the main corridor and stopped dead at the sight of Miss Marjorie Simpkins.

'I don't know how we're going to cope in such small quarters,' she was lamenting to Kate, who'd just emerged from the cabin doorway. 'I really must have a word with Mr Slater.'

'You'll do no such thing, Marjorie,' Kate told her severely. 'Our quarters are ample.'

'There are *bunks*,' Miss Simpkins said, her voice tremulous with woe. 'And you snore, Kate, you know you do.'

'I do no such thing,' she said, her nostrils narrowing. 'I'm not too thrilled to be sharing a room with you either, Marjorie. But adventure has its price.'

Miss Simpkins turned and saw me, and pursed her mouth disapprovingly. Then, with a small despairing moan, she hurried back into her cabin, closing the door after her. I stared at Kate in disbelief.

'I know, I know,' she said, walking towards me, hands raised as if to calm a dangerous beast.

'She's not coming,' I said.

'She's coming.'

'She can't.'

'She's coming. Or she'll tell.' Kate sounded about six years old. 'I was hoping I could just sneak out, and leave a note, but she caught me packing. Then *she* started packing. She said she could not possibly allow me to go off on such an outlandish trip, on a ship crammed with strange, sweaty men – without a chaperone.'

'What about the blind eye?' I demanded.

'She's had a miracle recovery.' Kate drew closer, lowering her voice. 'Do you know what I think it is? I think she rather fancies Hal Slater herself.'

'This is too much.'

'If she tells my parents, they will move me back home, and lock me in a room for the rest of my life. I'm quite serious.' She must have seen my smile, because she said, 'No, that would not be a good thing, Matt Cruse. No Sorbonne, no fame and fortune, no jollies whatsoever. My life would be over.'

'What did Slater say?' I asked.

'As long as she keeps out of the way, he doesn't care.'

'She doesn't even like flying!'

'I know. She thinks she's being a real martyr.'

'She probably wants a cut of the loot, too,' I scoffed. Kate winced. 'Actually—'

'You're joking!'

'I promised I'd give her something out of my share.'

'But you're only getting the taxidermy!' I reminded her.

'I'll give her a yak or something. She can turn it into a coat.'

I rubbed my forehead. This was far from ideal. 'Has Nadira arrived?' I asked.

'I haven't seen her.'

She wasn't late yet, but I couldn't shrug off the suspicion she might indeed be in league with the pirates, and meant to lead them to us.

'I'm off to help prep the ship,' I told Kate.

'Is that all you brought?' she said, looking at my duffel bag. 'Gosh, you do travel light.'

Stacked in the corridor outside her cabin were about eight suitcases and trunks.

'I'm amazed he let you bring all that,' I said.

'I have a great deal of gear. I thought I was very restrained.'

'I'm sure you were.'

Down the gangway I went, and found Slater talking to one of his crew, a short, compact man who looked of Himalayan descent.

'Cruse, this is my first mate, Dorje Tenzing.'

'I'm very pleased to meet you,' I said, shaking his hand.

'Dorje's been with me from the start,' Slater said, 'and there's no one in the world I trust more. I'd close my eyes and jump from the control car if he told me to.'

'It is often tempting,' Dorje said with a chuckle. I liked the way his almond eyes became crescents when he smiled.

'Most of my crew are Sherpas,' Slater told me proudly. 'No one's better at working high altitude. They were born to it. Dorje has summitted Everest five times, most recently with me. I carried his pack, I seem to recall.'

'Only because I was carrying you,' Dorje replied.

Slater gave me a wink.

'What can I do to help?' I asked.

'There's still plenty to load,' Dorje said.

I rolled up my sleeves and got to work alongside Thomas Dalkey, a fortress of a man, who greeted me with a friendly nod and sweaty handshake.

'Cruse,' he said. 'From Eire, are you?'

'My parents were.'

'Come over in the great migration?'

I nodded. 'And I was born halfway over the Atlanticus.'

'That's something. My family used to own an island in the old country. Castle and all. But that was six hundred years ago. The goats tend it now. Grab hold of this, lad . . .'

Dalkey talked a streak as we worked, and I enjoyed listening to him, savouring some of the same expressions I'd heard my parents use. There was something intensely satisfying about getting your ship ready to sail, bringing aboard the provisions, the extra tanks of aruba fuel, oil for the engines, reams of goldbeater's skin in case patching was needed – and knowing in your gut that your departure was near.

As I hefted aboard some crates of spare parts, Kami Sherpa came to help, and we introduced ourselves. He

130

was slender, with dark, grave eyes, short black hair, and the ghost of a moustache on his upper lip. I thought he looked even younger than me. But watching him lift, I could tell he had muscles and sinew of alumiron. He was not even breathing hard.

'How long have you worked with Slater?' I asked.

'Two years.'

'Two days,' said another crewman, joining us.

'This is Ang Jeta,' Kami Sherpa said, throwing his arm affectionately around him. 'He's my cousin. I put in a word for him with the captain.'

'I got tired of staring at mountains,' said Ang Jeta with merry eyes. He looked older than Kami, his face much more weather-lined, and I noticed that he was missing the little fingers of both hands. Frostbite, no doubt.

I met the final crew member, Jangbu Sherpa, as we were pumping the last of our fresh water. Slater was indeed fortunate to have Sherpas as crew; they had become legendary for their skills as pilots and navigators, guiding ships across the globe's sometimes treacherous skyways. The only person I hadn't met yet was the cook, Mrs Ram, whom I was told was best left alone until she'd put her kitchen in order. I wondered if all ships' cooks were as volatile as Chef Vlad.

Slater approached as I was coiling up the water hose.

'Your gypsy girl's late. I had to grease a few palms for an early launch slot and I don't want to miss it. My tow's coming now.'

I saw a motor truck with a huge towing rig backing

towards the nose of the *Sagarmatha*. In a hanger this size, it was necessary for the ships to be piloted in and out at specific times.

'We miss our slot and we might end up waiting till tomorrow,' said Slater. 'I can't wait for her. Go up to the catwalks and see if you can spy her.'

'I was just about to,' I told him.

I climbed the two hundred and fifty spiral steps to the catwalks. Inside the Heliodrome, illuminated by the great tungsten lamps fixed to the ceiling, it was brighter than the Paris afternoon. Through the vast hangar doors I could see ships being towed in and out. Atop the catwalk, I strolled to the centre of the Heliodrome and gazed down at the traffic below, looking towards the east entrance, where Nadira was most likely to enter, given her lodgings at the rue Zeppelin.

A huge group of tourists was being herded inside by a guide holding a scarlet umbrella. But there was no sign of Nadira.

I walked on, hoping I'd see her soon. Down below, an impressive ship caught my eye. She was long and lean and had a military aspect to her, yet I couldn't make out any markings on her flanks. Her crew wore no uniforms as they prepped her. Two men emerged from the gangway and paused at the bottom, talking. Right away, I recognized one of them by his size, and ginger hair and beard. John Rath.

I quickly turned my back to them, feeling as though a dozen spotlights were aimed at me. What if they looked up? I exhaled, glancing at the Heliodrome's ceiling – and realized I needn't worry. With the intense glare of the lamps behind me, I was nothing but a silhouette to those below.

I looked back. Rath was still speaking to the other gentleman. He was thin and frail-looking, and I got the impression he was elderly. In his camel-hair coat, he was the very image of a respectable gentleman, and I wondered what on earth he was doing with the likes of Rath.

Anxiously I looked back towards the east entrance, and saw Nadira just entering the Heliodrome. She wore her leather overcoat, and had a big haversack slung over her shoulder. She headed for the stairs up to the pedestrian catwalk, but stopped when she saw they were completely glutted with gawking tourists.

Feeling sick, I watched as she started across the Heliodrome floor – a route which, within seconds, would take her right past John Rath. I dared not shout out, for fear of attracting his attention. I stood frozen, watching in horror as Nadira strode through Rath's berth. I stopped breathing. She walked by, not three metres from the two men at the gangway. She didn't notice Rath; he didn't notice her. I let out my breath in little puffs, scarcely believing our good luck.

Suddenly there was flash of reflected light as a window opened in the ship's control car, and one of Rath's crew was shouting and pointing in Nadira's direction. Rath and the elderly gentleman whirled.

Nadira ran. She careened through berths and ramps and maintenance areas, moving so quickly she blazed a kind of trail as people and carts swerved to avoid her. In her wake came Rath and two of his men. Their fists clenched pistols. Their shouts wafted up to me, muted in the vast atmosphere of the Heliodrome.

'Gypsy thief!' I heard Rath cry out. 'Stop! Stop her!'

I lost sight of Nadira briefly, then caught her again as she vaulted a tow rig. She had a good lead, but the pirates weren't far behind. I started running back to the *Sagarmatha*, making better time than Nadira, for I had no obstacles in my path. When I was directly over our berth, I bellowed down at Slater.

'We need to go! Now!'

He squinted up at me, and seemed to grasp instinctively what was happening, for he started shouting orders at his crew and they all went running.

I grabbed the banister, lifted my feet off the steps and slid down the staircase, fourteen storeys, swirling faster and faster until my palms burned. Gasping, I ran for the *Sagarmatha*'s gangway.

'John Rath,' I panted to Slater. 'Chasing Nadira.'

'How many?'

'Three.'

'Will she make it?'

'Just.'

'Guns?'

'Yes.'

Slater turned to the tow truck driver, who was about to affix his rig to the ship's bow lines.

'No thank you!' Slater called out to him.

'You don't want a tow?' the man demanded irritably.

Slater whirled towards the control car and made a bullhorn of his hands. 'Dorje! Prime the engines!'

'You can't go starting your props in here!' the tow driver exclaimed.

'Difficult to fly without them,' Slater replied.

'There's no flying in the Heliodrome!' the driver shouted. 'I'll be reporting you to the harbour master, sir!'

A volley of gun shots rang out in the distance.

'Report *that* while you're at it. Now if you'll excuse me, we have to make a rather hasty departure. Cruse, slip her stern and breast lines.' Slater ran for the gangway. 'Get Nadira inside and haul up the gangway.'

'What about the bow line?' I asked, seeing it was still tied.

'It's on an automatic coupling,' he yelled back over his shoulder, 'I can free it from the control car.'

Luckily there weren't many lines on the *Sagarmatha*. There didn't need to be in the shelter of the Heliodrome. Frantically I loosed the knots. A low, well-oiled and intensely satisfying hum emanated from each of the six engine cars and the powerful propellers began to turn, very slowly at first, then with increasing speed.

Nadira came bursting into view, about three berths away, leaping over stacks of cargo and barrels of aruba fuel, swinging from mooring lines. She really knew how to move. She grabbed a high pressure water hose and wrenched it from its collar. It rose like a king cobra, thrashing and spraying a powerful geyser of water everywhere, creating chaos between her and the pirates.

'Come on!' I shouted at her, pointlessly, since it was clear she was running with the last vapour of her strength.

I heard a little mechanical snap, and saw the ship's bow line fall away from her nose. She was completely untethered now, hovering calm as a mirage, waiting. Another shot rang out and a metallic ping sounded above my head as a bullet ricocheted off the hull's alumiron exoskeleton.

Nadira threw herself on to the gangway stairs and we hauled each other up and inside. Before we'd even reached the top, I heard the crash of water ballast being dumped, and the ship started to rise. I turned the wheel to raise the steps, and swung the hatch shut. Turning, I nearly crashed into Miss Simpkins.

'Are we departing already?' she asked, alarmed.

'Yes.'

'But I needed to post these letters,' she said, waving a sheaf of envelopes in her hand.

'It'll have to wait,' I said, and smiled as the ship reared up and my stomach gave a giddy lurch. Miss Simpkins gasped and reached for the handrail.

'And who's this?' said Miss Simpkins, seeing Nadira for the first time, dishevelled and panting after her run.

'That's Nadira.'

'I had no idea there'd be so many Sherpas aboard!' exclaimed Miss Simpkins.

'I'm not a Sherpa,' Nadira said. 'I'm a *gypsy*.'

'Oh, my goodness!' said the chaperone.

'We're going?' asked Kate, rushing into the corridor, her face alight.

'Right now, yes!'

The engines' pitch had reached a deep crescendo and I felt it coursing through my legs and torso as I rushed forward, and down the ladder to the control car.

Through the tinted wraparound windows, I saw the vast Heliodrome spread before us. We were fifteen metres in the air now, still well below the metal webwork of catwalks. Far in the distance were the hangar doors that would release us into the sky. But our path to them was anything but clear. A Norwegian tanker was manoeuvring into the berth directly in front of us, and beyond that, a Dutch mail ship was being towed across the Heliodrome.

'Busy today,' muttered Slater.

Down to the left, I saw John Rath and his men, their fists raised high, sparks leaping from their pistols. A bullet shrieked off the window, scratching, but amazingly not shattering, the glass. Slater must have had it reinforced somehow.

'They're going to hurt someone doing that,' said Slater. 'Cruse, return fire, would you?'

He snatched a pistol from the wall and tossed it at me.

The weight of all that well-oiled steel in my fist made my stomach turn over.

'I don't think—'

'Quite right. Complete waste of time. We're already gone. Full ahead now!'

The *Sagarmatha* leapt forward like a wildcat, hurtling on a collision course with the tanker. My breath snagged in my throat.

'Give us another metre or so, would you, Jangbu?'

At the elevator controls, Jangbu tapped the wheel and the *Sagarmatha* jumped, cresting over the Norwegian tanker with not much to spare. Great horns sounded from the tanker, and alarms rang out across the Heliodrome. We'd all be thrown in jail for this stunt, but that didn't matter since we'd likely be killed within seconds. We charged straight towards the Dutch mail ship, which was being towed in high. There was no way we could rise above her at this speed.

'Goodness me,' said Slater. 'Under her, I think.'

His crew obliged instantly. The ship dipped and skimmed the Heliodrome floor, sending ground crew scattering. The control car couldn't have been riding more than five metres off the ground, and I could only stare, too shocked to close my eyes, as the distance between us and the mailship evaporated. Suddenly we were under her, and I had no idea how we managed to clear her.

'Truck!' I shouted, pointing at the aruba fuel lorry directly in our path. Manning the rudder, Dorje gave the wheel a little tug and the *Sagarmatha*, like a shark smelling blood, veered to starboard and we left the fuel truck safely to port.

'The hangar doors!' I shouted, almost cheering.

'Control yourself, Mr Cruse,' said Slater. 'No need to get excited.'

But there was, for a vast passenger liner was just being tugged into view. Within seconds she would block our exit, immovable as the Great Wall of China.

Hal Slater glanced at me. 'Full reverse, Cruse?'

'Full ahead!' I cried, scarcely recognizing myself.

'My thoughts exactly,' he said, pushing the throttles all the way.

We streaked towards the hangar doors, the prow of the passenger liner nosing into the opening. Alarms clanged all around us. Slater grinned and hummed a sky shanty. The *Sagarmatha* rotated slightly to starboard, and my body clenched, waiting for the shriek of metal on metal, the dull crumple of the ship's hull imploding, but suddenly we were through, and in open air, leaping sharply over the aeroport, banking around the flight paths of incoming airships and then, with another thrilling burst of speed, finding a clear swath of sky to take us up and away from Paris.

7

ABOARD THE SAGARMATHA

If the *Aurora* was like riding a cloud, the *Sagarmatha* was like riding a gale force wind. Not that her flight wasn't smooth. It was just that you could feel her speed, the sudden thrust of her engines and the pitch and roll of her. She made me want to give a whoop of delight.

'You like her, Cruse, admit it,' Slater told me.

'She's very swift,' I replied, not caring for his smug grin. It was clear he was a skilled captain, and had a splendid ship, but he was altogether too pleased with himself. What was it like, I wondered, to be so confident in yourself and your place in the world?

'Rath had a ship in harbour,' I told him. 'It looked fast. They may give chase.'

'By the time they're ready to cast off, we'll be long gone,' Slater said. He turned to Jangbu. 'It's nice and cloudy over Holland. Let's hide ourselves in that for the time being.'

'We need to talk now,' he said to me. 'Dorje.'

Dorje surrendered the rudder wheel to Dalkey, who had clambered down the ladder several minutes earlier to assume his watch. Slater led us back to the small navigation and radio room behind the bridge.

'So let's find out where we're headed.' Slater passed me a piece of paper and pencil and watched me expectantly. I was reminded unpleasantly of John Rath at the Ritz, and felt a quick chill of uncertainty. How well did I know this captain and crew? I looked over at Dorje and couldn't help trusting him. I scribbled out the longitude and latitude of the *Hyperion*.

Dorje's eyes flicked over the numbers. From one of the many neatly labelled pigeon holes beneath the chart table, he drew out a long narrow roll of parchment and unfurled it. He located the place almost instantly and touched it with his dividers.

'An interesting spot,' he remarked.

'The Devil's Fist,' said Slater.

'It nearly had us,' I said.

'What altitude was the *Hyperion*?' Dorje asked me.

'Seven thousand metres.'

'That's how she's survived all these years,' Dorje said.

'She's beyond the weather's reach,' I said, nodding. 'She might drift forever at that height.'

Dorje drew out a second chart from the pigeon holes, this one drafted on a kind of translucent paper, fine as onion skin, and ornamented with all manner of swirls and symbols, some of which I recognized as meteorological notations. Dorje laid it down over the first chart, so both could be viewed together.

'The date and time of your sighting?' Dorje asked.

I told him. With a quick hand he jotted this on a piece of paper.

'Her bearing?'

'South by south west.'

'Speed?'

'Maybe thirty aeroknots. I'm guessing now.'

Dorje reached over to his pigeon holes and took down even more sheets of onion skin parchment.

'I'll need some time,' he said.

'Let's leave Dorje to work in peace,' Slater said to me. He returned to the bridge and gave some instructions to Jangbu and Dalkey, then ushered me towards the ladder.

'Can he really calculate the ship's position?' I asked as we climbed up.

'If he can't, I doubt anyone can. He knows the winds, especially in that region. He knows them by altitude, time of year, planetary alignments. Not even those London gentlemen with their new-fangled Turing computer can calculate meteorological conditions like Dorje. Now then, let's have some dinner.'

Kate, Miss Simpkins and Nadira were all waiting in the lounge when we entered. Miss Simpkins, I thought, was looking a bit peaky, but the other two seemed untroubled by the *Sagarmatha*'s swift ascent. A wonderfully satisfying aroma wafted in from the kitchen, and my stomach gave a happy lurch.

'Ladies, shall we dine?' asked Slater.

'Well, I suppose so,' said Miss Simpkins, who looked as if just rising to her feet was a great chore.

Slater offered her his arm and escorted her to the table. I thought I saw a flare of colour on the chaperone's cheek, and remembered Kate's words about Miss Simpkins and her penchant for bounders.

Just looking at Slater made me feel smaller. His fine clothes, his dashing hair and easy smile: I could not imagine ever fitting clothes like that, or looking so confident. I wanted his boots; I wanted his jacket; I wanted his ship. I was a buzzing hive of covetousness.

'By tomorrow you'll have your sky legs,' Slater told Miss Simpkins. 'Now, I may as well tell you the ship's schedule. Breakfast between seven and eight, lunch from noon to one. We usually dine at six thirty, not so fashionable an hour as in Paris, but we tend to sleep and rise early here. Apart from that, you can plead for a snack from Mrs Ram, and she's usually happy to oblige. Please, ladies, do sit down.'

He pulled out a chair for Miss Simpkins. Not wanting to be outdone, I managed to reach Kate's chair before he did. We caught each other's eye, and his mouth gave a twitch, of amusement or annoyance, I couldn't tell.

I went to the serving window to retrieve our dinners, and there met Mrs Ram. I'd expected a stocky woman with powerful forearms, and was surprised to find she was altogether diminutive, and that her head and shoulders barely cleared the serving window.

'How do you do, Mrs Ram?' I asked. 'I'm Matt Cruse.'

'You could use some feeding up,' she said with a concerned frown.

'I look forward to it,' I said. 'This looks delicious.'

She beamed. I took two plates and placed them before Miss Simpkins and Kate. It was a kind of Kathmandu curry, with delicate slices of lamb mixed with yoghurt, fresh chillies, ginger and a bit of garlic. Kate thanked me. Miss Simpkins sat very straight, face tilted slightly back, as if trying to put as much distance as possible between her and the food.

I started back to get dinner for Nadira and myself but Slater waved me to my seat, went to the window himself and set plates before Nadira and me.

'Mrs Ram is a marvel,' said Slater, as he returned with his own meal. 'I met her in Nepal two years ago; she's Dorje's aunt actually. Never have I been so well fed.'

From a serving cabinet, Slater produced a venerable-looking bottle, and swiftly uncorked it.

'A little something I've been saving for a special occasion. I always like to start a new journey with a toast.' He poured red wine into all our glasses. He filled his own glass last and lifted it high. 'To a lucrative venture!'

'A lucrative venture!' I seconded.

'And a scientifically rewarding one,' Kate added, giving me a rather stern look.

We clinked glasses, then sipped the wine which, I was glad to note, wasn't particularly good. During my time aboard the *Aurora*, the chief steward had taught me quite a bit about fine wines. Not everything was perfect in Hal Slater's little airborne world. I felt quite bucked up, and enthusiastically began my meal.

'This is far too spicy,' said Miss Simpkins, putting down her fork. 'I can't eat it. Don't eat it,' she urged Kate.

'Don't be ridiculous, Marjorie. It's delicious.'

'It will ruin your digestion. It isn't wholesome. Is there any boiled ham?' Miss Simpkins asked.

'I leave the provisioning and cooking entirely up to Mrs Ram,' Slater said. 'I don't think she's familiar with roast beef and Yorkshire pudding.'

'Perhaps just a little gruel?' Miss Simpkins inquired.

'Gruel?' cried Mrs Ram from the kitchen. 'What is this thing, gruel?'

'I can't imagine how I'll last the journey then,' said Miss Simpkins faintly.

'Try eating,' Nadira told her.

'I'm sure it's quite agreeable to gypsy tastes,' said Miss Simpkins.

Nadira made no reply, just stared back balefully with heavy-lidded eyes until Miss Simpkins looked away. It was shaping up to be quite a dinner.

'The food really is excellent,' I said nervously.

'It certainly is,' Kate agreed.

Miss Simpkins sniffed. 'We'll all get gyppy tummy,' she said.

'What on earth is gyppy tummy?' Nadira demanded, unable to hide her contempt.

'It's what tourists in Egypt get, if they're foolish enough to eat the local food.'

'Miss Simpkins,' I said, 'we've just left Paris. All our provisions came from there.'

'Nonetheless,' she said. 'There are spices and so forth.'

'You're mortifying, Marjorie, you really are,' said Kate.

At that Miss Simpkins looked quite glum and I almost felt sorry for her.

'Miss Simpkins,' Slater said, 'I can promise you, there's never been any gyppy tummy aboard the *Saga*.'

'I'm sure,' she said, but let her fork lie, and gingerly plucked a piece of bread from the basket.

We ate in silence. I let my eyes stray to the walls, where there hung several framed prints of famous airships: the *Polarys*, the *Marie Celeste*. Along the entire length of one wall hung a mounted strip of airship skin, bearing the name *Trident*.

'My first ship,' said Slater, catching the bearing of my gaze. 'She was a heap of junk, but she saved my life and helped get me this ship, so it didn't seem right to go forgetting her.'

I got the sense he wanted me to ask more about this particular adventure, but I didn't feel like helping him boast right now.

'Hm,' I said, and nothing more.

'Well, you've piqued my curiosity,' Kate said to Slater. 'It sounds like there's a thrilling tale to be told.'

I stared straight ahead, dismayed.

Slater waved his hand. 'No, no. Old war stories. All

airshipmen have them, eh, Cruse? I won't bore you with mine.'

'You have to tell us now, Mr Slater,' Kate insisted.

'Please, call me Hal,' he protested. 'Being mistered by all you fine young ladies is making me feel old.'

'Hal. Please tell us.'

'She was a real wreck,' Slater said, launching right in. 'About as airworthy as an anvil. I didn't even own her. She belonged to a rogue who leased her to me for double her worth. But she was all I could afford. I did freight and a little salvage with her, small jobs mostly, barely enough to meet my costs. Do you remember Hurricane Kate?'

'Was it really called that?' Kate asked, delighted.

'Named after you, actually,' I said.

Kate didn't even turn to laugh at my joke, she was too busy shining her bright face at Slater.

'Hurricane Kate!' Slater exclaimed. 'Absolutely! She was notorious! She blew through the east coast of the Americas. I knew there'd be plenty of airships in trouble if they got caught. So out I went in my lead zeppelin.'

'You chose to go out in the hurricane?' Kate asked, eyes wide.

'Oh, I was hungry,' Slater said with a lupine grin. 'I needed to make something of myself and I was in a hurry. I could have died out there, it was that bad. By rights I should have.' He took a drink of his wine, giving us a little pause so we could marvel at his insane courage. 'But I was dead lucky. I came across a mailship in distress,

147

her skin all torn, and her rudder ripped off. She was in a slow spin to the sea. The captain was desperate; when I offered help, he took it. I got a tow line on her and started hauling her back to shore. Twice we nearly went down into the drink, but we made it. The Sky Court awarded me twenty-five per cent of the ship's value and cargo as salvage – and wouldn't you know it, she was carrying a shipment of Yukon gold. Enough for me to build a brand new ship of my own.'

It was a good story, I couldn't deny it. Slater had looked at no one but Kate as he'd told it. And she had listened, rapt, giving little sighs of excitement and appreciation throughout. It made me want to gnaw the rim of my glass. Slater wasn't the only one who had tales to tell, but I couldn't think how to get on to my own without looking like I was trying to one up him. I glanced at Kate, hoping she would chime in and help me out.

'And what about *your* war stories?' Nadira asked me. 'Crossing blades with the likes of Vikram Szpirglas.'

I turned to her in surprise, feeling immense gratitude.

Slater gave me a sympathetic shake of his head. 'Ah, you must be sick and tired of telling that one by now.'

'I wouldn't mind hearing it first hand,' Nadira pressed on. 'I heard rumours and read newspaper accounts, but I always wonder if they aren't tarted up by the gutter press to make a flashier story.'

'So true,' Slater said gravely. 'One has to be so careful these days.'

'Well,' I said, defensively, 'I don't know what the papers said, but—'

'From what I've heard,' Nadira said, 'Szpirglas was a powerful, very ruthless man. It's hard to imagine you besting him, unless you had a gun.'

'I had no gun,' I said. I had enough of the braggart in me to want to impress Nadira, but I could not lie, and I was worried my tale might not seem very glorious after all.

'So how did it happen?' she asked. Her questions had an urgency which seemed beyond simple curiosity.

'Well, he'd just shot our friend, Bruce Lunardi, and he came after me with his pistol.'

'You should tell them about how we got rid of the other pirates first,' Kate said.

'It's Szpirglas I want to hear about,' Nadira said firmly.

'He chased me up to the axial catwalk, and I managed to clog up his gun by heaving a bucket of patching glue at him. But he still had a knife and the look in his eye was not charitable.'

Slater gave a chuckle. The others were watching me. I felt the pulse of the story pounding in my temples.

'I climbed out the aft crow's-nest on to the ship's back, and started heading for the forward hatch. I was halfway across when the cloud cat lunged out and blocked my way.'

'Cloud cat?' she asked.

'You never read about them?' Kate said with just a touch of indignation. 'A new species of flying mammal over the Pacificus that I – I mean, Matt and I – discovered? One of them got aboard the *Aurora*.'

'I might have heard about this,' Nadira said, but I could tell she wasn't very interested. 'Go on,' she told me.

'Well, I dared not go any closer to the cloud cat. So I turned, and there was Szpirglas, coming out of the other hatch. A murderous carnivore on one side, an even more villainous pirate on the other.'

I paused, quite enjoying myself now.

'You had no weapon?' Hal asked.

'Nothing.'

'Why didn't you rappel down the side?' Nadira asked.

'There were no lines handy. Szpirglas came closer, his knife flashing. I had nowhere to go. He seized me and hurled me off the ship and I went flying.'

'You fell, you mean,' Nadira said.

'Fell, flew, it was hard to tell, but I crashed on the ship's tail fin. I was half dead by then, flat out on my belly, clinging for dear life to the elevator flap. And Szpirglas came down after me. To finish me off.'

Nadira waited. Her eyes had none of Kate's appreciative brightness. Her gaze unsettled me, it was so intent.

'He came down and kicked at my fingers, trying to break my grip.'

'That's ugly,' said Hal.

'But then I gave him a great kick, and managed to trip him up, and he started sliding off the fin.' I paused, wishing I could stop the story there, with a triumphant quick-witted blow. But Kate already knew that wasn't the end. 'Szpirglas regained his grip, though, and came back to me, and I saw his eyes and knew he was about to break my skull with his steel-toed boot. Then something brushed his shoulder. There was a whole flock of cloud cats passing over the *Aurora*, and one of them knocked him off balance. That time he truly did fall.'

'He just fell,' Nadira said.

I nodded.

'So really, you didn't kill him at all.'

'I survived him, that's all. I was lucky.'

'It was very cowardly of him,' said Nadira. 'To attack a boy like that.'

I didn't like her referring to me as a boy, but her eyes had lost their fierceness now. Far from seeming disappointed by my story, she seemed strangely relieved.

'Well, the newspapermen did their work well,' Hal crowed. 'Made a proper Hercules of you! Always good to have a pirate-slayer aboard – though you might have stopped John Rath from firing on us earlier.' He looked at Nadira. 'Those pistol enthusiasts of yours will have made me very unpopular at the Heliodrome.'

'With luck, they've been caught by now,' I said.

'Don't count on it. But enough pirate talk. I trust you ladies are happy with your stateroom?'

'Perfectly,' Kate replied. 'Thank you.'

'Actually,' said Miss Simpkins, 'I was wondering if there were any adjoining rooms?'

'Apparently I snore,' said Kate. 'She's worried I'll deprive her of sleep.'

'Just make sure she's on her side,' Nadira told Miss Simpkins. 'A good shove usually does the trick.'

'I'm sure it does,' said Kate indignantly. 'I'd be wide awake after that! In any event, I don't snore.'

Miss Simpkins made a little sing-song sound without opening her mouth.

'You're welcome to share my cabin, Miss Simpkins,' Slater said with a roguish grin, 'but I tend to speechify in my sleep and I'm told it's not always terribly polite.'

Miss Simpkins flushed crimson. 'I wouldn't dream of being parted from Miss de Vries,' she murmured.

'Completely understandable,' said Slater. 'Cruse, you'll be bunking with Dorje on the starboard side, and Nadira, you're on the port side with Mrs Ram. Bathrooms on both sides, and a shower on the starboard, just one I'm afraid. We'll all be a little snug, but as long as we change socks daily, we should be perfectly comfortable. We'll get you to the *Hyperion* in no time.'

It felt odd to be merely a passenger, and I didn't like it.

'If you need any help about the ship—' I began, but Slater was already shaking his head.

'We're a well-oiled machine, my crew and I. We'll work better without having a trainee about.'

I bristled. 'I've served three—'

'Thank you, but we've got everything well in hand.'

I said nothing more, afraid of appearing foolish. I felt my cheeks warm, and hoped no one would notice.

'I think you'll find the lounge very comfortable,' Slater was saying, 'and you have the run of it, of course. This should be quite a remarkable voyage.'

'And with such varied company,' said Miss Simpkins, looking at Nadira.

'I must say, I think it's fascinating you're a gypsy,' said Kate.

'Is it?' Nadira replied coolly.

I took a sip of water to help my food down.

'Absolutely. I've never met one before.'

'Well, if you've met one, you've met them all.'

Kate faltered, seeing she'd offended her. 'I only meant I'm curious about your customs and traditions and so forth.'

Nadira said nothing. I knew that Kate held no prejudices against gypsies, and was genuinely interested in Nadira's way of life – in the same way she was interested in so many things. Nadira had no way of knowing this, though, and so she assumed Kate was like most people, who saw gypsies only as thieves or street urchins. Nadira's silence seeped over the table like a malignant fog. I cleared my throat nervously. Slater seemed far from bothered. In fact he appeared to be enjoying it. He sat there at the head of the table, smiling faintly, looking over us all as if we were a collection of very odd family relations.

'Can you tell fortunes?' Miss Simpkins asked Nadira out of the blue.

I stopped chewing. Kate actually flinched. For a moment I thought Nadira was about to say something rude, but she only smiled.

'May I see your hand?' she inquired politely.

'Oh well, I don't know,' Miss Simpkins replied.

'Go on, Marjorie,' said Kate. 'She's going to read your palm!'

Reluctantly Miss Simpkins extended her hand. Nadira took it and studied it intently, stroking various parts. She frowned.

'Perhaps this isn't a good idea,' she said.

'What?' demanded Miss Simpkins.

Nadira folded Miss Simpkins' palm closed. 'It's very unclear.'

'What do you see?'

'I'd rather not say.'

'You must! Tell me, girl!'

With a reluctant sigh, Nadira opened her palm again. 'I see you will be enslaved to the idle and moneyed classes. You will tend their spoiled children. You will never free yourself from the tightening chains of fruitless labour and ignorance.'

Miss Simpkins pulled back her hand as though it were caught in the jaws of a wild beast.

'You impudent scamp!'

'Were you unhappy with your fortune?' Nadira asked, eyes wide with feigned surprise.

Cutlery and dishware clattered as Miss Simpkins pushed back from the table, stood, and left the room.

Nadira picked up her fork and continued eating. 'Anyone else want their fortune told?'

'Did her palm really say that?' I asked.

'How should I know? All those lines look the same to me.'

Laughter burst out of me, and Kate and Slater were quick to follow.

'I gather I was the spoiled child of the idle rich,' Kate said good-naturedly.

'Not all gypsies are fortune tellers,' Nadira told her. 'My mother's family have been metal workers for generations. Her people worked on most of the great skyscrapers of Europa.'

'Really?' said Slater with interest.

Nadira nodded. 'Whenever there was a job, we'd get in our caravans and go and the men would work metal up high. I grew up around construction sites. The buildings were our playgrounds.'

I nodded in admiration. 'You seemed pretty comfortable jumping rooftops.'

'That's nothing,' she said.

The door to the mess opened and Dorje entered, a chart under one arm, and a smile slowly unfurling across his face. Slater turned to him.

'You've had some success, I think, Dorje.'

We cleared away our plates, and made space for the chart on the table.

'She has drifted significantly,' said Dorje.

As I scanned the map it took me a moment to realize I was looking at the southern coast of Australia, and the great sea below it, seeping away to Antarctica. Dorje had pencilled in a theoretical course for the *Hyperion*.

'The Devil's Fist won't have kept her. It will spin her out to the south east, and from there, the trade winds will take her towards the Pole.'

'Dorje's the finest navigator in this hemisphere, or any other,' said Slater proudly, clapping the Sherpa on the shoulder.

'We should meet the *Hyperion* here,' Dorje said, planting the tip of his pencil lightly on the chart.

'That's a long trip,' Nadira said.

'The bottom of the world,' I said.

'Southern hemisphere,' Kate said. 'At least it'll be summer there.'

'Not where we're going,' Slater told her. 'It's as bleak a place as you'll ever encounter. We're bound for Skyberia.'

8

SKYBERIA

Skyberia was the name airshipmen gave to the altitudes over the Polar Regions, places where it was cold enough to stop clocks, and hearts, too. It seemed the *Hyperion* had set her ghostly course for Antarctica, and even though that icy continent would be enjoying summer, it would send its glacial breath to meet us on high. I remembered the cold that had filled the *Flotsam*'s control car, as we'd angled for the *Hyperion*. What we would face over Antarctica would be much worse.

My first night aboard the *Sagarmatha* I plunged instantly into sleep, heavy as an anchor after the day's rush and excitement. I woke only once, in the small hours of the morning. Dorje was on watch, so I had the cabin to myself. I was very grateful to him for sharing with me, since I knew, as first mate, he was used to privacy. The cabin was much like my old one aboard the *Aurora*: two bunks, a little sink, a chest of drawers that doubled as a desk. It was good to be aloft again, to smell the familiar ship's fragrance of canvas and aruba fuel and mango-scented hydrium. I rolled over to the wall and peered out my porthole to see the lights and spires of Prague drifting past beneath me, and then went happily back to sleep.

Before breakfast the next morning, Slater asked us all to assemble in the lounge. Aside from Mr Dalkey and Jangbu, who were at the helm, everyone was there. In one corner of the room, Dorje and Kami had just finished building a small temple of rocks. Colourful prayer flags, many of which bore the image of a winged horse, were strung overhead.

'This is called a chorten,' Dorje explained to us. 'It is a temple, to honour the gods. The sky we seek is as much a place as Mount Everest herself. There are deities who ride the wind at these heights, and it would be foolish to ignore them. Before we make our climb, we must ask their permission to break the sky.'

'Sherpa nonsense,' I heard Miss Simpkins whisper to Kate.

Kate frowned, as though a dog had barked, and took a step away from her chaperone.

Dorje lit incense and several sprigs of juniper. Sweet smoke filled the lounge.

'This is for good luck and purity,' Dorje said. 'Properly, the puja should be presided over by a holy man, a lama. In his absence, I will do my best.' He sat before the chorten, opening a small hand-bound book with coarse pages. Taking my cue from the other Sherpas, I sat down on the floor.

Kate seated herself on the floor, too, but Miss Simpkins

I noticed, chose an armchair towards the back. Nadira sat to my left. She must have just had a shower; her hair was still damp, and carried the heady fragrance of sandalwood. She wore a long colourful skirt, and a simple white blouse. She was very close. As she crossed her legs, her knee touched mine and didn't move away. I thought of shifting, but if she noticed she might think that was rude.

'Good morning,' she said quietly.

As Dorje began to read the ancient Tibetan script, he beat rhythmically on a small drum. Slater took up a large bowl of rice and, with his fingertips, pinched some grains and tossed them into the air. Then he passed the bowl to Mrs Ram, who did the same. When the bowl reached me, Kami said quietly, 'It's an offering to the gods, for good fortune on our journey.'

I tossed some rice and passed the bowl to Kate, who took it with great eagerness.

'Too much,' I mouthed, looking with alarm at her big fistful of rice. I was too late. Her clump of rice soared high in the air, and pattered down over everyone like a sudden rain shower. Dorje did not stop reading, but Slater raised an eyebrow.

'Sorry,' whispered Kate.

Ang Jeta chuckled and gave Kate an encouraging nod. Though the Sherpas were attentive to the ceremony, they all seemed completely at ease. Mrs Ram's face, eyes closed, was the picture of serenity. Nadira too seemed to be enjoying it, and several times when I looked over to her, I thought her lips seemed to be moving along silently with Dorje's words. Sandalwood, juniper, incense. The drum beat. Someone chimed small cymbals. I might have been on the foothills of Everest. I did not understand the Tibetan words, but I loved their sound, and the solemnity with which Dorje made his observances. All his movements were slow and precise and just watching him made me feel calm, as though some serene goddess was watching over us and granting us safe passage to the sky's upper reaches.

When the ceremony ended, Dorje stood and looked at Slater.

'We can begin our climb now,' he said.

'I hope someone will be cleaning up all the rice,' said Miss Simpkins, looking askance at the grains scattered on the floor.

Breakfast was boisterous with so many at the table at once. It was a kind of celebratory meal following the puja, with all sorts of foods I'd never tasted at breakfast – or any other time. Miss Simpkins nibbled. I liked the brouhaha at the table: laughter, and English and the Sherpa tongue overlapping. I was glad to become better acquainted with Kami and Ang Jeta; and Kate, for her part, peppered them with questions about their homeland, the meaning of their names, and the origins of their language. Dalkey joined us after he came off duty, and told a shaggy dog story that won all our laughter – even from Miss Simpkins, who quickly pretended she was coughing. I was sorry when it was over, and the crew disappeared back to their duties about the ship.

I was not accustomed to being a passenger, and I can't say I liked it. The lounge was comfortable and spacious, as Slater had promised, and windows in the floor gave us a large view. But I wanted to have the ship's prow before me, cutting the wind. I wanted something useful to do, to help us on our way. According to Dorje's calculation, our trip to intercept the *Hyperion* would last at least four days. It would be a long time to spend in one room.

Kate didn't seem to mind at all. She said she had a long list of reading and small experiments to conduct, and within minutes had turned a corner of the lounge into her own private laboratory.

'You brought a microscope?' I asked, as she unpacked her various cases of equipment.

'Just a small one,' she said regretfully. 'I had to pack light.'

After making sure all the incense and juniper sprigs had been snuffed out, Miss Simpkins sat alternately reading her novel and sewing. Nadira seemed content to lounge on the floor with a cushion, perusing the ample supply of newspapers and journals, but mostly staring out the window, watching the scrubland of the Balkans give way to the deserts of Arabia. It was a fine view, but right now I felt too restless to sit still. From the kitchen came the homey sounds of Mrs Ram chopping and stirring and clanging pots.

I walked clockwise around the lounge; then

anticlockwise, pausing to peer at the many framed photographs. There was an interesting series of the *Sagarmatha* under construction, and then a shot of Slater in all his finery, standing beside the gleaming control car, about to christen his new ship with a bottle of champagne.

There were also numerous photos of the Himalayas, some of which were obviously taken from an airship. In one picture, Slater was seated on a rock, draped in mountain climbing cloaks, the puckered fabric of a tent in the background. Beside him sat Dorje, on a much smaller rock, so he was lower than Slater, and had his arm resting on Slater's knee. Slater had his arm around Dorje. I assumed this must have been taken during an ascent of Everest. Both men were smiling at the camera. I didn't like it that Dorje was so much lower than Slater in the photograph. It made him look like a servant, crouched humbly at the foot of his lord and master.

'A bit nauseating, isn't it,' said Kate, coming up beside me. 'The conquering hero.'

But I noticed that her eyes had strayed to a photograph of Slater stripped naked to the waist, riding atop an elephant.

'You seemed impressed enough with him last night,' I said. '"Oh, Hal, do tell me about your thrilling adventures!"'

Kate's nostrils narrowed; her chin lifted. 'I was just trying to be polite. Keep the conversation going. In case you hadn't noticed, there was a little tension at the dinner table.'

The lounge was big enough that we could talk in private if we spoke softly, but I still felt self-conscious with Nadira and Miss Simpkins in plain view. And I did not trust Kate to keep her voice low if we argued: it wasn't her style.

'Sorry,' I said. 'I'm just grumpy. I feel like I'm in a jail cell.'

'It's a comfy jail cell at least.'

'Some of the inmates are quite charming,' I admitted.

That made her smile. 'You should try sharing bunks with Marjorie.'

'Who has the top?'

'Me. She's worried she might have to go to the lavatory in the night, and doesn't want to break her neck getting down the ladder. Which I told her was very unlikely unless I greased the rungs.'

'I'm sure that reassured her.'

'You seem very restless,' Kate said. 'Your eyes are getting that darty look. You always say you're happiest aloft.'

'I know. But I feel like luggage.'

'Why don't you do some studying?'

I thought of the textbooks I'd brought, the small lines of bickering numbers. 'I will. Later.'

'Hello over there, you two! Yoo-hoo!'

We both turned to Miss Simpkins' sing-song voice. She was peering at us over the top of her needlework. 'Whispered conversations in a parlour setting are considered a no-no in polite society. Kate, you know better than that.'

Kate looked at me, exasperation smouldering in her hooded eyes. 'I'm trying to hold my tongue,' she muttered.

'Make sure you've got a good grip,' I said.

'Nadira and I might wish to be included in your conversation,' Miss Simpkins said cheerily.

'Not me,' said Nadira. 'Sweethearts need time alone.'

'Oh heavens, they're not sweethearts.' Miss Simpkins gave a brittle laugh. 'Goodness, no.'

Nadira turned to me, smiling, and there was something so conspiratorial in her gaze that I felt both intrigued and deceitful. I looked away.

'I was just on my way to the control car,' I said. I could see that aboard the *Saga*, it was going to be near impossible to have a private conversation with Kate – much less a kiss. I started to wonder if Miss Simpkins' main reason for coming was to keep Kate and me well apart.

Leaving the lounge, I gave a great exhalation of relief, and made my way forward, and down the ladder to the control car. Slater was at the rudder, with Jangbu at the elevator wheel. Jangbu smiled, but Slater did not look pleased to see me.

'Anything I can do for you?' he asked.

'Just looking for a change of view, if that's all right.'

'So long as we're not too busy.'

'You've plotted a gradual climb, I suppose.'

'That's right. I'm timing it so we'll be at seven thousand metres when we meet the *Hyperion*. About thirteen hundred metres a day, nice and gradual to give our bodies time to acclimatize. In a ship like the *Aurora* you're used to flying at barely a thousand metres, no more. I hope you're fit. The height takes its toll. After three thousand metres, you'll start feeling it.'

He had a way of talking to me like he was teaching me a lesson, and it rankled. It made me want to shove back.

'Why not just pressurize the crew quarters?' I asked.

'No point,' Slater replied. 'If we're to board the *Hyperion*, our bodies need to be ready to work at seven thousand metres. We stay all comfy in a pressurized cabin, we won't last five minutes when the hatch opens and the air's thin as pauper's gruel.'

He was right. I gave a grunt, wishing I hadn't tried to be so clever. Better to keep quiet than have Slater correct me.

'Don't worry,' he said. 'The cabins are heated, and as we get higher, I'll start pumping in a little oxygen. Not too much. I don't want you getting reliant on it.'

I decided it might be best to stay away from the control car when Slater was on watch. I'd rather take my lessons from a textbook, which I did dutifully dig out from my duffel bag when I returned to my cabin.

Over the next thirty-six hours, I tried to play the part of the contented passenger, and it was not so bad. The meals were excellent. I worked at my studies. Staring out the windows, I saw Persia give way to India, and caught sight of Madras before our view became the blue creases of the Indian Ocean. We would not see land again until we crossed the northwest coast of Australia.

Sometimes I made out the sleek outlines of other airships, well below us, for we were already far above normal cruising altitudes. Often the view was obscured by wispy cirrus and thicker nimbus. Outside, it was getting close to zero, but the cabins were heated to a comfortable temperature. So far I'd felt no signs of altitude sickness; nor had anyone else, including Miss Simpkins, whom I expected would be the first to complain. Slater's acclimatization programme seemed to be working well.

Kate was always busy. Despite being trapped with Miss Simpkins in such close quarters, she couldn't have been more buoyant. At meal times she was full of questions for Slater: our speed and bearing, the weather reports, the state of the engines, the capacity of the cargo holds. Quite the little sky sailor she'd become. Now that she had her ornithopter's licence, I suppose these things held more interest for her.

Mid-morning of our third day, I was taking a break from my studies, paging through a Paris newspaper in the hopes of improving my French. I was struggling through an article about the Aruba Consortium, and understanding every third word or so. Apparently, they had been drilling for aruba fuel in the south seas and had just found a new, vast reserve. Now they were spending billions to extract it. After that, the language got more complicated and I couldn't follow it. I glanced up at the photograph – the usual picture of a row of smug, suited men in top hats, looking like they'd just eaten a big greasy meal.

'I think I saw him,' said Nadira, passing behind my chair. She pointed at the newspaper photograph. 'That frail old fellow with the bushy eyebrows – he was talking with Rath in the Heliodrome!'

'Really?' I said. 'He was thin, wearing a camel-hair coat?'

She nodded. 'I remember those eyebrows.'

'Who is he?' Kate asked, coming over.

I glanced at the photo caption. 'Says here, George Barton. He's on the Board of the Aruba Consortium.'

'It seems most unlikely,' commented Miss Simpkins, looking up from her needlework, 'that a fine gentleman from the Aruba Consortium would be dealing with the likes of John Rath.'

'I agree,' said Kate. 'It's not a very clear photograph. Are you sure, Nadira?'

She stared long and hard. 'Well, not entirely. But those bushy eyebrows . . .'

'Those are very fashionable now,' Kate said. 'All the old richies are doing it. The bushier the better.'

'I think they're fake, half the time,' murmured Miss Simpkins.

'Oh,' said Nadira. 'I just caught a glimpse of him really.'

Kate lost interest in the matter and went back to her camera. Miss Simpkins sewed. Nadira found a newspaper and settled down. It was very hard to believe Rath could have had anything to do with the Aruba Consortium, but I couldn't help remembering something he'd said to me at the Ritz, about how he worked for some of the finest people in Paris. A lot of rubbish, probably.

'Aren't you surprised we haven't seen cloud cats yet?' Kate asked after a moment.

'Well, not really,' I said. 'I sailed three years without seeing any. Besides, they may not inhabit these skies at all.'

'I sincerely hope not,' said Miss Simpkins. 'Horrid creatures in my opinion.'

Kate ignored her chaperone, as though her words were nothing more than the dripping of a leaky tap. 'I do hope we spot a few,' she said. 'I've been working on a little theory over the past few months.'

I knew she wanted me to ask. 'About what?'

'Well, the sea, as we all know, is simply teeming with life. Why shouldn't the sky be the same?'

'Not quite as many fishies, last I checked,' said Nadira, without looking up from her newspaper.

'Ah, but if the sky can sustain a large predator like the cloud cat, surely there must be other creatures aloft.'

'But the cloud cats seemed to find most of their food at sea level,' I pointed out. 'Fish and birds.'

'That's just where we happened to observe them. Birds and fish might only be part of their diet.' She paused significantly. 'The sky may hold more surprises than we think, especially at the higher altitudes.'

A year ago, I would have contradicted her. I would have told her that in all my years watching the sky, I had seen no signs of life apart from brave sea-faring birds. But after discovering the cloud cats with her, I could no longer make any easy assumptions. Still, with Kate, I always thought it best to argue, just to stay in practice if nothing else. She liked a good debate, and I wanted her to think me clever.

'It gets awfully cold up high,' I reminded her, 'and there's not much oxygen. Or water. Every living thing needs water. They don't call it Skyberia for nothing.'

'True,' Kate said, 'but just think of the deep sea. Granted, it never goes below freezing, but when you think about it, it's a far less hospitable place than the sky. Remember the discoveries Girard recently made in his bathysphere?'

I recalled the stories and photographs in the newspaper: the intrepid French explorer in his striped bathing suit, standing beside his odd, spherical submarine. Its metal hull was a good metre thick, fitted with reinforced portholes and lamps and motors that enabled it to be lowered to the sea's blind depths.

'He discovered things we never imagined,' Kate went on. 'A fangtooth fish that lives at a depth of five thousand metres. The pressure down there is over three thousand kilos per square centimetre. Imagine that. You'd be squashed into meringue. Girard found sea spiders at six kilometres below the surface. There's no light, and not much oxygen down there. I don't see why airborne creatures couldn't live at high altitudes. Certainly they'd have to adapt in ways we hadn't thought possible.'

'It's a very intriguing idea,' I said to Kate.

'Hmm,' said Nadira, looking at her newspaper.

'I'm hoping Grunel has some interesting specimens aboard the *Hyperion*,' Kate continued. 'It would help my research no end. And imagine if he had a cloud cat! It would be even more proof. Those stodgy old men at the Zoological Society would think twice before accusing me of jumbling up some panther and albatross bones.'

Nadira looked up. 'It's a strange kind of loot to risk your neck over.'

'Well, I already have lots of the other kind,' Kate said. Apologetically she added, 'Not that I earned it. It was just luck of the draw.'

'I don't remember getting a draw,' Nadira said wryly.

I laughed. 'I guess we missed it. So what will you do with all your newfound riches?'

Nadira said nothing for a moment and I worried I'd overstepped.

'I want to strike out on my own.'

'You mean leave your family?'

'But isn't your community awfully close-knit?' Kate asked.

170

'There's no one community,' Nadira said. 'There's four nations of Roma. The Kalderash, the Machacaja, the Lovari, and the Churari, and a dozen other groups besides. They're all different.'

'I see,' said Kate sheepishly.

'Anyway,' Nadira went on, 'the truth is, my own people don't even consider me a Roma.'

'Whyever not?'

'My mother married a gadjo. An outsider. And if your father's not a Roma, his children can't be either. My mother was considered impure.'

'Was it terrible, growing up like that?' Kate asked.

'It would have been worse if my father's work hadn't taken him away for long stretches. He started out as a merchant airshipman, and then he began working with John Rath, and his work became more unsavoury. After he left us, my mother remarried a Roma, but we were always considered beneath the others. Now my mother's in a hurry to marry me off. Because of my mixed blood, she knows there won't be many takers.'

Nadira was so pretty, it seemed hard to believe.

'Do you have no say in the matter?' Kate asked.

'None.'

'Quite sensible,' said Miss Simpkins, glancing up from her sewing. 'Marriage is far too important a matter to be left to the young.'

'My mother would agree with you,' Nadira said. 'That's why I'm already betrothed.'

'You are?' I said, feeling an unexpected pang.

'I'm getting married in three days.'

'You're not!' Kate exclaimed.

'Well, no, because I won't be there, will I?' She smiled mischievously.

'You ran away!' I said, with surprise and admiration.

'Oh! This is scandalous!' Miss Simpkins said, but she had put down her sewing and was leaning forward in her chair.

'If you saw the man I'm supposed to marry,' Nadira said, 'you'd run too. He has very bad teeth. He is also old enough to be my grandfather.'

'I'm completely sympathetic,' said Kate.

'Unless I marry and become a wife and mother, there's no future for me back home,' Nadira said. 'That's why I need Mr Grunel's gold.'

She was right. If she were to leave her family and make her own way, she would need plenty of money. An unmarried young woman would find it very difficult to secure reputable work, or a place to live. And as a gypsy, things would be even harder.

'Well, I think this is very loose behaviour altogether,' said Miss Simpkins. 'You're a very bold girl.'

'I was thinking of settling in Paris, actually,' said Nadira. 'Buying a nice place on the river maybe. We could be neighbours.'

Miss Simpkins started sewing with renewed vigour.

'And what about you?' Nadira asked me. 'What will you do with your share of the loot?'

'Buy a new school uniform,' I said decisively.

She laughed. 'And then what?'

'Well, it depends how much is left over, doesn't it?'

'More than you know what to do with!' she said, eyes alight.

'Oh, I'd buy my mother and sisters a house. A really splendid house up in the hills of Point Grey, with a view of the water and mountains. My mother wouldn't need to work any more. I'd have an eminent doctor cure her rheumatism. I'd hire someone to help her keep house. They wouldn't have to make their own clothes. I would buy them a new-fangled motorcar if they wanted!'

'But you must want things for yourself, too.'

'Just to keep flying,' I said, but I was lying. I wanted more than that, and felt ashamed of how much. I daydreamed about money all the time now. I would buy myself clothes like the ones Hal Slater wore. They were bound to make me look less like a boy. I would become manly. I would not endure Miss Simpkins' peevish looks, and comments about my unsuitability. I would not suffer the humiliation of having Kate pay my way. If I failed at the Academy, I could buy a ship and a crew to call me captain. Money would conjure my happy future like a genie's lamp.

9

AIRBORNE ZOOLOGY

Later in the afternoon, I was hunched over my physics text, trying to train my equation to perform like a troupe of circus monkeys – without much success. As I rubbed out my pencil scratchings for the third time, Kate bustled into the lounge carrying a glass flask and looking windblown and flushed and altogether pleased with herself.

'What've you got there?' I asked.

'Oh, just a few specimens,' she said, heading for her table.

Miss Simpkins looked sharply up from her book. 'What do you mean, specimens?'

Kate sat down and began examining her flask through a magnifying glass. 'This voyage has given me the perfect opportunity to test my theory. So I rigged up a net.'

'A net?' I said.

'Just outside my porthole. I waited thirty minutes and now I've got my first specimens.'

'What exactly do you have in there, Kate?' Miss Simpkins demanded.

'Come see,' she said, delighted. Miss Simpkins came no closer, but Nadira and I certainly did. Even without the magnifying glass, I could see plenty of activity inside the flask. Nadira and I bent close, our heads almost touching.

'Spiders?' I said in surprise.

'Yes,' said Kate. 'Those down at the bottom are still in some kind of frozen torpor, but these others seem perfectly happy.'

They were scuttling around inside the glass. Some looked familiar enough, but others were odd, spindly-looking things, with smaller bodies and longer legs than I was used to seeing.

'But they don't live up here,' Nadira said. 'They're just getting blown around by the wind.'

'Well, some of them,' said Kate. 'Which is fascinating in itself. They're light enough so that the wind can carry them, probably for thousands of kilometres. They could cross oceans. Colonize new continents! I don't think anyone's considered the spread of insect habitat by such means. But some of these other ones are very odd indeed.'

Kate tapped on the side of the glass, directing our eyes towards a spider I hadn't noticed yet.

'Are those *wings*?' I said in amazement.

'Spiders don't have wings,' Nadira said. 'It must be something else.'

'I think it's a winged spider,' said Kate. 'I'm not completely sure. Arachnids really aren't my speciality.

But if it is, no one's identified it before. And look at some of these other insects.'

There were many. They were bizarre-looking things, with compact little armoured bodies and multiple sets of sturdy wings. Their colouring was muted, all silvers and greys and milky whites. To blend in with the sky and cloud, I supposed. Nothing wants to get eaten. It amazed me to think of insects flying at such an altitude, assisted by powerful tail winds.

'Do you know what all these things are?' I asked Kate.

'No,' she said, 'but I can't wait to start dissecting some of them.'

'Kate, you're not going to cut them up!' exclaimed Miss Simpkins.

'Oh yes, it's quite necessary.'

'You'll not do it in our cabin.'

'It's unlikely any will escape.' Kate gave me a sly smile. 'That one does have nasty-looking mandibles though, I must say.'

'You'll keep them in their bottles!' said Miss Simpkins.

Kate ignored her. 'This is very exciting. This could mean there's a vast airborne zoology just waiting to be discovered.'

'They're just little bugs,' said Nadira.

'Not just any bugs though. Most bugs are very sensitive to cold temperatures, but lots of these are special. Look how active they are, even though it's below freezing outside.'

'You're right,' I said. 'They should all be frozen.'

'I'm thinking they might have some chemical in their bodies that lowers their freezing point.'

'Like ethylene glycol,' I said, delighted I remembered this detail from my studies. I could see Kate was impressed, because she stopped talking and her eyebrows lifted. 'It was invented by a Frenchman, Charles Wurtz. A chemical that stops liquids from freezing.'

'Then this would be the same, only produced biologically!' Kate said. 'And here's the other exciting thing about these little fellows. If they can live up high, so can bigger creatures. Predators.'

'Really?' asked Nadira sceptically.

'Think what the blue whale eats. Plankton. Krill. The tiniest creatures are enough to keep the biggest in the world alive.'

Kate's words sent a sudden thrill through me. I had to hand it to her, she had a way of spinning your thoughts in completely new directions. A creature as vast as a whale, sailing the sky.

'Now,' Kate said, 'I've got a lot of work to do. Classifying and so forth.'

Nadira and I looked at each other, amused. We'd been dismissed. Kate was already busy making sketches and notes, oblivious to everything else.

I glanced at the clock. It was still an hour before dinner. We went back to our reading. All was quiet. Occasionally Miss Simpkins, engrossed in her book, would give a little squeak or gasp and sit up very straight in her chair.

'Is it an exciting bit, Marjorie?' Kate asked after the twentieth gasp. Miss Simpkins ignored Kate, or perhaps was too excited to hear her. She turned the page and squeaked again.

'Is it a good novel, Marjorie?' Kate persisted in exasperation.

'Hm? Oh yes, indeed it is.'

'Really? What's it about?'

Miss Simpkins lowered the book to her lap and looked sternly at Kate.

'An ill-advised romance between a headstrong young heiress and a stable boy.'

'How riveting,' said Kate. 'How does it all turn out?'

'With heartbreak, disaster, and *death*.' She let her gaze drift across the room to settle on me.

'I must read it after you, then,' said Kate breezily. 'I adore stories about stable boys.'

'It's not at all appropriate for someone of your tender years,' said Miss Simpkins curtly and went back to reading.

I'd barely returned my gaze to my wretched textbook when the door opened and Slater strode in.

'My, what a studious lot we are today,' he said. I did not look up but watched him from the corner of my eye as he moved across the room towards me, chest thrown out, chin tilted high like the figurehead of some flamboyant ship. He bent to take a quick look at my textbook.

'What a lot of rubbish,' he said with a chuckle.

'It's rubbish I need to learn.'

'I can assure you, you don't need it,' Slater said.

'I do if I want to graduate from the Academy.'

Slater gave a sniff. 'They're probably still teaching Morse code.'

'They are, actually.'

'That's what I'm talking about. About as useful as a dead language. Dorje learned it back in Nepal when they still used telegraphs.'

For some reason I was rather good at Morse code, but I had to admit Slater was right. Nowadays, I'd never known it to be used aboard ship.

'Looks like you've done more erasing than anything,' Slater carried on. 'I might be able to lend a hand.'

'I'm fine, thanks.' I doubted he could make any more sense of the calculations than me, but I dared not run the risk of having him show me up in front of Kate.

'Suit yourself. Just remember, you don't need a scrap of paper from the Academy to fly.' He held his arms out. 'Look at me. No scrap, and I'm a captain, my boy.'

I hated it when he called me 'my boy'. I sensed there was nothing affectionate about it; it was meant only to keep me in my place. What made it more galling was that he was not much older than me.

'Well,' Slater said, 'I came to let you all know we've just crossed the equator, and that always puts me in a celebratory mood.' He went to the gramophone, sorted through the ample collection of records and placed one on the turntable. He cranked the handle. 'Miss Simpkins, would you do me the honour of a dance?'

Kate's chaperone flushed from her collar to her hair. For a moment I thought she would decline and mutter some excuse but she said, 'Very well, a bit of exercise would do me good.'

'Well, if I'm only a bit of exercise to you, Miss Simpkins, perhaps I should find a more eager partner.' Grinning, he took her hand and led her to the room's centre.

From the gramophone's horn soared a rousing waltz.

Hal Slater, I had to admit, was a very good dancer. And so was Miss Simpkins. Watching her in Slater's arms, I saw her for the first time not as Kate's irritating chaperone, but as a young woman. She was only a little older than Slater. Dancing made her graceful and attractive. She smiled. Her hair caught the light. I felt I was watching a miraculous transformation.

'Delightful,' said Kate, clapping as the dance ended. 'Well done, Marjorie. Well done, Hal!' As another waltz started up on the gramophone, she turned to me. 'Come on, Matt!'

'You'll have to teach me,' I said quietly as she walked over, hands outstretched.

'You'll get the hang of it instantly.'

I was glad of the excuse to hold her.

'It's called the box step. Feet together. Here we go. Take a step with your left foot. Now step out and over with your right, and now bring your left over. Good.

Now the reverse: back with your right, back and over with the left and bring your right over so your feet are together again. You see? One, two, three. One, two, three. All there is to it.'

We danced – or tried to at least. As Slater swirled Miss Simpkins effortlessly around the lounge, I staggered and lurched and stepped on Kate and bashed her into furniture. I felt like an imbecile automation with rusted limbs.

'Ow,' Kate said again.

'Sorry.'

'Would you mind stepping on my other foot next time?'

'Shouldn't I be leading?'

'Then lead.'

'I'm trying.'

I gripped her more tightly, counting in my head. I watched Slater, trying to copy him. The music didn't seem to be cooperating with my counting. There were more beats than I had footsteps.

'Well, that was very . . . vigorous,' said Kate when the waltz ended. 'Thank you.'

'I think I'm starting to get the hang of it,' I lied.

'Mmm,' Kate said.

'I'm quite puffed,' said Miss Simpkins, her eyes shining happily.

'It's just the altitude,' Slater told her. 'Let's turn up the oxygen a bit, so we can all dance some more. Three fine ladies aboard my ship. I can't let this opportunity pass.' He went to a small brass tap above the door and gave it a half turn. I heard a faint hiss as valves opened and oxygen slipped invisibly through the grates.

'A little treat! Don't get used to it!' Slater warned us jovially. 'Miss de Vries, may I have this dance?'

I did not like to see him hold her. Had our bodies been so close when we danced? In his arms, she looked suddenly older, someone I didn't quite recognize. Slater led confidently and Kate's movements surrendered to his as they glided around the lounge. They fitted together perfectly. She laughed, she smiled up at him, and I felt desperately, desperately unhappy. I could not look away. It was as if I'd touched something viciously cold and my fingers had fused with it, and I could not pull free, so it kept on burning with its coldness.

I asked Nadira to dance.

'Promise you won't kill me,' she said.

'That bad, was I?'

'You just need a little more practice,' she said, and placed her hand inside mine. I held her waist. It was a completely different feeling from holding Kate. With Kate I was aware of a stiff layer of clothing; with Nadira, I was aware of her skin beneath the clothing. I cleared my throat and concentrated on my dancing. I looked over her shoulder and tried not to think about her throat and face and hair being so close to me. I tried not to think about the warm, supple curve of her waist. One, two, three. One, two, three. Kate and Slater swished

182

across our path, chatting and laughing and I felt like a small boat swamped in their wake.

'You're doing very well for a beginner,' Nadira told me, when my feet found the rhythm again.

'Really?'

She nodded. 'After jumping rooftops, dancing's a breeze.'

I smiled back. When another waltz started up, Kate and Slater just kept going, so I did too with Nadira. Maybe it was just the giddy rush of the extra oxygen, but I thought I really was getting the hang of dancing.

We swirled, and all my sensations swirled too. I breathed the sandalwood of Nadira's hair; I saw Kate in Slater's embrace, and felt the icy burn of my jealousy. The music quickened, and so did our steps. Mr Dalkey and Kami came in, and now Miss Simpkins was dancing again. Slater roared for Mrs Ram to come out from the kitchen. Dalkey, though heavy-set, was an amazingly nimble dancer. We pushed back the furniture so we had more room. We all switched partners, though I never seemed close enough to Kate to claim her before the next song started up. I danced with Mrs Ram. I even danced with Miss Simpkins. I danced again with Nadira. I felt my feet lighten and become swift and sure. All of us were flushed and laughing, barely having time to catch our breaths between songs as Slater cranked the gramophone.

'Ah, here's something,' Slater said, putting on a new record. An altogether different sound flooded the room.

There were guitars and clapping hands and a wild keening woodwind whirling through it. 'You'll like this,' Slater called out to Nadira.

He was right, for her eyes lit up at once, and she began a dance of her own. I had seen Flamenco in Sevilla and belly dancing in Constantinople and this was like an exotic gypsy blend of both. Her arms lifted, graceful as stripling branches. Her fingers stroked and caressed the air, her feet stamped, and her body slowly swirled. Her bracelets flashed and jangled. She held her neck proudly, and her eyes and teeth flashed as she smiled. Her hips circled and swayed.

'Oh, this is quite inappropriate,' said Miss Simpkins, but she kept watching – as did we all. No one could turn away. It was hypnotic. For just a moment I worried Kate might catch me staring but then I thought: let her. All the time Nadira's eyes were on me as she danced. Music filled the room, as heady as incense.

And then Slater was on his feet trying out the dance for himself, and Kate too, and Nadira was teaching them as she swayed. Kami and Mrs Ram joined in. Nadira turned to me and crooked her finger, summoning me like a mesmerist. I came, and tried to match my movements to hers. The music seemed to be speeding up, and then I realized the gramophone was skipping. At first I thought it was just the stomping of all our feet, but then I felt the ship give a strange shrug.

I sought out Slater's eyes. He was too enthralled with the dance to notice. The gramophone's needle righted itself and the music careened on, but I felt a second shudder pass through the ship. Had it been a bigger shake I would have known it was just a gust, but it was the very slyness of the movement which put me on alert.

'What's wrong?' said Nadira, for I had stopped dancing.

'Did you feel that?' I asked Slater.

He shook his head.

'There's something not right,' I said.

'Nothing's amiss, Cruse. Don't be a spoilsport.'

The door opened and Dorje approached Slater and spoke close to his ear. Slater gave a quick nod.

'Please excuse me,' he said. 'Mr Dalkey, Kami Sherpa.'

As they all left the lounge I followed.

'What's wrong?' I asked as Slater strode aft along the keel catwalk. He scowled when he saw me.

'Go back to the lounge, please.'

'It's the rudder, isn't it.'

'It appears to be jammed. It's not serious right now, but it will be when we need more turning power. I'm sending Dalkey and Kami out to deal with it.'

'I'll go, too,' I said.

'There's no need.'

But there was for me. I had no doubt his two crewmen were competent. But I badly wanted to prove I wasn't just a useless boy. It shouldn't have mattered so much to me, but it did.

'I've no fear of heights,' I told him. 'They might need an extra hand.'

185

'You'll only slow us down.'

'I can handle myself on the ship's back.'

'At four thousand metres?'

'I've worked at such heights,' I lied.

'Looking to impress Miss de Vries, are you?'

'She's seen me do more difficult things than inspect a rudder.'

We'd reached an equipment locker and Dalkey and Kami were already slipping on coats, strapping on tool belts.

'She's certainly a fine young lady,' Slater said. 'And a woman's eye will always stray to the man of accomplishment and means.'

He said it with a lift of his eyebrow and I knew he wanted me to think Kate was interested in him. And for all I knew, maybe she was.

'I'm happy to help you out,' Slater said. 'Grab a coat. Gloves and goggles in there. Boots too. And get a safety harness on.'

'Thanks,' I muttered, reaching into the locker and suiting up.

'A word to the wise, though,' Slater said. 'That Kate of yours, I look at her, and you know what I see? A pretty face and a heart of steel. She knows what she wants. She'll take it, and I pity the poor wretch that stands in the way.'

'Try not to get in the way, then,' I told him. He gave a hearty laugh and clapped me on the shoulder.

My skin felt hot and my fingers trembled with anger

as I clipped my harness around my chest. Hurriedly I climbed after Mr Dalkey and Kami up the ladder to the crow's-nest. Slater's words were nonsense, but they wormed their way into my brain. I was eager for the cold cleansing wind that would greet me on the ship's back.

Out I went, pulling the goggles over my eyes. I glanced at the thermometer fixed to the domed hatch. The mercury hovered just above freezing. Bright sun reflected off the *Sagarmatha*'s silver skin. In the fleecelined coat I did not feel the cold, and the wind was lighter than I'd expected. Crouching, I clipped my line to the safety rail that ran along the ship's spine. Ahead of me, Dalkey and Kami made their way back towards the upper tail fin, which rose three metres above the hull.

I'd never been outside at such a height, and when I glanced down over the side, I saw glimpses of the Indian Ocean through the clouds. It sparked in me no vertigo or feeling of danger. As always when I was aloft, the vista of sky and cloud seemed completely natural. This was more home to me than any place on earth.

The rudder was hinged at the rear of the fin, and to reach it we had to make our way single-file alongside the fin, then down the slope to the stern. Dalkey and Kami proceeded more cautiously now. I paid out my safety line as I went, my rubber-soled boots giving me sure footing.

Not far from the stern, I saw a long wire slapping against the hull, and my first thought was that something must have ripped free – a landing line, or worse, part of the rudder assembly. The wire lifted in the wind, wavered, and then lashed against the ship's skin.

Dalkey waited till the wire was still, then drew closer, meaning to grab it, and tie it off. Before he could lay hands on it, though, it snapped high in the air, circled wildly, and whipped Dalkey across the face and torso. Above the wind, I could hear Dalkey's cry of pain. The blow brought him to his knees. He began to slide but grabbed hold of the rail with his hand. It was then I realized he had not secured his safety line.

Kami hurried forward to help his crewmate, but Dalkey was already rising to his feet and waving his hand to show he was all right. I caught sight of the livid welt running across the left side of his face.

'Your line!' I shouted out to him. 'Fasten your safety line!'

He ignored me, or maybe he did not hear me above the wind. It was possible that Dalkey never used safety lines, so confident was he of his skills. Intent on securing the loose wire, he stepped forward, hand outstretched.

Suddenly there was not one wire, but three.

They swirled briefly in the air, then, as if coordinating an attack, drew back like bullwhips and struck. Dalkey's arm flew up to shield himself. One wire hit his back, the other his stomach. Dalkey's coat and shirt exploded off him. Flames leapt from his eyes through the goggles, melting them. His body, as though viciously tugged by puppet strings, jerked three metres in the air. It all happened in a single beat of my heart. Then Dalkey fell, past the ship's stern, and was gone.

I realized with horror that he'd been electrocuted. The wires must be high voltage lines, severed somehow from the ship's circuitry. But as they arched high in the air, near the rudder's tip, I finally saw their source. These were not wires.

They were tentacles.

Billowing from behind the ship's fin was an enormous squid-shaped creature. Its upper body was almost translucent, a rippling sac which could easily have been mistaken for a weather balloon were it not for the green and blue bundle of intestines contained in its gelatinous lower regions. Trailing from its undersides were countless whip-like tentacles, some of which had been snagged in the rudder's hinged joint. The creature's body swelled, puckered, swelled again, as though breathing, and its tentacles flexed and thrashed in vain against the ship, trying to free itself.

I shouted a warning at Kami, but he too had seen the creature and was frantically backing up. I moved as quickly as I could, making room for his retreat, afraid of the full reach of those tentacles. No fewer than five were whipping around near the stern now. Two hovered overhead, their tips quivering, as if sniffing out prey.

'Look out!' I shouted.

Kami unhooked his safety line so he could move faster, and leapt. The tentacles struck in tandem, one lashing him across his lower legs, the other just missing.

There was a crack as a spark of lightning leapt from Kami's feet. Face twisted in pain he crashed down, rolled, and began sliding off the ship's back. His numb hands tried in vain to grab hold of something. I rushed for him as he went over the side, but was too late. Kami fell and landed hard on the ship's horizontal fin. In his current state, I feared the wind would blow him off.

Immediately I started rappelling down after him. High above me, the airborne monster was still thrashing against the rudder, but I seemed beyond the range of its tentacles. For the first time I felt the thinner air at four thousand metres. I was breathing hard, and my muscles felt pulpy. I was only halfway down to Kami when I reached the end of my safety line. It would let me go no further. I unhooked myself and left my line dangling. Carefully I started climbing down. I couldn't have done it if Slater hadn't caged his ship with alumiron filigree. It gave me good hand and footholds. A blast of wind pushed hard at me and I pressed myself tight against the hull. When it let up I kept going. I got to the fin and crouched beside Kami. His eyes were open.

'Can you climb?' I asked him.

'I can't feel my legs.'

I let out a long breath.

'I'm going to get a line on you, and then you can use your hands and I'll pull from up top.'

He nodded wearily. I took the end of his safety line, clipped myself to it, and scaled the ship's hull as fast as I dared. Halfway up I reached the dangling end of my own safety line, and clipped it to Kami's. I now had a single line running from Kami to the safety rail on the ship's back. Very cautiously, for I had nothing to stop me if I slipped, I kept climbing, watching the creature's thrashing tentacles. I reached the ship's back, exhausted. Double-checking the safety line, I looped the rope twice around a mooring winch.

I started reeling Kami in. Luckily he was light. I kept one eye on the squid-like monster snagged in our rudder. I was still out of its range, but I was worried it might tear free at any moment. With both hands, I cranked the winch, watching Kami's painful progress. He tried to help pull himself up, but he was weak, and when I finally dragged him alongside me, I was soaked with sweat, and shaking with fatigue.

I was wondering how best to get Kami back to the crow's-nest when Slater emerged from the hatch. He saw our huddled bodies and hurried towards us.

'What's happened?' he bellowed into the wind. 'Where's Dalkey?'

'Overboard!' I shouted back. 'There's an animal caught in the rudder!'

'What in God's name . . .' Slater said, staring at the writhing creature snagged behind the fin. Suddenly it elongated, and the gelatinous membrane around its lower regions gave a violent contraction. The tentacles thrashed in tandem and all at once the creature soared up and was free, and was quickly left in our wake. I felt limp with relief.

'Let's get him inside,' Slater said to me.

We each took a side and, crouched over, started carrying Kami towards the crow's-nest. We hadn't taken five steps when I noticed, dead ahead, vague splotches of green and blue. I blinked, but my eyes were not lying: a whole colony of squid-shaped translucent sacs, puckered and undulating, was drifting straight for us.

'Look!' I shouted.

Slater saw them and we doubled our speed, desperate to reach the hatch. The creatures were nearly upon us, hastened by the wind. But I could see they were not just drifters: they had their own means of propulsion, opening and contracting their membranous aprons in sync with their tentacles. They jetted through the air at an odd slant, their long tentacles trailing far below them.

Staggering and breathless we reached the hatch.

'Get in!' Slater shouted.

'Get Kami in first,' I said.

The first of the creatures sailed overhead now, its tentacles swishing past no more than three metres overhead. I felt its wake, a warm humid wind, tinged with the scent of mangoes. More were coming, many sailing lower than the first.

Slater hoisted Kami on to his back and swung the two of them into the crow's-nest. There was no room for me until he started down the ladder. My heart raced. In my peripheral vision I saw something shift, and ducked as a great fleshy tentacle whipped past my face.

I jerked up to see one right above me. I glimpsed a beak, and beyond that, within its translucent innards, a complicated tangle of writhing guts and something half-digested that had a bit of fur on it. One of its tentacles stroked the ship, lifted, and curled back for me.

I threw myself into the crow's-nest as the tentacle cracked against the open glass dome. I wanted to grab the hatch and slam it shut, but the tentacle was still there, lingering, its tip vibrating. It had only to reach down and it would have me. The stench of rotting food washed over me, making me gag.

I grabbed the speaking tube and shouted, 'Shed one hundred and fifty metres, now!'

A second tentacle sliced past overhead and then hovered beside the first, as if conferring with it.

They shot down for me.

And the ship dropped, suddenly and swiftly, leaving them dangling in empty air.

Giddy with the sudden plunge I watched these deadly floating creatures shrink into the distance, electricity sparking from their tentacles. I reached up, closed the domed hatch, and started down the ladder.

'Turn back, or go on,' Slater said. 'That's the decision I have to make.'

Assembled around the dining table later that evening,

we were a grim lot. I had never seen a man die before me in such a way. Caught in my nostrils still was the horrifying smell of seared flesh and melted plastic from Mr Dalkey's goggles. In my worst nightmares I had never beheld such an awful thing.

'Kami is very lucky,' Dorje said. 'He has mild burns on his legs, and a small wound on his foot where the current passed through him. But the fire cauterized it instantly so I do not think there is any risk of infection. Already he says he is regaining sensation in his legs.'

'If he needs a doctor's attention, we should go back,' said Kate, looking around for support. Nadira stared at the table, silent. Kate's eyes settled on me.

'She's right,' I said, though the thought of giving up was terrible to me. We had come this far, and with such high hopes. I did not want to turn around and lose our chance at salvaging the *Hyperion*.

'What do you think, Dorje?' Slater asked.

'Kami insists he's fine. He doesn't want us to go back.'

'But do you think he needs to?'

Dorje paused. I knew that the Sherpas were proud, and that they were fiercely protective of their reputations. Any sign of weakness was quick to be concealed, lest word spread and cost them future employment.

'I do not think a doctor will heal him any faster,' said Dorje.

Slater nodded, his face strained. 'This adventure has already cost a man his life.'

'Mr Dalkey is gone,' said Dorje. 'Nothing will bring

him back. But a good salvage will take care of his family's needs and bring them some comfort.'

'Mr Dalkey was married?' said Miss Simpkins.

'With three children,' Slater replied.

'How terrible,' Kate breathed.

Slater dragged a hand across his face. I could see the misery locked behind his eyes, and realized how deeply he cared about all his crew. And now he had lost one of them, and would have to tell the family the tragic news. The moment of Dalkey's death flared in my mind once more, and I thought I was going to be sick. I took several deep breaths and gradually felt the hot constriction in my stomach subside.

'We carry on then,' Slater said with a savage determination. 'We'll wrest a victory from this voyage yet. I'm short a man. Cruse, you've been hankering after work?'

'I have.'

'Then welcome to the crew,' he said.

10

WEATHER CHANGE

Up in the crow's-nest, I was the ship's eyes – as I had been so often aboard the *Aurora*. Despite the heating wires encased within the glass observation dome, small patches of ice glittered on the inside, intricate as lace. I scraped them away, then drew my fleece-lined jacket tighter about myself.

Below us Australia was enjoying a blistering summer, but at five thousand metres the mercury had fallen to negative fifteen. The crow's-nest itself was unheated, and my feet were never warm, though I wore two pairs of socks. I clenched and unclenched my gloved fingers to warm them, and thought of my mother's hands, her joints swollen with rheumatism. With money it wouldn't matter. I imagined all the treasures aboard the *Hyperion*. I would plunge my fists into a chest of gold, and the touch of it would warm my hands and heal my mother's, as quickly as a pond blessed by a saint. I scanned the skies, watching for unmarked vessels – vessels of any kind – always anxious now that someone would steal our prize.

In the distance I saw a brief flurry of sparks, and thought it must be lightning before realizing it was another colony of those squid-like floaters. I reported it to Dorje, who was on watch in the control car, but they did not seem to be coming any closer, so we held our course.

Though Kate was shocked by Dalkey's death, she was still devastated she'd missed seeing the creatures during our first encounter. I could understand her excitement – surely this was a high altitude species never before seen – but Dalkey's death was still too close at hand for me, and I did not like to remember it. I could tell Kate was barely able to control her curiosity, but she was kind enough not to pester me.

It was good to be busy again. I was delighted with my new duties aboard ship, though I couldn't help feeling guilty they had come to me through a man's death. With Kami Sherpa still bedridden, there was a great deal to be done, and Hal often put me up in the crow's-nest. Some of Dalkey's sailmaker duties also fell to me: inspecting the rigging and the gas cells and the valves. Once Hal even let me do a watch as navigator.

I found it soothing to be back amongst the working rhythms of a ship. I was also relieved to be away from Kate and Nadira.

Watching Hal swirl Kate about during the dance, I had felt he could just as easily swirl her away altogether. Before we'd departed, she'd told me her interest in Hal went no further than his ship, but I could tell she fancied him. She seemed awfully self-conscious whenever he was present, and kept touching her hair, and laughing more than usual. I had never known how deep jealousy could bite. So how was it, at the same time, I wanted to look at Nadira, and feel her gaze on me? How was it I liked remembering the sensation of her blouse shifting under my hand as we'd danced?

I felt pulled in different directions, and I hated it. I did not like myself. I wished I had Baz with me. He would be able to sort me out. He knew about these things. Obviously my heart had a fiendish bent, or else how could I adore Kate, and desire Nadira too? When I wasn't on watch, I started keeping to my cabin rather than join them in the lounge. At meal times, I ate quickly, and then made some excuse so I could slip away.

I let my eyes drift to the east. Dawn was almost here, a promise that was never broken. Soon the sun would crest the horizon, and bring colour back to the cloudless sky. It would be another day of smooth sailing for the *Sagarmatha*. I was startled to hear footsteps on the ladder, because my watch was not over for another two hours. I looked down to see Nadira climbing to the crow's-nest.

'Good morning,' she said, stepping on to the platform. She was a bit out of breath from the climb; the air was much thinner at these loftier altitudes.

'You're up early,' I said.

'When Mrs Ram wakes up, she starts humming, and

I can never get back to sleep. I was hoping to see the sunrise.'

'You really shouldn't be up here.'

'Why not?'

'I'm on crow's-nest duty. I'm supposed to be giving the skies my undivided attention.'

'Pretend I'm not here,' she said, and we both smiled, for the crow's-nest was not much bigger than a telephone booth. 'May I just stay for the sunrise? Then I'll disappear, I promise.'

I gave a curt nod and turned my gaze back to the sky, willing the sun to hurry up. I could no more ignore Nadira than a pillar of fire. From the corner of my eye, I saw her silently watching the eastern horizon.

Kate would have talked.

She would have made all sorts of observations and told me everything on her mind. She would have vexed me and made me laugh. There was no stopping her words. I loved her words. Harness their energy and you could light Paris. My feelings for Kate were so strong I could scarcely make sense of them. Being near her, I was filled with happiness and want and panic all swirled together. I wanted to talk to her, shout at her, touch her and kiss her. I wanted to flee from her. It was altogether exhausting.

The sun was taking an awfully long time.

'You must love it up here,' Nadira said. 'The view.'

'It beats studying.'

A few moments passed in silence.

'I can't read fortunes,' she said, 'but it turns out I'm pretty good with numbers. I might be able to help.'

I'd been trying to hide my difficulties from everyone, hunched over my textbooks, cursing only inside my head. But Nadira must have been watching carefully, and noticed my scratchings and crossings out. If Kate had made the same offer, I would have pretended I was getting on just fine by myself, thank you. She was quite brilliant enough already. I felt like I was doomed always to lag behind her. Flying was supposed to be my realm: my pride would not let her best me there too.

But somehow I didn't feel the same competitiveness with Nadira. Maybe it was because I didn't know her as well, or because I saw her more as an equal than a superior. And best of all, Kate would not have to know of my mathematical failings.

'It's complicated stuff,' I said.

'Maybe we can muddle through it together. My father schooled me, whenever he was at home. He was a good teacher. After that I picked up a fair bit on my own.'

'All right,' I said. 'Thank you, that's very generous of you.'

'Stable hands like us should stick together.'

I chuckled but felt sad, remembering Miss Simpkins' stern words of caution to Kate.

'Look, there's the sun,' said Nadira, the dawn's light upon her face.

I forced myself to look away. 'Yep, it's a beauty. You should probably head down now.'

She turned, her hair's fragrance ensnaring me. We could not have been closer if we were dancing.

'It's my wedding day today,' she said.

'So it is,' I said.

She smiled. 'Care to kiss the bride?'

I said nothing, thinking this must be a joke. I did not move. She leaned forward and put her lips against mine. Our noses rubbed. She tasted deliciously of sleep, of raisins and curry. Her hands came up to rest on my shoulders. It was impossible not to kiss back. I didn't want to hurt her feelings. I had not started this. Our bodies pressed together. My hands touched her face and hair. My heart paused, as if forgetting itself, then gave a kick and ran fast like some guilty thing. Our mouths parted for breath in the thin air, and when she tilted her face back towards me, I stepped away. I cleared my throat. I scratched at my neck.

'You look miserable,' she said.

'I'm sorry. I shouldn't have done that.'

'Why not? I'm the one who's betrothed.'

'No, but Kate and I . . .'

And I stopped, for suddenly it seemed presumptuous to say anything. I wasn't at all certain how Kate felt about me any more. Miss Simpkins certainly didn't think we were sweethearts, and perhaps Kate didn't either. Hal had half convinced me that he was her object of desire. I shook my head, too confused and dismayed to speak.

And then, for the second time that morning, I heard

distant footsteps on the ladder, and looked down in shock. Climbing up to the crow's-nest was Kate.

'Oh no,' I breathed.

'Should I step outside?' Nadira whispered, eyebrows arched with amusement.

I ignored her, and briefly considered hurling myself out the hatch.

'I thought I'd come and say hello,' Kate called up from below. 'I feel like I haven't seen you in ages.'

Her head emerged above the platform and her eyes moved swiftly from me to Nadira. She gave a big smile.

'Oh, hello! Did you come to see the sunrise too?'

'Nadira couldn't sleep,' I said.

Kate was flushed, and blowing hard, from the climb. She reached out a hand and I helped her up on to the platform.

'You know it's really surprisingly roomy up here,' she observed.

If two people was a squeeze in the crow's-nest, three was almost impossible. We stood all bunched together, shoulders and arms grazing. Despite the subzero temperature beyond the hatch, I was starting to sweat. Kate was quiet for a moment, still catching her breath.

'You just missed the sunrise,' Nadira told her.

'Did I? What a shame. I have a bad habit of sleeping late. Matt can tell you all about that. Remember the pirate village, when we were trying to escape?'

I forced a chuckle from my parched throat.

'It must have been stunning up here,' Kate commented. 'The sunrise.'

'Thrilling,' Nadira replied.

'Well, I'm so glad we both had the same idea,' said Kate. 'What fun. And what a view! I can see why you've been avoiding us, Matt.'

'I haven't been avoiding you,' I said. 'I've just been busy. And if you two don't mind, you really should go back down.'

'But I just got here,' Kate protested.

'If Slater finds out I've been entertaining up here, he'll have a fit.'

'Oh, Hal won't mind,' said Kate, sounding as if they were on very familiar terms now. 'I was hoping we could have a little chat about those floaters you encountered. I've hardly seen you since then, and I want a full account. I even brought my notebook.'

'What a surprise.' So she'd only come to press me for scientific details; once again, I was merely useful to her. 'I'll tell you all about it tonight when I'm off duty. Honestly, you two, it's very hard to see properly with so many people up here.'

'The glass *is* a bit steamed up,' Kate said. She wiped at it with her handkerchief. 'There you go. Is that better?'

'Loads, thanks.'

'I don't think Matt likes us up here,' said Nadira.

'Is the presence of two young ladies a bit distracting, Mr Cruse?' Kate inquired.

'I'm all aflutter,' I said.

'Maybe we should leave him be,' Kate said to Nadira.

'Good idea,' she agreed. 'Let's have breakfast.'

I watched as they descended the ladder one after the other, chatting amiably, leaving me alone up in the crow's-nest, feeling utterly confused.

'And its tentacles,' Hal said, 'were easily three metres long.'

I'd just come off my afternoon watch, and walked into the lounge, hoping for some dinner. I found Hal and Kate sitting side by side on the sofa, very cosy. On his lap, Hal had one of Kate's large sketch pads, and was drawing a picture of the airborne creatures which had killed Dalkey. Near the electric hearth sat Miss Simpkins and Nadira, one sewing, the other reading.

'You draw with a very fine hand,' Kate told Hal. 'You're a man of many talents.' She noticed me for the first time. 'Oh, hello. Hal's just been telling me all about this fascinating fellow.' She turned back to him. 'And how many tentacles exactly did it have?'

'I think eight, wouldn't you say, Cruse?'

'I'm not sure. When they're all flailing at your head, it's hard to do a proper count.'

'And sparks leaping from their tips!' Hal added.

'Not all of them carried electricity,' I said. 'Dalkey got struck across the face with one, and it didn't electrocute him.'

'Hmm.' Kate did not sound impressed. She looked back at Hal's drawing. 'Oh that's fabulous! Thank you so much. Now, tell me about this balloon-like structure at the top.'

She had a notebook of her own and busily took notes as Hal talked. I had to admit, he was a fine storyteller, and he did have a good eye for detail, even though he'd scarcely seen the thing at all, compared to me. Kate was listening to him, engrossed, and would frequently interrupt to ask for a more precise bit of information. She and I had talked just like this when we'd first found the bones of the cloud cat. I felt usurped.

'You've never seen anything like this before?' she asked Hal.

'Never.'

Kate smiled. 'This is an amazing discovery, you know. It's certainly very odd. It seems to combine the characteristics of a number of aquatic animals. The squid, the jellyfish, and the electric eel of South America. And yet, its element is air, not water! It actually flies!'

'Floats anyway,' said Hal. 'Likely just riding the winds. The thing was light enough.'

'No. It had hydrium,' I said.

'What was that?' Kate asked, looking up from her notebook.

'Hydrium. There was one right over me and—'

'A bit far-fetched, don't you think?' Hal interrupted. 'Hydrium comes from deep within the earth, Cruse! You're saying this thing produces its own lifting gas?'

'It smelled of mangoes.'

He compressed his lips, as though too polite to point

205

out how absurd I was. Then he turned back to Kate and began describing how the creature had moved through the air by contracting and dilating its apron-like membranes. Kate nodded, taking notes, asking more questions.

'Don't forget to tell her about the beak,' I said.

'It had a beak?' Kate asked Hal, ignoring me entirely.

'Absolutely,' he said. 'Sharp, like a squid's.'

Hal only knew this because earlier I'd told him myself. He hadn't been under its foul maw, about to be gored. But I could see that this was Hal's show, and I didn't feel like hovering around the two of them, trying to horn in. I went to the kitchen and asked Mrs Ram if I might have some food. With my plate, I returned to the dining room and started eating my meal alone, feeling miserable. I could see Hal and Kate through the archway, still talking excitedly.

'It should have a name,' she said.

'Of course,' said Hal. 'Would you do the honour?'

'Really the honour should be yours since you saw it first.'

'I insist.'

'That's very gallant of you. Thank you.' She thought for a moment. 'Aerozoan. Creature of the air.'

'Well done,' said Hal.

I wished I'd stayed away from the lounge altogether. Clearly in the two days I'd been working so hard aboard Hal's ship, he and Kate had spent a lot of time together. Every look she gave him, every kind word, was poison to me. I could not bear it.

Nadira walked in from the lounge and sat down opposite me at the dining table.

'Do you mind if I join you?' she asked.

'No, not at all,' I said, though I could feel my mouth go dry. It was the first time we'd spoken since the crow's-nest incident. I liked thinking of it as an incident rather than a kiss. It made me feel less guilty.

'I was wondering,' she said, lowering her voice, 'if you wanted to do some mathematics with me.'

I smiled when I saw she'd discreetly smuggled one of my textbooks into the dining room.

'It's awfully nice of you,' I said. 'Are you sure?'

She tapped the cover. 'I took a look earlier. I found the page you were on.'

'Ugly stuff,' I said.

'Very ugly. But I think I've got the hang of it.'

'Really?'

'Took about two hours to figure it out, but what else is there to do around here?'

I returned my dinner plate and cutlery to the serving window, thanked Mrs Ram, and sat down beside Nadira. From where we were, I couldn't see Kate and Hal, and I was glad, for I'd had my fill of them chatting, and wasn't eager for them to know I was getting help with my school work. Miss Simpkins, though, had a clear view of us through the archway, and would peep over at us occasionally. Doubtless she would tell Kate I preferred the company of gypsies now.

Nadira pulled her chair closer, and we bent over my

textbook. Our faces were very close together. She smelled nice. I forced myself to concentrate on the page.

She had not lied: she was good at math, and was a good teacher too, clear and patient. It was like she used the numbers to tell a story, with a beginning, middle and end, and suddenly it all made sense to me.

'My professor couldn't do that,' I told her gratefully. 'Explain it so well. That was brilliant.'

She shrugged, but I could tell she was pleased. 'Any time.'

We were still hunched over the book together, and for a moment, we just looked at each other, silent. The urge to touch her was strong, so I scratched at my cheek, and sat back in my chair. I tried to think up something to say.

'You must have plans,' I said, 'for when this is all over.'

Her gaze fell to the table. 'I don't know yet. It was all very quick, my leaving home, coming to find you. I don't know if I have a plan yet.' She nodded towards the lounge. 'I've been looking at all the newspapers, reading up on the world, trying to figure out how I might fit in to it.'

'I think you could handle anything you turned your hand to.'

She smiled, and for the first time I saw she was scared. When you've seen someone jump rooftops and dodge bullets, it's hard to imagine they could be afraid of anything. Maybe her home had not been a good one, but it was the only one she had, and she'd left it and launched herself on a very risky adventure. Anyone would be frightened; and lonely. I wanted to say something reassuring to her, but before I could figure out the words, Hal was standing in the archway.

'Cruse, come join us,' he said. 'I've worked you like a galley slave today. Come take a break!'

I could not escape without seeming rude or sulky, so I returned to the lounge with Nadira and sat down.

'How are you faring, Miss Simpkins?' I inquired.

'I'm flaking away!' she lamented. 'My skin's terribly chapped from this dryness!'

Hour by hour, the air grew thinner and colder. Last I'd checked, the outside temperature was nearly negative twenty-three. And with the cold came a terrible desert dryness.

'What about all your moisturizing creams?' Kate said. 'I hear you putting them on all through the night.' She made the sound of a jar lid being rapidly unscrewed.

'Only if I happen to wake up,' said Miss Simpkins defensively.

'After all that I'd think you'd be soft as a slug by now.'

'But my creams are running low,' said Miss Simpkins. 'Just look at my hands!'

Kate dutifully went to see. 'Gosh, you do look a bit mummified,' she said gravely.

Miss Simpkins withdrew her hands, affronted.

I did not care to admit it, after all Miss Simpkins' whining, but I too felt the dryness. The skin around my thumbs had split from chafing, and I was surprised how painful it was. My eyes burned faintly in their sockets, and my elbows itched, especially at night.

'It's devilishly dry at these altitudes, Miss Simpkins,' Hal said. 'There's not much to be done, I'm afraid. Drink lots of water. More important, keep walking. I know you're all feeling listless with the thin air, but you'll acclimatize faster if you stay active.'

'It's all I can do to walk across the room without wheezing,' Miss Simpkins complained.

'Make sure to take at least two walks a day, for at least twenty minutes each. Don't let yourselves get weak. On this journey, the sky itself will prove to be our greatest adversary.'

Miss Simpkins, I'd noticed, had developed a dry cough, and several times Kate and Nadira had complained of headaches. There would be no more dancing. Yesterday morning, when we'd passed four and a half thousand metres, I noticed the climb to the crow's-nest ladder left me out of breath. My heart beat harder and faster than usual. Throughout the day I'd occasionally felt light-headed. And that night I'd slept fitfully. But upon waking this morning, even though we continued to climb, I was myself once more. My body seemed to have acclimatized to these new heights, and I was hugely relieved.

'Do you feel the thin air at all?' Kate asked Hal.

'I'm used to it,' he said with a dismissive wave of his hand. 'I should have been born a Sherpa. Six hundred metres or six thousand, it makes no difference to me.' As if to prove his point, he added, 'You know, I fancy a cigar.'

'Oh, must you?' protested Miss Simpkins, giving a little cough.

'Afraid so, Miss Simpkins. Cigar, Cruse?'

'Yes, thanks,' I said.

'Matt, honestly,' said Kate. 'You don't smoke.'

'You've just never seen me.' I gave her what I hoped was a roguish wink.

'Good man,' Hal said, cutting off the tip and handing me a cigar.

Since I'd started working aboard the ship, I'd noticed that Hal was less likely to call me lad or boy. For my part, I'd started calling him Hal, though he hadn't invited me. If Kate was calling him Hal, I refused to call him mister and play schoolboy to his master.

I think he was satisfied with my work, and Dorje had told me that Hal had been impressed with how I'd helped save Kami Sherpa on the ship's back. Of course, all Hal had said on the matter was 'Good work up there, Cruse.' Much as he vexed me, I had to admit he was a good captain and a good leader. And he carried it off with such verve. I had to confess I rather liked him. Hated him too. For though he seemed to hold me in higher esteem now, it wasn't stopping him from flirting with Kate.

I made a big show of rolling the cigar and sniffing it appraisingly so I could watch how Hal lit his. I got mine fired up and sat back with a contented sigh. Kate was right of course, I'd never smoked a cigar in my life. I'd tried a cigarette once and had not enjoyed it. The cigar was worse. After a few moments my mouth felt like it had been sprayed by a skunk, and then the skunk had decided to curl up with a bunch of friends and spend the night. I wondered how long I'd have to carry on with this. I did enjoy the feel of the cigar poised between my thumb and fingers, and wondered if I looked terrifically suave.

'Ladies?' said Hal, humorously offering his cigar box to them.

To my surprise, Nadira stood and took one. She accepted Hal's lighter, flicked a flame from it, and ignited her cigar. Miss Simpkins watched, horrified. Hal and I watched, mesmerized. Nadira puffed meditatively a few times, and then blew out a series of perfect smoke rings.

'I think I'm going to be ill,' said Miss Simpkins.

'Have you been smoking long?' Kate asked with keen interest.

'Mmm,' Nadira said.

'Is it . . . traditional?'

'You mean is it a gypsy thing?' said Nadira. 'No. It's just the men make it look like so much fun. Want a puff?'

'All right,' said Kate with scarcely a moment's hesitation.

'Kate, no!' exclaimed Miss Simpkins. 'What would your mother say?'

'Someone would have to tell her first,' said Kate. She took Nadira's cigar and had a puff. She winced. 'You know, I rather like it.'

'You don't,' Nadira said.

'It's a very interesting taste,' Kate said bravely, taking another pull.

'Give it back before you're sick,' said Nadira. Kate surrendered the cigar.

'This is all most diverting,' said Hal.

Kate's cheeks, I noticed, had turned a rather minty shade of green.

'Excuse me,' she said, standing abruptly and leaving the lounge.

I stood to go after her, but Miss Simpkins stopped me. 'I'll see to her. Such foolishness, honestly.'

As she bustled out after Kate, Hal gave Nadira and me a conspiratorial wink. 'Cigars are best left to vagabonds like us, eh?'

Slumped back in our chairs, a hard day's work behind us, we suddenly seemed equals. Hal exhaled and sang:

> *Come all ye young fellers that follows the sky.*
> *Way! Hey! Blow the man down!*
> *I'll sing ye a song and I'll tell you why.*
> *Give us the time and we'll blow the man down!*

Hal looked at me expectantly. I knew the sky shanty well enough, and was glad of the excuse to stop puffing on my cigar, so I carried on:

> *'Twas in a Sky Trawler I first served my time.*
> *Way! Hey! Blow the man down!*

And in a Sky Trawler I wasted my prime.
Give us the time and we'll blow the man down!

Hal gave me an approving nod, and as we both careened on into the third stanza, Nadira chimed in with the Way Heys and the Blow The Man Downs. Hal started stamping his boot heel against the floor. Nadira and I clapped to keep time. We were risk takers, rule breakers, all three of us, bushwhacking our way through the obstacles thrust in our paths by polite society. This morning Nadira had kissed me. And I'd kissed back. Had it really happened? Hal stood and, still singing lustily, made his way to the bar where he poured three glasses of port. He was just bringing them over when Jangbu Sherpa stepped into the lounge.

'Everything all right?' Hal asked above our singing.

'We've picked up a strange transmission,' Jangbu said.

'Distress call?'

Nadira and I stopped.

'No. It's on the wrong frequency. It's almost off the dial. We only came across it by accident. There's no message. It's a single pulse, repeated every two seconds.'

Hal took another puff of his cigar, unconcerned. 'Cruse, what do you think?'

'It's not a distress call. Sounds more like a homing beacon.'

'We're probably picking up something from down below, Australia way,' Hal remarked.

'It's too strong,' said Jangbu.

'From another ship, then.'

'*Our* ship,' said Jangbu.

Hal said nothing.

'There's no other vessel in sight,' Jangbu continued. 'The signal's very strong. It could only be coming from our ship.'

For a moment Hal stood perfectly still, his face a mask. Then he carefully ground out his cigar. He turned to Nadira. His voice was dreadful in its calmness.

'Where's the transmitter?'

'What do you mean?' she said, startled.

'Where the hell is it?' he shouted.

'You think she brought it aboard?' I said, only now understanding Hal's lightning line of thinking.

'Of course she did,' Hal said. 'So John Rath could follow us.'

'I didn't!' Nadira cried.

'I never should have let you aboard my ship! Tell me where it is!'

Nadira's eyes were wide with fear. 'I don't know anything about this, I swear.'

'You're a gypsy liar.' He grabbed her roughly by the arm.

'Hal!' I said, rising to my feet. 'You can't be sure of this!'

'Of course I am. She's cosier with those rascals than she lets on.' He began pulling Nadira towards the door. 'You're coming with me. If you won't tell us where it is, we'll search your room and everything you brought aboard.'

'This can't be right, Hal!' I said.

'Get out of the way,' he said, pushing me to one side as he marched Nadira out of the room.

I stood there in the lounge, frozen. A part of me knew that Hal might be right. I'd trusted Nadira on a gut feeling, but we knew very little about her. She obviously had secrets, and maybe some of the darker kind. In league with pirates? It seemed far too nefarious. But who else could have brought the homing beacon aboard the *Sagarmatha*?

They'd been inside my room.

Back in Paris, standing in the Academy quadrangle, I had seen something shift behind my window. It had not been my imagination.

I ran out of the lounge, down the passageway, and threw open the door to my cabin. I dragged my duffel bag out from beneath the bunk, and loosed the drawstrings. Dumping all the contents on to the floor, I handled everything, opening the books, patting clothing for suspicious bumps.

I lifted the duffel bag to see if I'd missed anything, but it was empty. Still it felt heavy. And I remembered how oddly heavy it had seemed when I'd first hefted it over my back in Paris. Feeling sick, I took my jackknife and slit the padded bottom. When I pushed my hand between the layers of fabric I felt some kind of thin metal lozenge. I yanked it out. Despite its smallish size, it was weighty in my hands. From one side sprouted a long, whip-thin antenna whose end was still somewhere

216

in the bag. I tugged out more, and more, and more still, for it was very long, and ingeniously woven into the lining of my duffel bag, making it one enormous transmitter, and giving its infernal signal enough power to travel hundreds of kilometres through the sky. The antenna's tail end was snagged deep in the fabric and I could not wrench it free, so I left the whole lot on the floor. I ran out of my room and down the passageway.

I burst into Nadira's cabin. Hal and Jangbu were in the midst of ransacking her backpack.

'What's this then?' said Hal, holding a thin silver case aloft.

'Give it back!' Nadira said. 'That's personal.'

'I'm sure it is,' he snorted.

'Hal, wait,' I said.

Hal opened the case. It was a hinged picture frame and I glimpsed a photo of a man and a woman, elaborately dressed in wedding finery.

'I found it,' I told Hal. 'The transmitter. It was in my bag.'

'You're sure?'

Nadira tried to snatch her picture frame back from Hal, but in her haste she knocked it to the floor. I quickly bent down to pick it up for her. My eyes settled once again on the photograph. The woman was unmistakably Nadira's mother, and in the moment before the case was yanked from my hand, I recognized the man. Nadira's father. It was Vikram Szpirglas.

11

THE BOTTOM OF THE WORLD

'You can't keep her locked up,' I said to Hal.

'I don't want her sneaking about my ship. She could get to the wireless room and radio our position. She could tamper with our engines. She stays in there till we return to Paris.'

'Hear, hear!' chimed in Miss Simpkins.

We were back in the lounge, all of us except Nadira. Kate looked paler than usual but no longer green. At the table, Jangbu Sherpa was busy with his tools, trying to open the brass casing of the transmitter. It had no screw holes, nor any seam nor hinge I could discern.

'The transmitter was in my bag, not hers,' I said. 'Doesn't that prove she's got nothing to do with Rath? Or else why wasn't she carrying it herself?'

'She may not be working with Rath, but she's already deceived us, and I don't mean to be deceived again.'

'She knew if she told us about Szpirglas you wouldn't let her aboard.'

'With good reason. If Szpirglas gave her that key, others might know about it. Who's to say she hasn't made her own murky alliances? We're less than a day away from the *Hyperion*. We find her and Nadira might have a crew of rascals ready to snatch the ship from us. For all I know she's already radioed them the coordinates.'

'You're assuming the very worst about her,' I said. 'What about the rest of us? Why not lock me up? It was in my bag!'

'It did occur to me.'

'And just to be safe,' I added, 'better lock up Kate and Miss Simpkins, too. We might all be in it together.'

'I resent that!' Miss Simpkins protested.

'I'm just trying to be fair,' I said.

'You're very outspoken in her defence,' Kate said, staring hard at me. My heart sank. Of all the people at the table, I'd expected her at least to be my ally. I knew she held no prejudices against gypsies, but right now I could not fathom her.

'Let us not forget Nadira is the daughter of a notorious pirate,' Miss Simpkins said.

'What's that got to do with anything?'

'Don't be naïve, Cruse,' said Hal.

'It indicates very poor breeding,' Miss Simpkins informed me primly.

'We are not dogs or horses,' I insisted hotly. 'None of us gets to choose how we're born, it's what we make of ourselves afterwards.'

Hal looked thoroughly unimpressed. I glanced at Kate. She turned her eyes away from me and I felt as though I'd been slapped.

'She's a pirate's daughter,' Hal said. 'She's had ample opportunity to be influenced, corrupted and ensnared in all sorts of nasty enterprises.'

'But we have no proof she's engaged in anything unsavoury,' I insisted.

'Matt's right,' Kate said.

I looked at her, grateful, but her gaze was on Hal.

'I think she just wants her fair share of the *Hyperion*'s cargo,' Kate went on. 'She means to start a better life for herself. I like her.'

'You do?' I said, surprised.

'Very much. She's got good spirit.'

'You killed her father,' Hal said to me. 'If I were you, I'd wonder if she had a knife destined for my throat.'

Nadira had climbed the crow's-nest early this morning to see me. If she'd wanted, she could easily have slit my throat. I'd been completely unsuspecting. Instead she had kissed me. The daughter of the man who'd tried to end my life. I made my brain go over it one more time, just to make sure I understood. I had kissed Vikram Szpirglas's daughter.

'I don't think she means to kill me,' I said.

'Unlikely,' Kate agreed.

I remembered how intently Nadira had questioned me about my so-called duel to the finish with Szpirglas. She'd wanted to know every detail, every thrust and parry. Maybe, once I'd admitted Szpirglas had not died by my hand, whatever anger she'd felt for me had evaporated.

There was a sharp crack, as Jangbu succeeded in splitting the brass case apart. Inside was the smallest transmitter I'd ever seen. An ingenious thing it was, each tiny part nestled against the other, wasting no space.

'Shall I cut off the power?' Jangbu asked, pointing his chisel at the battery.

'No, not yet,' said Hal. He thought for a moment. 'We're going to change course, nothing too drastic. I don't want them suspicious. There's no moon tonight. We'll douse our running lights, just in case they're closer than I think. Then we'll kill the transmitter. They'll lose our signal. After that we resume our original course, and part company for good. Go tell Dorje, please.'

After Jangbu had left the room, Hal looked distastefully at the transmitter and its ungainly tangle of antenna.

'It's an expensive little toy, and it makes me wonder what other clever gadgets they have. They've got a fast ship, too, if they followed us all the way from Paris. A high flyer possibly. These fellows have money. I'd like to know where they got it.'

'What about that old gentleman Rath was talking to in the Heliodrome?' I suggested.

A few days ago, I'd shown Hal the photograph of George Barton in the newspaper. Like Kate, he hadn't been convinced Rath would have any dealings with the Aruba Consortium.

'You said Nadira wasn't even sure it was the same man.'

'No, but they've got the money to kit Rath out with fancy electrics and ships.'

Hal considered for a moment, then shook his head. 'I can't see the Consortium hiring pirates for a treasure hunt. They've got enough liquid gold in the ground to keep them happy.'

He got up to leave.

'What about Nadira?' I said. 'You've got to unlock her.'

'It's simply not fair,' Kate insisted.

Hal hesitated, then nodded.

'You two keep an eye on her then,' he said. 'And Cruse, watch your back. Gypsies have fiery hearts in my experience, and a healthy appetite for vengeance. Just remember, if she does kill you, I get your share of the loot.'

Hal left for the control car to oversee our change of course, and must have unlocked Nadira's cabin on the way, for a few minutes later, she walked into the lounge.

'Hello,' said Kate cheerily, as if nothing had happened.

Nadira walked over to the glass of port wine which Hal had poured for her earlier. She picked it up, and downed it. We all watched in silence, Miss Simpkins peeping over the top of her novel. Nadira smacked her empty glass down on to the counter, put her hands on her hips and glowered at us.

'You scurvy dogs better watch your step around me,

or I'll singe your guts with me pistol.'

For a few seconds no one spoke. Then Nadira grinned, and Kate and I started laughing.

'How very vulgar!' murmured Miss Simpkins and went back to reading.

'Better get used to it,' said Nadira. 'Now that I'm Szpirglas's daughter, I'll be talking like this all the time.'

'I expect a great deal of cussing,' I said.

'Did he cuss much?'

'No, not at all really.'

She nodded. 'I understand I have you both to thank for my liberation.'

'It was Kate actually,' I told her. 'She made a stirring speech. Hal was moved to tears.'

Nadira raised an eyebrow. 'He said he'd heave me overboard if he caught me sneaking about.'

'He's just a bit tense,' I said.

She gave a sniff and sat down. I tried to superimpose Szpirglas upon her, but could see no similarities. The shape of the eyes, the mouth, the hands were all different. Still, now that I knew who her father was, his name whispered insistently through my mind, and I felt his presence heavily in the room.

'I'm sorry,' I said, 'about your father.'

'It's not your fault. He chose a very wicked life for himself.'

'He certainly did,' said Miss Simpkins, muffled behind her novel.

'I don't think he ever set out to be a murderer.' I

wanted to make Nadira feel better. 'He was a thief, and he killed people if they got in his way. But he told me he didn't like doing it.'

'And then he tried to kill you,' Nadira said.

'Well, yes.'

'Not much of a virtue,' she remarked.

'Everyone has some good in them,' Kate said kindly.

'Yes, certainly,' I said. I thought about how Szpirglas had held his son, and told him stories. I would have liked to share this with her, but I did not want to cause her more pain. Likely she did not know her father had other wives and other children.

'He wasn't a bad father,' Nadira said after a moment, 'the little he was around.'

'You said he taught you your numbers.'

'And how to read. My mother's people couldn't. They didn't see the need. But he said it was important. He said there was a whole world in books. I'm grateful to him for that.'

'After he left, did he ever come to visit you?' Kate asked.

'No. Even if he'd wanted to, my mother's family would have lynched him. Partly I blame them for driving him away in the first place. They were not welcoming.'

'Lynching does tend to discourage people,' Kate said, and won a smile from Nadira.

'My mother said he had other wives. Other children too maybe.'

I kept quiet. So did Kate.

'Oh, he had a son,' Miss Simpkins piped up. 'That boy, what was his name? You know, Kate.'

'Theodore,' she said quietly, and gave her chaperone a withering stare.

For a moment Nadira was silent. 'Where was this?' she finally asked.

'In the Pacificus. On his island hideout,' I told her. 'The boy's in an orphanage now. The Sky Guard wouldn't tell me where.'

'How old was he?'

'He'd be six now.'

She nodded, her face smooth and unreadable.

'I'd wager he's not the only half-sibling you have,' said Miss Simpkins.

Nadira ignored her. 'And the boy's mother?'

'Szpirglas said she'd died,' I told her.

'A short life as a pirate's wife,' murmured Miss Simpkins. She laughed at her own rhyme, and then had a fit of coughing.

'Marjorie,' said Kate, 'that cough of yours sounds wretched. Perhaps you should go to bed and sleep for a long, long time.'

'I am rather tired, you know. This thin air.'

'Go ahead. I promise not to wake you when I come in later.'

'Very well. Don't stay up too late.'

We all watched Miss Simpkins leave the room.

'That was nicely done,' I said when she was out of earshot.

225

'She's really quite a masterpiece, isn't she?' Kate said. 'One day Madame Tussaud's will make a wax dummy of her.'

'In the chamber of horrors,' I added.

Kate laughed, and I smiled at her, realizing how much I'd missed her. She started to smile back, but then her eyes cooled, and this sudden connection between us crumbled like a cobweb bridge.

We talked on a bit, the three of us, but I sensed we were ill at ease with one another. I felt the *Saga* turn, and knew Hal was taking us on his trickster's course, to throw off our pursuers. It wasn't long before we all started yawning and saying we should get some sleep.

We made our way to our separate cabins, and for a few moments it was just Kate and me alone in the corridor. I wanted to say something. She was being so chilly with me. Maybe she hadn't liked the way Nadira had sat with me at dinner, or maybe – and my stomach gave a nasty squeeze – she really had seen us kissing in the crow's-nest. I wanted to apologize, but I dared not mention it, for what if she *hadn't* seen, and I was just opening up a Pandora's box of trouble?

'Are you angry with me?' I asked her.

'Why on earth would I be angry with you?' she said, looking at me strangely.

She seemed all surprise, so I assumed she couldn't know about the kiss. Kate would not lie; she was too terrifyingly straightforward. I should have been relieved, but only felt a keen disappointment. She was not angry with me. There could be only one explanation for her behaviour.

We stood in the corridor, facing each another. I wanted to ask her then and there if she preferred Hal to me. But I would not. I would not ask for reassurance, like a street urchin begging coins from the pretty rich lady.

'Oh,' I said. 'I just thought you seemed a bit vexed with me.'

'Not at all,' she said.

'No vexation whatsoever? Not even a little bit?'

'Not in the slightest.'

'You're sure?'

She gave me the politest of smiles. 'I'm just tired. Good night.'

'Good night, then.'

Inside my cabin, I washed my face in the basin. I could not remember a more ghastly conversation in my life. I beheld myself in the little mirror, wondering when I would see a man.

All the lights went out suddenly, and I knew that Hal had thrown a cloak of darkness over the *Sagarmatha*. Now, under cover of night, he'd be smashing the transmitter to pieces. Our pursuers would lose the homing signal, and be left with nothing but our phantom wake.

As I settled under my blankets a few minutes later I heard the drone of the ship's six powerful engines increase in pitch. I felt the *Saga* bank swiftly as Hal took us back to our true course.

I wished I knew my own true course.

★ ★ ★

Next morning, Hal posted extra lookouts. He wanted no chance of the *Hyperion* slipping by undetected now that we were nearing our rendezvous mark. In the control car, Hal and Dorje scanned the skies directly ahead. Kami, who was walking again, though slowly, was stationed on the starboard side of the bridge; I was on the port. You could not have asked for more favourable weather. The sky was completely clear. From our altitude of seven thousand metres, you could see all the way to the white shores of Antarctica.

It was a great relief to me that there was no sign of Rath's ship. Hal's ploy had obviously worked, and they were likely hundreds of kilometres off course by now.

But there was no sign of the *Hyperion* either.

As each minute ticked by, the tension in the control car coiled more tightly. With increasing regularity, Hal would seize the speaking tube and demand a report from Ang Jeta in the crow's-nest.

'Nothing fore or aft,' came the reply once more.

Two hours after we'd overshot the mark, Hal turned to me and said, 'Cruse, those coordinates you gave us, you're sure of them?'

'I wouldn't forget those numbers.'

'You've been having trouble with your numbers at school though, eh?'

'That's different,' I said indignantly.

'Then where the hell's our ship?'

Hal let his eyes rest on me longer than was pleasant, but I held his gaze, refusing to be rebuked.

'My calculations may be at fault,' Dorje said quietly.

'You've never been wrong in your life,' Hal said.

'I want to check again. Hold our course for now.'

Dorje went back to the navigation room and I heard the sound of his ingenious charts being taken out and unfurled on the table.

'Someone may have beaten us to it,' Jangbu said from the wheel.

Hal scoffed. 'There's only a couple of ships in the world that could make these heights. Before we left, I checked up on the locations of all the other skybreakers I could find. They're all tied up on long-haul jobs. They can't be seeking the *Hyperion* as well.'

I looked at Hal. 'I thought you said yours was the only ship that could work so high.'

'A bit of an exaggeration. There are several.'

'How many?'

'Maybe a dozen. Probably more. But they don't have the coordinates, do they? Those sensationally accurate coordinates of yours.'

Hal kept us on watch long into the afternoon. When finally Dorje emerged from the chart room, we all turned expectantly.

'I didn't account properly for our proximity to Antarctica,' he said. 'The cold air slides off the mountains there like an avalanche. No ship without power could cut those headwinds. The *Hyperion* will have changed her course. Bring us about east north east. We will find her yet.'

Up in the crow's-nest, the cold numbed my feet and fingers as I peered into the vastness of the sky. It was half past three in the morning. With only the stars and a sliver of new moon, it would be near impossible to sight an unlit vessel. Luckily, Dorje had said we would not come across the *Hyperion* before midday, soonest. Which was why, no doubt, Hal had put me on this watch. As far as he was concerned, it was my fault we hadn't yet found the *Hyperion*. Every ship takes on the mood of its captain, and with a ship as cosy as the *Sagarmatha*, Hal's ill humour was easy to detect. He had no tolerance for disappointment.

We were circling the bottom of the world, and earlier in my watch Hal had called up to report a storm festering over the Antarctic Ridge. I did not think it would bother us at this altitude, but suddenly I noticed whole swaths of stars disappearing along the horizon. The running lights on the *Sagarmatha*'s back reflected brightly against the mist that was quickly enveloping us.

'Crow's-nest reporting,' I said into the speaking tube.

'I know,' came Hal's voice. 'Just a little spume from the storm below. Should be through it before long.'

The *Sagarmatha* shuddered as she rode the turbulent air. Beyond the observation dome, the sky opened and closed as we sailed through the wispy cloud. Then, all at once, the cloud thickened and there were no more snatches of star-speckled sky. The ship's lights flashed against the mist in time with my pulse.

'Crow's-nest,' I said. 'I'm blind up here. Can we climb above it?'

'No need,' came Hal's voice. 'We'll be through in a minute.'

I did not like this one bit. We picked up speed as Hal tried to drive us clear. I caught myself counting seconds. Hal was right; it did not take long. Soon the cloud began to thin once more: white cloud, black sky, white cloud, and then we ploughed through the last of the high cirrus and were suddenly out in the open.

Off to starboard, a huge wall of night hurtled towards us.

I yanked the speaking tube to my mouth.

'Ship at three o'clock!' I cried. 'Collision course!'

Through the tube I heard Hal barking orders to his crew and then I could only stare in horror as the enormous vessel came at us broadside. She blotted out the sky as she came, looming above us, raven black and visible only for the ice glittering on her flanks. I saw her ribs, her flayed skin. We shed ballast so quickly I gave a shout. Our engines roared and we angled high, banking to port. I was tilted so far over I lost sight of the other ship for a moment but then I heard an unearthly moan, like the woodwind section of Satan's orchestra, as she began passing beneath us.

She struck. The impact threw me against the hatch.

My face hit metal, and the sight was momentarily dashed from my eyes. The iron taste of blood filled my mouth. I rallied my senses. Peering out through the dome I saw the ship, driven by the wind careening slant-wise through the sky.

From the speaking tube I heard the staccato exchange of voices in the control car.

'We've lost two and three on the port side!'

'The ship must've sheered them off when she passed.'

'Jangbu, go back and find out how bad the damage is.' That was Hal. 'I want all available hands for repairs. How're the gas cells?'

'We're tight. No leakage.'

'Elevators and rudder?' I heard Dorje ask.

'Seem fine.'

'Thank God,' said Hal. 'Get some lights on her, and bring us about so we can follow her. Cruse!'

'Here,' I replied.

'Any damage up there?'

'I don't think so.'

'You all right?'

'Fine.'

My tongue prodded for damage. I'd chipped a tooth and cut up the inside of my mouth. My skull was still intact, apart from a swelling behind my temple. Served me right. Served me right for not seeing the ship. What kind of lookout was I?

'A little more warning would have been useful,' Hal said.

I said nothing, feeling terrible.

'We were in a cloud,' I heard Dorje tell him in the control car.

'A feathering of cirrus,' Hal retorted. 'Nothing more.'

It was true, the cloud had been thinning, but the brief flashes of clear sky had not been enough for me to make out the ship, cloaked as it was in night. I was not sleepy. I had not let my eyes become bleary and unfocused. I'd been doing my best, but it was not enough.

'We saw nothing from the control car either,' I heard Dorje remind Hal.

'Don't make excuses for him, Dorje,' Hal said sharply. 'It was his watch, and we lost two engines on it.'

From the *Saga*'s bow, powerful spotlights blazed twin pathways through the night, and quickly fixed on the airship before us. On her flank, I could make out the name: *Hyperion*.

We hadn't found her.

She'd found us.

12

THE HYPERION

Beneath us the *Hyperion* rode the wind like a great airborne whale, cutting the icy sky with her flukes. From the windows of the control car, I watched as Hal brought us closer. Sometimes, as if aware of our harpooner's intent, the *Hyperion* dipped and slewed; other times, trying to scare us off, she crested, forcing us away from her massive sun-bleached back. Hal's crew were expert sailors and, even without a full complement of engines, they managed to mirror the *Hyperion*'s every movement. Through the night we'd kept well back, shadowing her, but now the dawn gave us enough light to attempt a boarding.

'Bring me in lower,' Hal told his crew. 'Bring me in nice and close now so I can get a line on her.'

'She's enormous,' I said. 'She must have two hundred and fifty metres on her.'

'Two hundred and seventy. And she'll be all ours soon.'

From the ceiling of the control car, Hal pulled down a periscope-like column of controls, bundles of cables entwining the central shaft. The control console hung at chest level studded with all manner of dials and levers, and on either side were manoeuvrable brass handles with rubber grips.

Hal grasped the handles and swivelled them forward in tandem. There was a harsh whirring sound beyond the control car windows, and I looked out to see a pair of mechanical arms unfolding themselves from the ship's hull like the limbs of a praying mantis. As they extended they seemed spindly things, but then I saw that their sinew was braided alumiron cable, near unbreakable. The limbs bulged with universal joints and massive shock absorbers, and were tipped with a thick loop of cable and pincers.

'Give Dorje a ring,' Hal told me, 'and tell him we're ready to lock on.'

I picked up the ship's telephone and called the aft docking station, near the *Sagarmatha*'s stern. Dorje was stationed there, and I assumed he was manning an identical set of arms, ready to guide them towards the *Hyperion*'s back. I relayed Hal's message to him, and hung up as the *Saga* made a sudden leap.

'Stay sharp,' Hal told Jangbu and Ang Jeta at the helm, 'she's lively down there.'

Through the windows in the control-car floor he had a clear view of the two mechanical arms stretching down towards the *Hyperion*. Hal squeezed the trigger on both his handles, and down below, the arms' pincers opened wide, aimed for the *Hyperion*'s forward mooring cleats. At that moment, the great ship dipped and shuddered, leaving the arms dangling over empty air.

'Bring her back, bring her back . . .'

Within seconds the *Saga* stole over the *Hyperion* once more.

'Come here, me darling,' Hal muttered.

I saw his fingers tighten around the brass handles.

'Just a little nudge to port . . . I'm almost there.'

He shoved the brass handles hard.

The arms suddenly lunged, pincers gaping like the jaws of some deadly eel. On both port and starboard sides they connected with the *Hyperion*'s mooring cleats and bit down.

'Got her!' cried Hal. 'Throttle back and hold tight, gents, we're on a Nantucket sleigh ride!'

Long ago when men had harpooned the great whales, they were often taken on a wild ride through the waves by their quarry, and so it was with the *Sagarmatha*. She'd just coupled with a ship six times her size, and was now being pulled through the glacial sky, dipping and rolling. I wondered how long it would be before Miss Simpkins was airsick.

The coupling arms were strong yet supple. Buffered by huge springs, they compressed and stretched as needed, but I realized they were also designed to hold the other ship at a distance. The *Hyperion* could only ride up so close before the arms locked and prevented a collision. I just hoped her ancient mooring cleats did not rip free.

The ship's telephone rang and Hal grabbed it.

'Good work, Dorje,' he said. He turned to me and gave a wink. 'We're locked on.'

'I'm not going to waste time lying,' Hal told us all in the lounge. 'The *Saga's* seriously damaged, and it's changed our plan of attack. I'd originally intended to tow the *Hyperion* back to a safe harbour and salvage her there. It's a tricky business at the best of times, and with only four engines, we don't have enough power to attempt it safely. That means anything we want from the *Hyperion*, we have to salvage from her mid-air.'

After the collision last night I'd helped survey the damage. The ship's alumiron exoskeleton had done its job well, for the hull was unharmed and the skin torn only in a few places. None of the gas cells had been ruptured. But as Hal had feared, the aft and amidships engine cars had been crumpled against the port flank, and now dangled from their twisted struts. We'd done all we could to lash down the wreckage, but Hal would need a dry dock to repair his custom-built engine cars. It made me sick to look upon them. Even though I was sure the collision couldn't have been avoided, I was up there in the lookout when it happened, and it would always feel like a failure.

'First priority is the money,' Hal continued. 'Gold, banknotes, jewels, that's what we'll be looking for. Everything else comes second.'

'That was not my understanding of our agreement,' Kate objected.

'Things have changed,' said Hal. 'I've lost a member of my crew; I've got expensive repairs to look forward to.' He held up his hand to cut Kate off. 'I know you wanted the taxidermy. Likely we won't be able to take everything. If it fits up the ladders we'll try it. Otherwise, it stays with the ship. And even that depends on weather and time. Every hour we stay up here, we get weaker, especially you lot who aren't used to these heights. Right now, the winds are light, but if the weather sours, we may have to break off our salvage. Could be a matter of life and death. Are we all clear on this?'

Kate's nostrils narrowed, and her eyes strayed to me for a moment. I wondered if she was angry with just Hal, or me too. Maybe she actually blamed me for the damage to the *Saga*. Maybe she thought I'd been up there smooching with Nadira, and not paying attention.

'Cruse, you'll be boarding with Dorje and me. The rest of you will stay aboard the *Saga*.'

'What?' Nadira said in disbelief.

'I'm going aboard,' Kate said angrily. 'I didn't come all this way to knit socks by the hearth.'

'I'm perfectly content to knit by the hearth,' said Miss Simpkins who was, in fact, knitting by the hearth.

'You're both brave, spirited young ladies,' Hal said, and I could tell he was somewhat taken aback by the ferocity in their faces. 'I'm just thinking of your safety. You've no experience working salvage. It's going to be hard work. You'll slow us down.'

'Kate, I think your parents would want you to stay behind,' her chaperone said. 'It's too dangerous!'

'I need to examine the specimens before I know which ones I want,' Kate said. 'Hal, I absolutely insist on it.'

'The cargo bay doors don't open without my key,' Nadira told Hal. 'And it stays around my neck until I'm on board the *Hyperion*.'

The two girls looked at each other and almost smiled.

'You'll take one look out the hatch and think better of it,' Hal said.

'They're equal to the challenge,' I told him. 'And we'll work faster with a few more sets of eyes and hands.'

'Fine,' Hal said. 'But if you fall behind, it's back to the *Saga* for good. I'll not be hindered playing nurse maid. I'll have Mrs Ram alter some sky suits for you. Cruse, we need to start assembling the gear. We board in one hour.'

'This is your sky suit,' Dorje said, holding a thick hide garment out to me. It was a single piece of clothing: trousers, coat and hood all painstakingly sewed together with the smallest stitches I'd ever seen. The hide was soft and tanned, and lined inside, from hood to heel, with a layer of fur, thicker and whiter than any I'd ever seen.

'It's snow leopard, from the Himalayas,' Dorje explained. 'Strip down to your underwear and put it on.'

'Shouldn't I keep my clothes on? For extra warmth?'

239

I'd seen the thermometer outside. It was more than thirty below.

'They'll make you too bulky,' Hal said, unbuttoning his shirt and revealing a well-muscled chest. 'They're designed to fit snugly.'

'Wear the leopard fur next to your skin and you'll have the heat of the leopard,' Dorje said.

We were in the boarding bay, just aft of the passenger quarters along the keel catwalk. The hatch was still closed, and the electric heating coils along the baseboards glowed and struggled vainly against the mighty cold. The hull might as well have been made of gauze. Kami Sherpa was checking the winch that would lower us the fifteen metres to the *Hyperion*'s back. Arranged neatly on the floor was all our gear, to be divided among our five rucksacks. Oxygen tanks and breathing masks were laid out.

Hoping Kate and Nadira would not come in as I was undressing, I hurriedly pulled off my trousers, wool sweater and shirt. I started shivering.

'You need some more meat on those bones,' Hal said.

I pulled the sky suit to me, and slipped my legs into the trousers. The fur caressed me, warming me instantly. I shrugged my arms into the sleeves of the coat and drew it around me. There were two rows of complicated clasps to do up, and by the time they were all done, I had almost forgotten the cold that had assailed me moments before. I felt the snow leopard's skin against mine, felt its heat gathering against me. I stood, worried the suit would make me clumsy, but it was amazingly supple, yielding to every bend of my knee or elbow or waist. It fitted me like a second skin. I stepped into the boots. They too were lined with leopard fur, their soles fitted with thick, vulcanized rubber treads to give me good footing on the ship's icy back.

'Gloves,' said Hal, tossing me a pair.

I slid them on. They did not even hamper the flex of my fingers. They *became* my fingers.

'Ah, here are our fine lady adventuresses,' Hal said. 'Looking very fetching in their sky suits I must say.'

It gave me quite a shock when I looked up and saw Kate and Nadira both clothed in their snow leopard garments, striding towards me. Their dark hair spilled over the white fur of their hoods. Their boots made them taller and the hide suits lent them the lithe power of mountain cats.

'Mrs Ram is very handy with a needle,' Kate said. 'Marjorie was most impressed by how quickly she did the alterations.'

'Let's suit up,' said Hal. 'Safety harnesses first.'

I helped Kate on with hers, showing her all the places where it needed to be cinched and clipped. I offered to help Nadira, but she just shook her head and seemed to be managing fine on her own.

Hal held up a small tank for all of us to see.

'Inside your rucksacks will be your oxygen tank. It's good for four hours. Half a turn opens the valve. Depending how acclimatized your bodies are, you may not need it all the time. I'd like you three to wear your masks at least until we're inside the *Hyperion*. I want you all at your strongest when we're on the ship's back.'

'You don't use oxygen at all?' Kate asked Dorje.

'I bring a tank, but I have no need of it,' the Sherpa replied. 'I grew up at altitudes not much lower than this.'

'Everest is nine and a half thousand metres,' said Hal. 'This is a stroll.'

'Hal finds oxygen unmanly,' said Dorje, and I wasn't sure if there was a glimmer of gentle mockery in his eyes.

'Inside the *Hyperion* you can take the masks off if you feel comfortable,' Hal said. 'But the moment you feel faint, or clumsy, or start shivering, the mask goes on again. If you need to vomit, remove the mask, and replace it when you're finished. If you have trouble breathing, or develop a blinding headache, or your vision falters, tell me. You'll need to go back to the *Saga* right away.'

We put on our rucksacks. The oxygen tanks within were surprisingly light.

'Goggles stay on until we're inside. Hoods stay up, gloves on at all times. You take them off, your skin will start freezing in seconds. When I give the word, we return to the ship, no argument. We take no chances in Skyberia. The cold is bad, but the altitude will kill you faster. It takes different people at different speeds. I don't know what we'll find, but it's likely unpleasant. There will be bodies. We don't know what happened to the ship. There may have been a mutiny, a skyjacking, plague, or some other form of disaster that brought death to the entire crew. We won't be able to hear one another outside on the ship's back, so here's what we're going to do . . .' Step by step he took us through the boarding procedure, as stern and relentless as a drill sergeant. I watched Kate and Nadira's faces for signs of fear. Nadira was composed, and Kate's forehead bore a furrow of concentration.

'Hoods up,' said Dorje, 'I'm about to open the hatch.'

I pulled up the hood, feeling the soft fur encase me. The lower portion buttoned up, leaving only a slit for my eyes, now covered by goggles. All sound was muffled. I was eager to get outside, for I was starting to sweat.

Dorje pulled a lever and the bay doors split apart and rolled flush with the ship's underbelly. Cold gushed in. But I felt it only against the exposed portion of my face, for the snow leopard suit protected me so well.

I looked straight down to the *Hyperion*'s back, shimmering like a mirage, glinting with ice. I could not understand how she had stayed aloft so many years, uncaptained, clawed and pummelled by the winds.

Dorje went first. He clipped his safety harness to the winch and sat down at the edge of the hatch.

'Ready?' Kami Sherpa asked.

Dorje nodded, and pushed off into open air. The winch paid out line quickly. We all watched. Though light, the wind still twirled him about some. From our vantage point, it looked like he was swinging far out over the ship's flanks. As he neared the ship's back, he bent his knees and set down gracefully, dead centre. He quickly cleated his safety line to an icy guide rail, then unclipped himself from the winch. He gave the signal and Kami Sherpa started rolling the cable back in.

'Are you all right with this?' I quietly asked Kate.

'Yes,' she said tightly.

'You don't have to, you know.'

'I daresay I'll quite enjoy it,' she replied with a vigorous nod.

'Cruse, you're next,' said Hal. 'Get that mask on.'

'See you all down there,' I said.

I reached back into my rucksack and opened the tap on my oxygen tank. The mask was a translucent glass shield, rimmed with rubber insulation, that fit snugly over nose and mouth. It hissed faintly as I strapped it on. Instantly I felt like I was suffocating. I yanked it down.

'I don't want it,' I said.

'Breathe deep. Slow, even breaths,' Hal said. 'You'll get used to it.'

'I'm fine. I don't need it.'

'Put it on, or you don't go down.'

Reluctantly I strapped the mask back across my face. I did not want Kate and Nadira to think I was afraid of the descent; truly, I was eager to be in the sky. It was the mask alone that scared me, the way it sealed off my mouth and nose from the air. It felt wholly unnatural. Claustrophobia clutched at my chest. I fought my panic and took a long pull through my mouth. The air had an unpleasant metallic tang.

After a few more breaths, I felt the oxygen enter my lungs and my muscles unclenched a bit. I did not like it, but I could do it.

'All right?' Hal said.

I nodded. Kami Sherpa helped me hook my harness to the winch. I sat, and pushed off over the edge and—

Sky.

Seven thousand metres of it, spreading out around me to all the horizons of the world. This high, it seemed the sky no longer had anything to do with the land or sea below it. It was its own kingdom up here. Here, above the clouds, it scoffed at the idea of earth. These were the wild deeps of the sky, where water existed only as unseen ice crystals, and the wind moved in secret aerial tides. I was but a speck. For a moment I felt I had no right to be here, encased within my fur suit, breathing tanked air. Yet this was my birthplace: not so high, of course, but here nonetheless, and the sky could not disown me. This was still my element more than the earth.

Down I went.

The wind met my face like a chisel. Even through the sky suit, I could feel the ferocious cold, just held at bay like some starving animal. Below me, far below the great bulk of the *Hyperion*, the clouds looked solid as sand dunes. I hoped none of those electrocuting aerozoans would cross my path, or another diabolical creature not yet discovered. It seemed whenever I was with Kate, some new species popped up and tried to eat us.

On the ship's back Dorje was waiting for me, crouched low. My feet had barely touched down when he was clipping my safety line to the rail. I unclasped myself from the winch and gave Kami the signal to reel in. Dorje pointed at the forward crow's-nest, and I began to make my way over while he stayed behind to help Kate and Nadira. Hal would come last.

Bent low against the wind, I stepped carefully, for the ship's skin was icy, gritty in places, in others sheer, as if a film of water had frozen instantaneously. I kept my safety line fastened to the rail, though it was rusty and pockmarked and I had to wonder at its strength after so many years. The wind punched at me; the cold etched a fissure of pain across my forehead. There was no sound but the muffled howl of the sky beyond the hood, and my own panting through the mask.

I reached the crow's-nest, its glass observation dome thickly matted with frost. I tried the hatch. Locked. Hal's instructions were to get inside as quickly as possible. I reached into my rucksack and drew out the small pry bar. I wedged it under the latch, heaved down, and felt the lock give way. Bending to get a grip on the hatch's rim, I put my face to the dome.

Through a clear patch in the ice, an eye was looking out at me.

I gave a cry and jerked back, spluttering inside my mask and fighting the urge to rip it off. I forced myself to take deep breaths. With the edge of the pry bar I scratched away more of the ice.

Inside the crow's-nest was a sailor, his head tipped against the glass, forehead frozen to it. His eyes were wide open. His skin was blackened by sun and time, but his body had been preserved completely. He was shrunken in his uniform. His mouth was slightly parted. One of his withered hands was frozen closed around the speaking tube. He seemed about to say something, only death had come along and interrupted him.

Looking over my shoulder I saw Kate cautiously shambling up beside me. Behind her, Nadira had just touched down, and soon Hal would arrive. I needed to get the hatch open. I removed my mask and shouted close to Kate's hood so she could hear me.

'There's a body!'

I pointed at the crow's-nest and she nodded. Then I bent down and heaved up the dome. Kate helped. Hinges shrieked and ice danced up in the air as the dome lifted. The sailor's forehead snapped free of the glass, and his whole body toppled forward, rigid as a mannikin. His face clunked against the metal rim of the open hatch, chipping a piece of his cheek away.

I looked at Kate to see how she was doing, but her face was hidden behind hood and goggles and mask.

The body had to be moved, for it blocked the ladder. I jumped down into the crow's-nest and began to shift it. It was difficult – he was heavy with ice, and his arms were sticking out. For a horrible moment I worried I might drop him and he would shatter into a hundred pieces before my eyes.

But suddenly Hal was in the crow's-nest with me. He grabbed the body by the armpits, hefted it up, and heaved it out on to the ship's back. Before I could even object, Hal gave the body a good shove and sent it skidding over the hull's curve into the great blue sky. Without further ado, Hal started down the ladder.

Dorje, standing near the hatch, gestured for Kate and Nadira to follow. Then I headed down myself. Out of the wind, it was not nearly as cold. The pain across my forehead eased. Light from the open hatch spilled down the thin rungs, and faintly illuminated the ship's wooden ribs and the sides of her enormous gas cells. They were made from a kind of goldbeater's skin that hadn't been used for more than twenty years. Some of the bracing wires, I noticed, were rope instead of alumiron cable. The *Hyperion* was a venerable ship, among the first large airships to ply the skies. She was a piece of history. And it was a testament to the craftsmen who built her that she was still aloft.

Above me, Dorje closed the hatch and the companionway would have been plunged into gloom were it not for Hal's torchlight aimed from below. He was waiting on the catwalk with Kate and Nadira, who had removed their goggles and masks. I did the same. After the tanked oxygen, the thin air seemed meagre fare at first, but within a few breaths, I was used to it once more. Seeing Hal and Dorje breathing normally without any help at all, I was determined not to use my mask again.

'Everyone all right?' Hal asked.

Kate and Nadira were breathing heavily, but they both nodded. In the frigid air, our breath plumed from our noses and mouths like dragon's smoke.

'I can't believe you threw that man overboard,' I said. My voice was small and hollow in the dark ship.

'He's not a man any more,' retorted Hal. 'He's ice. And he was in our way. It's not safe hanging about on the ship's back. The crow's-nest needs to be clear for us and our cargo. It's our main thoroughfare.'

'Everyone deserves a proper burial,' said Kate.

'We could have lowered him down the ladder,' I told Hal.

'If we snapped his arms clean off, maybe. That's time I won't waste. Now, all of you, stow your sentimentality and save your breath.'

'Hal's right,' said Nadira. 'The way needed clearing.'

I glanced at Dorje, hoping for his support, but he said nothing. He either agreed with Hal, or was too loyal to criticize his captain before others. I looked about in the dim light. Flanking the catwalk were the rippling walls of the gas cells, sparkling with ice crystals, forming a kind of canyon. We were on the axial catwalk, the maintenance corridor that ran through the very centre of the ship, from bow to stern. Beyond the reach of Hal's torch beam, the corridor stretched on into darkness and I felt the cavernous immensity of the ship all around me, a lair of unseen spaces.

'This way,' said Hal, starting down another ladder. 'To the keel catwalk.'

Maybe it was the ship's wooden ribs, or my sky suit, or the tanked air I carried on my back, but with every slow, careful step I felt like a deep sea diver. The air around me was as cold and heavy as arctic water.

'Take out your torches,' Hal said when we'd all reached the bottom.

I switched mine on. I had expected many things, but not the sight which greeted us. It was like the inside of a shipwreck, frozen at the ocean's floor. All the tanks and pipelines overhead had burst and their various liquids – water, fuel and lubricants – had congealed mid-flow. Great oily stalactites spiked from overhead, releasing phantasmagoric rainbows as our torch beams struck them. Walls and girders and wires bore coatings of frost in purples and oranges and blood reds that resembled strange coral and sea anemones. The aruba fuel had turned brilliant green as it froze, and shaped itself into bizarre spirals and arches and buttresses as though an army of pixie artisans had been hard at work.

'Control car first,' said Hal, unmoved by the unearthly beauty around him.

He led the way cautiously forward. Dorje, I noticed, was deftly making a map as he went. We paused only to throw open the doors of a few crew cabins. In two, my torch beam passed over the dark humps of sailors, frozen in their bunks. They looked like the bodies found in Pompeii after Vesuvius had erupted.

'That's how I want to go,' Hal said. 'In my sleep.'

Whatever it was that doomed the *Hyperion* forty years ago, it had happened swiftly, and at night.

We descended an icy ladder to the control car.

The high windows were thick with frost, but let in enough light that we could turn off our torches. Rivulets of frozen water corded the glass and walls. Icicles hung from the ceiling. Most of the crew lay twisted on the floor, their bodies fused with pools of ice. The captain, hat still atop his head, perched on the stool before the rudder wheel, his torso slumped against it. His hands gripped the spokes, though I saw they were no longer connected with his wrists. They had snapped off long ago.

'What happened to them all?' Kate wondered aloud.

The sight of all these dead men was truly terrible to behold and my mind became very practical and turned them into objects, or else I could not have looked upon them with a steady eye or pulse.

The captain twitched suddenly, and I gave a shout, but it was only the wheel moving, shaking his rigid body as it turned.

'That's good news,' said Dorje, watching the wheel turn.

'The rudder chains are still working,' I said, glad to be fixing my mind on concrete matters.

'We can steer her at least,' said Hal. 'We won't be at the mercy of the winds quite as much. I told Jangbu we'd heave to if we could. That should keep us out of trouble for the salvage.'

'What's heaving to?' Nadira asked.

'Bringing the ship into the wind,' I told her, 'and locking her rudder to keep her stationary.' Even with only four engines, the *Saga* would provide enough power to keep the *Hyperion* from blowing backwards.

Hal and Dorje unceremoniously took hold of the captain and wrenched him off his stool. They tipped him against the wall. Hal gripped the wheel.

'Let's see how she moves.'

For forty years, the winds alone had steered the *Hyperion*. Now she once more had a helmsman. Very slowly Hal turned the wheel.

'She's moving,' I said.

Knowing that Jangbu above needed to match the *Saga* to his movements, Hal brought the *Hyperion* about gradually.

'That should do it. Let's tie her off,' he said.

Dorje took two ropes from his rucksack and he and I worked together to secure the wheel. The *Hyperion* wavered in the wind, wanting to turn, but the rudder held her in check, aided by the *Sagarmatha*'s powerful engines overhead. We still drifted slightly, but no longer rode the sky like a porpoise.

'That's much better,' said Kate.

The ship's clock had stopped at 23:48 hours. I looked at the altimeter, the glass dome cracked, the needle frozen at 6540 metres.

'She went too high,' I said. 'That's what killed everyone.

This was no mutiny. No pirates either. Everyone was still at their posts, or asleep.'

'No,' said Hal. 'This altitude isn't fatal.'

'It is if she rose fast enough.'

'Why would she?' Hal asked.

'An updraft maybe. I saw it on the *Flotsam*. If they went from seven hundred to seven thousand metres in a minute, it might've undone them.'

'They froze to death, you mean?' Nadira asked.

'No,' I said, 'they would've suffocated long before that. Going up so fast, it would've been like having all the air sucked out of their lungs. They would've passed out. That's why everyone is on the floor. Only the captain managed to hang on for a bit.'

Dorje silently nodded his agreement.

'Well, it's a nice theory, anyway,' said Hal. 'I hope you're right. If they weren't attacked by pirates, it means we'll be the first to plunder her holds. Let's get moving.'

A sound, very much like someone exhaling, whispered through the control car.

We all went rigid. My eyes skittered over the bodies on the floor, half expecting them to stir and crack free of the ice. Hal, a pistol suddenly in his hand, whirled towards the ladder, which was the only way in and out of the control car. No one was poised on its rungs, or in the hatchway above.

'Who's there?' he shouted.

'Crowwwwsnessssss . . .' came the reply.

This time I caught its source, and gave a shout,

pointing. The unearthly whisper was emanating from an icy grille mounted on the side of the control car. It was the endpoint of the crow's-nest speaking tube. Heat flashed across my back and down my arms. I pictured the lookout, raising the mouthpiece to his frozen lips, exhaling his last sounds from his ice-crusted throat. We stared, mute, at the grille.

'. . . esssssssssssssss,' said the voice, and then it became nothing more than a shushing of dead air along the speaking tube.

'It's just the wind,' Kate said. 'Making voices.'

'Obviously,' Hal agreed.

We all cleared our throats and gave dry little laughs and generally tried to make light of it.

'You brought a pistol,' I said to Hal.

'Just a negotiating tool,' he said. 'You never know who else might show up, claiming right of salvage.'

'Look at this,' said Kate. She was standing at the navigation table, peering down through the thick ice floe that had formed over the chart. Its markings were all but obliterated, but I could still make out the telltale outlines of Norway and Finland and the coast of Russia. 'Grunel was supposed to be flying to America. So why would they have a chart of Scandinavia and Russia?'

'Curious, but it doesn't matter,' said Hal, barely taking a glance. 'I want to get to those holds.'

Back up the ladder we went, and aft along the ice-encrusted keel catwalk, past the companion ladder we'd come down, squeezing around stalactites. We soon reached a short stairway that led up to the main passenger deck, but Hal ushered us past, saying we'd return later. On either side of the corridor we passed the closed doorways of the kitchens and pantry and various other crew's quarters. Some of the doors were half-sealed behind frozen waterfalls, and it would take some doing to crack through.

Our five torch beams ploughed the darkness before us as we entered the guts of the ship. Cargo bays are usually built amidships, port and starboard, so their weight is evenly distributed at the ship's centre. On either side of the catwalk were built strong walls, much higher than the usual cargo bay. These ones were two storeys tall, and were not made of wood, but metal, studded with rivets. They looked impregnable as a battleship's armour.

Hal came to a stop. On the port side of the catwalk was a single door, glinting with mauve frost. There was no sign. In the door's centre was a metal plate with a handle, and below it a complicated circular keyhole.

'Here we are,' said Hal, 'the treasure trove.'

13

THE DEAD ZOO

Nadira lowered her hood so she could take the key from the pouch around her neck. The door's reinforced bulk was as defiant as any bank vault; I could well believe it was booby-trapped. I imagined trip wires embedded in the metal. Nadira slowly started to insert the key, frowned, pulled it back and bent to look inside the keyhole.

'There's ice,' she said. 'It won't go in.'

Dorje removed a small blow torch from his pack. Blue flame jetted from the tip and he slowly waved it before the keyhole, careful not to get too close. A trickle of water ran from the hole, and froze again before it was halfway to the floor.

Nadira put the key into the lock. It didn't seem to want to go very far at first, but then she rotated it slightly, and I heard small metal pieces clinking and falling. Then the key went in a little deeper. I found myself holding my breath. The lock was like a series of puzzles one behind the other, and they needed to be aligned in a special way. Twisting and turning the key,

Nadira slid it deeper, bit by bit, and when it seemed to go no further, she gave it a slow full turn, clockwise. It was almost musical, all the metallic pings and chirps of the lock yielding to the key's mysterious shape. The key went all the way around and Nadira gave a cry as it was swiftly pulled from her fingers, and sucked right into the keyhole.

For a moment, no one spoke.

'Was that good or bad?' I said.

'Maybe it didn't like the key,' Kate suggested.

'That's not a reassuring thought,' I told her.

From inside the lock came a distinct ticking sound.

'Run!' bellowed Hal.

But a great clunk from inside the door froze us all in terror. The key was spat back out and landed on the icy floor. Then, with a hiss of air, the door opened, popping back and sliding to one side, flush with the inner wall.

'That,' said Kate, 'is the cheekiest door I've ever known.'

Nadira bent down and snatched up her key. 'Aren't you glad I came along?'

A frigid mustiness oozed from the pitch black rectangle before us. I saw Dorje's nostrils flinch. This door had not been opened in forty years. Whatever was inside was undisturbed. We were the first. We stepped in.

Row after row of enormous display cases, ten feet in height, stretched back as far as our torch beams could reach. Their glass was mostly coated in glittering ice, but I caught the occasional flash of fur or bone. Along both walls, the mounted heads of all sorts of horned and antlered animals leered down at us. From the middle of the room, the neck and head of a grey giraffe thrust up above the cases. Suspended from the ceiling was the skeleton of some enormous leviathan. The entire chamber was arranged like a museum, with narrow aisles between the rows of cases. Old man Noah could not have crammed more birds and beasts into his ark.

'It's Grunel's personal collection,' Kate breathed, and then she was off, rushing from case to case, scraping at the glass, shining her torch inside.

'Why'd he bother putting all this mangy stuff under lock and key?' Hal grumbled. He'd expected a chamber stacked high with overflowing chests of loot and was clearly disgruntled. With Dorje, he began a circuit of the room, making a map, and no doubt scouting for anything more lucrative than animal hides.

'A quagga!' I heard Kate exclaim.

I found her staring entranced at something that looked like a small zebra gone wrong. Its head and neck were fine, white with black stripes, but the rest of it was plain brown.

'Now these fellows,' Kate said, 'were native to South Africa until they were exterminated by hunters. That was supposed to have been quite some time ago.'

'How did he find it then?' I asked.

'He paid big-game hunters all over the world to search for unusual specimens. If only he'd kept it alive, rather than shooting it. It would have been much better for science.'

'And for the quagga too, I suppose.'

'Mmm,' she said distractedly.

And she was off again, like a child in Hamleys giant toy shop, whirling from one thing to the next, unable to stay still.

'And look at this!' she cried out.

Nadira and I walked over.

'It's a dodo!' Kate exclaimed.

'It's a great bloody turkey is what it is,' scoffed Hal, who'd crossed paths with us.

'But I thought they'd been extinct for centuries,' Nadira said.

'Apparently not,' said Kate. 'I wonder where Grunel got himself a live one.'

'Mauritius, probably,' I said, pleased with myself for remembering this little detail. 'A couple of years back, we stopped there to provision the *Aurora*. A local guide told me this was the only place a live dodo had been discovered. But he said the last one was spotted in 1681.'

'Maybe it also inhabited other places,' Kate said. 'Anyway, animals are always being declared extinct, then popping up again. Pomphrey Watt said the Tasmanian tiger was extinct and then a whole group of them turned up in the Florida everglades. That was his career over with.'

Kate stared at the dodo. 'Do you know that all we have in the whole world is a single skeleton of a dodo, and that's made up of all sorts of little bits and pieces from other skeletons? Grunel's got a complete specimen!'

'He never showed it to anyone?' Hal asked.

'No.'

'Maybe he was saving it up for Christmas dinner,' I remarked.

Hal gave me a chuckle, but from Kate all I got was a pair of disdainfully narrowed nostrils.

'This is coming with me,' she said. 'And the quagga.'

Hal grunted. 'There's a lot of ship to cover first. We'll deal with them later.'

I don't know that Kate heard him, for she was already heading down the next row of display cases. They were beautifully built things, with stout wooden bases, slotted into deep, specially built anchoring bays bolted to the floor. Normally, in a cargo freighter, these cases and their contents would have been separately crated, wrapped, stacked tight, and strapped into a hold. Yet Grunel had taken a great deal of care so he could arrange them like a permanent museum. And he had done his work well: nothing was toppled or smashed or cracked. The *Hyperion* seemed to have found serene skies and altitudes through which to sail her ghostly course.

'Everyone!' came Kate's excited voice. 'Over here!'

When we reached her, she was scraping frantically at the ice, clearing a larger window for us.

Its feet were the first things I saw, two of them and impossibly huge, covered with reddish grey fur. Five toes, with the middle ones bigger than the others. You could have fitted six of my feet inside one of his. The legs were tree-trunk massive. I blushed when I saw his genitals, for they were enormous, and only half hidden in the dense fur of his coat. I couldn't help glancing over at Kate, but her eyes were rising higher as she cleared away more ice, revealing the creature's torso and finally his head. He stood three metres high.

His eyes were open, and gave the unsettling impression of staring directly at you, and the look was a baleful one. He must have seen his death coming, and met it head on. Indeed, in the jutting ridge over his left eye was a large precise hole where a rifle shell had entered his skull. Around the hole, the fur was singed. That was not the only hole either. I saw two more in the massive chest, around the heart.

The creature's power transmitted itself even through its dead, motionless limbs. He could shatter the glass with a single flick of a wrist. He could pick up a man and shuck him like an ear of corn.

'It's the Yeti,' Kate said.

'No such thing,' Hal snorted dismissively, glancing at Dorje.

Dorje stared at the creature, stricken. 'My father, to his dying day, insisted he saw one.'

'Surely it's a fake,' said Hal. 'Make someone a fine rug, eh, Cruse?'

'Grunel didn't have any interest in owning a fake,' Kate said. 'These things were for him alone. If it's in his personal collection, it's real.'

'I can't believe this is pleasing to the sky gods,' Dorje said angrily, 'to see a creature of the great mountain, stuffed and displayed like this. It robs the creature of all its dignity, and the man or woman who performed the task, too.' Dorje turned away from it. 'This Grunel is a monster. There was a reason this ship met with tragedy. I would not want to guess at what has become of him in the next life.'

This was sobering stuff, and I don't think anyone knew quite what to say. I certainly didn't much like the picture I was getting of Mr Grunel. A rich man with no wants in the world, going around shooting rare animals to add to his collection – and one that didn't even benefit the scientific world. It was ghastly.

'I have only the greatest respect for the Yeti,' Kate said, 'but I would like to bring him with me.'

'You won't be getting him up the ladder,' Hal told her. 'He's too big.'

'The bones then,' said Kate.

'You're going to dissect him?' I asked.

'This is very high quality taxidermy,' she said. 'They would have skinned him first, taken a plaster cast of the body, treated the hide, and then fit the skin back over the plaster model. The only thing real about this fellow is his skin and fur. The bones should have been preserved separately. I just hope they took photographs during the dissection. The organs and anatomy and so forth. Maybe here . . .'

In the base of every display case were several deep

drawers, and Kate bent down and pulled one open. Inside, under a layer of glass, were carefully labelled bones, nestled together in a bed of foam.

'He was an organized man,' I said.

'You can't have any objection if I bring these back with me,' she said to Hal.

'Mark them down on your wish list,' he said. 'We'll come back after we've finished inspecting the ship. I've wasted enough time in this dead zoo.'

I watched Kate's face, waiting for her reaction. I was eager to see her disagree with Hal, even though I shared his impatience. I wanted gold in my hands, not bones.

'This is a floating treasure trove,' Kate said coolly.

'For you maybe,' said Hal. 'But an oversized chimp isn't going to help the rest of us.'

'It's not a chimp at all,' Kate retorted. 'A relation to the gorilla possibly. Or someone more like yourself perhaps.'

'Very witty, Miss de Vries. Now let's move on.'

We left the dead zoo and continued aft along the keel catwalk. Only a few steps on we reached a second armoured door, this time on the ship's starboard side. Once more, Nadira took the key from around her neck, and, twisting and nudging, unlocked it. This time we were ready for the pomp and ceremony: the ticking, the great clunk, the key spitting.

Throughout the entire ship, there was a horrid sense of expectation, that time had been only temporarily frozen, and might at any moment bring all the ship's inhabitants gruesomely back to life. But I felt it even more strongly now, as I stood on the threshold of this room, waiting for the door to slide open. Something was in there.

Something was waiting.

14

THE VIVARIUM

Complete darkness did not greet us this time, but pale light, revealing a chamber even bigger than the last. Dark silhouetted shapes hunched everywhere, as if ready to stand, or spring. Our torch beams danced about nervously. Against the far wall was a bank of floor-to-ceiling windows, all iced over. Looming darkly in the corner was an enormous machine, bent like a gargantuan crone, peering out the window. It looked to me a little like a telescope. I'd seen the vast Lowell telescope once, and had even been allowed to gaze briefly through its powerful lenses at the canals of Mars. I wondered if Grunel was some kind of astronomer too.

We entered cautiously, moving around the many ropes and pulleys and chains dangling from ceiling tracks. Obviously Grunel had used them to lift heavy things about the room.

And there were many heavy things here. The airship yards at Lionsgate City did not have more tools. I saw drilling machines and grinders, lathes and riveters, welders, metal saws, all dormant now, their flanks flecked with rust and ice. Shelves and pigeon holes soared up the walls, filled with all manner of hardware, jars of frozen chemicals, powders and pastes, as well as things that were altogether mysterious to me. Workbenches were everywhere, some still scattered with tools.

'It's his workshop,' I said.

Again it struck me: the *Hyperion* was no simple freighter, hired to move Grunel's personal belongings to a new home. This workshop had been in full use. I watched Hal's face darken as he swept the room with his torch and saw nothing but machines and tools and labelled crates of copper piping and rubber hosing and metal plates.

We made our way carefully through all the dangling chains and ropes, around the machines and workbenches. I paused at some kind of high-backed chair, from which sprouted a pair of mechanical arms.

'What is that?' Nadira asked.

'Must be one of his inventions,' Kate said.

Luckily, Grunel was an obsessive labeller, for a small brass plate had been fixed to the chair's seat.

I shone my light on it and read aloud, 'Automatic Dresser and Undresser.'

'Does it do corsets, I wonder?' Hal asked Kate, which I thought very bold of him.

'Can't be rougher than Miss Simpkins,' Kate said.

We moved on, opening crates as we went, but none of them yielded crisp banknotes or gold coins – just more tools and raw materials for Grunel's inventions. In some boxes we found his finished creations, nested in wood chips. Grunel's labels were almost as odd as the creations themselves:

A vaporous and aromatic propulsion device for the extinguishing of fires large and small

and another:

A revolutionary watertight lock for bathyspheres, submersible vehicles of all types, and automated washing machines

and yet another:

A form-fitting nappy for domesticated birds, particularly well suited for toucans, parrots and macaws

Hal stopped before a huge wooden chest which looked uncomfortably like a coffin, for it was surely too ornamented to be a simple storage crate.

'Why would there be a coffin in a workshop?' Nadira asked.

'You don't suppose he buried himself in that, do you?' I said.

'Let's find out,' said Hal. 'Maybe he can tell us where he hid his loot.'

I didn't want him to open it; I'd had my fill of cadavers for one day.

'There's no lock,' Hal said and heaved up the hinged lid.

He swore when he saw it was empty. I breathed easier.

'It must have been built for a very large person,' Kate observed.

'Or meant to sleep two,' I added.

A roomier casket you could not have asked for. It was lined with red silk and looked invitingly soft.

'What's all that?' I asked, for built on the underside of the lid, near where the head would have rested, were all sorts of mechanical contraptions.

'Apparatus for Signalling from the Grave,' Dorje read from one of Grunel's useful brass plates.

'What kind of fellow would invent such a thing?' I said.

'He was very morbid, from all I've read,' Kate explained. 'He had a phobia about being buried alive. There's a scientific name for it, but I've forgotten.'

'I think I see how it works.' I pointed at a long narrow drill bit. 'You could make a hole with this. I guess you use these cranks and handles to turn it and you can keep going through the soil until you hit the surface.'

'And look,' said Kate, 'there's an extendable breathing straw you can send up through the hole. So you won't suffocate.'

'And a periscope!' I added, pointing. 'So you can see all the fun you're missing.'

'There's even a little signal horn you can toot!' Nadira commented in amusement.

'I hope it was loud,' Kate remarked.

I reached into the box and gave the bulb a squeeze.

The sheer volume of the toot made everyone jump. My ears rang. The sound echoed through the cavernous cargo hold.

Dorje looked at me sternly. 'If anything were likely to be awoken, that would do it.'

'Well,' said Hal, 'I'm sure the grave signaller would have been a huge success for old Grunel. Of course, it only works if your relations were actually sad to see you go. I can just picture the burial. "Well, thank goodness we're finally rid of the old cow." Toot toot! "What was that noise? It seems to be coming from her grave!" Toot toot! "Let's just keep walking, shall we?"'

I smiled, but managed to stop myself laughing: Kate was doing enough of that, and I could not bear to hear the sound directed at Hal. He was hugely taken with his little joke, and as we continued to explore the inventing room, he'd periodically give a vigorous *toot toot!*

'What's phrenology?' asked Nadira, peering at the plate on yet another odd-looking machine. There was an open-sided booth with a stool; mounted directly overhead was a contraption that looked for all the world like an enormous mechanical spider. The spider had too many legs, each with many joints, and tipped with callipers.

'Phrenology?' said Kate, coming closer. 'It's the study of the shape of the human head. Some people think you can tell an awful lot from all the bumps and ridges.'

'Like what?'

'Oh, intelligence, potential for success, bravery, secretiveness, loyalty and so forth.'

I ran my fingers over the sharp tips of the callipers.

'I wouldn't want my head being handled by these things.'

'I'm sure,' Kate remarked tartly.

'I've had enough of Grunel's little toys,' said Hal. 'Let's be moving on. I don't think we'll find anything of value here.'

'What about that?' I asked, nodding at the vast telescope-like machine in the far corner.

We drew closer. The huge bank of windows along the hull's curving outer wall was completely frosted and though we could not see out, enough midday light passed through so we could switch off our torches and save the batteries.

Grunel's machine towered over us by six metres. A catwalk encircled its upper reaches, with spiral metal stairs leading up from the workshop floor. Its base resembled an enormous steam boiler, bristling with a confusion of copper piping and red taps and gauges. Slanting up from the top was a great cylindrical shaft which met the ship's hull and fused with a specially built window there. The machine seemed to be gazing out, but it was not sharing its view with anyone, for I could see no eyepiece anywhere.

Unlike the other machines, this one bore no brass label.

'I've never seen anything like it,' Kate said.

'Nor I,' remarked Dorje.

'Don't know what it is, and don't care,' said Hal.

'He was a great inventor, you know,' Kate told him. 'This could be something remarkable.'

'Fifty dollars at a scrap dealer,' said Hal, already turning away.

I hoped Kate was noticing Hal's oafish behaviour. Surely she must have realized by now that, despite all his suavity, Hal did not share her enthusiasm for higher learning. In his current mood he was likely to say the Mona Lisa would make a nice dartboard.

But I also knew he was right. We could not take the machine with us, so there was little point wasting time puzzling over it. We were searching for something cold and unimaginative: gold. I turned to follow him, then stopped, peering back at the long bank of floor-to-ceiling windows.

Now that I was so close to them, I realized they were not flush with the ship's hull, but built back from it by a couple of metres. I stepped to the glass and scratched at the thick frost. I pressed my eyes to the peephole.

My view was a small one, but I could see there was definitely a chamber built between this glass wall and the ship's hull, which was itself fitted with floor-to-ceiling reinforced windows. The chamber was not deep, maybe two metres at most, but it extended out of sight on both sides, and I could not see the ceiling. It was difficult to tell what was on the floor, it was so thickly matted with frost and ice. I caught sight of several long strands of what looked like decaying corn stalks, or maybe sloughed snake skins, it was hard to tell. Then my eyes fixed on a small white object frozen into the ice. It looked distinctly like a beak.

Something drifted past, not two centimetres from the glass, and I snapped my head back in shock.

Tentacles, just the tips of them, trailed slowly out of sight.

'Hal!' I called.

Everyone was at the glass within seconds, clearing away ice. Between us we quickly opened up a wide viewing window. We stared.

'It's a vivarium,' Kate breathed.

'A what?' Nadira asked.

'Like a terrarium. Any place where you keep live specimens in their natural state.'

'Good God,' said Hal.

Hanging in the air were four aerozoans. It took me a moment to realize they were all dead. Their tentacles were inert, their diaphanous aprons did not ripple and contract. Their squid-shaped floating sacs were shrivelled, and yet they still held enough lifting gas to keep the corpses aloft. While three of them drifted about aimlessly, the fourth and biggest had been tethered from the ceiling in a kind of harness. Two of its tentacles were encased in thick rubber sleeves, trailing wires that disappeared into the vivarium's icy floor.

'He must have been studying them,' Kate said. 'They *are* fascinating creatures.'

'They're killers,' Hal snapped. 'And if I ever catch sight of a live one I'll put a bullet through its heart.'

'I don't think it has a heart,' Kate said, peering intently at the aerozoans. 'It's really quite primitive. But I'd have to dissect it to make sure.'

'Typical of Grunel to make pets of these freaks,' Hal said.

'I want one,' said Kate.

'You're not bringing one aboard my ship,' he told her.

'What harm can it do, they're dead!'

'Look at those,' I said, pointing. Floating high in the air was a cluster of small translucent spheres, no bigger than golf balls. As they drifted closer, I caught a glimpse inside one, and saw a tight bundle of tentacles and wrinkly membrane.

'They're eggs!' said Kate in astonishment. 'They must be filled with enough hydrium to keep them afloat. Ingenious! The eggs are laid in mid air and float until they're ready to hatch. Here's what I'll do. I'll bring back an egg or two. I've a specimen jar with me right now.'

'Eggs tend to hatch,' I said.

'Not these. They're long dead. You can't object to that, Hal.'

'Fine. *You* go in and get them.'

'Agreed,' she said boldly.

She walked along the glass wall, until she found the

outlines of a small doorway. She began scraping at the ice around the hinges.

'You're sure you want to go in there?' I asked her.

'Quite.'

'Be quick about it,' said Hal impatiently.

Hanging from a peg beside the hatch was what looked like a diving suit, including a helmet with a large glass porthole in the centre. The entire affair appeared to be made of thick rubber. Several long rubber-tipped poles hung next to it. I could not imagine willingly putting myself within striking distance of the aerozoans, even so armoured and insulated. I did not know if Grunel was a courageous man, or just foolhardy.

Kate pulled at the handle. The door was not locked. She gave a sharp tug and it snapped open in a shower of ice crystals. A faint sickly odour of mangoes oozed out over us.

'Smell that?' I asked.

'Hydrium?'

I nodded. 'They make their own, I'm sure of it.'

I wanted her to see that I'd been right all along, whatever Hal thought. But she just reached into her rucksack and produced a small glass jar. She stepped inside.

I could not let her go alone.

'What do you think you're doing?' she said as I came in after her.

'I thought you might like a hand.'

'I don't need a hand, thank you.'

'Here,' I said, passing her one of the poles. 'Just in case.'

'In case what?'

'There's still life in them.'

'They've been dead forty years. I doubt they're very sparky by now.'

She was being haughty with me, but she took the pole. I took one too. Hal, I noticed, had closed the door behind us. My boots crunched against the icy floor. Looking down I realized what I'd seen earlier were the husks of countless dead aerozoans, their gelatinous shells now thin and wispy. Here and there, a sharp beak poked up through the membranous debris.

I turned my attention back to the floating ones, drifting listlessly about the vivarium. There was nothing between us and them now. I knew they were dead, but I still did not like being so close to their tentacles. I remembered how a mere brush with them had sent electricity and flame exploding through Mr Dalkey.

One of them was wandering a bit too close to us for my liking. I raised my pole and gave it a sharp poke. The tip of the pole dented its soft body, and the aerozoan sailed away from me. Its tentacles made no move, its gelatinous apron not even a flutter. Still, we gave them a wide berth.

It was much colder inside the vivarium, and the whistle of wind drew my eye up to grilled vents all along the outer wall.

'Fresh air – and food too,' Kate said, following my gaze. 'See those funnels outside? They would've channelled all sorts of airborne insect life into the vivarium as the ship sailed.'

'I'm wondering if that's all they ate,' I said, glancing at the corpses underfoot. 'Some of these look like they've been gnawed at.'

'Possibly,' said Kate. 'Cannibalism is amazingly common. Even humans have been known to have a bash at it.'

We stopped and stared up at the floating cluster of eggs.

The ends of our poles were curved, like a hoe. Kate raised hers high and tried to catch one of the eggs, but she couldn't quite reach. She persisted.

'I'll have a try,' I said.

'I'm not tall enough,' she grumbled.

I managed to claw one of the eggs down through the air. The shell glinted with frost. Inside was a baby aerozoan, frozen forever in sleep. With her gloved hands, Kate gently guided the egg into her specimen jar, and screwed on the lid.

'There you are,' she whispered. She stared at the egg, enraptured. I would have liked to receive such a look.

There was a sharp knock on the glass and I looked up to see Hal, gesturing for us to hurry up. I was eager to leave. The sound of my boots treading on all these frozen aerozoan corpses made my skin crawl. We closed the door of the vivarium firmly behind us.

Hal checked his timepiece. 'We'll be heading back to the *Saga* in an hour. Dorje, can you assist Kate with hauling her taxidermy up on to the ship's back? Nadira, you'll lend a hand with that. Cruse, you're coming with me.' He was already walking towards the exit.

'Where are we going?' I asked.

'To pay a visit to old man Grunel.'

15

GRUNEL

We headed forward along the keel catwalk to the passenger quarters, climbed the stairs and stopped at an ornate oak door.

'I'm thinking,' said Hal, 'that maybe Grunel kept his goodies a bit closer at hand.'

The doorknob would not turn. Hal put his pistol against the keyhole and fired. The door opened. It was terribly dark. Our two torch beams united to form one giant spotlight. We stepped inside, and it was like entering the lobby of a grand house, except that it had no sweeping staircase. But everything else spoke of painstaking craftsmanship, luxury and, above all, the money to buy it. Persian carpets glittered on the hardwood floor, oil paintings in gilt frames hung from the high corniced walls. Grand archways led to lounges on both port and starboard sides of the ship, and I could see the faint glimmer of light filtered through frosted windows and drawn curtains. Our torches picked out elegant wing-backed armchairs, and a pianola. I remembered Kate saying the *Hyperion* had been custom built for Grunel, and since he was the only passenger, these elegant apartments must have been for his use alone.

Hal led us down one corridor, with several doors opening off it. One led to a serving pantry, with a dumb waiter that obviously carried Grunel's meals up from the kitchen directly below. Through another door was an enormous linen cupboard and laundry room. A third room, much smaller than the linen cupboard, was obviously the bedroom of Grunel's manservant. The bed was neatly made, and there was no sign of the fellow. I wondered glumly where he'd turn up. Perhaps we could look forward to him lurching frozen from a closet.

We retraced our steps to the lobby and set off down the second corridor. A single closed door stood at the end, with a lion's head knocker so imposing I almost felt like I should consult it before entering.

'Getting tired?' Hal asked me.

'No, I feel fine.'

'You sure?' He shone the light in my face to examine me and I turned away, squinting.

'Yes, I'm sure.' I was not lying.

'Take some oxygen if you need it.'

'I don't, thanks.'

Hal pushed the door wide and entered Theodore Grunel's bedroom. My torch beam skittered over the silk-covered walls, the chairs and settees upholstered in leather and velvet. I saw a grand four-poster bed, the sheets thrown back. The sight of that empty bed did give me a shiver. It meant Grunel was elsewhere. But where? One side of the room was given over to huge bookshelves, their frozen leather spines sparkling. Along the starboard wall, the curtains were drawn. Then my torch beam glanced off a hand. I stopped and prodded the darkness with my beam.

Dressed in red silk pyjamas and wrapped in a burgundy dressing gown, Theodore Grunel reclined on his chaise longue. His feet were slippered. His chin rested against his chest. His eyes were open, though one eyelid drooped. He appeared to be looking over the room rather disapprovingly. He was not a tall man, but stocky and powerfully built. He had a great block of a head, with long flared sideburns and a high forehead. His nose was broad and squashed-looking. Unlike the lookout in the crow's-nest, his skin had not been discoloured by the sun. Instead it was sallow and waxy, stubbled with frost, and only slightly shrunken. He looked pugnacious, even in death. I felt he might get up and shake a fist at us.

'There he is, the old toad,' Hal muttered.

He walked across to the curtains and pulled them wide, allowing pale sunlight to flood the stateroom. It was spacious, with an adjoining dressing room. Through the open doorway I could see it was lined with closets and drawers and shelves for top hats, of which he seemed to have many.

'Let's get to work,' said Hal. 'Look behind and under things. I'm after a safe or a vault.'

He started on the book shelf, sweeping row after row of leather-bound volumes to the floor. It shocked me to see books treated so, but I dared not say anything, for I could see in Hal's high good cheer a fierce impatience and simmering anger.

I started on a cabinet on the other side of the room, delicately pulling out drawers, trying to disturb as little as possible, probing at the back for hidden compartments. Finding nothing, I began putting the drawers back. All the time I felt Grunel's half-closed eye staring at me.

'This isn't maid service,' Hal said, coming over. 'Even Howard Carter had to break some walls to get at Tut's tomb! And we don't have all the time in the world. Get behind the other side. Now, push!'

Together we heaved over the entire cabinet. It crashed to the floor. There was no vault hidden behind it.

'It feels like thieving,' I couldn't help saying.

'You should have left your fine conscience behind in Paris,' he said. 'But let me tell you something. This ship doesn't even exist. It was declared lost at sea forty years ago, after it went missing. Know what that means? Grunel's family was paid off handsomely by the insurers, and at that moment they surrendered all further claim to the ship. The *Hyperion* belongs to no one but us. Take it, Cruse. Anything here is ours. It can't do anything for the dead. But it might do a lot for the living.'

He had pull, I could not deny. He was like a bright shining sun and I was a little planet, whirling around and around him, half wanting to break away and be free, half liking the ride. From across the room, Grunel stared at me balefully.

'Frozen Oldie over there's not helping,' I said.

Hal gave a laugh. He ripped a sheet off the bed and made to throw it over the rigid body.

'What's this?' he said, squinting at Grunel's right hand.

Between the dead man's clenched fingers I saw the dull flash of gold.

Hal tried to open Grunel's fist, but the fingers were like tongs of steel. There was something indecent about it, seeing him struggle with the dead man.

'Leave it, Hal,' I said.

From his rucksack he took his prybar and brought it down sharply on Grunel's fist. I winced as ice and frozen bone shattered. Grunel was left with a jagged stub. A gold pocket watch fell into his lap. Hal snatched it up and gave it a cursory look. He prised it open.

Inside the cover was a photograph, spider-webbed with wrinkles, of a young woman.

'Looks like old Grunel had a sweetheart,' said Hal with a coarse laugh. 'I was hoping for something a bit more helpful, but this is a nice enough bauble.' He dug out the photograph with his fingers and let it fall to the frosted carpet.

I picked up the photograph and slid it into my rucksack. It didn't seem right to leave it lying around on the floor. I didn't like to look at Grunel's shattered hand. Hal picked up the bedsheet and threw it over him.

'Better?' he said.

I nodded.

'Our first spoils, Cruse. There's more to come. Let's get to work.'

Side by side Hal and I searched the stateroom. Plumes of steam rose from our mouths. I went through more chests of drawers and cabinets, pulled back carpets, yanked paintings from the walls. Hal's words had stirred me, and for the first time I felt the excitement of being on an abandoned ship, knowing that somewhere on it was enough gold to make me rich. My mother would have her house, and I might buy my own apartment on a nice Paris street. And an airship, one that was just a little bigger than Hal's. I would no longer be a boy, but a man.

A faint whisper reached my ears, and I stopped working. Hal and I looked at each other. It grew louder. It became the sound of someone hissing, finger pointed, spittle flying from his mouth. My neck hair lifted in terror. Hal fumbled for his pistol and I whirled about, seeking out this banshee, wishing my torch beam were a blade. The hissing grew louder until I found myself shouting as if to keep it at bay. Abruptly it stopped with a loud thud.

The sound came from within the wall and our torch beams jostled frantically as we sought out the place.

'There!' I said.

Protruding from the plaster was a pair of copper pneumatic message tubes that I'd not noticed before.

The ends of both were sealed with ornamented hinged hatches. From one of them a little green flag had sprung up, and was still vibrating slightly.

'Good Lord,' said Hal, 'it's just a message capsule.'

Most airships, especially passenger liners, had a complicated network of pneumatic tubes for shuttling messages. I was so relieved there was no shrieking ghoul afoot, that it was several seconds before the dreadful question occurred to me.

Who exactly had sent us a message?

My heart, suddenly, was pounding so hard I could barely breathe. I wanted some tanked oxygen, but wouldn't take any unless Hal did.

'Must've been one of the others,' Hal said.

'Right,' I agreed. 'Amazing it still works.'

'There's probably an air turbine outside powering it,' Hal said. 'As long as the ship moves, it works.'

We nodded appreciatively at this feat of engineering.

'I suppose we should read it,' I said.

Neither of us, I noticed, seemed to be in any hurry. I took a deep breath, and unclasped the hatch. A streamlined rubber capsule slid out of the tube into my hand. I unscrewed the top.

'Empty,' I said.

'It's all bunged up, I reckon,' Hal commented. 'The pneumatics and so forth.'

I nodded. 'Probably shooting things around all over the ship.'

'Back to work.'

I wondered if Hal was as unshaken as he seemed, but if he could work, so could I. It wasn't five minutes before I heard his whoop of glee from the dressing room. Inside one of the closets, behind a false wall, he'd discovered a safe. It was the size of a pot-bellied stove, a solid cube of metal, resting on four squat legs. The door looked to be a good two centimetres thick.

'Suddenly I feel quite fond of old Grunel,' said Hal with a grin.

'Can you open it?'

'Didn't know I was a lock-picker, did you?' Hal gave me a wink.

'You're a man of many talents,' I replied.

'It's all a question of having the right tools,' said Hal, and from his pack he took, not a clever set of picks, but a big brick of some kind of grey putty, and a fat nest of wire.

'Oh sure,' he said, pinching off a bit of the putty, 'you can mess about with files and picks, but in the end, the important thing is to get at what you want.'

He rolled a bit of the putty into a cigarette shape, jabbed two wires into it, then shoved the whole lot into the safe's lock.

'Let's move off a-ways.' Hal fed out the wires as we retreated from the dressing room. We crouched behind the ottoman sofa in the bedroom. From his rucksack he produced a small box with a plunger and attached the ends of the wires to the terminals.

'You won't blow up the ship?' I asked.

'No, it's quite precise. Go ahead,' he said, gesturing to the handle. 'Give it a push.'

'Really?'

'Absolutely. It's quite a thrill.'

His enthusiasm was contagious and I grasped the plunger and pushed down hard. There was a flash of light and a surprisingly muffled bang. A wave of chemical vapours washed through the room.

'Good, wasn't it?' said Hal.

'I can't lie,' I replied with a smile.

Then we were up and hurrying into the dressing room.

The door of the safe was still perfectly intact; the only difference was that it was now slightly ajar, as if it had just been opened by the owner.

'Almost too easy, ain't it?' said Hal. 'Let's get the goodies, shall we?'

I noticed when it was just the two of us alone, most of his gentlemanly speech and niceties disappeared and he became what he really was: a street-smart entrepreneur, a self-made man. I liked him better this way than when he was sweet-talking Kate, Miss Simpkins and Nadira, holding forth in the lounge like an elder statesman.

Hal threw wide the door of the safe.

Nestled inside was another metal door.

'He's a cautious man, our Mr Grunel,' I said.

'Hats off to him,' said Hal, already preparing more explosive putty. 'You can never be too cautious. You and I, Cruse, are about to be very rich, very soon.'

'What'll you do with your share?' I asked, giddy with excitement.

'Well, I reckon a man in my position should take a wife.'

'Is that right?' I said, my smile fading.

Hal inserted the putty into the lock. 'I rather fancy an intelligent, spirited young woman who enjoys travel and adventure.'

'Mmm,' I said.

'Rich is also no bad thing.'

I looked at him in surprise. 'I thought you were rich enough already.'

He faltered a mere second. 'Well, more never goes amiss, does it? And what about you?' He was backing away from the vault now, feeding out wire. 'Your thoughts ever turn to marriage?'

'I'm only sixteen years old.'

'At your age, would've been the last thing on my mind, too. The young don't need that kind of responsibility.'

'Well, I was actually thinking of proposing,' I lied.

'That right?' Hal said, hooking the wires to the plunger.

'Why not? An engagement can go on for years.'

'True, but usually, before you propose to a lady, it's customary to have some wealth or form of livelihood.'

'Just hurry up and push that plunger,' I said. 'I'm going to be very rich, very soon.'

Hal grinned. 'But not as rich as me.'

He pushed the plunger, and the explosion blew the second door right off.

I walked over to the safe with Hal. I did not feel very buoyant any more.

'Icy old fart,' Hal muttered, for there, behind the second door, was a third.

'Harder to crack than you thought,' I said.

After the third door was blasted off there was a fourth. By this time, Hal had stopped speaking altogether, except to have a little cursing spree when his cold fingers had trouble squeezing his brimstone putty into the ever tinier locks.

'There's not going to be much room left for anything,' I remarked, after we blew the fifth door off and saw there was a sixth.

'There's barely room in there for a pair of slippers,' Hal said darkly.

'A child's slippers,' I added.

'I'll have it open,' said Hal doggedly.

He blew the door open.

'What's inside?' I asked, my eyes smarting from the fumes.

'Nothing,' he said.

'Nothing?'

'A key. Looks the same as Nadira's. And this.' He tossed me a small notebook, slightly singed. 'You're the bookish type, Cruse. What is it?'

I opened the book at random. The page was filled with close lines of small meticulous handwriting.

'Looks to be some kind of journal.'

'He puts his diary in the safe.' Hal cursed and gave the wrecked safe a kick. There was no more joviality in him. I put the journal into my rucksack.

A dreadful hissing sound once more filled Grunel's stateroom, and even though I knew what it was, it still raised a rash of gooseflesh across my back and belly. The green flag sprang up from the message tube. I took out the capsule, unscrewed it. This time there was something inside, tightly furled. Carefully I pulled out several sheets. They were blueprints, filled with complicated lines and notations. I caught sight of a large cylindrical shape which looked like the telescope from Grunel's workshop. But before I could make sense of it, Hal snatched the blueprints from my hands.

'More of his bloody silly inventions.'

He rolled the sheets up roughly and jammed them back into the capsule.

'Maybe a beard puller or an automatic nose picker, eh?'

'Hal, wait—'

He shoved it into the outgoing pneumatic tube, and yanked the tasseled cord. The canister was sucked back into the system.

'That might've been useful!' I protested.

'If it doesn't glitter, it's not gold,' said Hal savagely. 'Where'd you hide the goodies, eh?' he said to the blanketed form of Grunel. 'No good hoarding it now, you old miser. Your best days are behind you.'

We heard footsteps and swung our lights to the doorway.

Dorje entered. 'The girls are tired.'

'We're not done here,' Hal said.

'We can continue tomorrow,' said Dorje. 'We all need rest.'

Hal was about to say something, but then he just nodded. 'You're right. Let's head back to the *Saga*.'

16

TWO JOURNALS

It was good to be back aboard the *Sagarmatha*. After the unearthly cold of the *Hyperion*, the dining room and lounge seemed almost tropically warm. At dinner, we scarcely touched our food. We all looked haggard and our appetites had shrivelled. My trousers were already looser around my waist. And yet, I did not feel unwell. I dared not mention it, for fear Hal would think I was suffering from high altitude delusions, but I felt restless and filled with energy. I wanted to get back to work aboard the *Hyperion*. I wanted my gold.

As a little treat after dinner, Hal released some tanked oxygen into the lounge. Slumped in a wing-backed chair, I stretched my feet towards the electric hearth. Any closer and they'd be set alight. Even the snow leopard's fur had not prevented my toes and fingers from burning with cold by the end of our three hours aboard Grunel's ship.

Just before we left, I'd convinced Hal to let me enter the captain's cabin. On his roll-top desk I'd found the ship's log, locked at the base of a small frozen waterfall.

I'd managed to hack the journal free from the ice, and right now it was thawing in a roasting pan near the fire. That was Nadira's idea. I just hoped the paper would not dissolve into an unreadable inky mess.

The evening was calm and the two ships, tethered together, moved gently against the wind, steadied by the *Saga*'s engines. We couldn't have had more ideal conditions for the salvage. But my heart was not calm. I could not stop thinking of what Hal had said about taking a wife. Surely he had his sights set on Kate de Vries. Now, every time he opened his mouth, I half expected him to fall on one knee and propose to her. I don't know what terrified me more, the idea of Hal marrying her, or me marrying her.

Miss Simpkins sewed. By now I'd have thought she'd sewed enough clothing for all the Russian army. Nadira was watching the ship's log, turning it every once in a while so it thawed evenly and did not get singed. Near the bar Hal and Dorje conferred softly, looking over the map which Dorje had diligently made during the exploration. Kate was busy taking pictures of her aerozoan egg, jotting notes. With every flash of her camera, a faint chemical haze drifted across the room. The quagga and dodo and Yeti bones had been hauled up inside the *Sagarmatha* and were now safely stored in the ship's hold. But it was the aerozoan which had all Kate's attention at the moment.

In my lap was Grunel's diary, my one bit of treasure to show for the day. I was amazed that Hal had not snatched it from me to read himself. Instead he told me to have a peek and let him know if there was anything useful. He hadn't sounded very optimistic. He seemed to have a low opinion of Grunel, and of writing in general.

Glancing at the diary's first few pages, I almost agreed with him. It was not much like a diary, for there were no dates, and what few words there were he didn't even bother to write on the lines. They were scattered all round the page, amongst diagrams which made no sense to me. Quick stabs of ink, a flurry of odd symbols, and numbers everywhere. It was like trying to make sense of snowflakes in a storm.

'Haven't you taken enough photos of that little oddity?' complained Miss Simpkins, waving away the vapours from Kate's flash bulbs.

'It's no more an oddity than you, Marjorie,' Kate replied, taking another photograph. 'I want a record of what it looked like in its egg before I dissect it.'

'You're going to cut it up?' Miss Simpkins asked.

'Into little pieces, yes. I can learn much more about it that way. Though, really, I'm better with mammals. There's something much more primitive about this one.'

'You must be happy with all your new specimens,' I said to Kate, hoping to strike up a genial conversation.

'I could've had them all, if the *Sagarmatha* hadn't been damaged.' She gave me a look, as though it were all my doing. She was getting as bad as Hal. Really, they were perfect for each other.

'At least you got something,' I told her. 'I haven't found so much as a penny.'

'There's the old man's watch,' Hal said, without looking up from his map.

'There was a picture inside it,' I said, remembering. I took it from my pocket and showed it to Kate. 'Any idea who that is?'

She glanced at it. 'His daughter.'

'You're sure?'

'Absolutely. They have the same foreheads and noses. Anyway, I saw a photograph of her in a newspaper once.'

'This is the one he cut off without a penny?' I asked. 'The one he wouldn't talk to?'

She nodded.

I wondered if Grunel had made things right with her before he embarked on his final journey. She had clearly never left his thoughts.

'You know,' said Kate, 'I think it's rather low of you to sneak his personal belongings.'

'Isn't that exactly why we all came?' said Nadira from the hearth. 'To swipe all his things?'

This stumped Kate for a moment. 'Well, perhaps, but we don't have to be grave robbers. I mean, honestly, the man's pocket watch?'

For a moment I was speechless with indignation. Taking the watch hadn't even been my idea, but I wasn't going to tattle on Hal.

'Grave robbing?' I said. 'You're the only one digging up bones.'

'That's different,' Kate replied, with an imperious tilt of her chin. 'That's the pursuit of knowledge.'

I said nothing more. A fine, testy crew we were this evening. No doubt some of it was exhaustion, and the thin air of seven thousand metres. But it seemed all too easy to irritate Kate these days.

'Even if I can't salvage Grunel's whole collection,' she said to Hal, 'I can try to catalogue it at least. Can I bring my small camera tomorrow?'

'By all means,' Hal replied distractedly.

'I think this is properly cooked now,' Nadira said from the electric hearth. She picked up the ship's log. Its pages were warped and stiff and the entire book had swollen to twice its original size.

'Can you read it?' I asked.

She settled herself in a chair and turned back the cover to the first page. 'It's dated Edinburgh, 25 March. There's just some kind of loading register. Should I skip ahead?'

She was already turning the page.

'Wait,' I said. 'Go back. What does it say for aruba fuel?'

Nadira looked down the loading register, and read the weight aloud. The *Hyperion* had left harbour carrying over two hundred thousand kilograms of aruba fuel.

'And what about water?' I asked.

'Which do you want? Radiator water? Trim ballast? Fresh water?'

'Fresh.'

'Thirty-five thousand kilos.'

I looked over at Hal and Dorje. They'd both been listening.

'He wasn't moving to New Amsterdaam,' I said. 'That's obvious from the *Hyperion*'s chart. He was on some much longer journey.'

'Where?' Hal said. 'You could sail five times around the world with all that fuel.'

'Maybe he planned to live aboard her.'

Hal sniffed, thinking the idea ludicrous.

'Look at the museum he made for himself,' I said, 'and the workshop. Not even the *Aurora* had staterooms that luxurious. She's no simple freighter. She's a home.'

Hal shrugged, as if this wasn't a very interesting or useful piece of information.

'Listen to this,' said Nadira.

I asked Mr Grunel where he meant me to sail, and he said he had no destination in mind. I inquired as to whether he would care to choose one, and he replied that I could choose, so long as it was somewhere out of the way. 'It does not matter in any event,' he told me, 'since we will not be arriving.' When I said I was not sure I understood, he retorted, rather impatiently, 'Just keep us sailing, captain, that's all I ask.' I inquired what we were to do when our fuel and supplies ran

low, and he just gave an odd smile and said I was not to worry.

'Well, he's a complete nutter obviously,' Hal said. 'But we already knew that from his inventions.'

'He most certainly wasn't a nutter,' Kate objected. 'He gave us some of the greatest inv—'

'Yes, yes, I know,' Hal interrupted. 'But what kind of man loads his life on to a ship and aims to disappear into the sky?'

I had no answer to that, so I began to turn slowly through Grunel's diary. Page after page was covered by his odd notations. It seemed incredible they could make sense even to him. His strings of numbers and symbols made my physics textbooks seem all simplicity.

Nadira read some more:

Mr Grunel dined with me and the officers on our first night aloft. He reminded us that we were on no condition to telegraph our position to anyone on earth. As of this moment we no longer exist. Furthermore, we are to keep our current position and heading to the bridge officers, and let none of the other crew know our whereabouts. We had, of course, already agreed to these conditions when Mr Grunel hired us. At meal's end, Mr Grunel thanked us, and bid us adieu. 'You will likely not see me again for

**quite some time. I have a great deal of work
before me, and I do not wish to be disturbed
except for the most urgent of reasons. Good
evening, gentlemen.'**

When Nadira finished reading, I turned a page of
Grunel's diary and came upon a rare line of text, written
in his small, meticulous hand.

'Here's something,' I said, and read aloud:

*Aloft now, and can at last complete my work
without interruption, sneaks or saboteurs.
Not even B can find me now.*

'He was very paranoid,' Kate said, 'I remember reading
that.'

'Who's B?' I wondered aloud.

'Maybe someone trying to steal his ideas?' Nadira
suggested.

'He was convinced *everyone* was out to do that,' Kate
said.

'Another sign of lunacy,' Hal put in. For some reason
he seemed irritated we were reading the journals. He
listened impatiently, chewing at his lip, eyes straying to
the far corners of the room.

'What was he working on though?' I said. 'There
were dozens of things in his workshop.'

But automatically I thought of the enormous
telescope-like machine. It alone bore no label. It had no

name. Maybe if Hal hadn't bunged the blueprints back into the tube, we'd have some idea what it was.

Nadira turned the swollen pages of the ship's log. 'It's mostly just weather conditions now. Oh, here's something.'

Grunel is an odd fellow to be sure. Since the first night, we have not seen him. He keeps to his apartments, I suppose, waited on by his furtive little manservant, Hendrickson.

'We never did see Hendrickson,' I said to Hal. I thought it a bit strange, since we'd searched all the staterooms. Surely we should have seen him, especially since it was late at night when the *Hyperion* met her doom.

Hal just shrugged. 'Maybe Grunel had him down in the kitchen making hot chocolate.'

'Sorry for interrupting,' I told Nadira. 'Please keep going.'

However, my crew says they hear a great deal of noise coming from what Grunel calls his engineerium, though they have never seen him going in and out. He has the only key to this room, and the one opposite. Three weeks, and we've had no contact with the earth.

I remembered the poor captain, frozen to the rudder wheel, the last beat of his heart far in the past. I wondered if he'd ever started to wish he'd declined the command of the *Hyperion*. A more unusual journey would have been hard to imagine. His task was only to keep the ship moving. In some ways, it sounded like the grandest of voyages, for I loved to be aloft more than anything, and always felt a vague sadness when I returned to earth. Having been born in the air, I often wondered what it would be like never to have to land.

'Well,' I said, 'it seems Grunel meant to stay airborne until he finished his work.'

'It must have been something impressive,' Kate said. 'For him to go into such seclusion.'

'It might be worth a lot of money,' I said.

Kate directed a withering look at me. 'Is that the only value a thing can have? It might be an invention of huge scientific importance. We must find out what it is.'

'Doesn't interest me,' said Hal.

'I wonder if he ever finished it,' I said.

'How long would all that fuel last?' Nadira wanted to know.

'He could've hitched a ride on a tailwind and hardly used any fuel at all,' I pointed out. 'If staying aloft was his only goal.'

'What's the date of the captain's last entry?' Hal asked Nadira.

She flipped pages. 'April 20.'

'By then everyone assumed he'd already crashed,' Kate said. 'They were expected to arrive in New Amsterdaam

300

within four days of their departure. He was aloft much longer than anyone thought.'

'Read the last entry,' I asked Nadira.

Lookout reports we are being followed. With no success in identifying the ship, we assume it is a pirate vessel. It is slowly but surely closing with us. I have apprised Grunel of our situation. He was greatly agitated, and demanded we steam at full speed into the storm front which lies twenty aeroknots to the south east. I tried to discourage him, but he was adamant. He thinks we will lose our pursuers in the clouds. Our new heading now takes us towards the storm front.

For a moment, no one said anything, knowing these were the last words the captain's hand ever wrote. I turned to the end of Grunel's diary and began flipping backwards, until I came to his final entry. It was just a few handwritten lines, and I read it aloud.

It is what I have always feared. The captain thinks we are pursued by pirates, but I know better. It is B. He has hounded me on land for years, and now, somehow, he has found me in the skies. It is too cruel to think he might take my invention from me, when I have only now just completed it.

'But the pirates, or B – whoever it was – they never boarded,' Nadira said. 'They never reached the ship.'

I nodded. 'The *Hyperion* went into the storm, and got caught in the downdraft.'

'Updraft, you mean,' said Hal.

I shook my head, remembering what had happened to us aboard the *Flotsam*. 'No. First the downdraft. The captain panicked and dumped all his ballast to try to save the ship. I bet if we look at her ballast boards we'll see there's not a drop left in the tanks. She was light as a feather, and then she got caught in the storm's updraft, and was rocketed into Skyberia.'

'He could've valved hydrium,' Hal said.

'He might not have had time.'

'It's a theory,' said Hal.

'A good one,' added Dorje. 'I think you're right, Matt.'

Dorje's quiet agreement was like a benediction. I said nothing, only hoping that my face did not show the great hurrah of jubilation I gave inside. I glanced at Kate, but she wasn't even looking at me. She seemed not at all interested that I'd solved the mystery of the *Hyperion*'s disappearance.

'I'm tired of their little scribblings,' Hal said. 'Unless they tell us where the loot is, these journals are pointless.'

Nadira nodded in agreement, a flash of frustration in her dark eyes.

'They may yet yield some clues,' Dorje said.

Nadira exhaled impatiently. 'Is there anything else in

there?' she asked me, nodding at Grunel's diary. 'A map with a big X on it?'

I flipped backwards, and there, drawn across two pages, was one of the most beautiful sketches I'd ever seen. It was an entire city aloft in the sky, suspended beneath enormous cloud-shaped bags of hydrium. The buildings were connected with soaring articulated bridges and enclosed walkways. Lush garden terraces spilled flowering vines over the sides of the glass buildings. People stood on wide balconies and looked at the view, which was the everchanging sky, and whatever part of the earth they were floating over. There was an airship dock where several ships were moored. Ornithopters fluttered about, ferrying people between the city's many grand piers.

Everyone must have seen the amazement on my face, for they quickly came over to have a look.

'It's beautiful!' said Kate, standing at my shoulder.

And suddenly she and I were pointing things out to each other in the picture. It wasn't like we were really talking to each other, or having a conversation, but it was the closest I'd felt to her in days. Our mutual wonder bound us together, and I didn't want it to end.

Mesmerized, I turned more pages. There were no words, just sketch after sketch of this fabulous airborne city from every possible angle and distance. I squinted.

'Are those birds?' I asked.

'No, they're people!' said Kate.

She was right. What I'd thought were birds flapping about the city's spires were actually men and women, wearing artificial wings. It was as if these images were birthed from my own mind, for I could imagine no more perfect way to live. I was smitten.

'He had a fanciful imagination,' Nadira said. But far from sounding enthusiastic, she sounded angry. This was not the kind of thing she'd been hoping for.

'Was he planning to build all these things, do you think?' Kate asked.

'I don't know.' And all at once I felt wistful, for I didn't see how a city like this could ever be built. 'It would be impossibly expensive. You'd have to be shipping fuel to it all the time.'

'Not to mention fresh water and food,' Hal said. 'And what if something sprang a leak? Where would they get their hydrium? A storm front passes over it, and it's so much twisted alumiron. It's nothing but a pipe dream.'

But the impracticality of it made it no less beautiful – more so, if anything, for it was truly like something spun from the gossamer of the finest dreams.

'Put your pretty pictures away,' Hal said. 'We need to lay down plans for tomorrow.'

Reluctantly I closed the diary.

'There's a weather change coming, so we can't go squandering our time. We're going to split up. Cruse, you're with Nadira. I'm with Kate. Dorje can take care of himself. We'll cover more ground that way.'

I glanced over at Kate, wondering how she felt about me and Nadira being paired.

'That's a very sound plan,' she said, nodding.

Hal and I regarded each other for a moment, and I thought I saw a ripple of merriment in his eye. Was this a marvellous game to him? If so, he was not playing fair.

'Will I have time to catalogue Grunel's collection?' Kate asked.

'After we find the gold, you might get a bit more time. But I wouldn't get your hopes up. The longer we stay up high, the weaker we get. We lose muscle mass, stamina, and the ability to think and move quickly. Our bodies are dying. After forty-eight hours you'll be as close to death as you're ever likely to be – until you die, of course.'

No one said anything for a moment.

'That was an encouraging little speech,' I remarked.

'No use mincing words,' said Hal. 'Needs saying.'

'I have no worries about Mr Cruse,' Dorje said with a smile. 'I do not think he was suffering much today. He has a Himalayan heart. Like my people.'

I smiled, warmed by the compliment.

'Grunel squirrelled his money away somewhere odd,' Hal said. 'But I know it's there. So we're going to divide the ship and work through her till she gives up her treasure.'

Nadira started to speak, then stopped herself.

'What is it?' I asked her.

'It's just . . . I'm wondering if anyone else felt something in there. Something watching us.'

An icy rash swept my neck and shoulders.

'Ghosts?' said Miss Simpkins, looking up for the first time in ages. 'Are you saying the ship is haunted?'

'Gypsy poppycock,' said Hal, but I caught him glance quickly at Dorje.

'In the control car,' Nadira said, 'we all heard that voice over the speaking tube.'

'The wind,' said Hal.

'That's what we said to make ourselves feel better. It sounded like someone saying "crow's-nest" to me.'

'It did rather, I must admit,' agreed Kate.

'Listen to me,' Hal said angrily. 'This is a salvage, and a difficult one. We do not have time for superstitious fantasies.'

'It would have been better,' Dorje said, 'if we'd kept the lookout with his ship.'

Hal threw up his hands in exasperation. 'What was I to do? Leave everyone slipping about on the ship's back while we fussed with a corpse? What if one of you had fallen to your death? Would that have been preferable?'

'No,' said Dorje, 'but the ship is not tranquil. Nadira's right. I sensed it too.'

I hadn't forgotten the terrible sense of anticipation I'd felt aboard the *Hyperion*. I remembered the fearful gaze of Grunel's hooded eye.

'If anyone's frightened, they needn't come,' said Hal contemptuously. 'I don't want anyone ninnying about the ship.'

'I'm coming,' I said.

'We all are,' Kate said.

'The ship has seen great calamity,' Dorje said, 'and the souls of those men may still be confused and even angry at their sudden death. I don't think we can expect them to cooperate with us.'

That night I slept poorly, the thin air starving me of breath. I kept jerking awake. I should have taken Dorje's advice and used my oxygen mask. But I pictured Hal in his cabin, sleeping soundly without it.

I thought of Kate. I did not understand her, or what she felt for me. My heart beat hard. I wished it could telegraph me what I was meant to do. I wished it could tell me what manner of person I was.

In the hours before dawn, I drifted off once more, and dreamed I was walking through doorway after doorway. There seemed no end to them. With every new door I opened, fear coursed through me, for I sensed something was waiting for me on the other side.

I came to yet another door, and with the utmost dread, knew this to be the last. I turned the handle and pushed.

The door swung open only halfway before stopping with a thud. My mind and body sang out with panic. There was something behind the door. I tried to wake myself, but the dream would not release me.

Something stepped out from behind the door. It was some kind of half-formed man, and whether he was wearing clothes or not, I could not tell, because his whole body was so unfinished. It was as though he'd been moulded from clay and the hands of his creator had not smoothed him or given him proper shape. In his head, only the eyes and mouth were really apparent. His face was all pinches and gouges, and yet it wore an expression – not of malice, but of fear, as though he too had been caught by surprise. We stared, eyes mirroring each other's terror, and I did not know what he was, if he was friend or fiend.

17

FROZEN GARDEN

Clad once more in our snow leopard suits, Nadira and I made our way aft along the *Hyperion*'s keel catwalk. It was mid-morning and we'd just boarded. Hal had told us to start at the stern and work forward, checking every storeroom, cabin and locker methodically. The wind had picked up during the night, and the ship rocked and groaned in the sky's mighty swell. The timbers and girders and bracing wires trembled. Our torch beams struck rainbow colours from the ice. Our breath steamed before us. After my nightmare, I feared I would see some frozen crew member, revivified by anger or confusion, lurching towards us out of the shadows.

I thought of Kate and Hal exploring the ship together. If she were frightened, she might clutch his arm, press close against him. He would thrust out his chest and reassure her with his manly talk. She would feel safe with him. He had her all to himself. He could propose at any moment. And what would she say? If she said yes, maybe it would be a mercy to me. We had about as much in common as a fish and a kangaroo – that's what my good friend Baz had told me last year. I was thinking he might be right after all.

I glanced over at Nadira, strands of her dark hair escaping the hood. I thought of our kiss, as I often did. She was very beautiful. In many ways I had more in common with her than with Kate. We knew what it was to be underlings, to make our own way. We'd both lost our fathers. When I was with her, I did not feel I had to prove myself. I did not know what to make of our kiss in the crow's-nest. Perhaps she was just carried away by her joy at escaping a dreadful marriage, and it meant nothing to her. The thought disappointed me somehow. And yet my feelings were a puzzle. It was as if the *Hyperion*'s cold had frozen part of my heart, and my own pulse was lost to me. I tried to think only of the work ahead of us.

When we reached the last door on the catwalk's port side we stopped. I touched the handle, and felt a tremor of premonition. Gritting my teeth, I pushed the door wide.

We entered, and at first I was hopeful, for the room was filled with wooden crates. After I raised the nearest lid, though, I realized the crate contained not gold, but food. Sacks of cereals and rice were stacked high against the walls. Crate after crate revealed tins of all kinds: peaches, calves' brains, lettuce, whole rabbits, fur and all. There were provisions enough here to mount an expedition across Antarctica. I suppose I shouldn't have been surprised since, according to the captain's log, the *Hyperion*'s journey was meant to be a long one, and she would not be allowed to reprovision along the way.

We moved on. The next room we came to was a landing bay. A great track ran along the ceiling, and suspended from their docking trapezes were two of the oddest-looking flying machines I'd ever seen. The ornithopters I was familiar with were feathered, with a pair of wings that flapped to give lift and thrust. But Grunel's seemed more bat than bird. Their wings bore no feathers, but were made of some kind of supple leathery material, furled strangely, and ribbed. Two propellers were mounted above the wings and cockpit. Certainly it was an ungainly thing, flimsy-looking too. And yet I saw it had room for not one but four passengers, so obviously was quite powerful.

The ornithopters hung just a metre or so above the floor, and I took a closer look at one. There was a metal handle jutting from its breastbone, like the starter crank for a motorcar. Along the machine's leathery flank, I found a hatch, opened it and shone my torchlight into its sparkly innards: gears and pulleys and sprockets and more little parts than could be found in all the factories of Switzerland. There was no combustion engine that I could see.

'It's all clockwork,' I said to Nadira in amazement. 'It doesn't even need fuel.'

I'd never heard of such a thing: an engine that didn't rely on aruba fuel. In the floor of the hangar were the

311

launching bay doors, firmly shut and filmed in ice. Had these strange craft ever taken to the skies, or were they just another of Grunel's works in progress? I remembered his wonderful sketches of the aerial city, and the numerous ornithopters which had flecked the surrounding skies. And flying people too . . .

There, fixed to the far wall of the hangar was a pair of huge artificial wings. I walked over for a better look. Each wing was densely feathered, pleated like a fan so it could be retracted. They were connected to an elaborate frame which strapped on to your chest, arms and legs – for there seemed to be a tail segment as well, which could be steered with your feet.

'Does it work, do you think?' I asked Nadira.

'Care to take a test flight?'

I laughed. The crew of the *Aurora* used to joke that I was lighter than air. And some small, defiant part of me, even now, believed that if I were ever to fall, the sky would hold me aloft. I stroked the feathered wings once more. How I would have loved to try them.

Nadira had already moved on. She was like Hal. Grunel's inventions were just distractions to her. I joined her and we checked the rest of the hangar. There was not much else to investigate, apart from some chests of spare parts, and mechanics' tools. We took a short break, and Nadira breathed some tanked oxygen. I was feeling the altitude, and even walking was labour, but I was not out of breath yet, and I wanted to save my oxygen for when it was really needed.

'Do you think Kate's feeling all right?' Nadira asked, removing her mask.

'What do you mean?'

'She just seems a bit ill-tempered lately, especially with you.'

'Oh,' I said carelessly, 'I think she blames me for wrecking the *Saga*.'

Maybe Hal was right about her: she had an iron will, and I had come between her and her heart's desire. She wanted all Grunel's specimens; she wanted Hal.

'That's ridiculous,' Nadira said.

'She doesn't see it that way. And neither does Hal.'

'He doesn't give you the credit you deserve. You risked your life saving Kami Sherpa.'

I felt very grateful to Nadira, then, for Kate had never said those words to me.

'We should move on,' Nadira said, and I could hear the impatience in her voice.

As we left the ornithopter hangar, the ship gave a quick shudder. For the past hour, I'd been aware of the wind picking up, could feel it shaking the floor through the torn hull. The *Saga*'s engines would have to work harder to steady us. We crossed the catwalk to a door on the ship's starboard side.

I turned the handle and pushed. The door swung open halfway and then struck something hard. My nightmare awoke and beat against the walls of my chest. I swore and gave the door a violent kick. There was another sharp clunk, then the sound of something scraping along the floor as the door swung further open.

I stepped back, waiting. Nadira was looking at me wonderingly, eyes wide. I felt as though someone had grabbed my heart and squeezed it dry like a sponge. Nothing happened. No noise came from the dark room. From my rucksack I pulled out the pry bar and gripped it in my right hand. I lunged inside, stabbing torch light behind the door.

I gasped. Then I started laughing, and could not stop. A chicken, frozen hard as an anvil, was toppled against the door. Nadira was behind me, and her torch picked out several other chickens, settled behind the mesh windows of their coop. They looked as if they might give a cluck and start laying at any moment.

The room appeared to be a small barn. Straw was scattered around the floor, speckled with frozen chicken droppings. Feed and water troughs were set out. Against the opposite wall were two stalls, one containing a goat, the other a milking cow, keeled over on its side.

'Eerie,' said Nadira.

'Very.'

But I began to feel that *I* was the freak aboard this ship, moving and breathing when all around me were the frozen dead. It was unusual nowadays for a cargo or passenger ship to bring animals aboard. Still, it was all of a piece with Grunel's wish to be self-sufficient on his long journey. From the hen came eggs, from the goat and cow fresh milk, cheese, and meat if need be.

We made a thorough search of the room. Nadira even

opened the henhouse and sifted through the straw and nests in case Grunel had hidden some goodies in there. Impressed by her thoroughness, I slit the bags of feed with a pitchfork, lest they contain diamonds instead of seed. There were no pleasant surprises to be had here.

'Are you getting worried at all?' she asked.

'That there's nothing? I'm starting to wonder.'

'Should we try through here?' Nadira said, pointing to a door between the two stalls. It was not locked. I was startled by the light that spilled over us when she opened it.

We walked into an orchard.

The ship's hull had been generously fitted with windows, and the frosty glass shone brilliantly. The trees glittered. Their leaves had turned and were furred with ice. It was like some kind of faerie garden that had been put to sleep for a hundred years and would only bloom and thrive again when the king returned. I did not know much about trees, but could see there were several different kinds here.

'Look,' said Nadira, 'there's a vegetable garden, too.'

Beyond the orchard was a small rectangular patch of soil. Nothing had had a chance to grow much, just a few withered stalks and vines. But each furrow was marked with stakes bearing small handwritten signs: potatoes, tomatoes, carrots, spinach, rhubarb and corn.

I'd heard of cooks growing potted basil in their kitchen windows, but never had I known of airborne gardens and orchards.

'Must be another of his experiments,' I said, 'to see how trees and plants grow aloft.' I looked at the large windows. 'They had enough light I suppose.'

'But how did they keep it all watered?' Nadira asked.

'Plenty of water tanks aboard. They could collect it, too, when it rained.' Most ships had adjustable gutters. Fly beneath a single rain cloud and you could pick up water fast.

Suddenly I thought of Grunel's sketches, the lush gardens, the greenhouses.

'He wanted to build his aerial city,' I said with certainty. 'That's why he came up here. To see if it could be done. Water from the clouds. Food from his farms. The only thing he wouldn't have is fuel. Without fuel, it could never work.'

Nadira shrugged. She didn't seem particularly interested. Kate would have understood my wistfulness. She knew me of old, knew the part of me that longed to be airborne at all times.

'Maybe he buried his treasure,' Nadira said.

I looked over the orchard in dismay. If Hal saw this he'd probably want us to dig it all up. Grunel was so strange a fellow, I supposed it was possible he'd entomb his treasure in the earth. Still, I did not have the heart to embark on it right now. 'Why don't we save that treat for later,' I said.

'It's beautiful,' she said, gazing at the faerie orchard.

'Are you all right?' I asked, for I noticed she was shivering.

'I'm just a bit cold.'

'Take some oxygen.'

I waited while she fitted her mask and took some deep breaths. I felt guilty. I should have stopped more often for breaks. When you see a person jump rooftops and kick up their heels at bullets, you do not think anything can stop them. After a few minutes she took the mask off.

'How's your headache?' I asked, remembering how she'd winced and rubbed at her temples before we'd boarded the *Hyperion* this morning.

'Not too bad.'

'You sure? Do you want to go back to the ship?'

She looked at me. Her green eyes.

'You're very kind,' she said.

I gave an awkward laugh. 'No.'

'Yes you are. You stood up for me when no one else would.'

'I'm surprised you can think well of me, after what happened between me and your father.'

'Anything you did was self defence. When I first met you, somehow I knew there wasn't a cruel bone in your body. You're too decent a person. You're like . . . the Statue of Liberty.'

'Well, I don't usually wear a gown. Are you sure you're not feeling light-headed?'

'She's like a beacon, standing there gazing into the future. I like the way you think all things are possible.'

I marvelled at her words, for as much as they flattered

me, they seemed untrue. Lately my thoughts had taken a gloomy turn.

'Ah, well,' I said, 'I feel like I'm cheating.'

'How?'

'Looking for treasure, I'm no better than a pirate. I'm not earning it. If I played by the rules, I'd be back at school studying for my exams.'

'The rules,' said Nadira. 'If I followed the rules, I'd be married right now.'

I grimaced. 'The fellow with the bad teeth.'

She nodded.

'Some rules really should be broken,' I admitted.

'If we find gold here,' she said, 'you won't need to go back to the Academy. You won't have to fly rich people around the rest of your life. You can do exactly what you want. Buy your own ship. You won't have to answer to anyone but yourself. You'll blaze your own trail!'

She was conjuring a glorious picture of my future, one that I had started sketching for myself the past few days. But there was still something mirage-like about it. It still felt beyond my grasp – or was I just too timid, too blinkered to seize it?

'You and I are rule breakers,' Nadira said. 'The world's hard. We might not be able to change it, but I think we'll make a dent in it.'

'I hope you're right,' I said.

She touched my face.

I wanted to be touched.

I felt like crying, for at that moment I knew it was

Kate's touch I wanted, and I could not have it. Despite how mismatched we were, despite my disloyal heart, it was her I wanted above anything, and I worried I'd lost her.

I cleared my throat, and nearly fell over as the ship gave a violent shudder, and did not stop. The sun shone just as brightly through the windows, but the invisible wind had the *Hyperion* in her claws and was not willing to let go.

'Come on,' I said.

With the ship's floor heaving, we lurched towards the door and out on to the catwalk. The wind was gushing in through the tears in the ship's fabric and playing devil's fiddle in the rigging. I caught sight of Dorje struggling along the catwalk towards me.

'We're leaving!' he called out.

We reached the forward ladder at the same time as Hal and Kate.

'Blowing a bit hard,' said Hal.

'Did you find anything?' I asked.

He shook his head and grunted. I didn't care. I was looking at Kate. I half expected her to announce an engagement.

'Lead the way, Cruse,' Hal said. 'We'll wait this out on the *Saga*.'

I started climbing for the crow's-nest, the ladder swaying like a metronome as the ship pitched and fell. Beneath the observation dome I peered out at the sky, and did not like what I saw.

As the wind pummelled the two ships, the *Saga*'s four coupling arms were stretching and compressing like springs. They managed to keep the two ships from colliding, but they were being sorely tested. The sky shrieked. The *Hyperion* was like a wild thing thrashing for its freedom.

Overhead I could see Kami Sherpa peering down from the *Saga*'s hatch, starting to lower the winch. The line came down askew, blown by the wind. A sudden gust cracked it like a lion tamer's whip.

'Get the girls on first,' Hal said from the ladder. 'Let's be quick about this.'

'Make sure your harnesses are snug,' Dorje said. 'I'll take you out one at a time. Oxygen. Goggles. Get them on. Kate, you're first.'

I made room for Kate beside me. She looked out at the maelstrom, as she fumbled with her goggles.

'It's going to be bumpy,' I said.

'I can see that.'

'Be careful,' I said, adjusting her mask for her.

She looked at me, far away behind her goggles, and then Dorje opened the hatch. I crouched instinctively as the glacial sky hit us.

Dorje hooked his safety line to the rail, and Kate's too. Side by side, hunched low, they made their way along the ship's back. The wind was full of malice, beating at the ships. Dorje caught the winch cable and was about to hook Kate to it, when I saw one of the forward coupling arms jerk free of the *Hyperion*'s back. It had slipped its mooring cleat.

I pulled my mask from my mouth and shouted to Dorje with all my might, but the wind stole my words. I clipped my line to the safety rail and hurried out. The other forward coupling arm was bearing a double load now, and it could not last long.

I reached Dorje and pointed. Without a word, he left Kate in my care, and scuttled across to the loose coupling arm. As he pulled it back towards the mooring cleat, there was a snap loud enough to beat the wind's howl, and the second forward coupling arm ripped its cleat right off the *Hyperion*'s back. Dorje held tight as he was lifted high into the air.

I could not leave Kate. We grasped the safety rail, terrified. There was another wrenching shudder and I looked aft to see the two remaining coupling arms tear loose. We were free of the *Saga* now, and I saw her slide off into the sky above us. Dorje, clinging to the mechanical arm, was carried away from us.

There was nothing to do but get back to the crow's-nest. With the ship rolling, we flattened ourselves against her back and crawled, praying the safety rail did not tear loose. Hal and Nadira were waiting to haul us inside.

The wind tearing at our faces, we peered up at the *Sagarmatha*.

'He's all right,' Hal shouted, watching Dorje. 'They're bringing him in.'

I saw that the coupling arm carrying Dorje was slowly being retracted, and when it was alongside the control car, a window opened, and Dorje nimbly leaped inside.

The *Saga* dipped closer, but Hal started bellowing and waving his arm.

'No! Take her up! Take her up!'

They could not have heard his words, but they must have realized the same dreadful fact. It was far too windy to attempt another docking.

The four of us were marooned aboard the *Hyperion*.

18

MAROONED

We slammed the hatch shut and climbed back down to the axial catwalk.

'They'll be back for us as soon as the gale blows itself out,' Hal said.

I said nothing. Nadira and Kate were breathing hard, struggling to keep their balance as the *Hyperion* heaved and trembled. We'd taken her captive only briefly, and now she was free once more and appeared to be revelling in the storm winds. She's been through worse, I told myself. She's spent forty years aloft, pummelled by the sky, and she's survived. Ominous shrieks and groans wafted through the ship like the cries of a tortured man.

'When will the wind die down, do you think?' Kate asked Hal, trying to sound like she was just making polite conversation.

'Could be an hour . . .'

'Oh, that's not so bad.'

'. . . or twelve. Dorje will keep us in sight, but he won't try to dock unless it's safe. If the *Saga* gets wrecked, we're all finished. Is anyone hungry? I think Mrs Ram packed us some sugared almonds and dried fruit.'

The ship lurched to port, and Kate staggered against me.

'We should find somewhere safer to wait this out,' I said. 'What about Grunel's apartments? There are blankets if we get cold.'

'I'd rather not go back there,' Kate said, with surprising firmness.

I looked from her to Hal. 'What happened?'

'Nothing,' Hal said, sounding exasperated. 'Remember the sheet I threw over Grunel? When Kate and I went in, it fell off, and gave her a bit of a fright.'

'It didn't just *fall* off,' Kate objected. 'My back was turned, and I heard a sound like someone *ripping* off the sheet. When I looked around, it was on the floor.'

I felt my scalp prickle.

'Things move aboard a ship,' Hal said. 'Especially in storm conditions.'

'He'll be tap dancing next,' said Nadira.

'Surely there's somewhere else,' Kate insisted. 'Preferably without dead people.'

Had it been left up to me, I would have stayed perched in the crow's-nest. It would be viciously cold, but at least there, I could see the open sky. I dreaded descending further into the ship's darkness.

'Somewhere with windows would be good,' I said. 'That way we can save our torches for night. If it comes to that,' I added, seeing the alarm in Kate's eyes.

'Why not his engineerium?' Nadira said. 'We can finish searching it while we wait.'

'I'm not sure that's a good idea,' I said. 'There's a lot of heavy equipment in there. I wouldn't want any of that ripping free in the storm and crushing us.'

'It looked pretty well tethered to me,' Hal said. 'Nadira's right. We can put our time to good use and check it thoroughly. Seems Grunel spent most of his time squirrelled in there; that's where he'd hide his riches. So far I've found nothing but the contents of the captain's safe. Petty cash and the crew's wages for three months.'

'That's something at least,' I said.

'It's not enough to repair even one of my engines.'

We climbed down the swaying ladder to the keel and worked our way aft, the catwalk pitching beneath us. We entered Grunel's apartment to take as many blankets as we could carry from the linen cupboard. Though we did not enter the actual bedroom, I felt clammy just imagining him sitting on his reclining chair, with his hollow cheeks and watchful eyes. I wondered if his sheet was on or off him.

Back on the catwalk, we stopped near one of the fresh water tanks and managed to chip away some icicles to suck. We were all very thirsty. But the icicles were so bitterly cold against my lips and tongue, it felt hardly worthwhile. We entered the engineerium and turned off our torches. I gazed up worriedly at Grunel's immense telescope-like machine. Though it vibrated slightly in the bad gusts, it seemed anchored solidly to the floor – like every other piece of equipment in the room.

'I wouldn't mind a cup of tea,' Kate said, and sat down with her back against a crate.

Nadira pulled sugared nuts from her rucksack and offered them around.

I handed out blankets, studying the girls' faces, wondering how their strength was holding out.

Hal had walked off. Against one wall he'd found a ladder that ran on a track in front of the shelves. I left Kate and Nadira, and made my way over to him. He tried a few times to climb the ladder but it was rolling back and forth too much. Eventually he gave up with a curse, and decided to forage with both feet on the ground. Really, he should have sat down, but I could tell he was in a dangerous mood. He needed to find something big.

Beyond the ship's hull the wind screeched and whistled and thumped, wanting to be let in.

'I don't think this is going to blow itself out soon,' I said.

'No,' he agreed.

'Would Dorje try to dock at night?' I asked.

'He'd wait till dawn's light.'

He was infuriatingly calm, and I admired him, even as I tried to quell my own growing fear.

'If we're here overnight,' I said, 'it's going to get even colder.'

Hal grunted. 'We're out of the wind at least.'

'I'm worried about the girls. If they start needing oxygen, we'll run out.'

'They can share mine. I don't need it.'

I went back to Kate and Nadira, and told them I was going to make a fire. I needed to be doing something. I broke some crate lids into kindling, and arranged them on a piece of sheet metal. Inside the various crates was plenty of shredded paper and packing sawdust. That would catch fire easily enough.

'You're a good man to have around in a shipwreck,' said Nadira.

'This isn't a shipwreck,' Hal said jovially, taking a blanket and settling down beside Kate. 'We're still skyworthy. All we need to do is keep warm. Now, a trick you learn fast enough on Everest is to stay close and conserve body heat.' He snuggled up beside Kate, and waved for Nadira to come closer. She raised an eyebrow at him.

'Trust me,' Hal said, 'this is standard mountaineering practice. We stay warm, we stay alive.'

Nadira chose to sit beside Kate. Hal heaped more blankets around them. Kate smiled and seemed to be enjoying herself. My pulse beat hard and fast in my ears.

'Come on in, Cruse,' Hal said, 'the more the merrier.'

'Where's the butane torch?' I asked.

'Why? What're you up to?'

'Making a fire.'

Hal shook his head. 'Not with the ship pitching like this. Some embers spill and the fire gets out of control, we're as good as sunk. Anyway, you won't get much of a fire going in this thin air. Smoke is all you'll make.'

I hadn't thought of that. I felt a proper idiot.

'What we can do,' said Hal, 'is make a brew.'

'What's that?' Kate asked.

'It's what we call making water on Everest. Go find a metal can now, and we'll use the torch to melt some ice for drinking water.'

I started scouting around for a likely container, one that didn't already contain some vile-looking chemical sludge. *Make a brew*, I muttered resentfully to myself. *That's what we call it on Everest.* Of course Hal would know all about how to survive at high altitude. He was perfect. He was also right. We needed water. At these altitudes it was very easy to get dehydrated. Sucking snow or ice just wasn't enough.

Beyond the large windows, the sun still blazed, bobbing up and down as the ship cavorted through the storm. Near the enormous telescope machine, my eyes swept across the complicated control panel. I wished I knew what all those buttons and gauges meant. Hal might not give a toss, but I certainly did. I had a feeling that this was the machine Grunel had been labouring over when aloft. From the brass panel I brushed away some frost – and saw a keyhole.

'I think you should see this!' I called out to the others.

They threw off their blankets and joined me. The keyhole looked remarkably similar to the one in the doors to the dead zoo and engineerium.

'Well, isn't this intriguing,' said Hal, casting his eye over the machine's bulky lower regions. 'Big enough for a vault, do you think?'

'You think it's full of money?' I asked, surprised.

'Gold preferably,' remarked Nadira. She was already reaching into her hood to extract her key.

'Can't see hinges anywhere,' Hal commented, shining his light all around the control panel. 'If there's a door, it's well hidden.'

Nadira slid the key into the keyhole. By now she'd learned all its tricks: she twisted and prodded until the key was fully inserted, then gave a complete turn.

All across the machine's surface, lights silently blinked on. I heard a sudden gurgle of water and traced the sound to a pair of broad pipes running from the machine, up the wall to a large mounted tank.

'Should be frozen,' I muttered.

'What's it doing?' Hal said, with the utmost suspicion.

Light suddenly filled the room as the hanging lamps along the ceiling snapped on. A drill came to life and made us all jump. I rushed over and managed to turn it off. There was a sharp crackling sound: along the baseboards was an electric heater, its coils slowly turning orange as they warmed up.

'He's got electric hearths,' I said. There must have been others placed all round the chamber, for already I could feel a welcome current of milder air moving past my pinched face.

I rushed to the engineerium's door and peered out into the dark catwalk.

'Nothing's on out here,' I called back. Whatever was powering the lamps and heaters, it was confined to the engineerium.

'It must be a generator,' Kate said.

'But where's it getting its fuel?' Hal demanded.

'Some kind of battery,' I suggested.

'No battery holds its charge for forty years.'

'This one seems to,' Nadira said.

I'd done some reading on batteries in my electrics class. Most of those built in the early days were not very efficient, and they tended to give off poisonous fumes. I had a sniff and caught only a faint whiff of mangoes, which I assumed was leaking from the vivarium.

'Well, we've got light and heat,' Hal said. 'And that's the first bit of welcome news all day.'

Hal asked me to go and close the door so we didn't lose the heat. I made sure there was a handle and keyhole on the inside, but even so, I felt a bit anxious when it slid shut. I didn't trust Grunel's doors, and dreaded the idea of being entombed aboard his dead ship.

The heaters were working hard, and already I could feel the change. It was still well below zero, but there is all the difference in the world between minus sixty and minus twenty.

Once Hal knew the machine wasn't a bank vault, he lost interest. He set about searching the engineerium again. Even as the ship continued to shudder and jolt, I knew we all felt more cheerful now that the room was well lit and warming up. Nadira didn't look so pale. Kate seemed tired, but in good spirits. I was heartened to know we would not be facing the coming night with just our electric torches.

Nadira had been exploring the engineerium, and came to a stop at the phrenology machine, with its many spidery arms.

'Thinking of having a go?' Kate asked pleasantly.

'You know, I think we should *both* have a go,' Nadira said with a smile. 'What do you say? Since I'm no good at fortune telling, maybe this can help predict our futures. Just for a lark!'

Nadira was being awfully friendly, but I wondered if there was just a hint of a challenge in her invitation. Certainly, I wouldn't have wanted to put my head in Grunel's contraption. But Kate was never one to back away from anything.

'Why not?' she said brightly, walking over.

'We have better ways to pass the time,' said Hal, sounding annoyed. 'Cruse, what about that water?'

'I don't imagine this will take long,' Kate said. 'Matt, can you come crank it up for us, please?'

'Who's going first?' I asked, grasping the handle and turning.

'After you,' said Nadira to Kate.

'No, no, I insist,' said Kate, ushering Nadira towards the machine.

The stool adjusted up or down by spinning the seat. It must have had some kind of sensor, for the moment Nadira sat, a clockwork ticking emanated from inside the machine. Its many mechanical arms, each tipped with callipers, slowly unfolded, circling Nadira's head. There was something decidedly menacing about them.

'Stay very still,' I said, reading the instructions on the side of the machine.

With a sudden jerk, the first set of callipers came down, and the two points jerkily adjusted themselves to the width of Nadira's head and slowly began to revolve.

'It tickles actually,' said Nadira, biting her lips and trying not to giggle.

The first set of callipers withdrew. The mechanical spider above her head turned one way, then another, and a second pair of instruments dropped down and gripped another part of Nadira's head. This time she winced as the revolving points tweaked her ear. The callipers lifted away and now a thick rubber cap descended and covered the top of her skull. Through the rubber I could see odd little knuckles kneading Nadira's head quite firmly.

'It feels like someone's got their fingers all over me,' she said.

'Are you all right?' I asked.

'It's rather nice. Could be a bit more gentle though.'

While the rubber cap was massaging her skull, two more pairs of callipers dropped down on either side of her head. For a moment they looked like they were going to veer into her ears, but at the last second they twirled off to one side and began measuring her temples. One arm of the callipers caught in her hair and began twisting it into a knot, tighter and tighter.

'Ow!' she cried, pulling away and getting jabbed on the other side. The rubber cap seemed to tighten its grip on her skull, the metal knuckles kneading more furiously than before.

I tried to untangle her, but the little prongs were stubborn and surprisingly strong and I could not stop them turning and yanking her hair.

Nadira struggled to stand, but the rubber cap pushed down hard and kept her locked in her seat.

'I've had enough,' she said. 'Turn it off.'

Hal, watching from a distance, just laughed, but I could tell Nadira was alarmed. Kate and I started tugging and pulling at the arms of the mechanical spider, and trying to pry the cap off her head.

'It hurts!' Nadira cried out. 'Get it off me!'

Hal stopped laughing and ran over to lend a hand. None of us really knew what we were doing, but suddenly, Nadira came flying off the seat. The mechanical arms jerked to and fro resentfully, the callipers jabbing the air, searching for their victim.

'I can't see this catching on in a big way,' I said. 'Are you all right?'

Nadira was rubbing her head, touching her ears, making sure everything was still there. She turned and kicked the machine. There was a busy clicking sound from somewhere inside, and a ribbon of ticker tape shot out and landed at Kate's feet. She picked it up.

'It's your personality assessment,' she said, eyes flicking over the scroll.

Nadira snatched it from Kate's hand. 'It looks like you get a score out of ten in different categories. Vitativeness: nine. What's vitativeness?'

'Love of life and power to resist illness, I believe,' said Kate. 'That's a very good score.'

'Benevolence: seven.'

'Who does better than that?' said Hal, amused.

'Self-esteem: eight. Tune, ten. I never knew I was musical!' said Nadira, pleased. 'Secretiveness . . .' She trailed off.

'Ten,' said Hal, peering over her shoulder. 'No surprise there.'

Nadira took a step away and kept reading. 'Individuality: ten. Cautiousness: three. Combativeness: nine.' She looked over and gave me a wink. 'Well, what did you expect from a pirate's daughter? Hope: eight. Amativeness. What's that?'

Kate actually blushed. 'I think it has something to do with your attractiveness to the opposite sex.'

'Ten,' said Nadira, smiling modestly.

'Gosh,' said Kate, 'I'd say you scored awfully well.'

'It's just a silly machine,' said Nadira, folding away her piece of paper. 'Are you going to have your go?'

'Absolutely not,' I insisted. 'The thing's murderous.'

Kate looked crestfallen. 'I really did want to see my scores.'

'I suppose Matt's right,' said Nadira. 'What a shame.'

'Load of nonsense,' said Hal. 'Cruse, there's a bucket over there, perfect for water. Grunel's machine is making me thirsty.'

And me as well, for within its vast metal innards the contraption made a faint but constant gurgle. The bucket Hal pointed out was full of sand. I suppose this was what Grunel had used as a fire extinguisher before he invented his own. I banged out the sand in a solid block.

'Someone needs to go with you,' Hal said, as I headed for the door.

'I'm fine.'

'No one goes alone. Kate, go with him. I'd send Nadira, but with all that amativeness, she and Cruse might get up to mischief.'

Hal chuckled at his own joke, but Kate could not have looked less amused. She grabbed her torch from her rucksack and walked over, staring past me. I felt very glum. The engineerium's vault-like door opened easily, and I left it ajar as we ventured out on to the catwalk.

After the lighted room, the darkness and cold were even more oppressive. In silence we walked towards the water tanks. I used the sharp end of my pry bar to chisel at the ice. Kate picked up the pieces and put them in the bucket.

All around us the ship was alive with sounds I did not recognize. I felt as if the storm had awoken the ship and ghostly crew. My hair raised at the sound of an odd clanking.

'What was that?' Kate asked, trying to sound merely interested.

'Just a loose elevator chain,' I said.

'What about that wheezing noise?'

'Air blowing against an intake vent.'

'Are you lying to me?'

'As best I can, yes.'

'You don't need to lie to me,' she said testily, 'I'm not a child.'

'Fine. I have no idea what these sounds are. That thumping noise? For all I know it might be the dead, marching towards us.'

The ship heeled over, righted herself sharply, and somewhere, a door slammed shut with the force of an explosion.

Kate clutched my arm. I clutched back.

'The wind,' I told her.

'It sounded like it came from Grunel's apartment.'

'He's just trying to stay fit.'

She did not laugh.

'Don't be scared,' I said, touching her shoulder. 'I'd never let any harm come to you.'

She turned away from me. 'You're a liar,' she said tightly.

'What do you mean?'

For a moment she said nothing. 'I saw you. Kissing her.'

I was glad she had her back to me, for the face I wore must have been the stupidest, gape-mouthed thing in the world.

'But . . . I asked if you were angry with me, and you never said anything!'

She turned to me, eyes flashing. 'Of course I saw you kissing her. I was halfway up the ladder! How could I have missed it?'

'I didn't hear you!'

'I'm not surprised. You seemed thoroughly engrossed.'

'And what about you and Hal?' I said, starting to feel some indignation of my own. 'The dancing, all the compliments and cosy little chats!'

'Why not? I could see the way you looked at Nadira. Even before you kissed her.'

'She kissed me, actually.'

'Perhaps I should've let Hal kiss me.'

'You wanted him to?'

'He's very appealing.'

'Maybe you should marry him then,' I said recklessly. 'Or has he already proposed? He means to take you for his wife.'

'Take me for his wife?' Kate said with a laugh, which I hoped was disdainful. 'He said that?'

I nodded miserably.

'As if I had no say in the matter?' she exclaimed.

'And what would you say?' I couldn't stop myself asking.

The ship lurched and groaned around us. I waited for her answer.

'I'd say no,' she said.

I started to smile.

'I have no intention of marrying anyone just now,' she added. 'Least of all a wretch like you.'

'I'm sorry,' I said.

'It's not your fault you're attracted to her. She's very beautiful.'

I shook my head. 'It's you I crave.'

'Then why've you been avoiding me?'

'I've just been busy. And you've been so unfriendly. I thought you'd lost interest in me.'

'You're such an idiot. I was just trying to make you jealous.'

'It worked.'

Her face lit up. 'Did it? I was never sure. Were you utterly miserable?'

'Utterly.'

'So was I.'

I took her hand. 'If my heart were a compass, you'd be north.'

'That,' she said, 'is a very romantic thing to say. But it seems the needle swings a bit to Nadira too.'

'A little magnetic disturbance,' I said. 'Nothing more.'

'She scored a perfect ten, Matt.'

'You'd have scored eleven. Anyway, what about you and Hal?'

'I do hope he proposes!'

'Kate!'

'Only so I could say someone's proposed to me. You know the answer's no.'

'Just for now?'

'Just for ever. He's a bit of a bully at heart.'

'Old Hal's not so bad,' I said, feeling incredibly generous.

'He's a natural leader,' she said. 'They're all arrogant. They need to be.'

I was suddenly so happy I put my arms around her and pulled her furclad body against mine. 'I've really missed you,' I said.

'Likewise.'

It was not the most satisfying kiss. Our faces were numb with cold, our lips chapped, but it did not matter. I was just so glad to have her close and breathe her in. Better than oxygen she was.

'We should get back,' I said reluctantly.

The ice made surprisingly little water once it was melted. But it was enough for each of us to slake our thirst. Now that I knew Kate and I were all right again, nothing seemed so bad – not the ship's violent rocking, not the fact that our treasure hunt had so far brought us next to nothing. As soon as the wind died down, the *Saga* would be back and take us off – and what happened after that, I did not care to think about.

Hal set us all to work, searching different areas of the engineerium. He looked a bit weary, and did not seem as big as before. As the room warmed up, everyone was pulling off their hoods and gloves, and unbuttoning their sky suits a bit. My toes were starting to thaw. It felt almost balmy. I was busy checking through some crates when a hissing sound pulled my gaze to the aerozoans' vivarium. Inside, water was spraying against the glass, running down in rivulets that melted the frost. Kate had noticed it too. Together we ventured to the door and cautiously pulled it open. We peered inside. The ceiling here was dotted with small sprinklers, now vigorously spinning and sending a dense mist through the chamber.

'That makes sense,' said Kate. 'Every living thing needs water. He'd have to water them in captivity.'

The sprinklers turned off. They must have been on some kind of clockwork mechanism.

'How do you think they got their water in the wild?' she asked.

'Probably rain clouds,' I replied. 'Do you suppose they froze to death, trapped up here?'

Kate was shaking her head. 'Remember those bugs I collected? They weren't frozen. The aerozoans must produce the same kind of anti-freezing chemical.'

'They'd keep getting food through the vents,' I said.

Kate nodded. 'But if the sprinklers didn't work, they'd eventually dehydrate and die.'

It was good to be talking with her like this again, puzzling over things, just like old times. She was so curious, and full of wonder. Making sure no one was watching, I took her hand in mine, and felt her fingers squeeze back. And I thought: *home*. It took me completely by surprise. But I suppose that once you bid farewell to your first home, you're always looking for another – that place where you can feel happy and strong and at your best. For three years I'd called the *Aurora* home. Now that I lived in Paris, it was not the city itself that was home. It was Kate.

Grunel's machine gave us light and heat, but it could not make the air any less thin. We'd been aboard the *Hyperion* more than eight hours now, and night was coming on. As the temperature outside plunged, the heaters struggled just to keep the engineerium at freezing. We were all exhausted.

A few hours earlier, Kate had asked Hal if she could go to the dead zoo and itemize Grunel's collection. Grudgingly, he'd given her half an hour. I'd accompanied her, and held the torch as she hurriedly scribbled details about the cretaures in the display cases. Her portable camera, it turned out, was useless in the intense cold. When she tried to take a photograph of the Yeti, the shutter wouldn't even open. Though Kate had complained bitterly that it wasn't nearly enough time, when the half hour was up we were both shivering violently and Kate could barely hold her pencil. We'd retreated to the comparative warmth of the engineerium.

Now, huddled under blankets with the others, I noticed that Kate and Nadira were taking more frequent sips of their tanked air. Hal had not touched his oxygen, nor had I mine. I worried we might run out before we were rescued. We all had dry coughs by now, though Nadira's was the worst.

We needed sleep desperately. I volunteered to take the first two-hour watch. Kate and Nadira put their masks on, and slept. Hal slept too, without oxygen, coughing and mumbling in his dreams. The sprinklers in the vivarium came on every half hour, melting the frost that was constantly reforming on the glass. I had a clear view of the dead aerozoans, drifting listlessly. The storm slackened some, but still the ship moaned and muttered. I was glad of the lights.

I wished I'd brought Grunel's diary with me. I would've liked to look at his sketches of the floating city. His giant machine made an ominous creak, and I glanced over at it, still worried it might rip free from its moorings and squish us as we slept.

If Hal hadn't bundled away those blueprints so quickly, we might have known how this machine actually worked. I got up to examine its lights and instruments, and listened to the constant burble of water through the pipes. It seemed to be circulating the water to and from the great tank mounted on the wall. The generator gave off heat, too, like the side of a pot-bellied stove.

The hydrium smell I'd noticed earlier was stronger now. I didn't think it was coming from the vivarium. Sniffing, I tracked it to the back of Grunel's machine. A thick hose ran from the machine to a vent in the ship's hull. Some water had frozen against the coupling and cracked the rubber. I heard the hiss of escaping gas and put my nose closer. The smell of ripe mangoes wafted over me. The fissure was a small one, and I didn't think there was much risk of hydrium filling up the entire room and suffocating us, but there was precious little air as it was, and I wasn't taking any chances. I ferreted around the worktables until I found some sealing tape, and wrapped it three times around the crack. The hissing stopped; the smell faded.

This machine produced hydrium, I realized in wonder.

I'd never heard of such a thing. Hydrium came from deep fissures in the earth, and was refined before its use as a lifting gas. Somehow, Grunel had figured out a way to make his own. What else this generator of his did, I could not imagine.

When I woke Hal later for his watch, I told him about it.

'I'd be happier if it made gold,' he said. 'Get some sleep.'

Lying down, I felt the thin air more acutely than before. I was tempted to use some of my tanked oxygen, but wanted to save it for Kate or Nadira if they needed it. It took me quite a while to fall asleep.

I dreamed we were all sleeping in the engineerium, and were woken by a dreadful honking sound. It came from the enormous coffin. I was frozen with terror, but Kate and Nadira and Hal seemed calm enough, and said someone must be inside. They told me to go and let the poor fellow out. I did not want to go, but without even moving my feet, I found myself upright and skimming over the floor to the coffin. The honks had become more and more frequent and urgent, like the sounds of a giant and demented goose.

I knew what I would find.

I heaved up the lid, and there he was again, the same malformed creature I'd seen behind the door. He was half encased in ice, and trying to speak, but his throat and mouth were frozen and he could not make any words. I wrenched myself from the dream and woke up with a shout bottled in my throat.

Kate was staring at me.

'You made a very alarming sound,' she said. 'Nightmare?'

I nodded, not wanting to describe it, for it still hovered with frightening clarity in my mind. I looked over at the enormous coffin, its lid closed. The lights and heaters were still running. The machine blinked and gurgled water.

'The wind's died down. And we're rising,' I said. A ship's movements had never been a secret to me; I'd always been able to tell when she was climbing, descending, turning, no matter how slight the motion.

'I hadn't even noticed,' said Kate.

'It's very gentle,' I said, not wanting to alarm her. Still, I wondered how long this had been going on. With every thirty metres, the air thinned even more. I looked at Nadira, still asleep under her mask. Her breathing was fast and shallow.

'Hal told me to turn off her tank at half past three,' Kate said. 'But I didn't have the heart.'

I nodded, but was calculating how much oxygen we had left. The longer we stayed up high, the more we'd come to rely on tanked air. I couldn't quite understand why I didn't feel dizzier. I did take longer to do things, every step an effort, but I was still all right. Kate looked very tired, the skin beneath her eyes smudged with purple.

'How are you feeling?' I asked.

'I wish I knew more chemistry,' she said.

I had to laugh. 'That must be very distressing.'

'I'm just trying to figure out how they do it. The aerozoans.' I saw she had one of her little notebooks out. At that moment I felt very fond of them; they seemed almost as much a part of her as her hair or imperious nostrils.

'Its diet seems so small. A little food. A little water. Yet it produces enough energy to keep itself alive; it produces hydrium, and also a huge amount of electricity – to keep away predators, I suppose. I wonder if it somehow draws energy from the sun. Really, it's a perfect little machine.'

If she hadn't used the word machine, I probably wouldn't have made the connection. At last I understood.

'He got the idea from them,' I said, pointing to the aerozoan Grunel had collared with wires. 'That's why he kept them. He was studying them to find out how they produced so much electricity. And he copied them!'

'What's going on?' Hal said, squinting over at us.

'Matt's having a brainstorm,' said Kate.

'The machine,' I said excitedly. 'I've figured out what it does.'

I expected Hal to turn over and go back to sleep, but he gave a sigh and sat up.

'He uses the sun. He collects the light with that big telescope, just like the aerozoans must collect the sun's energy. Something happens inside there. It's like a giant generator, but it only needs air and water to make an electrical charge. I have no idea how. Then as a by-product, it makes heat, more water, and hydrium.'

'Hydrium?' Kate asked.

'There's an exhaust pipe at the back that vents hydrium. And the water just keeps going round and round to keep the process going.'

'It's a big battery,' Hal said with a shrug.

'No, not just a battery,' I said. 'It makes power out of nothing. Well, not nothing. Just air and water!'

'Well, I'm glad the old fart came up with something useful,' said Hal, getting up and stretching.

'You don't understand, Hal. This is an eternal supply of electricity. Enough to run engines. Enough to power tools and generators. And enough extra hydrium to lift a platoon of airships.'

'Or an aerial city,' said Kate.

'Exactly!' I said. 'This machine is Grunel's treasure!'

But Hal wasn't listening. He was looking over my shoulder.

'Something moved,' he said.

We all turned to the vivarium. The four aerozoans dangled limply in the air.

'They always move a little,' I said.

Then one of them flinched – and I flinched with it. This was no shifting with the wind. The creature's gauzy apron flared, then contracted sharply, and it jetted higher. Its tentacles flexed.

'Oh my goodness,' breathed Kate.

'They're supposed to be dead!' Hal shouted. 'You told me they were dead!'

'It's the water,' Kate said, excited. 'I don't believe it! It must be anhydrobiosis.'

'What're you talking about?' I demanded.

'Some creatures put themselves into hibernation when there's not enough water. I read about this. It's called anhydrobiosis. And then when there's ample water, they revivify. But this is remarkable. Usually it only happens with very small, primitive organisms.'

'Then let's stop watering them!' Hal said.

'They're not machines,' Kate told him. 'You can't just turn them off.'

I ran to the glass door to make sure it was securely shut. It was. The aerozoan was now jetting about the vivarium like an airborne squid. It nudged one of the others, and seconds later, that one jerked to life too.

'This is fascinating,' Kate said.

A few seconds later, the third aerozoan jerked to life. Only one didn't stir: the one harnessed by Grunel. The other three circled round it. The biggest flew in close,

347

squatted against it, and ripped away some of its withered flesh with its beak. The other two aerozoans closed in as well, and started feeding. There was a great deal of fighting between them as they jockeyed for space, lashing out at one another with their tentacles.

'After being so long in hibernation, they're bound to be voraciously hungry,' explained Kate.

'I could've done without the voracious bit,' I said.

'What's going on?' Nadira asked, sitting up, only half awake.

'Kate's pets have woken up,' Hal said, taking out his pistol. 'But not for long.'

'Put that away!' Kate said. 'They're safely behind glass.'

'Don't do it, Hal,' I said. 'Shatter the glass, and we'll have all of them out in the open. Save your bullets.'

Reluctantly he holstered his gun. Nadira watched the aerozoans with a mixture of fascination and horror. Kate was entranced. In a matter of minutes they had stripped the dead one, leaving only its balloon sac. Then they pierced that with their beaks, tearing it to shreds as it sagged slowly to the floor. Even with a glass wall between us, I felt sickened being so close to them. Their feeding noises were muted – a rapid clicking of their beaks, the rustle and slap of membranes and tentacles jostling.

'Have any of you seen the floating eggs?' Kate asked.

'Likely they got eaten,' I said dully.

The aerozoans seemed to be sated, for they had stopped foraging about the vivarium floor, and drifted up to the ceiling. Their balloon sacs, I noticed, were fuller, as though they'd already produced more hydrium for themselves.

I wouldn't have noticed the break in the glass if an aerozoan hadn't drifted right past it.

'Up there,' I blurted in alarm, pointing. 'There's a hole!'

It was small and jagged, no bigger than a billiard ball. The aerozoans were too big to fit through, but the glass around it was cracked and weakened by ice, and I knew the power of the creature's tentacles. I ran to get the sealing tape. The maintenance scaffolding that ran around Grunel's telescope was almost flush with the vivarium wall, and I figured I could reach the hole from there. I started up the spiral stairs.

'I'm going to patch it,' I said. I reached the scaffolding, puffing hard. As I leaned out over the railing towards the glass, the aerozoans did not move, but I noticed that their tentacles drew up a little closer towards their bodies, as if tensed. I tore off a strip of tape with my teeth and leaned way over to patch the hole.

'Matt! Watch out!'

From the floor, Nadira was pointing at something behind me. I whirled, instinctively dropping to a crouch. Above me was a small translucent shimmer – a tiny aerozoan. It didn't seem to have any dark designs on me, for it was bobbing away, gossamer apron flapping, tentacles waggling like a baby's chubby fingers. It was no bigger than a small jellyfish, but I didn't care how harmless it looked. I wanted it far away.

'It must have hatched,' Kate called up.

And found its way out through the hole. How many eggs had there been? I tried to remember. They were all in a cluster. Eight or nine maybe? Cautiously I scanned the room, wondering if any others had hatched and escaped.

Near the top of the telescope, I saw the glimmer of balloon sacs and tentacles.

'There are three more,' I yelled.

Taking my piece of tape I leaned out to seal the hole in the vivarium. A gust of warm mango hit me in the face, and a split second later, a tentacle lashed against the vivarium's wall, centimetres from my face. I heard a crack and recoiled. An aerozoan billowed against the glass, tentacles writhing.

'Get down from there, Cruse,' shouted Hal. 'You're just making it angry.'

The glass now bore a network of hairline cracks. The tentacle struck again. This time, glass splintered and the hole doubled in size. The creature's tentacle shot clear through, getting slashed against the sharp edges. It pulled back, but the tip remained in the hole, delicately tapping the edges as if mapping it.

'Matt!' Kate called, 'I really think you ought to come down!'

I couldn't have agreed more. I backed towards the stairs, for I wanted to keep my eye on the big one in the vivarium. To my relief, it seemed to lose interest in me, and sailed away. Then it stopped. It turned. It jetted straight for the glass, stretching itself as long and skinny as a spear. I cursed under my breath and started running. The aerozoan gave one last great contraction of its apron and tentacles, compressed itself into a tight bundle, and soared clean through the hole, over my head and into the engineerium.

'Everyone out!' Hal was shouting. 'Get to the door!'

I hurtled off the spiral stairs and rushed to join the retreat. We took nothing, just ran for the catwalk. Hal had his pistol at the ready and was trying to take aim. The aerozoan swelled back to its normal size and jetted up to the ceiling amongst the cables and pulleys. For a second I lost sight of it. Then it moved, and I saw its dangling tentacles sweeping towards us fast.

'Out, out!' Hal shouted, wielding his pistol.

'Don't shoot!' I yelled. 'You'll pierce the gas cells.'

Hal took a shot anyway, and missed, the bullet whistling through the ship's innards.

I rushed Nadira and Kate ahead of me through the doorway, and then turned to see where Hal was. He was intent on taking another shot. One of the aerozoan's tentacles hit a circular saw, and the electric current brought it briefly to life, sparks flying off its metal surface.

'Hal, come on!' I ran back to grab him and haul him out of the room, yanking the door shut behind us. It slid into place with a well-oiled hiss, and we were plunged into total darkness. The cold came upon us like a hammer's blow.

Only Nadira had had the presence of mind to snatch up a torch. We stood there in the pale light, shaking and panting, numbly pulling up our hoods and fastening buttons. We still had our sky suits, but in our panic to flee, we'd left behind our rucksacks, our gloves – and all the oxygen tanks. No one needed to mention any of this. We were all thinking it. We knew we could not go back inside.

Kate slipped her hand into mine. I squeezed back.

'It's all right,' I said, 'it's nearly dawn. The *Saga* should be coming for us soon.'

'At first light, we'll be back aboard,' Hal said. 'A couple of hours at most. The wind's lost all her puff.'

'Let's go to Grunel's apartments, and get as warm as we can,' I said, my teeth starting to chatter.

Kate did not object this time. After the aerozoans, our phantom fears seemed far less threatening.

'Good idea,' said Hal. 'There are windows. We'll have some light soon.'

Wearily, we made our way forward. My nostrils crackled with the cold. My face felt brittle as china. I pulled my hands up inside my sleeves, hoping to ease the icy pain that coursed through them.

The windows in Grunel's quarters let in some star- and moonlight, and also the glow along the eastern horizon. We did not venture into the bedroom, but settled in the starboard lounge. I fetched all the remaining blankets from the linen cupboard. Hal draped a huge rug over the furniture and made a kind of tent for us, insulated with cushions. We huddled together, trying to keep the cold at bay.

We were all too dispirited to speak. Even Hal seemed completely exhausted. My heart beat faster than usual, strained but undefeated by the meagre air.

I did not know if we actually slept, or merely all lapsed into a kind of semi-conscious stupor. I was aware of everyone's laboured breathing. I was aware of the cold gripping my face and feet and hands. And yet I could not keep the image of Grunel's machine from my mind. Hal hadn't understood how important it was. If only we had the blueprints. Where had Hal sent them? Half awake, I slid out from my blankets and made my way to Grunel's bedroom. The door was closed. I opened it. Inside I could make out only shadows. I saw the dark form of Theodore Grunel, hunched over in his chaise longue. I went to the message tubes.

Beneath the outgoing tube was a little row of buttons with the names of all the rooms where you could send messages. I found the button that was still pressed in.

Anger and disappointment gripped me.

Of all the places Hal could have sent the blueprints: he had sent them straight to the engineerium.

19

THE PROMETHEUS ENGINE

As I left Grunel's bedroom, a ship's horn blared in the distance. The long blast was followed by two shorter ones. I hurried back to the lounge. Everyone was stirring, woken by the sound. I started scraping frost from the window, my fingers so cold I could scarcely move them: they seemed more claw than hand.

'That's the *Saga*,' Hal said.

I expected him to leap up, but he stood slowly, as if dizzy. When he reached the window, he helped me clear a viewing hole. The cloudless sky looked like it had been carved from ice, and was just beginning to show the first signs of colour. The *Sagarmatha* sailed towards us, the rising sun directly behind her, setting her metalwork ablaze. In all my life I'd never been so glad to see a ship.

'Thank God,' Hal murmured.

I couldn't wait to get aboard her. It wasn't food I longed for. I would go straight to the shower and let the warm water fall over my head and shoulders. It would stream down my arms and unlock my knuckles.

It would pool at my feet, thawing my toes. Afterwards I would climb into my bunk. I would put on my oxygen mask and let it send me into a deep oblivious sleep.

Nadira and Kate joined us at the window, both puffing as if they'd been running.

'Oh good,' said Nadira, and then started coughing.

'Are you all right?' I asked her.

She waved me away. 'My throat's just dry,' she croaked. 'I'm fine.'

'We should be docked in less than an hour,' Hal said, rubbing his temples. 'This has been a right fiasco. Two days and all we've done is play with Grunel's toys. It's his gold I want.'

'There might not be any gold,' I said. 'Grunel came up here to finish work on his machine.'

'It won't fit aboard the *Saga*.'

'But the blueprints will. You sent them to the engineerium.'

Hal was silent for a moment, realizing what he'd done.

'We need to rest up first,' he said. 'Then we'll come back with some proper firepower and finish off those bloody squids. I want those blueprints.'

'Why?' Nadira asked, and suddenly I realized she didn't know anything about what the machine really did. Back in the engineerium, she'd been asleep when I had my brainstorm.

'It makes electricity from air and water and sunlight,' I told her. 'Power from nothing. An unlimited supply.'

Nadira nodded slowly. 'That's worth more than a shipload of gold.'

'It better be,' Hal said, and turned back to the *Saga*. His eyes widened in alarm.

I looked. The sun had climbed higher now, and out of its glare materialized another ship. At first all I could make out was her hazy silhouette but as she pulled closer, fast, her lines grew sharp and large and powerful. I squinted at her flank, looking for markings, but saw none. It didn't matter – I recognized her. Rath's ship from the Heliodrome. I wondered if the *Sagarmatha* had even noticed her against the sun's blaze.

'No . . .' Hal whispered, and then gave a great shout. 'No!'

Swift and sure, the ship closed on the *Sagarmatha*. Her nose dipped pugnaciously, like a bull charging, then she skidded slightly as she turned broadside. I caught a flash of light from two hatches on her flank and saw cannons jut forward. Quick coronas flared from the iron snouts and at the same moment a thunderclap cracked fissures in the glacial sky.

'Did they hit her?' Kate cried.

The ship fired a second volley at the *Saga*. It was hard to tell what was hitting and what was missing – I just heard the cannon's thunderclaps and then the *Saga* was listing and sinking. There was no smoke, but I saw that her hull was crumpled amidships. Her gas cells had been pierced and her hydrium was gushing into the sky. She fell fast, right past the *Hyperion*, close enough that I could see a smudge of frantic movement in the control car. And then she was gone.

'Marjorie!' Kate gasped. Her hands flew to her face and she burst into tears.

I felt as if my lungs had been trampled. My heart beat so quickly I feared it would run away from me altogether. Hal was staring right at me, but didn't see me. I knew he was furiously calculating what Dorje and his crew would be doing. We started talking at the same time.

'They missed her fuel tanks,' he said, 'or she would have blown.'

'The control car was intact,' I said.

'Her fins were fine,' he said, 'I'm sure of that.'

'I didn't see her engine cars—'

'They didn't get hit. She's got power, and helm.'

'They breached the hull, but it didn't look too bad.'

'Two or three gas cells torn,' Hal said, 'no more.'

'You said she had plenty of compressed hydrium in reserve—'

'If they can patch her fast enough—'

'She was falling fast.'

'Dorje put her into a dive,' Hal said. 'To get away from their cannons.' He did not sound entirely certain, and I hoped he was right.

We stopped and watched the other ship as it sailed for us. Those wretches would not have an easy time docking: the wind was brisk, and the *Hyperion* lively in the wind.

Kate was still crying, gasping in the thin air. I wanted

to calm her. I took her shoulders and leaned my hooded head against hers. 'They may be all right,' I said.

'How did they find us?' Kate asked.

'They knew exactly where we were,' Hal said grimly.

He was staring hard at Nadira, the muscles of his jaw rippling dangerously. 'Secretiveness: ten,' he said.

Nadira just shook her head, breathing hard, mute.

'Hal,' I said.

'She's been one of them all along, you idiot! She led them to us.' He seized Nadira by the shoulder and shook her. 'Did you raise them on the *Saga*'s wireless while we all slept? Give them our coordinates?'

I was worried he might strike her so I stepped between them.

'Nadira,' I said, 'it's not true, is it?'

I was not proud of doubting her, but I couldn't help it. I stared her straight in the eyes, and was glad of the anger and defiance I saw there.

'No,' she said, and then glared at Hal. 'No!'

'Then how did they find us?' he demanded.

'Hal,' I said. 'they've got expensive toys aboard, you said so yourself. They might even have an echolocator. Even after we killed their homing beacon, they could have found us if the range was good. Or they could have come upon us by sheer luck.'

Hal stared at Nadira, his nostrils flaring and contracting. 'I'm watching you,' he said.

Nadira turned away in disgust. 'The thin air's starving your brain,' she muttered.

'They'll be aboard soon,' I reminded them. 'We have an hour, no more. We should try to raise the *Saga* on the wireless.'

Some of the anger leeched out of Hal's face. 'There's no power,' he said.

'We've got one torch. We might be able to use the batteries.'

He nodded. 'Good. Let's do it then.'

We were exhausted and half frozen, but we moved as swiftly as we could. We reached the keel catwalk, then climbed down the ladder to the control car. I hadn't even noticed the wireless gear on our first visit, and I was dismayed by what I saw now. It should have occurred to me sooner: the equipment was forty years old. The radio was little more than a transmitter and spark key for telegraphing messages.

'This is a dead loss,' said Hal. 'You can't even talk over it.'

'I know Morse code, remember?' I told him. 'It's one of the useless things they teach at the Academy.'

Hal snorted. Nadira started fumbling the dry cells out of her torch. I found the telegraph's ancient battery, and with my numb hands pulled the wires loose. I showed Nadira how to hold them to the torch batteries.

There was a bright flicker from the tuning dial, and a crackle of static from the headphones. After forty years it still worked.

'Whenever the crew's separated, Dorje and I have an emergency frequency,' Hal said, turning the dial for me. 'No one else uses it.'

I put the headphones over my ears. How long the batteries would last, I didn't know. Not long probably. I hoped the antenna was still intact below the control car. The spark key was near frozen, and I tapped at it to loosen it up.

Nearby was a pad of frosty paper, and a pencil, which I pulled towards me. I was nervous and wanted to write my message out first so I'd make no mistake while coding it. Once done, I started tapping.

Saga. Cruse here. Reply.

I was sure I muddled a few letters, but hoped the message would be understandable. Could they hear it in the control car? Was Dorje even there? If he wasn't, surely someone would fetch him. But likely it was all chaos aboard ship, and maybe everyone was patching madly, trying to stave off a crash.

I sent the message a second time, then a third.

Only static played against my ears.

'Save the battery,' I said. 'There's no reply.'

'They've got their hands full, I reckon,' said Hal.

'We can try again later.'

He nodded, and for a moment no one said anything, because we were all thinking the worst.

From overhead came the dull drone of engines, as Rath's ship tried to lock on.

'They'll be aboard soon,' Hal said.

'They won't know we're here,' said Nadira. 'They'll

think we were on the *Sagarmatha*. That's good for us.'

'Except we've left all our things in the engineerium,' I said. 'They'll go and find our gear, and the lights and heat on, and everything cosy – we may as well bang a gong and offer a hot meal.'

'They go in there,' said Hal, 'and that aerozoan might finish them off for us.'

'We need to get our things back,' I said. 'We need the oxygen.'

I hadn't wanted to say it, but there seemed no time now for delicacy. Kate was struggling, but it was Nadira I was most worried about. Her breathing was fast and shallow, and she was coughing more and more. Unless she had some oxygen, she'd get even worse. And if the *Hyperion* continued to rise, we would all need tanked air before long.

'I don't fancy getting electrocuted,' Hal said.

'Look, if Rath figures out we're here, he'll come looking. We won't have a chance. And there's the blueprints,' I said, sensing that Hal needed a lot of convincing. 'They're in the engineerium. We go in, grab our stuff, grab the blueprints and get out. Then find somewhere to hide until the *Saga* comes back for us.'

The plan sounded good until the last bit. Even if the *Saga* weren't mortally wounded, how could she retrieve us if a pirate gunship lay in wait for her?

'I'd certainly like my gloves back,' said Kate.

'How many bullets do you have?' I asked Hal.

'Four. This is madness.'

'We'll open the door. You'll shoot the aerozoan. We'll get our things, and then wait it out.'

'The bow,' said Hal. 'They'd never look up there, there's no point.'

From overhead came the blunt sounds of coupling arms trying to grab hold of the *Hyperion*'s frame.

'We've got half an hour or less,' Hal said. 'Let's go.'

The distance to the engineerium was not great, but it seemed like a trek across Antarctica. Every few steps, we'd stop and catch our breath. I kept my eye on Kate and Nadira. Aboard the *Flotsam* I had seen what high altitude could do to seasoned airshipmen: their minds strayed, their judgement failed, and they blacked out with scarcely a second's warning. Hal was trying to hide his discomfort, but he looked grey. I wondered how I looked; I certainly felt pinched and parched. A ragtime tune started playing in my head, over and over, and I let its peppy rhythm guide my footsteps.

The door was before us. Hal gripped his gun. I hoped his aim would be true, for doubtless his hands were numb. With difficulty, Nadira turned the key in the lock. The door slid open. We all stood back, and sighed as the room's heat washed over us.

Hal and I peered around the doorframe. I was hoping to see the aerozoan dangling in the centre of the room. I wanted an easy shot for Hal. But I saw nothing. I wasn't so worried about the hatchlings; I figured they were too small to give much of a shock.

Behind the walls of the vivarium were the other two aerozoans, thrashing about. That was good. We just had the one loose. Where – that was the question. I grabbed a loose hunk of ice from the catwalk and tossed it deep into the room. It made a lot of noise as it clattered along the ground, but nothing moved.

I saw our rucksacks and oxygen tanks.

'I could run in and grab it all,' Hal whispered.

'No,' I said, shocked at his recklessness. 'We should stick to the walls, stay away from all the chains and ropes.'

They worried me, for it was hard to tell them apart from the tentacles. One gentle brush, and we'd be finished.

'There it is,' said Nadira, pointing.

She was right. The aerozoan was way over by the vivarium, bobbing up against the ceiling. Its apron rippled hypnotically.

'They don't have eyes do they?' I asked Kate.

'Oh yes,' she said. 'But not like our eyes. If they're anything like jellyfish, they have very simple eyespots on the tips of their tentacles.'

'How much can they see?'

'Probably just light and darkness.'

'Can they hear us?' Hal asked.

'Jellyfish can pick up vibrations. They rely on their tentacles to taste and smell as well.'

'So if we move slowly,' Nadira said, 'it might not notice us.'

'You and Nadira turn off Grunel's machine,' Hal told me, 'and find the message tubes. Kate and I will grab all the gear.'

'Slowly,' I said, and started in, keeping my back to the wall. The others followed. We kept our eyes glued to the aerozoan. It didn't move. I hoped Kate was right, that it didn't even know we were there. As we worked our way around the room, the aerozoan was almost completely hidden around the far corner of the vivarium. I could just see the very top of its squid-shaped balloon sac, rustling near the ceiling.

We crouched behind Grunel's enormous coffin. We were as close as we were going to get to our oxygen tanks and rucksacks. Kate and Hal ran to pick up the gear; Nadira and I headed for Grunel's generator.

At the control panel, Nadira pushed her key into the lock. Turning it off was simpler than turning it on; all it took was an anticlockwise half-turn. Immediately the lights on the console faded; the overhead lamps that illuminated the engineerium blinked off, the gurgle of water petered out.

'Cruse, catch,' Hal said, and tossed me an unlit torch.

The heating coils all along the floor were clanking as they cooled. Already I could feel the temperature plunging. Now to find the message tubes.

'They'll be somewhere against the wall,' I told Nadira. 'I'll check down this way.' We split up, keeping our torch beams low to the ground, lest the aerozoan sense the light.

Mercifully I did not have to look long, for they were not far from Grunel's machine, half hidden behind a small desk. Above the incoming tube, I saw the little green flag raised.

'Found them!' I called softly to Nadira. I could see she was breathless, so I waved her towards Hal and Kate, who were about to head out with the gear. 'Go on, I'll be right there.'

I lifted the hatch and saw the end of the message capsule. As I reached for it, the ship jostled and slewed in the sky, and just before my fingers touched the capsule, it was sucked away from me.

'No!'

I bent down and shone my torch light into the tube, but the capsule was long gone, spirited away into the whistling maze of the pneumatics. The whole system was malfunctioning, the air flowing in all directions depending on the movements and mood of the ship.

I thumped at the wall. I pressed buttons and yanked the tassel pull, vainly hoping the capsule would come jetting into my hands. Kate was at my side, her rucksack slung over her shoulder.

'You all right?'

'It was here, and then it got sucked back in. It could be anywhere!'

I looked over and saw Nadira and Hal halfway to the exit. He gestured impatiently for us to follow. I peered into the empty message tube once more, then turned to head out. After two steps I stopped.

'What's wrong?' Kate asked.

'It's not there.' I was staring at the place where we'd last seen the aerozoan.

'Oh no,' Kate breathed.

Hal and Nadira were already safely through the doorway. I stood frozen with Kate, my eyes roaming everywhere, trying to find the aerozoan.

'Run,' Kate said, but I pulled her back.

'No,' I hissed. 'Look.'

Dead ahead, some tentacles shifted amongst the cables and chains. My eyes lifted. The aerozoan's body hung near the ceiling, cloaked in the shadows. I killed my torch, for fear it would act as a homing beacon.

I took Kate's hand and started stepping backwards for the wall.

'Cruse!' Hal called from the doorway. 'Come on!'

I pointed at the aerozoan and he fell silent. I made a circle with my hand, telling him we were going around. We were halfway, and the aerozoan still seemed unaware of our presence. Maybe it had noticed the draft from the open door, and thought it might escape back to the sky. Maybe it was following the light of Hal's torch.

A sound passed through the ship: the hammer of feet on ladder rungs. We were boarded. Hal heard it too. I saw him pull his pistol and take aim at the aerozoan.

'Hal, no,' I hissed. 'They'll hear!'

For a moment I thought he was going to fire anyway, but he stayed his trigger finger.

The aerozoan inched closer to the doorway, as if intentionally blocking our path.

The footsteps grew louder. I couldn't tell which ladder they were coming down, fore or aft, but they would be at the keel catwalk soon, and find Hal and Nadira in plain sight.

'Go!' I whispered to him. 'Go! We'll meet you up there.'

They disappeared. I looked at Kate.

'It'll be all right,' I said.

Without warning, one of the aerozoan's tentacles silently retracted and whipped out in our direction. It snapped back not one metre from us. Kate gasped. The aerozoan tensed and glided towards us. For a split second, I wondered if we should run for the door, but I did not like our chances. Those tentacles were long. I touched Kate's arm and we stealthily moved back deeper into the room. I dared not make too sudden a movement.

From the catwalk I heard voices and looked around for a place to hide. But the aerozoan seemed to have a pretty good idea of where we were, and stalked us patiently. Maybe it was tracking our wake. Maybe it was tasting us. Its long tentacles nearly brushed the floor. As the tips passed close to metal, sparks flew.

The voices were getting louder. I realized the aerozoan was backing us into a corner. I looked over my shoulder and saw Grunel's coffin. My decision was instant. Three more steps and I grabbed hold of the coffin lid and heaved it up.

'Get in!' I told Kate.

She hesitated for a split second only, then we swung ourselves into the casket. I lowered the lid as gently and quietly as I could. We were in total darkness. The thickness of the coffin and its plush lining muffled all sound. We backed against opposite ends, our legs touching. I could feel Kate's knapsack against my feet.

I turned on the torch, illuminating the silky red interior. Over our heads, we both heard a faint rasping noise.

'Tentacles,' I said, and with a shiver pictured them slithering over the wooden lid.

'This wasn't a good idea,' Kate said.

'I just saved our lives!'

'How are we going to know when it's safe to come out?'

'Well, we'll just have to use Grunel's nifty little grave signalling apparatus, won't we?'

'Ahhhh. You're brilliant.'

'Can you hold the torch?'

As Kate aimed it at the ceiling, I lay flat on my back to examine the controls. Maybe it was being in such confined quarters, but I felt rather flustered by the array of knobs and gears.

'Honestly,' I muttered. 'Look at all this! Do you think someone who's just woken up in a coffin could figure this out?'

'You probably wouldn't be in top form,' Kate agreed.

'It'd be pitch black. You wouldn't be able to see anything.'

'Maybe he meant to add a reading light.'

'Why not throw in a few good books too, in case you had to wait a while?'

I found a knob marked 'periscope' and started turning. I heard the sound of well-oiled metal moving within the wood casing.

'I think I'm raising it,' I said. I figured I only needed to put it up a little way since we weren't buried six feet under. Then I pulled the retractable eyepiece down to my face.

It took a while for my eyes to adjust, for the light in the engineerium was quite dim, and the lens on the periscope gave a strange warped view, as though the room itself was a little planet, everything curving away at the sides. But it did let me see a great deal at once.

'Where's the aerozoan?' Kate asked.

'It's hard to see. It's not like a spyglass. Everything's all bulgy.'

'It's a fish-eye lens. I've used them for photography. Do you want me to have a look?'

'I'm fine. I've spent three years in crow's-nests.'

'I think this swivels the periscope,' Kate said, and I heard her turning something. The room careened suddenly to the left, and I instinctively rolled the other way and whacked my head against the casket.

'Stop that,' I hissed. 'You're going too fast. I can't see anything.'

'Let me have a look,' she said. 'You're hogging.'

'Hogging? We're not sight-seeing. Just keep turning. Slowly.'

I went all the way around the room without seeing the aerozoan. Then, a tip of a tentacle dangled before my eyes.

'It's right over us,' I breathed.

'Oh dear.'

'No, wait, it's moving.' I watched as the aerozoan, looking much fatter and squatter through the odd lens, drifted away from the coffin, back towards the vivarium. Already, the glass walls were frosted, concealing what was inside.

'Shall we make a run for it?' Kate asked.

'Hold on. Swivel me to the right . . . a little more . . . there.'

Through the engineerium's doorway, torch beams swept the catwalk.

'No. They're coming.'

'Are they inside?' she said.

'Not yet.' I watched as the blaze of their lights strengthened. Two figures stopped in the doorway. More were behind them. They seemed enormous as Yetis in their reddish mountaineering garb, fur-rimmed hoods all but concealing their faces. Oxygen masks hung at their throats. The two in front were talking, pointing at the open door.

A third man came forward and inspected the doorway. He wore special lighted spectacles, like a jeweller, and he took his time.

'I think they're checking the door for booby traps,' I whispered to Kate. 'I can't hear what they're saying.'

The walls of the coffin were too thick and well-insulated to let sound in.

'Wait, they're coming in. I wish we could hear them.'

'Grunel had a horn,' said Kate. 'Maybe it also doubled as a listening trumpet.'

'Do you think?'

'Well, it would've been nice to know what people were saying about you at the funeral. What's this here?'

I could scarcely believe it, but Kate was right. Behind a small hatch was a little trumpet which could be pulled down and placed against your ear.

'I want to hear as well,' she said. She started sliding towards me, and I shifted to make room for her.

'Careful,' I whispered.

'What?'

'You nearly tooted the horn.'

'That would be bad. Extremely bad.'

She lay down beside me. It was a tight squeeze.

'Well, isn't this romantic,' I said.

'Side by side in our very own coffin.'

We had a little giggle. Being so near her, I felt absurdly happy. It made no sense, given the peril we were in. It must have been the thin air, finally taking its toll on my brain. I should have been terrified by our predicament, but it seemed far away, as if the walls of the coffin formed our own impervious little world. I leaned closer and kissed her.

We shared the listening trumpet, and I pulled the periscope's eyepiece once more to my face. I was getting the hang of it, and could reach up with a free hand and swivel it myself now. I only hoped the periscope jutting up from the coffin did not catch their attention. I suddenly realized what a conspicuous hiding place this was – a coffin in the middle of a workshop. Anyone would want to have a peek inside.

There were eight of them, walking into the room, laden with gear. My heart sank. Giants they seemed, carrying portable battery packs and tall pole lamps. I could not make out faces yet. They moved slowly, like arctic explorers bogged down in snow. Even with their tanked oxygen, their bodies were struggling with the altitude and thin air. I wondered if they'd climbed too quickly, and hadn't had a chance to acclimatize as we had. We were weak, but without their oxygen, they'd be even weaker. It didn't matter though, because holstered in each of their belts were large pistols.

Their torch beams spun a spider's web of light around the room. I could not see the rogue aerozoan anywhere. I watched all this as I might watch a film in the cinema. I was somewhere else, safe. *You need to be afraid*, a voice inside my head told me, but it was not a very loud voice, and I did not want to listen right now. I was feeling calm and controlled.

A thin man fixed his torch beam on Grunel's huge machine, then turned to the larger man beside him.

'Set the lamps up over here!' the big man shouted to the others.

The sound through the listening trumpet was surprisingly crisp. Grunel was a genius.

The big man turned, and light washed over his face. His ginger goatee was frosted with ice.

'It's Rath,' I said to Kate. I was not surprised, but it still made my guts contract to behold his big, brutal face. 'They seem to know what they're looking for.'

As the crew busily set up the lamps, Rath and the thin man stepped back out of the way, stopping near the coffin. I'd been hoping we could make a break for it – but not now.

The man beside Rath nodded. 'This is it, most certainly,' he said, his voice thin as bone china. He turned. Within his fur hood I saw an elderly frail face and bushy eyebrows.

'It's the old fellow from the newspaper!' I whispered to Kate.

'And now that we've found it,' said Rath, 'perhaps you can tell me what it is, Mr Barton.'

'Barton,' Kate breathed in amazement. 'George Barton?'

I nodded. Nadira was right. There could be no question now: he was the same man who'd been speaking to Rath at the Heliodrome; he was the man from the Aruba Consortium.

'This machine,' said Barton, 'is Theodore Grunel's greatest invention. It creates power from nothing but water.'

Rath gave a chuckle. 'I wouldn't have thought such a thing was possible.'

'None of us did at first,' said Barton. 'But Grunel was an unusually brilliant man. I knew him well. The Consortium funded his work on the internal combustion engine, and it made us all rich. But he was never satisfied with it. He said it was dirty and wasteful. That there were purer forms of power. We wanted to know what he had in mind, but he wouldn't share his designs with us. Later we learned he was secretly working on some new form of engine, one that didn't require aruba fuel. Of course we were eager to acquire it.' He gave a reedy laugh. 'It only took us forty years.'

The speech seemed to tire Barton out, and he put the oxygen mask over his face and breathed deeply.

'Let's have some light!' Rath shouted at his men.

All the portable electric lamps came on at once, and shadows leapt for cover in the room's corners. There was no sign of the aerozoan, and no one had noticed the vivarium yet, for its glass walls were now completely frosted over. Everyone's attention was directed at Grunel's enormous machine, gleaming in the lamp's glare.

'It's an impressive-looking thing,' Rath said, 'but how can you be sure it works?'

Barton lowered his mask. 'Our fine locksmith Mr

Zwingli should be able to resolve that question shortly. Grunel was well known for his extravagant locks. Luckily, in the forty years since his demise, locksmiths' tricks have advanced somewhat. Mr Zwingli! Might I prevail upon you to see if the machine functions?'

The man with the lighted spectacles nodded and proceeded to Grunel's machine. From his rucksack he removed a bristling tool belt and set to work on the control panel.

'They're trying to turn it on,' I whispered to Kate.

'Without the key?' she asked.

'I don't know that this fellow needs keys.'

'You'll forgive my scepticism, Mr Barton,' said Rath, 'but it sounds a lot of make-believe to me.'

'Not at all,' said Barton. 'In theory, nothing could be simpler. Were you well schooled, Mr Rath?'

'Until the teacher had a nasty mishap.'

'It was one of Grunel's most amazing discoveries. Water contains both oxygen and hydrogen atoms. But it's a deucedly difficult business to separate them. Grunel focused the sun's light to split them.' He pointed at the enormous brass cylinder that looked like a telescope. 'Miraculous. So now he has hydrogen and oxygen in abundance and he uses both of them to create an electrical current. I won't bore you with the details, but the process creates power, water, heat and hydrium, which is stripped from the air. There are no moving parts, no soot, and no end to the supply. He called it the Prometheus Engine.'

Again, Barton lifted his mask to his face, and breathed hungrily.

'I'll believe it when I see it,' said Rath.

As if on cue, the ceiling lights in the engineerium flared on; the heaters clacked, water gushed through the pipes.

'Good Lord,' said Rath.

Barton stared at the machine in sheer admiration. 'As you can see, Mr Rath, it's an act of genius. Grunel did it. That's why you and I are here. To finish the job I failed to complete forty years ago.'

'What do you mean?' Rath asked.

'Grunel went aloft to finish the engine in secret. To get away from the Consortium. I pursued him.'

I glanced excitedly at Kate. 'He's B.,' I whispered. 'From Grunel's diary. Grunel was right. It wasn't pirates. It was Barton stalking them!'

'I was nearly upon him,' Barton told Rath. 'But he flew into a storm, and we lost them. Like everyone else, we assumed they'd crashed. Until the ship was sighted last week. And now we're here, Mr Rath, to make sure Grunel's invention never reaches earth.'

'You mean to destroy it?' Rath said, and his astonishment matched my own.

'Correct,' replied Barton.

'Seems a pity,' Rath said.

'We're not paying you to have an opinion, Mr Rath.'

I caught my breath, hearing him speak to Rath like this.

'Certainly,' said Rath, and I saw all his dislike and anger compressed into a frigid smile. 'But perhaps you wouldn't mind satisfying my simple-minded curiosity, Mr Barton. I can see how it might be a threat—'

'Not a threat, Mr Rath. An end. The Aruba Consortium has spent over sixty years drilling and refining aruba fuel. At great expense we now control the vast majority of the world's supply.' He paused to suck some oxygen from his mask. 'We've just discovered a huge new aruba field, perhaps you've read about it in the papers. Finding it nearly bankrupted us – *that*, you wouldn't have read in the papers. All will be well once we extract and sell the fuel – but how can we sell it if Grunel's water engine comes along and makes us obsolete?'

'But presumably,' said Rath, 'only you would have the machine. You would still be the world's power brokers.'

'A seductive thought,' wheezed Barton, breaking off to take frequent puffs of oxygen. 'But if the secret of this machine were to get out – and it surely would, given time – we would lose our monopoly. Anyone could build their own Prometheus Engine. And we would have nothing to sell them. Huge fortunes would be wiped out, nations would collapse, thousands would be out of work. It would turn the entire world on its head.'

Rath gave a wry smile. 'Ah, I see. You're acting for the good of all mankind.'

'For such a moralist, Mr Rath, you seemed to have no trouble opening fire on the *Sagarmatha*.'

'That was your order, Mr Barton.'

'And my machinery that made it possible. Do you think we would've found the *Sagarmatha* without my echolocator?'

Kate caught my eye. 'Nadira wasn't lying,' she said. 'She didn't help Rath find us.'

I nodded, relieved I hadn't been foolhardy in trusting her.

'The echolocator is a handsome device, to be sure,' Rath said placatingly.

'As is the skybreaker,' Barton went on, 'which is yours upon completion of this enterprise. Until then, you're required to do nothing but follow orders.'

'When the pay's this handsome,' said Rath, 'I have no opinion on the matter.'

'Very good. Turn off the machine now, Mr Zwingli! And destroy it!' Barton turned back to Rath. 'Instruct your men to search the ship for the blueprints. Any technical drawings or plans must be brought to me.'

'But the ship will be scuttled,' Rath told him. 'We'll blast it to pieces. Nothing will survive.'

'That is not an assumption the Board can afford to make. The machine's blueprints will come back with us to Brussels.'

Barton was wheezing now like a veteran smoker, and he put his oxygen mask back on. Rath turned to his men and relayed Barton's orders.

'I want a look,' said Kate, and pulled the eyepiece

from my grip. 'They're starting to cut into the machine. Oh, Matt, they're tearing it apart!'

I didn't like it at all, but right now I was more concerned with how we might escape. Getting out of the coffin would be a major production – pushing the lid high, leaping out, running for cover. How could we do it without being spotted?

'Oh no,' said Kate suddenly.

'What?'

'One of them's looking right at me.'

'Don't move the periscope!' I wondered how obvious it was, jutting up from the lid of the coffin.

'Let me see,' I said. 'Could you move a bit?'

Kate pushed up with her elbows and tried to shift herself out of the way, but she lost her balance and fell right against the horn's bulb. A great honking noise echoed through the engineerium.

Kate and I stared at each other, frozen.

'I tooted the horn,' she said in a very small voice.

I grabbed the eyepiece. Rath and his men were looking around in bewilderment.

'What the blazes was that?' someone said.

'Where'd it come from?' another asked.

There seemed to be a huge amount of confusion over the source of the noise. Pistols were drawn, some aimed at the catwalk, others at the vivarium.

One fellow pointed straight at the coffin. 'It came from over there.'

'What's a coffin doing here?' asked Rath angrily.

'The sound came from there!'

'Then go and open it if you're so sure,' Rath said testily. 'It's big enough to fit the Vienna Boys' Choir.'

The pirate gripped his pistol and started walking over.

I looked at Kate. 'This is going to be bad,' I said.

She nodded.

'When he opens the lid, just run.'

'He'll think we're ghosts. He'll be scared witless.'

'More likely to squeeze the trigger.' My hands were shaking as I pulled a pry bar from Kate's rucksack. I would try to smack the pistol from his hand, and buy us a few moments.

'We could just surrender,' said Kate.

I peered through the eyepiece. Just as the pirate neared the coffin, there was a shout from one of the others. The man before us whirled in alarm and the next thing I knew he was screaming and convulsing and tentacles were flailing about with great lightning cracks. A terrible smell reached me even through the coffin.

Kate gripped my arm, terrified.

'The aerozoan got him,' I said.

A chorus of curses and exclamations rose from the other pirates and gunfire cracked the air. Several bullets smacked the coffin's wall but amazingly didn't come through.

I kept watching. The aerozoan had been hit and was slewing around the room like a punctured weather balloon.

'Get ready,' I said. 'We're making a run for it.'

We crouched.

'Oh!' said Kate.

Worried she'd been hit by a stray bullet I looked over.

'Something poked me,' she said, and I spotted a tiny switch jutting from the side of the coffin. Before I could stop her, Kate reached over and touched it. A door dropped open in the coffin's bottom, and she disappeared.

20

Blueprints

Through the trapdoor I saw stairs, and quickly threw myself down them. Kate was picking herself up at the bottom and shining her torch around. We were in a tunnel. I could almost stand upright, but had to stoop a bit. I pushed the trapdoor firmly shut, just in case the pirates opened the coffin.

Kate began to speak, but I hushed her. We were directly beneath the floor of the engineerium, and I did not know how easily we might be heard. One passage led forward, another led across the ship to the port side. I took Kate's hand and started forward. The corridor was narrow but, like everything in Grunel's ship, very well constructed, with wall panelling and light sconces, now dark. The floor was a metal catwalk, and beneath our feet I could see the *Hyperion*'s ribs and her outer skin. I paced out the distance as I walked, keeping silent until I reckoned we were well past the engineerium.

'No wonder the crew never saw Grunel,' I whispered. 'I can't fathom this fellow. He has a perfectly good passageway along the keel, but he'd rather scuttle about like a ferret.' I nearly brained myself on a low beam, and cursed under my breath.

'He was very short, you know. This would have been perfectly comfortable for him.'

'Odd little man,' I muttered.

'I feel extremely grateful to him right now. Where do you think this leads?'

'Right back to his stateroom. And I bet that other branch back there keeps going to the dead zoo. He probably popped up inside the Yeti case.'

The passage ended with a spiral staircase, and at the top was a small landing and door. I reached for the handle, praying it would not be locked. It turned, but when I pushed, the door didn't move. I put my shoulder to it, with no effect.

'Try pulling,' suggested Kate, and I felt a fool, for I could now see the hinges were on my side.

I pulled hard, but the door was stubborn. I heard a faint crackling of ice and the door shifted a smidgin. The effort left me winded. Kate grabbed hold too and we hauled with all our weight. Loose ice showered down on us as the door slowly swung open.

Kate was wheezing from exertion, and held her mask to her face so she could catch her breath. We stepped into Grunel's bedroom. The door was not simply a door, but an entire bookshelf. A burst water pipe had filmed it with ice. Hal had swept most of the shelves clean of books when searching, but had never noticed they hid a secret passageway.

Kate gasped when she saw Grunel. His sheet was on the floor, a metre or so from his body, as if he'd thrown it off in a fury. He was staring at us. It seemed no matter where you were in the room, he was looking at you. I hoped he hadn't heard me call him an odd little man. I saw the snapped fingers on his right hand, where Hal had wrenched the watch from his grasp. I wished I had the photograph of his daughter to return to him. I did not like to think of him separated from it in death. Of all the things he'd taken aloft with him, this was what he'd clung to at the end.

'I'm sorry,' I said to him, under my breath.

Before I closed the secret door, I had a quick look around to find out where the catch was. Now that the shelves were empty, it was easy to discover that one of them could be tilted up slightly, and behind it was a little brass button.

'We should go,' said Kate. 'They'll come looking for the blueprints here.'

Warily, listening all the time for Rath and his men, we left the apartment and made our way forward. Once past the officers' quarters, and the ladder down to the control car, the keel catwalk began its upward curve to the ship's bow. We laboured up the steps, pausing several times so Kate could gulp some tanked oxygen. I was breathing hard, and my temples throbbed. We reached the top of the stairs and were inside the ship's nose cone. There was a small landing and workspace here, where the crew could tend to the mooring lines and forward gas cells. Running aft, through the ship's very centre, was the axial catwalk, disappearing quickly into the gloom.

'Where are they?' Kate whispered.

'Cruse,' hissed Hal.

I turned to see his head sticking out from a large storage locker. We'd walked right past it. Hal ushered us inside, and slid the door shut. The locker was filled with harnesses and fleece-lined coats and patching gear, but deep enough to fit all four of us. Hal's choice of hiding place was a good one, for even if the pirates did search the bow, we had two possible retreats: back the way we'd come to the keel, or along the axial catwalk.

'You had me worried,' wheezed Hal. He did not look at all well.

'We hid in the coffin,' said Kate, and quickly told him of our escape.

Hal nodded, though his eyes seemed unfocused. I didn't think he was taking much in.

'So Nadira had nothing to do with Rath finding us,' Kate told Hal pointedly.

'Good to hear,' said Hal vaguely.

Nadira's breathing was quick and shallow, even though she was sitting, and breathing tanked air.

'How are you feeling?' I asked her.

'Fine,' she said, her voice muffled through the mask.

'She's not fine,' said Hal. 'She fainted when we got up

here. She came round once I got the mask on her. I think her lungs are filling with fluid.'

I nodded calmly, hoping my face did not betray my worry. I knew that at its worst, hypoxia could drown you, or make your brain swell fatally. Nadira was still conscious, which was a good sign, but I didn't know how long she could last. I had no idea how high the *Hyperion* was now; at least she was no longer climbing, held in check by Rath's ship.

'Is there anything else we can do for her?' Kate asked.

'Just keep her on oxygen and resting,' said Hal.

'The only real cure is going down,' I said.

'A bit beyond our control right now,' Hal added grimly, and started coughing.

'Hal,' I said, looking at him, 'do you need some oxygen?'

'What? No, I'm fine,' he spluttered. 'Save it for the girls.' He looked at Kate. 'How're you making out? Getting enough air?'

'After wearing a corset, this is a walk in the park,' Kate said.

I chuckled. Maybe that was why she was faring surprisingly well. I'd always assumed it would be Kate who flagged first, that Nadira's harder life would make her more resilient. But altitude sickness could strike anyone at any time, even the most fit.

'Cruse, what about you?' Hal asked.

'I still feel all right.'

'Lying's not going to change anything.'

'I'm not lying.' It vexed Hal that I wasn't harder hit. He'd spent far more time at high altitudes than me – or so he said – but maybe not this high, or for so long. I felt the altitude sorely, I surely did, but it was not crippling me the way it was the others. I felt as if my body was calibrated for lofty heights. For me, the cold was the hardest part.

'Did Rath see you?' Hal asked.

'We're still the ship's ghosts,' I told him, and regretted my choice of words. The possibility of the *Hyperion* adding us to its eternal crew seemed far too likely right now.

'We're all going to die if we don't get down soon,' said Hal. 'That's the long and short of it.'

'We need to radio the *Saga* again,' I said. 'They might be able to pick us up.'

'What if they can't?' said Kate.

'There's two ornithopters,' I said uncertainly.

Kate's eyes widened. 'But they weren't even invented in Grunel's time!'

'Well, he invented his own, and kept it quiet. Nadira and I saw them in a hangar near the stern. Weird-looking things.'

'You'll not get me in one of those,' said Hal. 'We don't even know if they work. And where would you propose to land? We're in the middle of the Antarctic Sea.'

'We need some way off, Hal,' I said.

'I'd rather try to steal Rath's ship. There were eight

men, you said? So probably at least three back on board . . .'

I started shaking my head, the idea seemed so impossible. 'How would we board her in secret, Hal? Anyway, they're all heavily armed.'

'I've still got four bullets. Their ship may be the only way off this floating morgue.' His anger billowed from his mouth like dragon's smoke.

'The *Saga* may be all right,' I said. 'We need to find out at least. I'll try to raise her again.'

'I'll come with you,' said Kate.

I looked at Hal; he nodded. I was the only one who knew Morse code, and someone needed to stay with Nadira in case Rath came. It took all her strength just to breathe.

We would have to be careful. Even at this minute Rath's crew was probably fanning out through the ship, looking for the blueprints. The control car wouldn't be an obvious place to search, but they might have their own reasons for making a visit.

We took the stairs down to the keel catwalk, and then the ladder into the control car. With Kate's help, I hurriedly connected my torch batteries to the wireless. I put on the headphones. Kate climbed the ladder to keep watch. I did not want to be cornered down here.

I sparked out my message to the *Sagarmatha*, then paused for a minute to listen to the static. After transmitting a second SOS, I heard only more dead air. Fearing the worst, I sent a third distress message, and the

moment I lifted my fingers from the spark key, I heard a
return beep.

I snatched at the notepad, and wax pencil, so surprised
I almost missed the first few letters.

```
Dorje here. Cruse?
```

Yes, I typed back jubilantly.

```
Others OK?
```

```
Yes. Hiding. Rath aboard. Oxygen almost
gone. Can you come?
```

```
Need three hours. Will come.
```

Decoding the last two words I almost started crying.

```
Will dock under control car. Be ready.
```

```
Yes.
```

I unhooked the batteries, took the message pad, and ran
to the ladder. Kate looked down at me expectantly.

'You got through!'

I nodded. 'They're coming to get us.'

The news warmed me. We hurried back up to our
hiding place in the ship's bow, and I told Hal and Nadira
of our good fortune.

'She's well made, the *Saga*,' Hal said with pride. 'They'll be patching like mad.' He looked at his watch. 'Three hours.'

'Won't Rath see them coming?' Kate asked.

'Not if Dorje brings her up from below,' I said. 'Rath's right on top. He's got no sightlines straight down.'

'And their cannons will be useless,' Hal said. 'They'll have no clear shot. Dorje will nudge up beneath the control car. It'll be a tricky business.'

I knew there was an emergency hatch in the control car floor. We'd have to get a line between the two ships, and then clip on with our harnesses and lower ourselves down.

'Just three more hours,' I told Nadira.

'They still don't know we're here,' Hal said.

'Exactly,' I said, wanting to reassure Kate and Nadira. 'All we have to do is sit tight. They'll never find us.'

'We can sit tight,' said Hal, looking at me, 'or we can get the blueprints.'

I would be a liar if I said the thought had not occurred to me, but I wouldn't have been bold enough to voice it.

'They could be anywhere,' I said.

'How many of those . . . things . . . buttons were there on the pneumatics?' Hal wanted to know. His sentences were starting to falter, which I knew was a bad sign. I recited all the buttons I'd seen below Grunel's message tubes: servant's room, engineerium, dead zoo, gardens, animal paddocks, captain's cabin, landing bay.

'But Hal,' I reminded him, 'the capsule might be trapped inside the system.'

'It's too dangerous,' said Kate. 'Why risk getting caught?'

'You got what you came for,' said Nadira, removing her mask and looking fiercely at Kate. 'If we don't get those blueprints, I'm sunk. I've got nothing to go back to. You've got your specimens. You've got each other.'

Her eyes drifted over to me. I looked down, not knowing what to say. I suppose she'd seen Kate and me holding hands, or maybe just noticed the way we'd been talking – and that had been enough. I somehow felt responsible for Nadira. She was alone in the world, and hadn't had any breaks – and wouldn't unless we found the blueprints. I wanted to make things right for her.

'I don't want anyone's pity,' Nadira said, starting to wheeze, 'but I do want a nice big pile of gold.' She fixed the mask over her mouth and breathed hard.

'Nadira's right,' said Hal. 'This job's yielded nothing for the rest of us. But those plans are worth a lot.'

I could not deny my own temptation. It wasn't just the money the plans would bring, it was the notion of preserving Grunel's Prometheus Engine. The machine would change the world, and make all sorts of wonders possible. The aerial city of my dreams.

'There's not that many places to check,' said Hal. 'What was it? Seven or eight? It's done easily enough if we're careful. And Rath still doesn't know we're here.'

Kate was shaking her head. 'There will be other salvages, Hal.'

'No,' he said savagely. 'There won't. All my hopes were hanging on this one.' He looked at me. 'I've not done as well as you might think. The *Saga's* mine in name alone; it's the bank that nearly owns her. I was counting on this trip to clear my debts. If I go home empty-handed, they'll seize my ship. I clawed my way to where I am, through luck and sweat, and I'll not be ruined.'

I did not know what to say, I was so shocked. All along I'd imagined Hal to be as strong and triumphant as the Eiffel Tower. He was all success: suave, handsome, wealthy, the captain of his own ship. I didn't know whether to pity or hate him, for his big talk had made me feel so puny and worthless. And yet, I did not like to see him laid low.

'I'm still against it,' said Kate.

'For,' huffed Nadira.

'For,' said Hal. 'Cruse, what d'you say?'

'For,' I said.

Kate stared at me, shocked. 'Matt!'

'We can't let Rath destroy the blueprints as well as the machine.'

'Is that it, or is it the money?' she demanded.

'Both,' I said. 'It's both.'

'That's three out of four,' said Hal. 'Clear majority.'

'Oh, it's a democracy now, is it?' said Kate.

'Not at all. I'd have done it my way regardless.'

'You should stay with Nadira,' I told Kate. 'We can't leave her alone.'

Nadira was shaking her head. 'I'm coming.'

'You're not going anywhere,' I said.

'I'm fine on oxygen!'

'Cruse's right,' said Hal. 'You'd be a danger to yourself and the rest of us.'

Angrily, Nadira started to rise. I watched, awed by her determination. She made it halfway up, then staggered off balance. I caught her and helped her back down. She wouldn't meet my eyes.

'You'll get your share,' Hal told her with surprising gentleness. 'You needn't worry.'

I knelt beside Nadira and checked the oxygen tanks. I figured she'd have enough to last until the *Saga* came.

'You're doing great,' I said.

'Not really,' she replied.

I could see she was scared. 'You're a rule breaker, remember? You'll be fine.'

She nodded tiredly. I don't think my pep talk cheered her at all.

'Go!' she said to Kate through her mask. 'No point you staying.'

Kate sighed and looked at me. 'If you're hell-bent on doing this, we'd better do it quickly.'

I did not like to leave Nadira alone, but she was right. There was nothing more we could do for her, and three sets of eyes were better than two – though I had no intention of letting Kate go off alone.

'You've got the gun,' I told Hal, 'you're on your own. Kate's with me.'

'Fair enough,' he replied. 'We'll split up and meet back here.'

We agreed on how to divide the ship, and then Hal set off down the steps to the keel. Kate and I headed silently along the axial catwalk, keeping our torches off so we'd see Rath's men before they saw us. The thought of ghosts and spectres no longer scared me. We reached the aft companion ladder and cautiously started down.

First stop was the orchard, but the blueprints weren't there, so we made our way to the landing bay. Inside, Kate's eyes lingered on the two ornithopters.

'Strange-looking birds,' she whispered. 'I wouldn't call these ornithopters. Chirothopters, maybe. More like bats. The wing structure is quite different.'

'No time for this,' I hissed at her, searching the walls for the message tubes. It didn't take long – but the blueprints weren't here either. I imagined them hurtling endlessly through the labyrinth of pneumatic piping.

As we headed for the dead zoo, I heard a great deal of noise coming from the engineerium. Rath's crew would still be dismantling Grunel's machine, and turning the entire room on its head, trying to root out the blueprints. It wouldn't be long before their search took them into the rest of the ship. We'd have to be quick.

Getting to the dead zoo was the riskiest bit of all, for the keel catwalk was the only way, and if Rath's pirates left the engineerium, we would have to press ourselves into the shadows and hope they wouldn't see us. We moved as speedily as our oxygen-starved bodies let us.

We reached the door safely and slipped inside amongst the huge, frozen display cases. We were halfway along the back wall, trying to find the message tubes, when we heard voices from the catwalk. We halted. Footsteps entered the room. Many rows of cases were between us and them, and light sparkled through the panes of frozen glass.

We crouched low behind a display case. The footsteps moved deeper into the room, and it sounded like there was someone coming down each of the three aisles. All escape routes were cut off. If they came all the way to the end, we were sure to be caught.

'What's all this, then?' I heard one of them call out.

'Dead animals,' said another.

'What a freak show,' said a third.

'Whole ship's a freak show.'

'As long as there's no more of them that got Harrison.'

I reached up for the latch of the display case and turned it. It was not locked. I swung open the large glass door. Inside was some kind of wolf, jaws wide.

Kate needed no explanation. Silently she climbed in. I followed. There was just room enough. I could not latch the door properly because there was no handle on my side. The frost on the glass was thick, though patchy in a few places. It was too late to change cases now. The men's voices were getting closer.

We stayed on all fours. I hoped that, through the frost, our silhouettes might be mistaken for animals. I heard a fast heartbeat, and for a confused, hair-raising moment thought it was coming from the wild creature beside me. But it was only my own pulse, pounding in my ears.

'What's that in there, the great fat fellow?' I heard one of them say.

'That's a Yeti, that is.'

'Crikey, he's an ugly bastard.'

'I've seen one in the wild.'

'You haven't.'

'Alaska. Mt McKinley. We took a few shots at it from the ship as we passed.'

'These drawers underneath are just bones,' came the voice of the third man. 'We won't be finding any blueprints here. Let's head out.'

'No. We need to be thorough. Rath's orders.'

I could hear them scraping ice from some of the other cases, muttering darkly about the specimens. I wondered if they'd notice the cases Kate had left empty from her pilfering. Surely they would not check each and every one.

They were coming down our row now. I tried to slow my breathing. I locked eyes with Kate. She gave a long silent exhalation and her warm breath rose like smoke. I reached out and put my hand over her mouth, my eyes wide with alarm. She understood. We each held a gloved hand to our lips so we would send up no signals.

I tried to be still. I tried to look like a wolf. It was not

396

so hard to imagine myself petrified, it was so cold. The ice lit and sparkled as torch beams swept the case. On the opposite wall, our animal silhouettes stretched and shrank.

All I could think was what a fool I'd been. A boy playing at pirates. But it was all dross to me now, the fluttering confetti of bank notes I'd imagined. It seemed greedy and reckless and ugly. I was no pirate, and I would have given anything to be back where I started, in the Eiffel Tower with Kate, and I would say, Let's not. I don't want the *Hyperion*'s cargo. Let's stay here and keep things as they are. I will work harder at my studies, I will master my numbers. I will become a junior officer and work my way up. It will be enough.

'This one's ajar,' said a voice outside our case, and I could see the man's bulk silhouetted against the frosted glass. His arm lifted to the handle.

My haunches tensed; I was ready to spring at his throat, snarling like a wild beast.

'There's nothing here,' came another voice. 'Let's head out. We've got plenty of ship to search yet.'

For a moment the arm did not move, and I feared he was going to open the case anyway, but then he turned and his shadow dissolved into the general gloom. I listened to their fading footsteps. The cold air seared my lungs. My face was a mask welded with ice to my skull. I imagined I must look like one of those ancient mummies found in glaciers, charred by time and terrible to behold.

Their footsteps evaporated and I heard no more talking. Kate nodded. We pushed the door wide and quietly swung ourselves out. I pointed my torch beam at the floor so my light would not splash around too much.

'Let's just get back,' Kate whispered. 'This is too risky.'

I let my torch light seep up the wall, and saw, in the corner, the two message tubes we'd been searching for. On the incoming tube, the green flag was raised.

'Just a second,' I said, and hurried over. I reached through the hinged door to pull out the message capsule, but there was nothing there. I closed my eyes in frustration. Grunel would not release his secrets to me.

Light hit me in the side of the face. Stupidly I looked, blinding myself.

'Drop your torch!' a familiar voice said. It was John Rath. 'I've got a pistol! Put up your hands!'

I dipped my head so the hood gave me some shadow. From the corner of my eye, I saw Kate, still hidden from Rath behind a case. She stepped back. I dropped my torch and raised my hands as he strode closer, keeping his light right on me.

'Who the hell are you, then?' he said. 'Head up!'

There was a trace of fear in his voice, as though I might have been some spectral beast, escaped from one of the displays. I wanted to run. But if he gave chase, and others came, they'd see Kate too, and we'd both be caught.

I checked on her. She was backing away quickly. She

turned and hurried out of sight. Good. She would run back to the others.

'Head up, I said!' Rath was close now, and I saw a flash of his ginger beard before he struck me in the temple with his torch. My knees buckled. I felt my hood being yanked off.

'Ah,' he said. 'I see. I thought the *Saga* was just arriving. But she'd already put aboard her landing party. She was just coming back to take you off when we scuttled her.'

I said nothing.

'How many others are here?'

'It's just me,' I said.

He snorted impatiently. 'We'll see about that. What've you found?'

'Not a single gram of gold,' I said, and it was not hard to muster venom. 'It's been a complete waste.'

'Should've taken my offer at the Ritz.'

The mention of the hotel barely made sense to me, it seemed so impossibly warm and long ago.

'So you're all alone and you've found nothing. What a shame,' said Rath, putting the muzzle of his pistol to my forehead. The cold metal burned against my flesh like a brand.

'My employer will be very displeased to learn there are others aboard,' he told me. 'I know what his orders will be. But if you've come across anything you think I might value, maybe we can help each other. How were you planning on getting off the ship? Flying perhaps?'

I kept my mouth shut.

'I can get you off if you tell me where Grunel's gold is.'

'There's no gold.'

He rapped the pistol hard against my skull. Tears sprang to my eyes, freezing on my eyelashes.

From the wall came a strange, hair-raising whistle and then a thud. Before I could stop myself, my eyes flicked to the message tube. The green flag vibrated.

'Expecting something, were you?' Rath said. 'Go ahead, take it.'

As Rath watched, I pushed the hinged door aside and pulled out the message capsule.

'Open it,' he said.

I removed the cap and pulled out the blueprints.

'Hold them up,' he commanded. Rath played the light over them and gave a satisfied grunt. 'Put them back in the tube,' he said. 'You've just saved me a great deal of time.'

He snatched the capsule from my hand and jammed it under his belt.

From somewhere in the ship came the sound of a gunshot, then another.

Kate.

'You're coming with me,' Rath said angrily.

There was a second whistle and thud from inside the wall, and the green message flag sprang up once more.

'You're very popular,' said Rath.

Keeping his pistol trained on me, Rath tucked the torch under his arm, thrust his free hand into the message

400

tube, and started screaming. He yanked his hand out. An aerozoan hatchling clung to his fist, tentacles flexing. I had not thought the little ones would be so potent, but Rath flailed, his jaw grinding. His torch fell to the floor, spinning light.

Rath tried to smash the aerozoan off with his pistol, but its metal sparked with electricity and he dropped it in agony. The message capsule containing the blueprints flew free from his belt and skidded across the floor.

I snatched it up, along with my torch, and ran.

Rath's screams had brought his men running. As they came charging into the dead zoo, I doused my torch. They had not yet seen me, so I slunk into the shadows, cloaked in my hide suit. I waited for them to rush past, then ran for the door.

'He's got the blueprints!' I heard Rath roar. 'It's Matt Cruse!'

I made it through the doorway. The keel catwalk was empty, but I heard more voices coming from the engineerium. I ran the other way, the dim glow of the ship's skin my only guide. I reached the aft companion ladder, climbed to the axial catwalk and then staggered forward to the bow, the message capsule clutched in my hand. The run had sapped all my strength. Six steps. Stop. Breathe. Six steps. Stop. Breathe. I had the blueprints. Soon the *Sagarmatha* would be soaring to meet us. But we'd been spotted now, and Rath's men would come looking. And what was that gunshot I'd heard?

I reached the ship's bow and knocked quietly on the locker door.

'It's me, Matt.'

I slid the door open and went inside. Hal was slouched against the wall next to Nadira.

Kate was not with them.

21

HIMALAYAN HEART

Hal looked up at me, face ashen, and saw the message capsule in my hand.

'You got it?'

'Kate's not here?' I asked.

'Let's have a look. Open it up!'

Hal reached for the capsule, but I pulled back. 'Did Kate not come back?'

'No. She was with you, mate!'

I staggered back out to the landing, listened for her footsteps, shone my light into the darkness. I'd just assumed she had gone on ahead.

'Turn your torch off,' Hal hissed, limping after me.

'They must've caught her,' I said, feeling sick. I quickly told him what had happened in the dead zoo. 'There was a gunshot.'

'That was me,' said Hal. 'You're not the only one who was spotted.'

For the first time I noticed the right shoulder of his sky suit bore a dark stain.

'You're shot!'

'My arm's broke, but I'll live. Better off than the other fella.' He tried to smile but it came out all crooked.

'Dead?'

'If I'd done it sooner my shoulder wouldn't be peppered with lead. I took his oxygen tank for Nadira. Got his gun too.'

'I'm going back for Kate,' I said.

Hal caught me by the arm. 'Hold up. She may just be biding her time. Wait a few minutes. Rath's men'll be everywhere.'

Reluctantly, I followed Hal back to the storage locker.

'We were idiots,' I said bitterly, 'to do this.'

'You got the blueprints,' he said.

'It doesn't matter.'

'It will,' Hal said fiercely. 'Maybe not right now, but when we get off this wreck and back to Paris, it will. Trust me. The *Saga*'s here in fifty minutes.'

'We've got to find Kate. You've already killed one of them. That leaves only six. The locksmith fellow, and Barton, they're not up for a fight. And Rath might be dead. An aerozoan hatchling got him. So just three or four of them now. We've got two guns. The odds aren't so bad.'

A voice welled up from the darkness, sounding as though it were carried by a bullhorn.

'We have the girl . . . We have Kate de Vries . . .'

Even though it was distorted by the bullhorn and its own echoes, the voice was plainly Rath's. The wretch hadn't died as I'd hoped.

'We will kill her,' Rath said, 'unless you surrender yourselves and give us the blueprints.'

It was as if a gale force wind had swept through my head, clearing all thoughts and words. I sat down hard, staring, empty. I thumped at my forehead with my fist. My mind must be going. Words and shards of thoughts swirled about, storm-tossed, but I couldn't catch hold of them. They had Kate. That was all I could grasp.

'Bring us the blueprints and no harm will come to the girl!' Rath bellowed through the ship. 'We're your only way off. Give us the blueprints and we'll give you safe passage home!'

'They're lying,' Hal scoffed. 'They mean to kill all of us.'

'Bring the blueprints to the engineerium! You have fifteen minutes.'

'I'm going,' I said.

Hal grabbed me with his good arm.

'They will kill you.'

I said nothing.

'The *Saga*'s coming. We have one chance of escape, that's all. If we miss that, we all die.'

I stared at him in horror. 'Are you saying we should leave her behind?'

'It's not right,' wheezed Nadira, taking the mask from her mouth. Her eyes flashed angrily at Hal.

'Right's got nothing to do with it,' he said. 'I'm talking about survival. Morality is a nicety we can't afford just now.'

I shook my head. 'I don't want to hear that, Hal.'

He snatched the blueprints from my grasp. 'You're not giving them these.'

'Of course I am. I'm going to trade them for her life.'

'Don't be a fool! If you go, you won't come back.'

'Give them to me.'

'I'm saving your life, Cruse!'

I lunged at him, and he fell back against my sudden weight. We both crashed to the floor. He tried to beat me off with his good arm, but he was weak, and my heart was pumping furiously. I grabbed the hand that held the message capsule and banged it against the metal grille until his fingers lost their grip. Seizing the blueprints, I stepped back and away from him, panting. He looked crumpled and forlorn on the floor.

'I'm sorry,' I said.

He made no answer. My fury left me. My knees shook. I tossed the blueprints back to him. 'You're right. These aren't going to help. But I'll not lose her.'

'I lost a man,' he panted. 'I hate it, but sometimes it's the nature of the beast.'

'I'm going to beat the beast. Give me one of the guns,' I said.

He shook his head wearily. 'You're outnumbered, Cruse.'

'Give. Me. The. Gun.'

Hal stared into the darkness, looking lost. He steadied himself against a girder, and retched twice, bringing nothing up. He swore.

'We'll both go,' he said.

'You've got a busted arm. You're ill. You should take some oxygen.'

'I'm fine.'

'Stay here with Nadira in case I don't come back. You can help her on to the *Saga*.'

'You should be weak as a kitten,' Hal said, in plain bewilderment. 'Why aren't you?'

'The sky knows me,' I said.

Hal snorted and passed me a pirate's gun. 'Four bullets in this one,' he said, and showed me how to use it. I tried to listen attentively, but my concentration was poor, my mind already chanting its own war dance.

I had a Himalayan heart. I was strong and they were weak. They needed tanked oxygen; I needed none. Their backpacks made them slow and cumbersome. I felt the leopard's fur against me and became the leopard. I was lithe and strong. I would be fast. I would bring Kate back.

Slinking down the steps to the keel catwalk, trying to keep my thoughts tethered.

We had broken the sky. We had angered the gods, just like Grunel. He'd taken light and air for his Prometheus Engine. The mythical Prometheus stole fire from the gods and was punished for an eternity. Maybe Grunel was being punished too. His unhappy spirit roamed the ship. He had come aloft with every hope of building an aerial city, and had only succeeded in constructing an airborne grave. All his gold and glory and fame hadn't been able to stop that.

But we had the blueprints, we could let the world know his secrets now. They were good secrets. Why should anyone be punished for such a thing?

I reached the door to Grunel's apartments without seeing any of Rath's men. Once inside, I listened, watching, my eyes so accustomed to the darkness I imagined my pupils as dilated as an owl's. I pulled down my hood so I could hear without the fur interfering. I touched the wall to help guide me, the silk paper shushing against my gloves.

I paused and felt a great welling of dread. Turning to face the wall, I saw it was no wall, but some kind of window. And standing on the other side, in the near dark, was the fiend from my nightmare.

He was cut from ragged bits of hide, clumps of potter's clay. He stared back at me, and his expression bore the look of terror I remembered from my dreams. I could not scream, though a strangled whimper escaped my mouth. I thought this was surely the end of everything, for what defence could I have against such a spectre?

Without any hope, I lifted my gun, and the creature too lifted its arm and great blocky fist, as if trying to ward me off. I faltered, and he too faltered, and then I knew I was not peering through some portal, but into a cracked, discoloured mirror. The unfinished man was me. I touched my face, scarcely recognizing myself, and hurried on.

In the bedroom, Grunel did eternal sentry duty in his

lounge chair. I found the secret catch in the bookshelf and pushed. Inside the passage, I closed the door behind me and turned on my torch. The ship was rising again, ever so slightly, and I felt it in my ankles. I walked. The *Hyperion* gave a shake and I stumbled against the wall. The wood panelling made a hollow thump. I tapped it with my gloved fingers, saw a small knob, and slid the entire panel to one side.

My torchlight picked out cables and the great rudder and elevator chains between the control car and tail. Above them, I saw the underside of the engineerium's titanium floor. Stuck to it at regular intervals were bundled sticks of dynamite, connected by a network of wires.

Nadira had been right: the entire engineerium was booby-trapped. If anyone tried to break through its walls, windows, doors or ceilings, it would mightily explode.

As I pulled back my torch, something glittered. Nestled snugly between the ship's wooden ribs was a collection of crates. The one nearest me had its lid missing – and inside glowed lustrous bricks of gold. The top few layers were uneven, bricks askew, like someone had already helped himself.

I looked up and down the secret passage in alarm, but I was quite alone.

I stared back at the gold. Here was our treasure. But the sight of it gave me no satisfaction. The opposite.

I could hurry back and tell Hal. He could fill our rucksacks at least, and bring them aboard the *Saga* when it came. But I would not go back and tell Hal. That would take more time and energy than I could spare.

I could step in right now, and grab a few slim bricks for myself. But I had no pockets to hold them. And even if I'd had my rucksack with me, I knew I would not take a single piece. The fuel of my old dreams was too weighty, and I needed to be as light as possible for what was to come.

I closed the panel and carried on, my stomach clenched tight as a walnut. Reaching the stairs, I silently opened the trapdoor, and climbed up into the coffin. I slid beneath the periscope and pulled the eyepiece to my face. I hooked the listening horn to my ear.

The portable lamps still illuminated the room. Grunel's Prometheus Engine had been gutted. Its innards lay strewn about, its huge brass cylinder toppled and hacked apart. Barton was studiously sifting through various pieces of the wreckage with Zwingli, the locksmith.

About fifteen metres from the coffin was Kate, sitting in a chair. They had stripped off her oxygen tank, to keep her weak, and I could see her chest rising and falling rapidly as she struggled for breath. Standing nearby was John Rath. Both his hands had been clumsily swathed in bandages. He held no pistol.

I swivelled the periscope, looking for the rest of his crew. On the floor I saw two dead bodies, one of which was horribly charred. The other must have been shot by Hal. The remaining three men were ranged on either side of the catwalk's doorway, pistols at the ready for anyone foolish enough to enter. Hal was right. They had no intention of bartering. They would shoot us as we stepped inside.

The vivarium was still frosted over, and intact, and I felt huge relief. Rath and his men had not bothered to see what lay beyond the icy glass. I saw no sign of the hatchlings. Perhaps they'd all found the pneumatic tubes and gone sailing through the ship.

The *Hyperion* lurched higher in the sky. From beyond the hull came the muffled sound of a ship's horn blaring.

'Storm's coming,' I heard Rath tell Barton. 'The ship wants us back. It'll be damaged if we stay tied up to the *Hyperion*. We need to cast off.'

'Not until we get the blueprints,' said Barton.

'Lads, five minutes,' Rath told his men. 'Then it's back to the ship.'

'Those are not my orders!' Barton said.

'I'll not have my ship wrecked.'

'That ship,' said Barton, 'is not yours until our venture is concluded.'

'It'll end in death if we're foolhardy,' said Rath menacingly.

The ship gave another ungainly gallop, and everyone staggered off balance.

'Your friends don't seem very concerned for your welfare,' Barton said to Kate.

Wisely, Kate said nothing.

Silently I lifted the lid of the coffin, and jammed it open with the end of my unlit torch. I peered out and saw Kate, and Rath, who, luckily, had his back to me. I had a clear view of the vivarium.

Not even my oxygen–starved brain could think my plan a good one. It held about as much promise as Pandora's box, but it was all I had.

I had never fired a pistol. My fingers stiff and clumsy, I took aim and held tight, for Hal said it would kick something terrible. I quickly fired four times, trying to aim a bit to the right with each shot. The noise was as loud as cannon fire, and its reverberations all but drowned out the sound of shattering glass.

A jagged hole gaped in the side of the vivarium. Even as Rath's pirates looked frantically around, trying to find the source of the gunfire, an aerozoan jetted out through the opening.

Barton saw it first, shouted, and ran out of the way. The creature's tentacles whipped Zwingli. His oxygen tank exploded, sending flaming debris and body parts across the room.

'Kill it!' Rath bellowed.

His three men advanced cautiously, unleashing a hail of bullets. Thrashing, the aerozoan slewed through the air, catching one of the men with its tentacles. He made a terrible leap into the air, electrocuted. I could smell the hydrium gushing from the creature's sac as it sank to the floor. Its tentacles lashed against the portable lamp batteries. Giant sparks flew, smoke billowed, and then the lamps went dark all at once. Shadows leaped across the room like hungry animals.

As I'd hoped, Kate saw her chance, stood, and made for the coffin. Rath had his back to her, watching the aerozoan, still in its death throes at the room's centre. But Kate was very weak, and she managed little more than a hobble.

I pushed the coffin lid high, and swung myself out. The air was thick with smoke and embers, and the terrible smell of burning flesh and hide. Kate saw me as I ran to her, but luckily did not call out. Rath still hadn't turned round. I grabbed Kate by the arm and hurried her back towards the coffin.

'Stop!'

It was Rath, but I knew he didn't have a pistol, and hoped the smoke would shield us from his men. We didn't look back. I pushed Kate inside the coffin, and got one leg over myself. Kate screamed. An arm hooked around my chest and dragged me back. Rath's hands were bandaged up like a mummy's, but he was still dreadfully strong. He threw me to the floor, and gave me a kick in the ribs.

As I scrambled about to avoid his boots, his men finished off the aerozoan and began striding over with their eager pistols.

'Go!' I bellowed to Kate.

I heard the sound of whips cracking, and when I looked I saw the quicksilver glimmer of the last aerozoan streaking from the breech in the vivarium. Tentacles trailing low, it struck one of Rath's men dead before he could run. Then the aerozoan tilted itself so it was perfectly horizontal, and came jetting low across the room, straight towards me.

Rath bolted. I scrambled to my feet, but knew there was no point running. I could never escape the reach of its lethal tentacles now. It came at me head-on like a steam engine. I ran to meet it.

I hurled myself at its hydrium sac. It was no flimsy diaphanous thing as I'd expected, but firm as a rubber tyre. I nearly bounced off, but clutched at the ridged membrane with both hands, and wrapped my legs tight around it.

The aerozoan felt my weight and its balloon sac swelled against me as it produced more hydrium. Up we went. A few of its tentacles whipped high, trying to knock me off, but mercifully I was just out of their reach, perched as I was atop the creature's squid-like summit. Through its translucent hide, I saw the writhing green tangle of its intestines, and further down, the hinges of its ghastly beak, snapping.

I rode the aerozoan as it veered round the engineerium. Kate ducked back inside the coffin to avoid its flailing tentacles. Gunfire pattered all round me as the aerozoan swerved back towards Rath's last remaining man. A bullet sliced through the creature's hydrium sac and passed within two centimetres of my belly. In a matter of seconds I'd be shot. But the aerozoan strafed the pirate, electrocuting him in its frenzy.

I tried to see Rath or Barton or Kate, but the aerozoan was whirling around so fast now, trying to throw me off, and the room was ablur. I held on as long as I could, for I knew that once off, I would be back within range of its tentacles. I saw the cables hanging from the ceiling, some of them quite close. The aerozoan gave a violent shrug, and I let go – and flew.

I sailed through the air, reaching for any metal chain, and caught one. It swung forwards with my momentum, and I let go, flew again, and flailed to grab another. I heard the aerozoan behind me, clattering cables as it came. I needed to get to the floor. I loosened my gloved grip on the chain and slid. My feet touched down, and I released the chain seconds before a tentacle electrified it.

The aerozoan was between me and the doorway, so I headed back through the cables for the coffin. From behind the phrenology machine, Barton stepped out before me. The pistol in his hand was pointed at me. I brought myself up short, looking wildly back over my shoulder, expecting to see the aerozoan in pursuit. But it had cunningly disappeared amongst the tangle of pulleys and cables.

'There's one still alive!' I shouted at Barton.

His eyes were cold and fearless and did not leave my face.

'Give me the blueprints,' he said.

I heard the ship's horn blare once again.

'We're leaving!' shouted Rath, striding towards Barton.

'Not without the blueprints,' the frail old man said. With his free hand he pushed the oxygen mask to his mouth and sucked hungrily.

'It doesn't matter, you fool!' Rath shouted. 'We'll blast the ship to pieces once we're clear. Everything will be destroyed. There's a trapdoor over here in the coffin, and I suggest we take it.'

I could only hope Kate had been smart enough to flee when she had the chance.

'The Aruba Consortium wants the plans,' Barton wheezed, looking at me.

'Put down your weapon!'

I turned to see Kate, standing beside the coffin, a dead man's pistol gripped in both hands. She was aiming at Barton – or me, it was hard to tell. I wasn't at all sure this was a happy turn of events.

'I'll certainly not put down my pistol, young miss,' Barton said. 'But you might want to put down yours before you hurt yourself.'

'I'd wager I'm as good a shot as you,' Kate said firmly.

The entire ship was so wind-racked that I doubted even a marksman could take a good shot.

'Try your luck then,' said Barton, and he walked up to me so we were practically face to face and pushed his gun against my chest.

'Kate, don't shoot!' I cried out.

Rath stood frozen, looking from Kate to Barton.

'The blueprints,' Barton said to me, as we both teetered and lurched to keep our balance.

'I don't have them.'

'Take me to them, and I'll see that you get off this ship.'

'We don't have time for this!' Rath shouted, staggering towards the coffin, and Kate.

'Not one step closer!' Kate shouted, levelling the gun at him.

He kept coming, and Kate shot him. His hood went flying back off his head, propelled by the bullet's force, but Rath was still standing, unharmed. His hand flew up to his skull, to make sure it was all there. He went no closer.

I looked back at Barton, wondering what he would do to me. The hairs on the back of my neck lifted, for I was half convinced the hidden aerozoan would flail out at me any second, and kill me before Barton could.

Something shifted behind him, almost invisible against the floor. The aerozoan's translucent sac had collapsed flat. It looked almost like an enormous, discarded snakeskin, blown along by the breeze. But I could see it was actually crawling, long tentacles splayed out, pulling itself across the floor towards the phrenology machine – and Barton. He must have seen my eyes, and thought I was trying to distract him. He would not look.

'Barton, behind you!' Rath shouted.

I had thought the aerozoan mortally wounded by gunshots, but I was wrong. With impossible speed, its balloon sac swelled with hydrium. It jetted off the floor and hovered over Barton.

He whirled. A tentacle shot out and snapped beside his boot. Barton gave a nimble jump, but as he did, the ship lurched again and he stumbled backwards on to the seat of the phrenology machine. Instantly the machine exploded into life, clamping its rubber cap over his head, covering his eyes.

'Rath! Help me!'

Barton fired wildly at the aerozoan but his blind shots missed. His legs kicked, his hands clutched at his head. The mechanical arms snapped up and began to circle and dart towards his skull with a ferocity I had not seen before. The calliper tips pierced his hood once, then again and again.

Perhaps the aerozoan thought the machine was some strange new predator, and it lashed it with its tentacles. The wooden arms had no fear of electric current; though they smoked, they continued their deadly work.

As Barton's screams grew fainter and his limbs went limp, the aerozoan made its fatal mistake and drew closer. The machine's spidery arms, whirling, got tangled in the tentacles and started dragging the aerozoan closer to the callipers. It was reeled in as surely as a squid on a line. The callipers punctured its balloon sac and membranous flanks. Hydrium hissed out, and the creature's intestines uncoiled explosively across the floor.

When I looked up, I saw Rath running for the catwalk. He wore his mask, the oxygen fuelling his escape. No doubt he was desperate to get back to his ship, for we were shaking violently now. I knew what damage the *Hyperion*'s unruly bulk could do to another vessel. Even though Rath was buoyed by his tanked air, it would take him some time to climb the ladder to the crow's-nest and get lifted off. After that his ship would cast loose and open fire on us. I had no idea if the *Saga* would reach us before then.

'Are you all right?' Kate gasped, suddenly at my side.

I nodded, coughing. I could only guess at our height, but figured we were well over seven and a half thousand metres now. We needed oxygen. Born in the air as I was, even I had my limits. I staggered over to the dead men, and stripped off two of their tanks. I fixed Kate up first, then myself.

Three deep breaths of tanked air and the leaden weight disappeared from my limbs. My vision sharpened, almost painfully so. Everything had an aura to it: the dead men's bodies, the aerozoan, Grunel's machinery. The whole room pulsed.

The ship jolted. As Kate and I stumbled along the keel catwalk towards the bow, I saw things. A chicken stepped out of sight around a corner. A vaporous sky sailor disappeared up a ladder. I swore I heard the grave signaller tooting back in the engineerium. It was as if the ship had finally unleashed all her spectres.

I could not tell if these things were real, or merely hallucinations projected by my brain. I did not think Kate was aware of them. I did not ask. I gulped my oxygen, like a man dying of thirst. I knew we were all in terrible danger, yet my body was just watching, patient, curious to see what would happen next.

During the gruelling walk up to the *Hyperion*'s bow, I

felt like time itself had ripped free of her moorings. The walk took forever; the walk took no time at all. I was an old man, gasping for breath; I was a young boy racing to the top of a hill.

Suddenly we were standing in the storage locker with Hal and Nadira. Their faces could not have looked more surprised had we been ghosts. Maybe we were ghosts. I truly felt lighter than air.

'Everyone's dead but Rath,' I said through my mask. 'He's leaving the ship. He means to scuttle us.'

Hal looked at his wristwatch. 'The *Saga* should be here in twenty minutes.'

No one said anything, hoping this would be soon enough, knowing it probably wouldn't be. I did not mention the gold. I did not want Hal tempted, especially in his weakened state. Getting off the ship was as much as we could hope for now.

'We should get to the control car,' I said.

I offered Hal an oxygen tank, and the stubborn goat faltered for a moment before strapping it on. I helped him to his feet. He was wobbly, and leaned on me. Kate helped Nadira, who was struggling for breath through her mask. It was very slow going down the steps to the keel. The ship's ribs and spine creaked and moaned. Her body trembled.

We reached the catwalk. The ladder down to the control car was in sight. There was a thunderclap, then another, and almost at once the sound of great trees toppling in a forest. We were all thrown to the floor.

All the way along the keel catwalk I saw rigging and timbers and girders explode as the ship's side was stove in by cannon fire. Seconds later there was a terrible rending of metal and glass beneath our feet, and I knew the control car was gone. I dragged myself towards the companionway and looked down. Glacial wind howled up at me. Only twisted wreckage hung from the ship's belly, the ends of the rudder and elevator chains whirling in the sky.

The smell of hydrium was suddenly overwhelming. We were breached. The wind held us for a few seconds, pushing and yanking, and then slowly the ship began to fall. Kate clutched at my arm, and for a moment we were all silent. There was no hope of patching the ship: the damage was too extensive, and all of us so wretchedly weak.

'The ornithopters,' I gasped.

'Yes,' said Kate.

There could be no rescue by the *Sagarmatha* now. For a moment I thought Hal was about to object, but he gave a nod.

The stern was starting to dip; she was losing hydrium faster there. But it made our passage aft quicker as we lurched down the catwalk, clambering over wreckage. I thought of the explosives wired beneath the engineerium. If they took a direct hit, they would turn the *Hyperion* into a firestorm. Wind galloped through the ship, gleeful as the Four Horsemen of the Apocalypse, knocking us over, freezing our tongues in our mouths.

Nadira fell and seemed too tired to get back up. I helped Kate haul her to her feet.

'Almost there,' I told her.

The *Hyperion* was picking up speed. It was lucky we were so high. The wind would brace us some, but soon we would be plunging too fast to do anything at all.

We lurched into the hangar – and my heart sank. The end of the launching track had been completely mangled by cannon fire. The two ornithopters themselves seemed unharmed, dangling from the track by their trapezes. But now there was no way of moving them the ten metres into launch position over the bay doors.

'It's all right,' Kate said, taking stock of the situation. 'We'll just unclip one from the track, and I'll fly it out. Straight out the bay doors.'

'You can do that?' I asked.

She nodded.

'And you've flown ones like this before?'

'Absolutely.'

'Are you lying to me?' I asked.

'As best I can, yes,' she said. 'We'll take that one.'

She pointed to the larger of the two. It had four open-air cockpits, one behind the other. Kate scrambled up the boarding steps, peered into the front cockpit, and screamed. I jumped up beside her. Crumpled over in the seat was a frozen corpse.

'Who's he?' Kate demanded angrily.

Beneath his icy leather coat, the dead fellow wore what looked like a butler's uniform.

'Hendrickson,' I said in amazement. 'Grunel's manservant.'

No wonder we'd never found him in the staterooms. He'd tried to make a break for it when the *Hyperion* was being chased. But he'd lost consciousness, like everyone else, as the ship had hurtled skywards.

'Well, get him out of there!' Hal croaked, stomping up the steps.

With his good arm Hal grabbed one side of Hendrickson, and I grabbed the other. We heaved him out and he landed on the hangar floor with a nasty *thunk*.

'Anyone have a problem with that?' Hal asked.

Kate leapt into the pilot's cockpit, quickly studying the controls.

'So how's this thing work?' Hal demanded.

'Crank start,' I said, pointing at the handle on the leathery fuselage.

'And after that we pedal,' Kate said.

'Pedal?' I exclaimed.

'If we want to keep flying, yes.'

She pointed at the two pedals jutting from the cockpit floor. I glanced into the seat behind hers, and saw an identical set.

'Dear God,' muttered Hal.

I didn't know if any one of us had enough puff to keep going for long. But I could not think about that now. We had no choice. My ears were starting to pop as the air pressure increased. I thought it best to get everyone settled in their seats, before cranking up the ornithopter and opening the bay doors.

Hal and I helped Nadira into the rear cockpit, and then Hal climbed into the one in front of hers.

'Buckle up,' I reminded them.

'Let's get going,' Kate said, staring at the various throttles and gauges and levers.

Hopping off the ornithopter, I grabbed the crank handle. I gave it a single, sharp turn, as I'd seen people do with motorcars. Nothing happened. I tried again, fearing I was weaker than I thought. There was no reassuring sound of combustion.

'Not like that!' Kate called down to me. 'It's like a clock. It needs winding!'

'Winding,' I muttered. I'd forgotten. I took the handle and turned it round and round, and I could indeed hear a tiny precise clicking sound inside the machine's body. As I panted for air, I pictured all the little gears meshing and revolving, and wondered how on earth this would be enough to power the craft. After a minute the handle could turn no more.

'It's done,' I said.

'Right,' said Kate. 'Here we go.'

She seemed to be pushing and pulling things, but nothing was happening. I staggered as the *Hyperion*'s stern dipped even lower.

'Now would be good,' I said.

'Maybe this one,' she said, and suddenly the great leathery wings twitched. Ice crystals leapt. In tandem, the wings slowly and creakily began to rise, as though this bat were arthritic and very close to death. In fits and starts, the wings lifted until they could go no further. Then their leading edges angled forward, and jerked slowly back down.

I looked worriedly at Kate. 'Those wouldn't lift a dandelion puff!'

'They're just warming up,' said Kate uncertainly. 'And look, the props are going now.'

Sure enough, the ornithopter's two overhead propellers began to spin, quickly becoming a circular blur. The wings flapped again, faster this time.

I ran across the hangar to the bay doors, and seized the wheel. It would not turn. The metal was welded with ice. I banged and kicked, but could not open the doors.

'Cruse, what's the problem?' Hal roared, lifting his mask clear of his mouth.

'Frozen solid!'

Reaching under his seat, he hauled out his rucksack and heaved it over to me.

'Blow the doors!'

I loosened the drawstrings and yanked out Hal's block of explosive putty, the wires and plunger. I took a breath. I had no idea how much to use, so I was generous. I stuck a great blob of putty dead centre where the bay doors joined, jabbed in the wires, and uncoiled them to the far end of the hangar.

'Cruse, how much did you put on there?' Hal shouted, straining to see from his seat.

'A fair bit!'

'Good Lord!' Hal said when he caught sight of my handiwork.

'Too much?' I shouted.

'Why not!' Hal said. 'Everyone duck!'

I crouched and pushed the plunger. The blast bowled me right over. When I looked up there was smoke everywhere. The ornithopter was swinging wildly from its trapeze, but seemed unharmed, as were all on board. Best of all, the bay doors had been blasted away, and a tsunami of icy wind was crashing into the hangar.

I rushed back to the ornithopter, whose wings were beating much more vigorously now. The propellers droned loudly.

'Get aboard!' Kate hollered.

I climbed up, slipped into the cockpit behind hers, and buckled up.

I'd thought Rath was through with us, but just at that moment another fusillade of cannon fire hit the *Hyperion*. The ship heeled over. The explosion was so intense I knew instantly what had happened. The engineerium had been struck – and the dynamite which lined its floor. The ship would soon be an inferno. There was a terrible din of rending timbers and shrieking metal and the *Hyperion* buckled violently in mid air. Then, through the open bay doors, I watched in horror as the entire forward section fell flaming seaward.

We were only half a ship now, spinning through the sky.

'Go!' I shouted at Kate.

She reached up and tugged at the handle which was supposed to release us from the launching track.

'It's not working!' she cried.

I unbuckled myself and reached for the handle, but could not grasp it from my seat. Scrambling out, I crouched awkwardly atop the hull. The ornithopter was lurching up and down now as its wingbeats became more powerful, and I struggled to keep my balance and stay clear of the whirling propellers.

I grabbed the handle and saw the rod was thick with ice. I pulled hard, then once more with my full weight. The trapeze snapped free, and the ornithopter dropped. I lost my balance and slipped. I hit the starboard wing and was swatted on to the hangar floor.

'Get back on!' Kate yelled.

It was not so easily done. The ornithopter was hopping about like a giant, crazed bat.

'Keep it still!' I bellowed.

'Hurry up!'

It seemed Kate had completely lost control, for the ornithopter was bouncing along the floor, heading right for the open bay doors.

'No!' I yelled.

Kate reined the ornithopter in, bringing it to a halt at the very brink of the hatch. I ran towards it.

'Hurry, Matt!' I heard Kate yell, 'I can't—'

Then, with a single flap, the ornithopter leapt forward, plunged down through the hatch, and disappeared.

I stood there, gaping in total incomprehension. The ornithopter was here just a second ago. Now it was gone. I was alone on the *Hyperion*. A sinking ship. Stupidly, I ran to the edge of the hatch and peered down, as though the ornithopter might be right there, just waiting for me to step on. I could see it, but it was already far, far below, circling jerkily.

The *Hyperion* would crash. I would crash with it. I looked wildly around the hangar at the other ornithopter, and then—

Grunel's winged suit, hanging undamaged from the wall. I ran over, took it down, and pulled it over my sky suit, fastening the clasps with my numb, trembling hands. I slipped my feet into the stirrups which attached to the tail segment. Hurriedly I stroked my new wings, shaking out the ice.

I ran clumsily for the open hatch.

Just then the *Hyperion*'s stern dropped so sharply, I fell over and started sliding aft. I shouted and cursed as I tried to scrabble up the tilted floor. Things came loose and avalanched towards me. A few more moments and the *Hyperion* would be standing on her stern. Then she would truly plummet.

I was a mountain climber now, grabbing at floor cleats and metal seams to help me get higher. My head pounded and popped with the speed of the ship's fall.

I reached the lip of the hatch, now slanted at a forty-five-degree angle. The ship thrashed and tried to throw me off. I made sure my oxygen mask was snug. Then I pitched myself forward hard and tumbled out into the sky.

22

ICARUS

I fell.

I was aware of the vast bulk of the *Hyperion*'s stern hurtling alongside me, but I was faster and soon had left it behind. Instinctively I spread my arms wide and my wings opened. I felt some kind of powerful cross-brace within them snap into place and hold. Instantly my fall slowed – so drastically that the *Hyperion*'s wreckage came plunging down straight towards me.

I had but seconds. I tilted my wings, angling my feet to swing my tail rudder, and banked sharply. The ship's severed body careered past, not fifty metres distant, and its massive turbulence completely capsized me. Somehow I managed to right myself, and veer clear of the aerial whirlpool in the ship's wake.

I cannot say how I knew these things; only that it was second nature, and I felt as though the wings had always been upon me. Riding atop my terror was a soaring joy, for I had known this feeling all my life in dreams.

I was still sliding steeply through the air. With difficulty I angled my wings and felt the speed of my fall decrease even more until I was flying level. I experimented. My arms did not have the strength to power a climb, so I began a series of loose, jerky circles. The wind was very strong; it would have smothered me were it not for the mask over my mouth and nose. My eyes were slits. High above me, I thought I made out the dark profile of Rath's airship, and I prayed they could not see me – or Kate and the others.

I cast about desperately, trying to spot the ornithopter. Below, I saw the two halves of the *Hyperion* sinking seaward, the forward section spewing flame and smoke. The stern section was tipped over even more now. All that kept her from plunging like a skyscraper was a few intact hydrium cells amidships.

Would Kate think I was still aboard? Surely she wasn't reckless enough to attempt a landing, for it would be impossible, given the *Hyperion's* angle and speed. I hoped she was sensible enough to stay well back – but not so sensible as to give up on me altogether. Kate was my only chance.

Round and round I went, buffeted by the wind. Below, the Antarctic Ocean stretched to all horizons. I searched in vain for the dark wrinkles of the ornithopter's wings. The intense cold squeezed me with the force of a glacier. I could not stay aloft forever. The sky would defeat me. My veins would turn to ice, my heart would stop, and my mind would empty of all its thoughts and memories and treasures.

The *Hyperion's* forward section hit the ocean first,

crumpling soundlessly against the waves. In less than a minute, the ship's stern joined it, piling into itself. After sailing the skies of the world for forty years, the *Hyperion* was reduced to flotsam in a matter of seconds. The inventions, the taxidermy, the bodies of the doomed crew: all lost. I marvelled at how such a big vessel could suddenly become so pitifully small. Really, I supposed, it was nothing but hydrium and the dreams of Theodore Grunel that had kept it aloft.

My mind was drifting, my thoughts already congealing in the cold. I spotted a pair of wings in the distance and shouted out, even though I knew they could never hear me. My only hope was that Kate and the others were also searching for me, and would somehow see the little speck I made in the vast sky. I could no longer see the wings, and looked all around in despair, not knowing which way to go. Perhaps they'd never been there at all.

A feather whipped past my face, and then another. I was surely hallucinating now. But when I glanced over my right wing, in horror I saw that I was moulting. Fast. As I gazed at my left wing, three more feathers went whirling off.

The ornithopter seemed to come from nowhere, cutting across the icy blue sky before me. Kate must have spotted me, because the wings waggled, and the flying machine made a steep turn and came alongside on my left. Hal was waving at me frantically, and I saw that Kate was bringing the ornithopter into the wind. She pulled ahead, dipping a bit lower.

My feathers flew. I could see bare patches on both wings now. Before long, I'd be about as airworthy as a plucked turkey. I was slewing all over the place. The ornithopter was dead ahead, and I had only one try. I was slipping too far to starboard. Steering with my wings and tail, I veered to port to compensate, and then came diagonally at the ornithopter. When I was almost overhead, I took my chance, drew in my wings, and dived.

I aimed for my empty cockpit behind Kate, but didn't quite make it. Instead I came crashing down in front of Hal, willing my frozen fingers to unclench so I could grab hold of something. Hal had only one good arm, but I felt it lock around me tight. With both hands I clutched the rim of my cockpit. My wings fluttered and billowed and I was nearly blown off the ornithopter. I had to jettison them. I kicked my feet free of the tail stirrups, and then swung my legs into the empty cockpit. My numb fingers fumbled with the suit's clasps – and suddenly my Icarus wings went sailing off behind us. I collapsed into my seat.

Kate turned around, her eyes wide with joy and disbelief.

'You made it!' she shouted.

'I'm OK!' I shouted back.

'Thank God! Start pedalling!'

Our touching reunion was over and she returned to the controls. It was my first time in an ornithopter and I can't say I found it reassuring. It rode the sky like a small boat on water, humping through the air as its wings pounded. I put my feet to the pedals and started churning, winding up the clockwork engine. It was a marvel, that Grunel had found a way of generating such power from the turning of tiny gears. I looked high in the sky, and saw no sign of Rath's ship. I hoped he was long gone by now, thinking we had gone down with the *Hyperion*.

I leaned forward and shouted beside Kate's ear.

'What's the plan?'

She turned her head slightly. 'Find the *Saga*!'

Hal was thumping my shoulder, and I turned to him. He made a circling motion with his hand, and I knew he wanted Kate to stay in a holding pattern so we could look for his ship. I relayed his message. Kate just nodded and put the ornithopter into a slow turn. I had to admit, the flying machine was more supple than I'd expected, and it responded smoothly to Kate's commands, despite the fierce wind.

I glanced back at Nadira, and was relieved to see she was still conscious, though far too weak to pedal much. The rest of us would have to make up for her. I reckoned we were flying at about five thousand metres now, and though the air was richer, we kept our masks on. We needed all our strength for pedalling, and the extra air would keep our vision sharp.

I scanned the sky for the *Sagarmatha*. If she'd been steaming for the *Hyperion*'s last position, we were in the right place at least, though I was unsure at what altitude she'd be approaching. My great fear was that they'd see the *Hyperion*'s wreckage on the waves, and assume we'd gone down with the ship.

I knew we couldn't keep pedalling forever, but said nothing. We would never make landfall. My legs sang with pain, and I was sorely tempted to pause and rest. I had survived one freefall, only to face another. But as I stared at the back of Kate's hooded head, bent intently over the controls, I felt strangely calm. It would be a quick death, hitting the hard waves. We would be together.

'There!' Kate cried, pointing.

We all started waving and shouting like imbeciles, but the *Sagarmatha*, three hundred metres above us, sailed on. Dorje was flying her with a skeleton crew, and he would have precious few pairs of eyes for lookout. They would certainly not be looking for something as small as an ornithopter.

'Go higher!' I shouted at Kate.

'Pedal harder!' she shot back.

The ornithopter humped and struggled to rise, but it was obvious our exhausted legs could not supply enough power. It was all we could do to keep it level. Unless we were spotted, the *Saga* would sail away and take our last hopes with her.

A red rainbow shot up into the sky, and my soggy mind took a moment to understand it had come from the ornithopter. Hal and I both turned round and saw Nadira, holding a flare gun. She lifted her mask from her mouth.

'Beside the seat!' she shouted, pointing down to where she'd found it.

I gave her the thumbs-up.

The crimson flare soared high, arching over the *Sagarmatha*'s bow. We all waited breathlessly, praying we'd been spotted. Slowly the *Saga* began to turn. Her bow dipped and she headed towards us.

Overjoyed I was, but I also knew we were no longer flying level. Hard as I pedalled, we were still slowly but surely falling. We didn't have much time. All my numb indifference evaporated now that rescue was so close at hand. I wanted it more than anything.

'I'm not so good at landing,' Kate shouted at me.

'You're fabulous!'

'Remember the Eiffel Tower?'

'Thing of beauty!'

I pedalled hard. I didn't know if it was killing me, or keeping me alive, staving off the cold which otherwise would have frozen me solid. I leaned back to Hal.

'Does the *Saga* have a landing rig?'

'Dorje can rig one amidships, from the cargo bay doors!'

I told this to Kate and she nodded without looking back. I felt sick. An aerial hook-on landing was one of the trickiest manoeuvres. It was one thing to do it at the Eiffel Tower in light winds, but up here, the sky was powerful and unforgiving.

'Can I help?' I shouted to her.

'Just pedal!'

And then we did not talk any more, for we were

making our approach. The *Sagarmatha* was before us, and Dorje had slowed her down and put her on our altitude and heading. We flapped towards the stern. I was about to tell Kate to watch out for the fins, but she beat me to it, veering nimbly around the tail. We skimmed beneath the *Saga*'s belly. Fifteen metres ahead, I could see a makeshift docking rig suspended from the open cargo bay doors. Kate throttled back; the propellers' drone deepened. Time seemed to slow. We rocked crazily from side to side as Kate tried to line us up with the rig. A gust of wind shook us, and we were suddenly too low.

'Pedal!' Kate bellowed.

I gave it my all, and Hal and the others must have done the same, for the wings thrashed, and the ornithopter jumped. I watched the *Saga*'s landing rig and the ornithopter's trapeze nearing each other and willed them to connect. They did.

With a jerk the ornithopter was hooked on. Kate killed the clockwork engine and the wings went limp; the propellers sputtered to a standstill.

'Welcome aboard!' Dorje roared down at us through the bay doors and he and Kami pulled lines and started to winch us up inside.

I took off my mask, leaned forward and pressed my frozen lips against Kate's hood.

'Couldn't have done it better myself,' I said.

She turned to me, beaming. 'You couldn't have done it at all,' she replied.

'You're right,' I said. 'You're absolutely right.'

* * *

Dorje, Kami, Mrs Ram and Miss Simpkins were all on hand to help us off the ornithopter, for we were so cold and stiff, we could not bend our legs to climb out.

'Marjorie!' Kate cried, and threw her arms around her chaperone.

'Goodness! Yes, there, there,' said Miss Simpkins, giving Kate little pats on the back, and trying to look impatient. But there was a smile hiding in the corners of her mouth.

'We saw the *Saga* get hit,' Kate said, 'and I worried you'd all gone down.'

'Your chaperone,' Dorje said, 'is a very accomplished seamstress, and fast too.'

'You helped patch the gas cells?' I asked in amazement.

'Oh, it was nothing,' she said. 'They hauled me up into the rigging on a little swing and I just sewed up the holes. It was perfectly straightforward.'

'It was a very close thing,' said Dorje.

Kate looked at her chaperone, shaking her head. 'Well done, Marjorie. You're a hero.'

There was no more talking, for Nadira and Hal both needed tending to, and Kate and I could scarcely stand. Miss Simpkins helped escort Kate to their stateroom. Mrs Ram took charge of Nadira and led her off. Dorje was looking at Hal's shoulder. I leaned on Kami and he helped me back to my cabin. At the doorway I thanked him, but he had no intention of leaving. He seated me on the lower bunk and proceeded to strip off my sky suit. I protested, telling him I could undress myself, but he just ignored me, knowing, as well as I did, that I couldn't.

'You saved my life,' he said. 'This is the least I can do.'

My hands were stiff and curled, and I felt as bent and stooped as an old man. When I was down to my underwear I started shivering uncontrollably, and Kami told me to lie down and pulled thick blankets over me. He examined my hands and face with a studied eye. I didn't know what happened next, for moments after my head touched the pillow, I began falling asleep. I was vaguely aware that Kami Sherpa was tending to me, and putting a bed warmer under the sheets beside me, and applying ointments and bandages to my skin. But nothing could keep me awake, and my last feeling was of warmth and tremendous well-being.

When I woke, I had no notion what time it was. The light beyond the porthole was dim; it might have been dusk or dawn. I just lay there, my mind windswept. I was alive. I was also ravenously hungry, and my throat felt dry as Skyberia.

It was no easy thing to sit up and swing my legs over the bed, my bones and muscles were so sore. Getting dressed would be a challenge. Several of my fingers were bandaged, and my left foot too. I stood before the mirror. My face was badly burned by the cold and wind, my lips chapped, one of my eyes swollen half shut. There were dark bruises all over my chest and arms. I didn't know if

I was looking at a man or a boy, but it was me.

It took fifteen minutes to get my clothes on and do up my zipper and buttons. The ship was silent as I limped my way to the lounge. I wondered if everyone else was still sleeping. I opened the door and the delicious smell of fresh bread wafted over me. My mouth started to water. I didn't expect to find anyone here, but the electric hearth was on and sitting beside it, all by herself, was Kate.

'Hello,' she said, 'how are you feeling?'

'Fantastic,' I said.

'Me too. Mrs Ram's preparing breakfast. Are you starving?'

'Thirsty, too.'

Beside her was a jug of water, and she poured a glass and handed it to me. For several seconds I was lost to the sheer pleasure of the water filling my mouth and sliding down my throat. At that moment I could not imagine a more satisfying experience. Kate took the glass and filled it up again for me.

'Thank you. What time is it?' I asked her.

'About seven in the morning. We slept eighteen hours you know. I ran into Dorje. He took out Hal's bullet and set his arm last night; and he said Nadira's already much better.'

'Good.'

For a moment we didn't say anything. Then I started laughing.

'I can't believe you flew off without me!'

'That ornithopter had a mind of its own! I couldn't stop it. I was trying to circle back for you, and then I just saw you throw yourself out of the hatch.' She looked at me, shaking her head. 'It was the most idiotic thing I've ever seen.'

'What did you expect me to do? Go down with the ship?'

'Only *you* would throw yourself into thin air.'

'Well, I did have wings on.'

'Sometimes I think you've always got wings on,' she said and gave me the nicest smile. 'Of course, angels don't usually moult. But it was very lucky you did. I only spotted you because of all those feathers in your wake.'

'You were amazing,' I told her.

'So were you, coming back to get me in the engineerium. That was quite ingenious, freeing the aerozoans. Of course, I might easily have been electrocuted.'

'It wasn't the greatest plan,' I admitted.

'It did the trick, though.' She paused. 'We saved each other. I like that.'

I took a deep breath. The air seemed so rich now. 'We're much lower,' I said.

Kate nodded. 'Dorje said two and a half thousand metres. We're headed back to Paris.'

'I suppose I've made my fortune,' I said.

'I should think Grunel's blueprints will make you quite wealthy.'

441

I grinned, wondering how much it would be. I imagined the house I could buy for my mother and sisters, the thick stacks of money I could lay aside for them in a bank. I thought of the future I would build for myself, high and magnificent as a skyscraper.

'Will you even bother going back to the Academy?' Kate asked.

'Yes,' I said at once, surprised by my own certainty. But I knew it was true. For most of my life, I had longed to attend the Airship Academy. It was one of the dreams that had kept me aloft, and I would not abandon it now. I'd been very lucky to get my chance, and if I did not complete my studies, and master all their challenges, I would be a lesser person somehow.

'I intend to graduate,' I told Kate.

She nodded. 'Good. You're a finisher. And after that, your options are endless really. You'll have an Academy diploma, and be very wealthy to boot.'

I looked at her carefully. 'Am I better wealthy?'

Before she could answer, Hal came into the room. His left arm was in a sling. His hair was mussed, and he seemed decidedly flustered.

'Cruse, you've got the blueprints, yes?'

'You put them in your rucksack, didn't you?'

'Yes, but I can't find my rucksack,' he said.

'Didn't we just leave them all aboard the ornithopter? After we landed?'

'I was just there,' Hal said impatiently. 'I checked all the cockpits, and found everyone else's rucksack but mine. You sure you didn't take it to your cabin last night?'

'No,' I said. 'I didn't.'

'Nor I,' said Kate.

Hal rubbed at his head. 'If it's that wretched gypsy girl—'

'Hal,' said Kate severely, 'you can't honestly still think—'

I let out a sudden gust of breath. 'No,' I whispered.

'What's wrong?' Kate asked.

Seconds ago, I'd felt my life to be a gleaming, glorious thing. Now, all of a sudden, it seemed shrivelled and joyless.

'I know where your rucksack is, Hal,' I said.

'Where?' he demanded.

'At the bottom of the Antarctic Sea,' I told him.

I had dined once with Vikram Szpirglas and his murderous pirates, in fear for my life and Kate's the entire time, but the morning meal aboard the *Sagarmatha* was much more unpleasant. Nadira, Hal, Kate and I sat around the table, touching our food with our forks, eating little. Hal had a bottle of whisky open beside him. He did not offer it to anyone else. He filled his glass, emptied it, and refilled it.

'When we reach Paris they'll seize my ship,' he said. 'What's left of it.'

'Hal, I'm sorry,' I said yet again.

I could not remember ever feeling such shamefaced

dismay. And it wasn't just Hal I was sorry for; it was Nadira and myself too. Not a cent would we see from Grunel's blueprints – nor would his beautiful aerial cities ever sail the skies. All our dreams had dissolved at the ocean's icy bottom.

The door opened and Miss Simpkins bustled into the dining room.

'I'm very sorry I'm late,' she said brightly, and took her seat. 'I slept in, you see, quite unlike me, and had some trouble getting enough hot water from that wretched shower, so it was rather an ordeal to wash my hair properly.' She looked around the table. 'What on earth's the matter?'

I closed my eyes and exhaled.

'Ah, Miss Simpkins,' said Hal, pouring himself another whisky. 'You haven't heard our little tale of woe, have you? Perhaps Matt Cruse can enlighten you.'

I stared at him, amazed at his appetite for torture.

'Very well,' Hal went on, 'since Cruse can't bear owning up to it. We were aboard the *Hyperion*, about to escape in an ornithopter. I threw my rucksack down to Cruse so he could get my explosives and blow apart the hangar doors. Inside that rucksack, Miss Simpkins, were the blueprints to Grunel's machine.'

'Oh yes,' said Miss Simpkins, 'Kate mentioned those last night. Worth a fortune, she said.'

'Indeed,' replied Hal, looking balefully at me. 'Except that Mr Cruse here decided to leave my rucksack and all its contents on the hangar floor.'

'No!' said Miss Simpkins, staring at me, aghast.

I was almost too weary and despondent to reply, but I could not let Hal go unchallenged. 'It was chaos,' I insisted. 'The ship was sinking. Time was scarce. I was trying to get back on the ornithopter before it flapped off. And then there was the explosion. The rucksack was not uppermost in my mind! And, Hal, I didn't hear you reminding me.'

'That's because I assumed you had it,' he countered. 'I assumed you were a man and not a child. And that you'd remember our fortune was inside!'

'It might be a mercy in disguise,' said Kate.

'Might it now?' Hal asked. 'Do tell.'

'Trying to sell Grunel's plans,' she said, 'could have been very difficult. First of all, would anyone believe such a machine actually worked? Second, and most important, if the Aruba Consortium found out you had the blueprints, your lives might be in grave danger.'

Hal said nothing for a moment. 'I'd rather have the blueprints and take my chances.'

'Me too,' said Nadira.

I was glad to see she was looking so much better, and only hoped she did not loathe me forever for this terrible turn of events.

'We're alive,' Kate insisted. 'We should be jolly grateful for that.'

'I don't think anyone's brimming with jolliness right now,' I said. 'And I can't blame them. I'm really very sorry.'

'Stop apologizing,' said Nadira irritably. 'It wasn't your fault.'

I stared at her in amazement and gratitude. 'Well, technically—'

'Whose fault was it then?' Hal demanded.

'Anyone would have forgotten the rucksack,' Nadira said.

'Absolutely,' Kate agreed.

Hal shook his head in disgust. Pouring himself another drink, he slopped whisky outside his glass. 'Let's not add insult to injury,' he said, his words thick. 'I've just been ruined by a boy's stupidity. Let's call it what it is!'

'I've heard quite enough of this nonsense,' said Kate.

'How is it nonsense?' Hal said, slapping the table. 'He's paupered me.'

'I think it's pathetic of you to blame Matt for this. He's man enough to admit he forgot the rucksack *and* apologize, even when he needn't. Nadira's right. It's no one's fault.'

'Why don't you go off and *pet* your taxidermy, Miss de Vries,' said Hal.

'I believe I will, thank you.' She stood to go.

'You are drunk, Mr Slater,' said Miss Simpkins, standing. 'It is breakfast, and you are drunk. I think it unmanly – and completely beneath you.'

She followed Kate out of the dining room. Hal stared sullenly at his glass.

'The rich,' he muttered darkly. 'Kate de Vries doesn't

have a clue what this means to us. She's never taken a risk in her life.'

'That's not true,' I said indignantly. 'She's from a wealthy family, yes. But if she played by the rules, she'd be sitting in a parlour, doing needlework, waiting for someone rich to marry her. Her parents don't seem to care much about her. She's set herself against her family and all they expect, because she's different, and wants to study and travel and learn.'

'A moving speech,' Hal said. 'But if she fails, she has a very soft landing.'

'She risked her life aboard the *Hyperion* like the rest of us,' I reminded him.

'But what *about* the rest of us?' He jabbed a finger at Nadira. 'What have you got to look forward to now? Work in a sweatshop? Life on the street?'

'I'm not going to any sweatshop,' Nadira said with a regal sniff.

'Ah, you have grand plans, do you?' Hal asked mockingly.

I truly hoped she did.

'I've got a few ideas,' she said.

'Will you go home?' I asked her.

'That would mean marriage, or utter disgrace.' She shook her head. 'I think I can do better.'

'I'm sure you can,' I said, but my smile faltered, for I knew her future was anything but certain, despite her many talents. I felt I'd betrayed her, blighted her prospects for happiness.

'I'm a pretty good dancer,' she said.

'You certainly are.' I almost blushed, remembering the mesmerizing dance she'd done for us in the lounge not so long ago.

'I could get a job at the Moulin Rouge,' she said. 'I hear they're always looking for new faces.'

'Not just new faces,' smirked Hal. 'They like to see a bit more than that.'

The music hall was famous, and infamous too, for its raucous parties and flamboyant dancers. I did not like to think of Nadira there.

'I'm not saying it's perfect,' Nadira said, 'but it's better than performing on the street. I've heard belly dancers can make a lot of money at the Moulin Rouge. I can save my wages and figure out what I really want to do.'

'It's a good plan,' I said, hoping it was.

'And if it's not,' she said, 'I'll get a new one. I'm going to make a dent in this world.'

'I think it'll be more than a dent,' I said with a grin, feeling suddenly that she really would be all right. And I felt a twinge of regret, too, for I knew we would soon be taking different paths.

'You'll go back to the Academy, I suppose,' Nadira said.

'Yes.'

Hal gave a dyspeptic grunt. 'How inspiring. You're destined to become a chauffeur to the rich.'

'I don't see it that way,' I said.

'Ah, who am I to talk?' Hal replied morosely, taking

another snort of his whisky. 'I'll likely end up serving as second mate on someone else's ship to pay off my debts.'

'I can't believe you'll be down for long,' I told him. 'You'll have some great scheme and buy the *Saga* back. I once heard someone say that the man who is dealt bad luck, but makes good despite it, is the most noble of men.'

'Pretty talk,' Hal scoffed.

'It was you who said it,' I reminded him. 'In Kate de Vries' library. I remembered your exact words. Because I agreed with them.'

'Make good,' he muttered. 'How can I make good? With what?' Hal slammed the table. 'I risked my life and my ship and everything I owned for this salvage. There was treasure within my grasp.' He looked at me, and his features were saggy and mean with drink. 'But you came between us. Go back to your Academy, Cruse. You'll not amount to much. You've not got the wits. The blueprints gone – and not even an ingot of the gold you promised!'

'Oh, there was *gold*,' I said vehemently. I hadn't meant to tell anyone, but I was finally fed up with his bullying accusations and insults.

'What?' Hal said, squinting at me.

'*Tonnes* of it,' I went on. 'Behind the wall of the secret passage. That's where Grunel kept it.'

'You're just trying to madden me,' Hal said.

'No. Must've been twenty crates. I discovered them when I went back for Kate.'

'Is this true?' Nadira asked.

449

I nodded, suddenly ashamed of my outburst. I'd just wanted to get back at Hal, but I saw now how this news pained her. She said nothing, but her eyes were bright with tears.

Hal was breathing heavily. For a moment, I thought he might lunge across the table and strangle me. Then all the fire seemed to go out of him. 'You were right there! Why didn't you take some?'

'Heavy stuff, gold.'

'Just twenty bars would have fixed my ship, and eased my debt!'

'I was rescuing Kate,' I said. 'There wasn't time.'

Nadira gave a quick nod. 'You did the right thing,' she said.

Hal snorted. 'Ah yes, very valiant of you. But let me give you my opinion. Man to man, you understand. I think you may find that Kate de Vries would admire you more if you'd taken some gold.'

I found Kate in the cargo bay, sitting in the cockpit of Grunel's ornithopter, studying the controls.

'Oh, hello,' she said, turning and looking down at me. 'This really is an amazing machine, you know. I don't think Hal appreciates it. He might be able to sell the design to someone.'

'I don't think the pedal idea will catch on,' I said. 'It was no easy thing, keeping it aloft.'

'It did feel heavy,' she admitted. 'But if he'll let me, I'd like to buy it. I'd give him an excellent price, and then at least he'd have something to split between you all.'

'I'm sure he'd appreciate that. It's very kind of you.'

'Not at all. I feel quite attached to it.'

'It saved our lives,' I said. 'With you at the helm anyway.'

'Those things Hal said about you – you mustn't listen to him. He's being hateful.'

'If it were my ship, I'd probably get drunk too.'

'You asked me a question earlier,' she said.

It took me a second to remember. 'Oh. "Am I better wealthy?" I don't think you need to answer that any more.'

'It still seems an important question to me.'

'You have the answer?' I asked.

'Yes. Well, no. Because it's completely up to you.'

'Is it? Just say you had to choose. The rich or poor Matt Cruse.'

She smiled. 'It doesn't matter to me in the slightest. It never has.'

'Really?' Just looking at her, I realized she was telling the truth. 'But it matters to other people,' I said. 'It matters to me. More than I'd care to admit, and that's a fact.'

'That's important to know,' she said.

'Hal thinks I'm destined to be a chauffeur. Does that repel you?'

'Not at all,' she said. 'It's always best to be in the driver's seat, isn't it?'

I laughed.

'Although,' she went on, 'right now, *I* appear to be in the driver's seat.'

'You certainly do.'

'Climb aboard,' she said, 'and tell me where you'd like to go.'

I smiled. We had the hangar all to ourselves. I saw a foothold in the ornithopter's flank, stuck my toes in, and started to heave myself up to the cockpit. But something gave way beneath my foot with a bang, and I slipped back to the hangar floor.

'Are you all right?' Kate asked, peering down.

'It's some kind of cargo hatch,' I said, squinting into the small compartment I'd unwittingly opened. There were two white sacks inside and I pulled them out, one at a time, for they were heavy.

'They're pillow cases,' I said.

'What's inside?' Kate asked.

I opened one and stared in utter disbelief.

'Gold,' I said.

'No, really. What's inside?'

I grinned and held it up to her so she could see the lustre of the smooth bricks.

'Oh my goodness!' she cried. 'No wonder the ship felt heavy!'

'Hendrickson,' I said, 'that little sneak! Grunel's manservant filched some gold and tried to make off with it!'

'Where did he get it though?' Kate wanted to know.

I hadn't yet told her about the store of gold in the

secret passage, and as she clambered down from the cockpit, I quickly filled her in.

'How many bricks are there?' she asked.

We dumped them out on the floor and counted them. Forty. I did the math.

'That means thirty-two for Hal, and four each for Nadira and me.' My heart was beating fast. 'That's enough for Hal to fix the *Saga* and get out of debt.'

'And it's a very nice windfall for you and Nadira,' Kate said. 'You won't be the richest young man in Paris, but you certainly won't be the poorest.'

'I don't think I'll mind that at all,' I said.

Kate and I just looked at each other. The gold's glimmer was nothing compared to the brightness of her face. I took her hand in mine and felt once more that sense of homecoming. I wanted to pull her tight and kiss her, but that would have spoiled it somehow, because I wouldn't have been able to see her eyes. And as long as our gazes met we were like a current. We were electricity, and together we could have powered an aerial city. My Himalayan heart felt big as the sky, and just as strong.

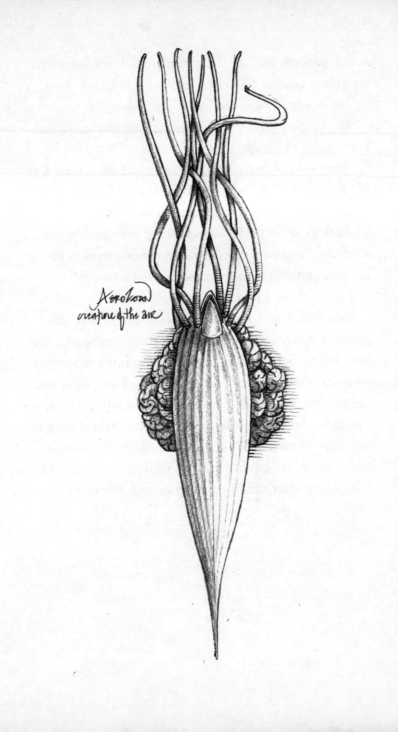

Agrokorn
creature of the air

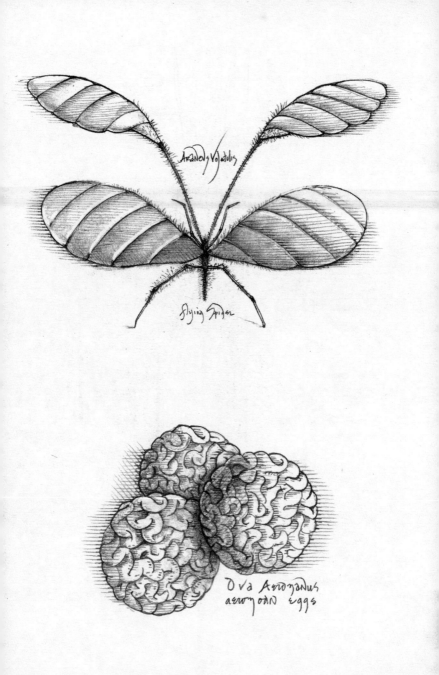

Aranevs Volatulis

Flying Spider

Ova Aeronavus
aeronaut eggs

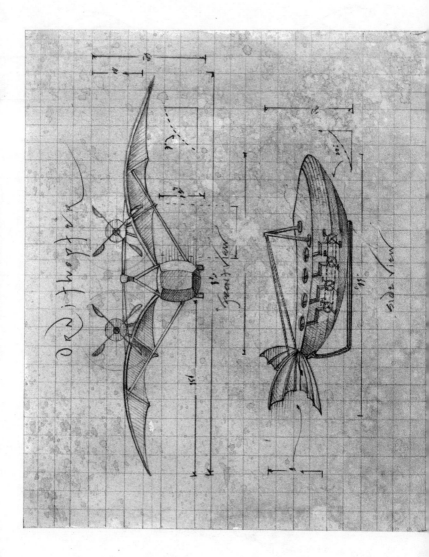